THE
STARS
WE
SHARE

THE
STARS
WE
SHARE

Rafe Posey

PAMELA DORMAN BOOKS / VIKING

VIKING

An imprint of Penguin Random House LLC
penguinrandomhouse.com

A Pamela Dorman Book/Viking

LIBRARY OF CONGRESS CATALOGING-IN-PUBLICATION DATA

Names: Posey, Rafe, author.
Title: The stars we share / Rafe Posey.
Description: [New York] : Pamela Dorman Book/Viking, [2021]
Identifiers: LCCN 2020013337 (print) | LCCN 2020013338 (ebook) |
ISBN 9781984879622 (hardcover) | ISBN 9781984879639 (ebook)
Classification: LCC PS3616.O827 S73 2021 (print) | LCC PS3616.O827
(ebook) | DDC 813/.6—dc23
LC record available at https://lccn.loc.gov/2020013337
LC ebook record available at https://lccn.loc.gov/2020013338

Printed in the United States of America
1   3   5   7   9   10   8   6   4   2

Designed by Cassandra Garruzzo

For Paula

BOOK ONE

1927, *RMS* Jaipur

Quiet, then, on the decks at night. Alec Oswin plays balancing games on the broad planks outside his cabin, always aware of the vibrations of the ship wallowing through the water like a great steel ox, carving its way west and north and west again. England feels like the invention of a cruel older child, and he had not wanted to go. His parents had friends around the garrison who spoke of England as a lost paradise, cursing the dense humidity and the fevers and the fecundity of the mud in India, and his mother had always nodded politely. But later, when her friends had gone, she would bundle herself around Alec where he lay half asleep beneath a mosquito net. Together they would whisper stories back and forth, listening to the sounds of the night.

The creaks and groans of the ship's night sounds are a world away from what he wants. Alec closes his eyes, the stars unfolding above the ship. In his trunk, tucked close under the edge of his bunk, there is almost nothing: four sets of clothes picked out by his uncle; a picture of his parents, younger and golden with affection; a small steel box full of his mother's jewelry and his father's medals and buttons. In his memory, Alec carries his mother's voice, which tells him stories in the gloaming or from books now lost in the chaos of his leaving.

Sometimes in the night the sea comes up and reminds them all where they are, and how small they are. Most nights the ship feels as safe as houses (although in Alec's experience, a house is no more safe than anywhere else), and sometimes it feels like a wad of paper bobbing in a river. But tonight is quiet. Tonight if Alec closes his eyes and ignores the lapping of the waves against the hull, he can imagine the stars singing. He sits with his back to a lifeboat mount and watches the sky. He has not yet learned all the constellations, although he knows the Great Bear, and the north star Polaris, and the Saptarshi, who inhabit the heavens and mark the bounds of the Great Bear's shape. He knows swans and hunters and fallen heroes.

Years ago, his father had given him a notebook with a soft leather cover that curled at the edges, and on that stiff white paper he draws the stars. They might be the same in the English sky, but he isn't sure. Alec is no longer sure of anything, and the stars are as close as he can get to fact. The stars, he feels certain, will not lie to him.

The stars are what he has now.

So he draws Polaris and the Bear, and then everything else outward. His mother called Polaris her lodestar, a word he will always trust. The sky doesn't change much from night to night—black indigo and the dots of impossible brightness chasing across it. Maybe it's Heaven up there, if the Right Reverend Mr. Hume and the congregation in Bombay could be believed. Alec is not convinced, although he needs to believe in Heaven because otherwise, where are his parents?

Somewhere belowdecks his uncle Roger is playing cards, and probably losing badly. Alec's father made excuses for his friend's gambling and drinking; they had served together from the first Somme onward, and so Martin Oswin knew Roger better than almost anyone. Alec's mother insisted that her younger brother was merely misunderstood. But now Uncle Roger is charged with escorting Alec to his aunt, somewhere in the east of England, a country as distant and unlikely as the stars Alec can't yet name.

. . .

On the third night out of Bombay the wind strikes sideways at the ship. Uncle Roger comes into Alec's cabin haloed with the juniper scent of gin and tonic and takes the boy back up to the deck with him, his palm cupped around the bony knob of Alec's shoulder. Alec hangs back, until he remembers the way the monsoons had shuddered their compound in Bombay, the household relieved by the dance of rain on roof. His uncle leans close, the black sheen of a day's growth of beard mesmerizing. *I miss them, too*, he shouts against the noise of the storm. He drops down to sit with his back against a bulkhead and pulls Alec close beside him, unleashing a deep well of sorrow over the loss of his sister and his best friend, all of it half-heard and barely understood. After, Alec's faith in his uncle has deepened.

Four days later Alec wakes to find his skin aching and tight, his throat clenched and as dry as stones. For a long time he lies in his bunk on fire, awake and asleep blurring together in a series of miserable dreams of the cholera that slashed through their house like a tiger. They were so happy, and then everyone was gone, and Alec had been left alone. In his cabin on the ship, stinking of illness and fear, he is never alone; he is always vaguely aware of his uncle and the ship's physician watching him, checking him, laying their big, rough palms against his clammy brow. But sometimes the fever takes him deeper and he believes Mr. Hume is there. Then Alec shouts at him, or at the shapes he imagines are a man. He is too weak to speak the curses the stableboy taught him, but he holds them in his heart for the clergyman who promised him his parents would be in Heaven, when what Alec wants is simply for them to be alive. But Mr. Hume had taken him from the house when everyone else was sick and dying, and his parents had been gone by the time the awful telegram had reached Uncle Roger in Mardan.

The ship has reached the Mediterranean the next time Alec sees the sun. Uncle Roger helps Alec make his way to the deck, the companionways and ladders he had scampered up like a monkey a week before now nearly beyond him. He sits back on his deck chair, enveloped in the bustle of other passengers around him. Alec is eight years old, and he wants his mother's voice and the light touch of her fingers on the back of his neck. He wants to go home.

There are other boys on board, some who sit quietly with their families or governesses, and some who run wild in a pack in the night. Before the fever, Alec had been tempted to join the wild boys, but he had known that his mother would worry. Would have worried. But now the fever has left him so tired his hair hurts, with aches in every joint, and his chest clatters with loneliness. One evening it gets the best of him and, when he has escaped from the closeness of the dinner service, he makes his way slowly along the passageways and through the hatches until he finds them in the cargo hold, climbing on crates and smoking cigarettes they've stolen from someone's auntie. Their leader, a boy he has heard called Charlie, jumps down fluidly from the crate until they stand face-to-face. Charlie is older, twelve or thirteen, much taller and at least two stone heavier, and he regards Alec with amusement.

"You've come to draw us, then?"

The other boys laugh. Alec looks at them all, one by one. If they know he draws, they've been watching him. He knows his mother would not want him smoking stolen cigarettes in a cargo hold. But he also knows she would not want him to be so lonely.

"No," he says. But what does he want? He wants his vengeance on the cholera, and on Mr. Hume, and on the whole of the world, for letting all of this happen to him, but there is no way to say that to this confident boy with mussed black hair. "I just wanted to know what else there was to do on the ship."

"Left it a bit late," Charlie says.

"I've been ill," Alec says.

"Right," Charlie says. He looks more carefully at Alec, who tries to puff himself taller, despite the fact that his knees feel full of thorns.

Another boy slides to the floor and saunters over. Where Charlie has regarded him with curiosity and reserve, this boy looks at Alec like there's something wrong with him. Alec meets his eyes, his shoulders back.

The boy jerks his chin upward roughly. "My brother says your uncle is a scoundrel and ought to be whipped."

"That's not true," Alec retorts. There are a lot of things his uncle does wrong, but if he were actually bad, Alec's father would have stopped him.

"You're no better," the boy says.

Alec knows that everything that happens next is wrong, but it is too much, all of it, the emptiness and the losses and the yearning. He looks at Charlie, and looks at the other boy, and at the boys gathering to watch, drawn by the scent of tension and the thrill of accusations, and he wishes he had stayed on deck.

The boys are waiting, all of them, and Alec knows that this is the moment that will determine the rest of his passage from his old life to whatever his new life holds. He opens his mouth, trying not to think of his mother, and utters the most horrible phrase the stableboy taught him, a thick warble of Urdu and loathing.

Charlie smiles. A boy perched on the nearest ladder laughs. And the one who called Uncle Roger a scoundrel blinks.

There are not many more days left before the ship will slide into its berth on the Thames. England is almost upon them. Alec has, as Charlie said, left it a bit late. But the boys accept him, the newest and smallest dog in their pack. By Gibraltar, the pain in his bones has receded, and he has learned how to stampede through the lounges or along the decks without letting any of the aunties or governesses grab his ear. He knows he will never see these boys again—that's what life is, as far as Alec can tell, never seeing anyone again except possibly for Uncle Roger—but it doesn't matter.

A s the ship settles against the dock in London, Uncle Roger tightens his hand around Alec's. His voice low and quiet against the chaos and press, he asks, "Are you excited about seeing your aunt Constance?"

There is a right answer and a true answer. Alec trusts his uncle with the truth. "No."

Uncle Roger lets his breath out slowly. "Your parents thought this would be best," he says softly. "Safest and best. It's a thing parents do, sometimes, make an arrangement like this just in case. I expect when they made this plan they didn't imagine it would ever need to come about."

Alec nods. How impossible and scary would it be, to look at the unthinkable and know what to do in the face of it? How could he have decided who would get his mother, if something had happened to him, instead?

1927, *Fenbourne*

The world smells like water, loamy and dense. Alec lies still in the slanting angle of sunlight that creeps through the curtains, the light too low over the water, the chattering of birds too loud in the sagging hedges that line the lane on the other side of the dark stone wall. He's been here in Fenbourne for two days. Shipboard feels like a dream, a stack of weeks he almost can't remember. He had three days in London with Uncle Roger, the city smoking with industry, crowded in a way Alec doesn't understand. Bombay was full of people too, sometimes so many it felt as though the whole world had come to live in the streets outside the compound, but they were tangible in a way that the London masses are not.

He's lying in the patch of sun, thinking about the train from London to Ely, and the skyward reach of the old cathedral, when his uncle taps on the door and leans in.

"Time to face the day," he says.

Alec pulls the thick woolen blanket tighter against his chest. He's not sure the day needs facing, least of all by him. He can smell the English breakfast downstairs, and his treacherous stomach growls. Uncle Roger smiles. Alec pulls the blanket over his face. He wants the echo of the chaiwallah and the bright yellow birds that used to call to him from the moringa trees outside his bedroom window. Not two months before the cholera he had sat in the courtyard of his father's friend, a merchant who told stories of the gods as if he had been part of them. Alec had rubbed the trunk and knees of an elderly elephant while his mahout told stories of the elephant's youth and the campaigns they had fought together. India is all Alec knows.

"Alec," his uncle says. "Time to get dressed." He steps into the narrow room and pauses. Alec breathes in the slight mustiness of the blanket. It smells like water, too. The day before they had driven to Ely, the three of them in Aunt Constance's Rover, and in a shop full of the fug of old cigarettes he had been fitted for what his aunt called "proper clothes." She had bought him a jumper, the drape of its collar soft despite the innate scratchiness of the wool.

"They itch," he says out loud, without meaning to. He means the wool and starched bright cotton of the clothes, but he also means England, and the cottage, and the low gray sky. The truth is that it's the deep end of autumn outside, and he can tell already that the heavy clothes are better suited to the Fenlands than the flannels he wore in India, even in the cooler climates. He almost smiles, remembering the hill stations in Kashmir, when his father had galloped bareback on his tall black gelding with his collar open, singing songs that made his mother blush. Those summer mornings had made Alec feel as though he was closer to being a man like his father, the pair of them striding the mountains, his mother watching them with a smile, a light shawl bundled up around her shoulders against the faint whisper of a Himalayan breeze.

Uncle Roger sighs. "That they do."

Alec lowers the blanket and looks at his uncle, who is staring out the window, lost somewhere else. Probably India, where he will return after Christmas to rejoin the Guides Cavalry in Mardan. *Take me with you*, he almost says, but then he thinks of his mother, who wanted him here if he couldn't be with her. He takes a breath and holds it as long as he can, trying to acclimate himself to a world full of water.

. . .

He sits in a high-backed chair in Aunt Constance's dining room, moving bacon and beans around on his plate. Uncle Roger has heaped his own plate with food, and Aunt Constance turns her attention from Alec to watch her brother eat, her plate nearly empty but for a poached egg and half a tomato.

"Honestly," she says, after he goes back for more, "you're going to make yourself as fat as Father."

Uncle Roger laughs. "Never, darling Connie."

Alec, who never met his mother's parents, looks down at his bacon. The elder Tennants had left India and passed away long before he was born. Aunt Constance had visited once, after the Great War, when he was much younger. He only partway remembers her in Bombay, talking late into the night with his mother. Now, it's the first time Alec truly understands what it means that Aunt Constance is his mother's sister, not just Uncle Roger's. Not just his aunt. He examines her face, looking for traces of his mother.

She turns her focus to Alec, lines forming between her eyebrows as she watches him with concern.

"You must eat, love."

Uncle Roger says, "She's right, Alec."

"We have to go on," Aunt Constance says quietly. She looks down into her coffee. "They would want us to."

Alec blinks, the sharp welling of tears almost too much. What can he say to that?

As they make their way to visit Fenbourne's vicar late that afternoon, Alec trails behind his aunt and uncle, kicking at small stones with his sturdy new boots. His aunt's cottage sits at the northern tip of the village, just within sight of the spires of St. Anne's, and the lanes they cross as they walk into Fenbourne run toward an impossibly distant horizon. The adults talk, laughing sometimes when one brings up something the other only half remembers. Alec falls farther behind, bewildered by the wholly flat world around him, and the lowness of the sky. He turns his attention to watching the way Aunt Constance walks, the way she carries herself, the deep chestnut of her hair where it peeks out from beneath her hat. Her shoulders are straight under her brown velvet coat, and she strides almost like Uncle Roger. His mother had walked like that, too. When they reach St. Anne's, his aunt points at the bell tower, and Uncle Roger nods and says something about ringing changes. Alec follows the lines of the church with his eyes, memorizing them and wishing for his notebook. Later he will draw the dark and light of the stones, the sweep of the willow tree over the churchyard, the way the spires jut into the sky.

When his aunt and uncle step away from the church and cross to the vicarage, Aunt Constance puts out a hand to Alec. He takes it, startled by the strength of her grip. She pauses, bends a little at the waist, meets his gaze. He's sure she's going to say something—she has the look of having practiced a speech—but instead she smiles. He nods as if her smile is a covenant, overwhelmed. She has his mother's dark eyes.

There's a massive bronze lion's head on the door, and Uncle Roger lifts it as high as it goes and lets it fall with a gratifying metallic thump. Alec smiles, and his uncle winks at him.

After a moment the door opens and a maid in a starched white apron appears. "Mrs. Fane." She ducks her head.

"Good afternoon, Mary," Aunt Constance says. "I believe Mrs. Attwell is expecting us."

Mary ducks her head again and steps aside. Alec follows everyone into the house. It's dark in the front hall, and almost as cold as it is outside. Mary leads them along a deep red carpet into the drawing room, where a woman stands, smiling, her hair pulled up into a complicated knot.

"Constance," she says. She and Alec's aunt embrace.

"Imogene," Aunt Constance says, "you already know my brother, Captain Roger Tennant, and this is my nephew, Alec Oswin."

"I am so pleased to see you again, Captain Tennant," Mrs. Attwell says.

Uncle Roger bows gallantly over her hand. "The pleasure is mine."

"And, Alec," Mrs. Attwell says. She looks down at him. "I am very pleased to meet you."

"Hello." He puts out a tentative hand, which she shakes. "It's nice to meet you, too."

Mrs. Attwell smiles, but it's a sad smile, nowhere near her eyes. She and Aunt Constance sit together on the long sofa, talking about the local hospital, and Uncle Roger settles himself into a chair. Alec, left standing, has no idea what to do with himself. He drifts closer to his uncle, who grins at him as if they're sharing a secret, but Alec doesn't know what it is.

Mary brings a silver tray laden with a tea service and sets it on a table near the sofa. She hovers, waiting.

Mrs. Attwell nods. "Thank you, Mary." As the maid turns to go, the older woman says, "Please tell Mr. Attwell our guests are here."

Mary slips out of the room, and Alec watches her go. In India most of the servants had been Hindu or Muslim men, except for his ayah and his mother's maid. There had been a whole staff. At his aunt's house there is only Mrs. Whittleton, cook and housekeeper both.

The heavy wooden door opens again, but this time it's not Mary. Instead a man wearing tweed over the black and white of his vicar's garb bustles in, followed by a girl in a blue dress with a sailor collar. She regards Alec with interest.

"Captain," the man says, "Mrs. Fane. I'm so glad to see you." His watery blue eyes cruise over Alec. "Well, young man, I am awfully glad to make your acquaintance, although I very much regret the circumstances."

"Thank you," Alec says.

Mrs. Attwell turns to the girl. "June, darling, why don't you show Alec the conservatory?"

June nods, her eyes still on Alec. There is something about her gaze that holds him in place. Not just the color of her eyes, but their steadiness. They remind him of a piece of ocean glass he found for his mother when they went to the sea at Kerala.

"My name is June Attwell," she says, as she leads him out of the drawing room.

"I'm Alec Oswin."

"Yes," she says. "I know."

He treads quietly behind her, ever deeper into the house, trying to remember the way back to the others, distracted by the rows of portraits hung along the hallways.

"My mother says you're from India." She pauses beneath a picture of a stag, the oils dark and heathered, and looks him over again. "You don't look it."

"I've never been to England until now," he says, although this does not answer what feels like a question. "It's awfully gray."

June leans hard on a golden-glassed door. "Not everywhere," she says, as the door slowly opens. Alec follows her into the bright, open space, gravel paths and greenery dappled red and gold and blue by panels fit at random into the mullioned glass of the walls and ceiling. It takes him a moment to realize that he's finally starting to feel warm again.

She watches him patiently, as if she can feel how much he wants to curl up under the massive leaves of an unexpected palm. It's not India, it doesn't smell like India, but it's not the watery blur of the Fens either. He might cry.

June smiles. "Come look." She moves along the paths so surely, the dark fall of her hair curling down against the broad collar of her dress. When she stops, she points down into a low marble fountain, where carp the color of sunrise swim just beneath the surface. "I call that big one Loomis because he looks like my father's deacon."

Alec laughs, surprising himself. June grins.

They stand together quietly, watching the carp.

"Tell me about India, Alec."

He closes his eyes, concentrating on the smell of green things growing around him. "I don't know how," he says at last.

"Well," she says, "in books, there's ever so much jungle and wild animals. And soldiers."

He thinks about it. "Sometimes."

She waits, bending to pick up small handfuls of the pea-sized gravel and arranges it in shapes on the lip of the fountain.

"In the Himalayas, there is always snow," he says, "and leopards."

June stops making shapes. "Have you seen them?"

"Yes," he says. There is a hill station at Gulmarg where the summer is full of flowers, and in the winter the snow there drifts as tall as his father, the Himalayas rising in the distance. "Here there is so much mud. There's mud there too, but it's not the same." He pauses, thinking of the old men he saw from the car, catching eels and chopping at sedges. "Is all of England like this?"

"I expect not," June says. "I've only ever been as far as Cambridge. Perhaps one day we'll find out about the rest."

"Perhaps," he says. He likes the *we*.

June nods, and shifts a piece of gravel from one shape to another. She stares at the pattern for a moment, looks at Alec, frowns. "My father says you don't have a mother or father anymore."

He almost cries out. He concentrates on breathing, trying to count the stones on the fountain, watching the fish.

Her eyes pained, June says, "Mother says I ask too many questions."

Does she? Alec doesn't know. He has known her only a few minutes, but it feels like longer. For a split second he thinks he will ask his ayah if she can explain, and then he remembers everything again. It hurts.

"My mother died," he says. "They all did."

"I'm sorry," she says. Her frown deepens. "Your aunt's husband died in the War, in Palestine."

Alec starts to speak, stops. He keeps forgetting that Aunt Constance has lost people, too.

"Well," June says, "shall we get some cake?"

It's impossible to keep up with her, but he wants to try. When June looks at him, he can feel his edges. He hasn't felt this real in months. Since before his parents died.

She nods again, as if she's reached a conclusion. "To the kitchen, then, Alec. Let's see what Cook is doing."

1931, *Fenbourne*

The River Lark cuts a neat line across the northern half of Fenbourne. June likes to stand on the banks of the river and watch the water curl past. At home she has a map of what the village used to look like, before they dredged the Lark and changed its course. When she watches the Lark now she thinks about the ways even a river can change direction, and about the more distant rivers Alec has told her about. She would like to see the Ganges, or a bright cold stream making its way from the Himalayan snow to the plains. Right now the River Lark is her river, the water coursing green and brown through her veins, or it might as well be. Will these currents eventually be replaced by others, by a twisted set of rapids or a broad, smooth stream? Perhaps someday. People tell her parents that she is too clever by half. Sometimes they mean she's destined for something bigger than Fenbourne, or she hopes they do. Sometimes they mean something else.

Today she's on her way to a spot where the light hangs differently against the water, just south of the bridge that crosses the Lark and connects the northern tip of Fenbourne to the rest of the village. The week before she had seen an unusually large pike in the shallows where the riverbank has been cut away, and she wants to see it again before someone catches it. She's brought a blanket to sit on, in case the pike makes her wait.

When she gets to her spot, though, she finds Alec there, almost knee-deep in the shallows, his shoes and socks wadded up against the old bricks of the bridge. He's singing to himself—it sounds like some kind of dubious music hall tune, echoing off the bricks. She should have known he would be there, and she smiles, trying not to be cross about the fact that he has almost certainly frightened off the pike. He is so occupied with whatever he's looking for under the bridge that he doesn't see her at first. She waits.

After a moment, he emerges from the shadow, the August sun lighting his hair like white gold, and stops mid-verse. He blinks up at her. "June!"

"Hallo, Alec."

"Do you remember the first time we skated here?"

June puts her head to one side. Of course she remembers. "Yes."

He grins at her. "Come and look?"

She spreads out the blanket on the almost flat place she likes on the bank, shaded by the bridge on one side and by an alder sapling on the other. She hadn't planned to actually go into the river, but why not? It's a warm day. She slips off her socks and shoes and puts them neatly on a corner of the blanket.

Alec puts out a hand and helps her step into the water. It's cool against her legs, and she tucks away a hint of remorse that there will be mud on the hem of her skirt. She follows him as he wades back into the shadows, gesturing at the rough bricks arching over their heads. June looks up.

"Oh, Alec!"

She gives him an affectionate smile, and they stand together, the river coursing past their calves, and look at the constellations he's drawn fresh against the dark underside of the bridge. The first time he'd done it had been that first winter nearly four years ago. The Lark had frozen, and June had taught Alec how to ice-skate. They had explored the riverbanks and canals for a mile in both directions out of

Fenbourne, Alec awkward at first in his skates, and then suddenly sure of himself. By the second winter, he'd joined the boys who waited all year for the fens to freeze so they could race. But that first winter, when they were eight years old, he had come out by himself on the ice one morning and drawn the stars he remembered from his journey west, and that afternoon he had shown them to June.

"I fixed them for you," he says bashfully.

"But how?"

He grins at her. "Tall enough now."

"Oh," she says. She steps back and looks at him more carefully. Of course she's noticed how much he's grown over the years; she sees him nearly every day. But she had not realized that where he had once been eight and not tall enough to reach the arch without the added height of ice and borrowed skates, he is now a week away from twelve and able to put his palm to the lowest row of stars. She tilts her head. "But . . ."

"I borrowed a punt for the higher ones," he says. "Frank Burleigh let me take it for a day."

Frank Burleigh is the smith's son, much older than June and Alec. He seems an unlikely ally. And, as if he can see that realization on June's face, Alec blushes and looks away.

"I told him I needed it for a surprise, but he made me give him tuppence." He shrugs. "Don't tell Aunt Constance."

"I certainly won't," June says. He is so impetuous, and she wishes he would think things through. What if a sudden summer storm had swelled the current and something had happened? Well. That does not bear thinking about. She looks at him, at the anxious creases on his forehead as he waits to see if she will scold him or praise him. "Oh, Alec. Thank you."

His face goes pink with relief. June smiles and goes back to looking at the stars. In Aunt Constance's parlor, there is a globe, and June has not forgotten the afternoon she spent there with Alec showing her his India, and the long sail to England. All those places, and she knows how much the shipboard stars meant to him. She feels it somewhere deep in her heart that he keeps giving them to her, one way or another.

1933, *Fenbourne*

That summer it seems as though everywhere Alec goes there are small stands of rock—slate, most often, or the smooth gray pebbles that he has taught June to skip across the surface of the Lark—always waiting. Here, one at the corner of the churchyard wall where it juts into the lane. There, one in the shade of the yew the postmistress refuses to trim. Alec knows the cairns are for him, that June does not perform random acts, that there is a message in the precision with which she has laid them out. He hasn't seen her often enough; they are only lately back in Fenbourne for the summer, and the Attwells have kept June as busy in these weeks as Aunt Constance and Roger, here on a month of leave from Kashmir, have kept him. But the cairns are always somewhere they've recently seen each other, somewhere she knows he'll be again. Always, he knows, for him.

But knowing is different from understanding. He knows what he wants the stones to tell him. He knows that he feels June's presence differently now, that how he missed her when they went away to school last autumn is not how he will miss her when he goes back to St. Paul's in September. And he knows that the week before, when he'd squared off with his cricket bat on the pitch just outside the village, the grass defiantly emerald despite the beginnings of drought, he had turned back from the arc of the ball as it soared across the river and found June in the small crowd, her eyes and her smile on him.

He is still not used to the racket and bustle of London, although he has learned to make his way through it. He wants to tell June that *she* is how he does it, that it is by finding the small treasures that he wants to share with her—a cat painted on the wall of a pub, the tremble of light on the old glass of the window in his bedroom, the way snow and ice cathedraled along the Thames during that hideous cold winter—that he navigates the space she does not inhabit.

He wants to tell her that he would rather she inhabit all the space there is.

He's contemplating the newest cairn—quartz, pale pink and shimmering against several layers of sheared-off sandstone—when his afternoon breaks open with the sound of hooves. He looks up, shading his eyes, although he knows who it is; Roger has brought a horse with him to Fenbourne, an Arabian mare with delicate ears and wicked eyes. And nobody races through the village like Roger and Noor, the midsummer sun warming the deep bay of her coat. Twice now Roger's been seen keeping company with Melody Keswick, the youngest daughter of the local squire, but Aunt Constance says that Melody is not made for India any more than Roger is for England.

"Afternoon, Alec," Roger says. "I've been looking for you." He leans forward, holding Noor in check with his knees, and offers her a lump of sugar from his pocket.

Alec greets him and stands, mostly so Roger won't notice the cairn and ask him about it.

Roger smiles, the horse restive beneath him. "You should come out with me sometime."

"I'd like that," Alec says. He doesn't know if the galloping impresses Melody Keswick, but he can't help but wonder if it might impress June. He eyes Noor, tossing her head in the sunshine, and Roger, keeping his seat without apparent effort. The horses at the stables in the village are a docile bunch; who there could keep up with Noor and Roger? But he is bold enough for a faster horse, and he knows it. Sometimes when he watches Roger on Noor he can imagine himself crouched over the arched neck of a horse like Roger's, letting her guide them over hedgerows and ditches. The idea of the speed, the endless motion, calls to him.

"I daresay you'd like the course at Brooklands," Roger says. "Motorcars and racing and so forth." He grins at Alec, then shifts in the saddle, looking out over the landscape as if he's trying to decide what to ask Noor to jump next. "I'm going down there for a few days tomorrow, if you'd like to come along. You seem as though you might not mind some excitement."

"I saw the new Aston-Martin just before I came back from London," Alec says. "The Le Mans."

"Bloody lovely machine," Roger says. "Two-seater?"

"Yes," Alec says. It had sat idling in a street not far from school, and the rumble had got into his bones.

A bevy of sparrows jerks into the air; Noor startles. Roger tightens the reins around one hand and rubs the other along Noor's mane. "Come down with me tomorrow, if your young lady can spare you, and we'll see if we can't get you closer."

"Brilliant," Alec says, rattled by *your young lady*. Is June anyone's young lady? Could she be? June has always seemed to him to be just her own. He is June's to his core, but he's less certain that she is his. It's an uneasy thought, though an intriguing one, so he concentrates on the cars he'll see. In his mind, the engines expand into a barrage of sound. He has always loved that thrum and thunder. The idea of speed washes over him again, but this time he imagines himself in the low-swooping seat of an Aston-Martin, roaring along the straightaways in a dusty fever.

Roger leans down and claps him once on the shoulder. "Good lad. I'll see you at home, yes?"

Alec nods absently. Noor whickers, and then she and Roger are gone, the sound of hooves retreating into the distance.

Brooklands is a grand spectacle, a shiny world that smells of petrol and rubber. Roger knows everyone, knows everything, and Alec follows him from car to car while Roger smokes and chats with the drivers. These are men Roger has known for years, and they talk about liters and speeds, about the patches in the concrete track that have left it so rough that cars leave the earth for seconds at a time. It's hot in the sun, and a line of sweat creeps along Alec's spine. But being too warm is better than the too-cold of recent winters, which left him raw with longing for India. He blinks the dust out of his eyes and listens to Roger. There are quiet exchanges of pound notes, gibes about bad bets and long shots.

Roger seems closest to a group of men gathered around a brace of Alfa Romeos, bright racing red and green. He pauses to sip from someone's flask as they drink in memory of a man they call Tiger Tim, recently dead of septicemia after a racetrack injury in Tripoli that spring.

"Heroic," a man says. He looks at Alec. "Had a glory of a Bentley."

Roger nods, drinks. "Used to get up to nearly a hundred forty," he says, shaking his head in admiration. The men murmur.

"Track's not good for it," the other man says. "But Tiger Tim, he broke his own record time and again."

Alec absorbs this quietly. What must it feel like to move so quickly? To roar like lightning across the track and feel the pull of gravity and the car on the steep banking curves?

That afternoon he sits with Roger and his friends and has a pint like the other men. He watches how they move. There are boys at school like that, nearly men, who fill the space around them, and boys who don't. Alec knows he is somewhere in between; he has just begun to feel the way he occupies his ground. Cricket helps, because everyone knows who he is. His height helps too; he's nearly as tall as Roger now, and looks older than a few weeks from fourteen.

"Tomorrow afternoon there's women racing the course," one of the men says. "Reckon there might be some good motors, though."

Another man leans off to the side and spits. "No place for ladies here," he says. "Although . . . A woman who wants to race isn't much of a lady." The group nods, grumbles. Alec watches their faces, puzzled by the distinction he doesn't understand. His aunt drives fast, and there is no doubt that she is a lady. And Melody Keswick, too—she is gentry, but he has heard Roger laud her recklessness on horseback and behind the wheel. Is it the act of competition that changes things? Is it the difference between wanting to go fast and wanting to go faster than someone else? He makes a note to ask June.

After lunch the next day Roger takes Alec to a stable near Byfleet. Alec nearly protests missing the afternoon's races—he wants to be able to tell June about the women and their cars—but the idea of watching Roger with horses pulls at him, too. Roger seems reserved and a little wary, and gradually Alec realizes that there is probably a gambling issue here as well. Perhaps, judging by Roger's face, a less happy story than whatever is between him and the men at Brooklands.

The stable itself does not provide any answers; Roger is his usual bluff self with the bandy-legged trainer who walks them through the barn, and Alec finds himself as absorbed as ever with the way Roger touches the horses. He wants to know anything as well as Roger knows horses. Cricket is close—how the bat feels in his hands, the way he can almost sense how the air and grass and men will work together with every bowled ball . . . Yes. It's close.

But that night, after the drive back to Fenbourne, he realizes that what he most wants to understand is June. He wants to know what she is telling him with the cairns, and what each of her smiles means.

He curls into the corner of his bed, watching the moon, wondering if June is watching it, too. Most nights, he tells himself the stories his mother used to tell him—Kipling, sometimes, or tales of Vishnu and Shiva and the Monkey King, but most of all an ever-changing tale of a princess and a bear and their life along a river somewhere. He can't remember where, and the loss of that detail gives him a pang every time he thinks of it. The maharani and her bear, the river cold as mountain ice. But tonight the details don't stick, and when he finally sleeps, his dreams are full of the blue sky above the Himalayas, of an avalanche shuddered into life by the sound of motorcycles, of the fire he never saw that consumed his parents and the cholera that had taken them.

I t's the next evening that they go to the vicarage for dinner. As they get ready, Aunt Constance fusses over him as if he were much younger, until Roger pulls her away with a laugh. Alec watches Roger, freshly shaved and gleaming in his dress uniform. The men he sees most often are the masters at school, or tradesmen or farmers either in the City or here in Fenbourne. But Roger is the kind of man he can see himself becoming—an officer, like his father, his shoulders broad in the uniform. Perhaps a horse, a commission in the Guides, a return to India.

At the vicarage, June enters the drawing room with her father, exactly as she had the first time he saw her. But she's elegant now in a way that startles him to the core, in a dress the color of coffee, her hair pulled back. He is not prepared for either the lines of her beneath the fabric or the way he feels when he notices. When she turns to greet Aunt Constance, Alec tries to catch his breath. He is not prepared for June at all.

They fill the room with chatter, Alec and June together by the window with their thimbles of sherry, the adults islanded on the furniture. Alec keeps stumbling over talking about the races, and each time she regards him with her level eyes, waiting, even while he knows she's listening to Roger and her father talk about what's happening on the Continent.

Finally she says, "Alec?"

"Yes?" He looks down at her, and realizes for the first time that it's been a while since they were eye to eye.

"I'm glad you're here." She smiles softly at him. His heart larrups.

"I am, too," he says, feeling the insufficiency. June's smile broadens as if she feels it too, through him, and forgives it, and she sips at her sherry. Her hair looks so soft, and he's glad when he hears Mr. Attwell say something about the Ashes and England's win against Australia last winter. Talking about cricket will be so much easier.

"Australia are looking strong again for the next series," Mr. Attwell says mildly.

"Alec can fetch 'em back if Australia win," Roger says, reaching out and poking at Alec's shoulder.

Alec grins obligingly. Playing for England would be grand indeed. And playing for the Ashes would take him back through India.

Mr. Attwell acknowledges Roger with a nod. "Say what you like, I prefer my cricket the old-fashioned way."

Roger grimaces. "Nothing wrong with body-line."

"I shouldn't like someone bowling at me like that," Alec says quietly, and the men both stare at him. Mr. Attwell's thin mouth curves into a smile.

"In any event," Aunt Constance says, her words clipped, "isn't what's happening in Germany more important?"

"We beat them once," Roger says, shrugging and lighting a cigarette. "If need be, we'll do it again."

"But the cost," Aunt Constance says. "Another generation, lost."

Alec turns and meets June's eyes. It feels good to be included as an adult, more or less, but it was easier when they could slip off to the conservatory together, away from the politics. He takes a step closer to her, wishing, although he's not quite sure for what.

She smiles again, as if she knows his thoughts, but then she moves nearer to where Roger is talking about the last war. Alec follows.

"If there is another war with Germany, mightn't it mean the end of empire?" she says, and the adults stop talking and turn. Alec realizes abruptly that they are listening as if she is one of them. Of course they are.

She continues. "Whether we win or lose—"

Mr. Attwell says, "We'll win handily enough, if it comes to it."

"That great wally at Downing Street will give the Huns his own bloody children if we let him," Roger mutters. Mrs. Attwell frowns and murmurs something about language, and Roger goes red.

"In India they've begun to partition the electorate," June says. "I should think that another war in which we expect the Indians to fight for Britain might make that fragmentation more pronounced."

"The end of the Raj," Aunt Constance says.

Alec doesn't know what to say—India has been part of his family forever. He is the third generation of Oswin to be born there, the fourth to feel the shattering rains of the monsoons. Intellectually he understands, almost, but in his heart, it's a bewilderment.

"Speaking of India," June says, eyeing him, "or, not India, quite, they've nearly made Everest this time."

"They might manage next time," Alec says.

"Lady Houston should be credited more," Aunt Constance says. "I expect she would have liked to see them succeed. It's quite an investment."

"It's a faith," Mrs. Attwell says tersely. "Imagine such a life." Alec nods. He had followed the trip closely in *The Guardian*, the pictures ranging through his memory. Impossible photographs of impossible acts, biplanes soaring above the clouds, the sharp prow of the mountains in the background. He can't look at the pictures without thinking about the crystallized kernel of absence his parents' deaths left in his life, but also he can't help thinking about what it must be like to fly. To be human, but other, thousands of feet above the surface of the earth, freed from all of it.

"On top of a mountain is not a good place for a woman," Roger says. He narrows his eyes at his sister, who looks like she wants to interject. "Don't look at me like that, Connie. Basic matter of strength, that's all. Women aren't suited to adventure."

June frowns, clearly vexed. "What about Gertrude Bell? Or Amelia Earhart?"

Roger smiles indulgently at June. "Exception proves the rule."

"We have our roles for a reason," Mr. Attwell says. June looks away, her lips pressed into a thin line.

Alec smiles at her. "There were women racers at Brooklands. Mechanics, too."

"When the next war comes," June says, glancing at Alec's aunt as if seeking her approval, "I suppose we'll see what women are capable of, if all the men go to the front and we're needed again for factories and farms."

"That's enough, June," Mr. Attwell says mildly, and June blushes, looking down at her hands.

Mary comes in to announce dinner, and as they all rise to their feet, it feels as though the room has let out its breath. As they sit, June leans close and whispers to Alec, "Every time I see a picture of Everest, Alec? I think of you."

Two mornings later, when a cairn made of sharply angled shears of slate appears beneath the willow in front of the cottage, he thinks of Everest, and something shifts in his chest, as joyous as an otter. Perhaps he doesn't have to ask her what it means after all.

1934, *Fenbourne*

I n flood years, the River Lark and the various rills and streams and minor tributaries that feed from it creep into the roads and lanes of Fenbourne. June has lost count of how often the bells of St. Anne's have rung the alarm when the river has crested too high, and twice that she can remember the water has edged up nearly to the steps of the church. Everyone knows the council needs to fix the sluices and clear the canals, or the flooding will just get worse, but so far they are mired in inaction like the tangles of branches and scummy dross that catch in the gates of the lock.

June wakes one morning the summer she turns fifteen to find the half-familiar stench of muck filling the air. She lies still, breathing it in. Not a flood yet, or the alarm would have rung, but something. And the floods are a winter problem, for the most part, when the rain fills the ditches and the wind brings more water in from the Wash. She stands and goes to the window. There's a ginger tom lying in the lane that runs alongside the vicarage, basking in the bright yellow morning and washing his paws. But no mud. Maybe she's dreamed it?

Today is the day Alec comes home. He's been away at school in London, and his absence has cut her to the bone. It's unfair, of course; she's been at school too, far to the west in Winchester, and no matter how often they write each other, the letters are no real substitute for what they have when they're together. They can't meander along the riverbank or explore the lanes, and she can't watch his dark eyes spark with interest when she shows him one of her maps or talks about someone they both know in the village. But she's also been back in Fenbourne longer, and it feels like an entirely different place with Alec not in it. She's surprised by how unsettling it is to move through a day here without seeing him, or without feeling the curious weight of his seeing her. The year before had been harder; there was the adjustment to being away from home completely, not just the shift of being apart from one's shadow.

June settles herself into the window seat, watching the cat. He has stretched himself out like a bow, a proud arc of fur and sinew. A breeze pushes over him, ruffling a tangle of wild roses that tumbles into the lane. The cat stands, stretches fore and aft, and meanders away, his tail waving behind him like a periscope. June looks out over what she can see of the village, but most of it is behind her—her window faces north toward the river. Toward Alec.

O n the north bank of the river lives a boy who carries with him a stub of pencil and a battered notebook. Inside it, he draws pictures of the stars and moon, of boats he remembers from what seems like a lifetime ago, of the lines he sees in the bark of the larches and oaks that stand outside his aunt's house. On the south bank, waiting, June makes maps of the world around her and lays them out across the ancient, creaking atlas in the study where her father composes his sermons. He is a dry man, and his sermons read accordingly, but his study is full of the deep smell of leather and books, and the small thunder of letting a map roll itself back up. She opens a notebook and lists the railway timetables from Ely to Norwich and King's Lynn and London by memory.

Her father teases her sometimes about her need for information, the hunger she has to know everything. She can't explain it, any more than she can explain the way maps unfold in her head, or the stories she sees in equations. Alec never asks her why she needs to know—he quietly tries to find the answer. She maps the cities for which she's listed the times. Compared to hers, Alec's drawings are like puzzles, lines that leap and curl, stars that don't exist, imprecise but somehow perfect even when she doesn't understand them. She looks down at the paper on which she has been making her own lines, satisfyingly straight. She smiles.

The maps keep her attention, as they always do, until Mary Hubbox bursts in an hour or so later.

"Begging your pardon, Miss," Mary says, "but Master Alec is here for you."

June looks up, a little lost. She's been deep in re-creating a particular street in Winchester, not far from school, where she and her friends go to buy ices on the rare afternoons that they can leave the grounds of St. Swithun's. The vicarage seems almost imaginary. As does Alec, and then he pokes in his head behind Mary.

"Thank you, Mary," June says. Mary bobs a light curtsy and leaves.

Alec has grown again. His jaw is thicker, and his hair, which he has always let fall how it will, is now carefully combed back over his head and neatly parted. He is not quite a man, but not the boy he was last summer, either. Over the Christmas holidays June had noticed that he was changing, but this seems abrupt. She can't decide how she feels about this new version of Alec.

"I say," he says, and June's eyes widen at the new depth of his voice, "can't just leave a fellow standing around. Got scooped up by the pater."

"Hello, Alec," she says, wondering what her father had to say to him. "Welcome back."

He strides forward as if he's going to hug her, then stops himself.

June has a bristle of feeling—not panic, exactly, but a new kind of confusion. An embrace from a young man, even this young man, perhaps especially this one, is another thing entirely now. She can almost see him look through the floor as if seeking out her father. Ah—perhaps he has given Alec some kind of hint about keeping to himself. But Alec is suddenly bigger, more assured, more like his own person than she's ever seen him. For an instant, she hopes her father's speech, if there was one, doesn't stick.

"June," he says. He exhales, and then it's as if he's himself again, the affected public school chap gone and replaced by the boy with stars in his eyes.

They have developed rituals for these reunions. They go to the kitchen and bother Cook, who adores Alec and has made his favorite cake, a sandwiched Victoria sponge, special for him. Alec and June sit at the heavy oak table in the kitchen with thick mugs of tea, and June's heart warms at the way he trails his fingertips through the extra jam at the seam of the layers. Then, full of cake, Alec and June lie on benches in the conservatory and talk about their schoolmates, working their way back to the way they are here, in Fenbourne, at home. For the first time, Alec is quiet about school, and she can't quite put a finger on why.

Later, they stop at the cottage and spin the globe in Aunt Constance's parlor, Alec quizzing June about the geographical details he knows she loves. After a while, he stops the globe with his palm across India and sighs. "In India my ayah told me stories about painting the world with mud and saffron, so I wanted to show you, but . . . I haven't any saffron, and the mud here is all wrong."

"But . . ." June frowns. "Why is that bothering you today in particular, Alec?"

Alec shrugs, the small boy showing through for a moment. "There's a new fellow at school, from Pondicherry. He was talking about the monkeys who lived out behind his house." He looks down at the globe, his fingers tracing the equator.

Now his reticence about school makes sense, if there is some new talk of India, or any of the kaleidoscope of things that makes him fall into memory. Sometimes June wishes he could be more here, more now. He's been in England for almost seven years, and now and again she feels as though he thinks he's working out a punishment for something, and then he can go back, join the cavalry with his uncle or some such idea. But how could he be so far from her? What would either of them do? But then he'll smile, or perform spectacularly for his side in the annual village cricket match, and she'll go back to believing he almost feels at home here.

"It's not just mud," she says, hoping to distract him. "It's all the present and past of the riverbank, all at once."

He grins at her. "Historical mud, then? Possibly some old Normans catting about in it?"

June laughs. "Quite." Something is shifting between them, and June knows he can feel it too, this new thrum of tension between them.

"I missed you." He stares down at the globe, his ears red. June has never made a boy blush, as far as she knows. Or at any rate, not like this. Not in a good way.

"I missed you too, Alec. I'm glad you're back."

He smiles at her, and June, abruptly aware of how near he is, says, "It's awfully warm up here, isn't it?"

"We could go sit in the garden," Alec says, and June nods. They make their way outside and sit beside each other on the old bench beneath the larches. After a moment, he says, "Once upon a time, there was a river, and on that river there lived a bear."

He had been taken from the forest as a cub, but he was too small to fight the other bears in the pits. And there was a keeper, a man named Rowland who had spent too much time among the animals of the forest, and he believed that a bear was almost like a human.

On the south bank of the Thames, Rowland's bears were known for being smarter and larger than the other bears, but as likely as a wild bear to take off a man's head. But the small bear, who Rowland taught to dance, was known to be his favorite.

The Thames froze hard that winter, and tents sprang up almost overnight between the boats held captive by the ice. A group of men from one of the theaters built a pit out of rocks and ice and bags of ash. They asked Rowland for a bear, and another man for a brace of hounds to torment it, and when Rowland said no, they spat at his feet.

He walked the ice for two days, wondering how to keep the little bear safe. A princess from India watched Rowland from her sleigh, pulled by immaculate white oxen. The glassy eyes of the furs she wore shone so bright Rowland nearly believed she balanced an actual leopard around her shoulders. Maybe she was a witch, he thought, and he pulled his tattered coat around him and walked on.

He pauses, and June reaches out and puts her fingers on his wrist. The air tightens between them. Then, as he leans closer and her face turns up to the sun and his smile, a clatter of lorry and work boots pounds along the lane. Alec jerks away, his face going crimson.

And June reminds herself to breathe. *All in good time,* she thinks. Like the ends of the bear stories, like everything. All in good time.

. . .

The summer they turn eighteen, Alec takes her up the River Lark in a borrowed punt. The water is running high again this summer, and she trails her hands in it like a Victorian heroine. Alec grins down at her, his shirtsleeves rolled up over taut forearms, and she's glad to have this time to spend with him. She has seen the way other girls in the village look at him, and soon he'll be off to university, where she imagines he will cut a dashing figure. He'll play cricket for his college at Cambridge, and she can see already how he'll look in the whites, standing ready with his bat on the endless green of the pitch. She is going to Oxford, to read mathematics at Somerville College. She would have liked it if Alec had come to Oxford too; she can imagine them punting on the Thames and wandering the ancient town together. But he will be happy at Clare College, following in his father's footsteps. At least he is staying in England. When his uncle Roger had visited over Easter, full of tales about the Frontier and the bandits of the Hindu Kush, June had felt Alec's longing for India to be as dense as the thick weave of a tapestry.

She closes her eyes and listens to the water, to the shush of the pole against the current and the riverbed, imagines the light splashing of a frog somewhere, or a fish. The afternoon climbs through her like a film, all crystalline black and white.

Alec whistles quietly. Then he says, almost under his breath, "June? There on the bank."

At first she doesn't see it, but then the otter moves again, gliding into the water with a suspicious glance at Alec, the punt, everything.

"It's good luck," Alec says, and goes back to guiding them up the river. And then, before she's really ready to be there, wherever *there* is, he adroitly steers the punt into the bank and ties it to a willow tree's convenient branch. He anchors himself on the riverbank and reaches down for her. She takes his hand, and for just a moment, there's a shift between them.

"Look," he says, pulling his gaze from hers, and helps her up the gentle slope of the bank. In the field opening before them, there are five horses the color of sugar just before it burns. They're grazing, and then one tosses his head and sends his mane sparking out from the arch of his neck. He whinnies, his ears pricked forward, and then he runs, gathering speed. She is still holding Alec's hand, and she knows he will not let go.

When he turns to face her, his eyes questioning and all brown and gold in the sun, she says nothing. And when he bends to kiss her, his hand still tight around hers, she lets him.

Is this how it happens, then, falling in love? In stages for years and years, then one swift tumble of feelings at the end?

BOOK TWO

1940, *Fenbourne*

The news from Dunkirk is appalling—German forces everywhere, the French and English shoved off into the docks in chaos, equipment abandoned. June has never felt more useless in her life. At the vicarage, she tunes in to the wireless with her parents, greedy for news about where the Germans are, hoping always for a morsel of new information about Alec's squadron. If she thinks too much about the peril Alec is in, the war threatens to swallow her.

With her father in his study more, drafting sermons meant to help the village through the darkness, June is untethered. But she doesn't need the scroll of maps, except to act as a sort of rosary to ward off her fears—all of Europe exists in her mind, the borders and fronts porous and shifting as she ponders the span of the war. Yet the vicarage feels claustrophobic, and she's glad to escape to the comforting shimmer of midsummer sun on toadflax and yarrow when her worries become too vast.

She bicycles through the village, visits Alec's aunt, does sums in her head. For the first time, she regrets the way she accelerated through university; had she taken her time, she would have the possibility of school in the autumn. Although—the war might have stopped that too, the way it's stopping everything else. She feels selfish, sometimes, fretting about that. After all, Alec's path through university has been interrupted, his service in Cambridge's student RAF cadet program transferred to the No. 600 City of London Squadron. They fly sorties as the war in the air fills the skies with menace, and when a cluster of planes passes overhead, June stops what she's doing—is Alec among them, just out of reach? His squadron changes bases so frequently that she is often a step or more behind, but the dots on the maps in her head help. But then in the night she worries—Alec is doing his part, risking his life every day for King and Country, but what is she doing?

Her mother has taken in a ragged cluster of children evacuated from London, and the press of that duty helps June, although the chaos sometimes leaves her feeling a bit strangled. Her mother says they're doing good work, important work, providing a place for the children. And June knows the truth of that—these children may well be alive because they're in Fenbourne, bedded down on cots in June's old nursery, surrounded by wallpaper with pictures of rabbits and cats in woolly jumpers and ridiculous hats. June has always hated that wallpaper, and she doesn't wish it on the evacuees. When eight-year-old George Cowan, a banty little Cockney, takes a pen and a bottle of India ink to the animals, she secretly supports his cause. Other than George, though, June finds the children daunting at best, and she's glad enough to accept the help of the girls from the village, who seem perfectly able to navigate the tumult.

Letters come from Alec, always a combination of his tendency to tell her everything and his need to be relatively circumspect about his squadron. She stores the letters in a small wooden box, keeping them close to try to hold the worry at bay, even as it blurs with her frustration that she's not doing more.

It's a damp Sunday in August, the sun too hot through the rain, the sound of birdsong and frogs from the fens almost too much to bear, when her father sends for June. Waiting in the drawing room with her father is an old friend of his from his own university days.

"June," Mr. Attwell says, kneading his hands anxiously before him, "you remember Sir Reginald, I'm sure?"

"Of course," June says. She puts out a hand, and one of Sir Reginald's eyebrows quirks upward as he reaches to shake it.

"Can't say when I last saw you," he says. "A dog's age."

"Quite," June says. She stands before the men, wondering whether she should look bold or demure. Her mother would counsel demure, but . . .

"You've just done at Oxford?"

"I have," she says. "Applied mathematics."

He laughs quietly, his mustache bristling across his upper lip. "Don't be shy, Miss Attwell. You took a double First, if I'm not much mistaken? And Firsts in languages as well?"

June blinks. Her academic honors at Somerville College are a source of pride for her, perhaps too much pride, if her father's sermons are any indication, and she is unused to talking about them. They often seem to have no real purpose in the life she sees playing out before her, although sometimes there is a tug from an unseen string, pulling her toward something bigger that she can't quite name. Hearing her accolades from someone else is new, and doubly so in the case of someone like Sir Reginald Cooper-Byatt, whose career at Whitehall is something June's father has never described clearly; it is incomprehensible that he knows, or cares, what she did at Oxford.

June nods, trying to find her way through the conversation. Next to Sir Reginald, her father frowns, his hands wringing together so intently that June idly wonders if they might burst into flame.

"I believe we have a mutual friend," Sir Reginald says. "Floss Corbett."

"Oh, yes," June says. "He was one of the Fellows at Balliol. He took me under his wing." Floss is the Honorable Alastair Corbett, an earl's youngest son, twelve years June's senior, and, outside of Alec, her closest friend. One of the lecturing Fellows in the mathematics department, nominally attached to Balliol and not part of the faculty at Somerville, he had read her research and challenged her endlessly. There had been innumerable nights when their insular group of mathematicians had stayed up together until nearly dawn, drinking sherry and building ever more complicated puzzles to challenge one another. By the start of her third year, she had become his confidant, despite their age difference, and he her mentor.

"Corpus Christi man myself," Sir Reginald says. "Any rate, Corbett speaks quite highly of you. Said you might be just the girl we need."

June smiles, pleased by the reference Floss has given her, and even more curious as to what Sir Reginald might be asking.

"It's clerical work mostly," he continues, "lot of Foreign Office claptrap, but we need girls who will do it right the first time."

"Anything," June says, startled and confused. She glances at her father. He nods encouragingly. Clerical does not sound like much, and yet. The words *Foreign Office* seem magical, quite the opposite of Fenbourne. And she will be helping, doing her part, performing her duty. For a moment she is lost in the idea of living in a flat in London, going to Whitehall or somewhere else where people are actually doing something.

Sir Reginald smiles. "Good girl." He looks at her father again, more serious now. "You worry too much, Attwell. We'll take care of her."

Her father regards her with a watery, benevolent smile. "It will be good for you, I imagine, keep you busy while you wait for your young man to come home."

Sir Reginald chuckles. "Yes, I expect she'll be considerably occupied. Lots to do."

The three of them discuss it a bit more before Sir Reginald leaves, and June's mind turns to the lists she needs to make, the whole unknown future for which she must plan. She'd been away from home for school, but this will be very different. This time it will stand for something.

The next few weeks pass in a blur of aptitude tests in London—drills to test June's acumen at Morse and simple codes like the Caesar shift, complicated crosswords run on very tight clocks, stilted conversations in German about the weather or what she might find at the greengrocer. It would all feel so basic, except that everywhere she goes there is an undercurrent of tension. It already seems so long ago that she'd gone downstairs to find Sir Reginald waiting with her father. Not a week later she'd gone up to London, to the Admiralty, where a liveried page had led her through the hushed corridors to Sir Reginald's office. He had sat behind a wide ocean of mahogany and slid a paper across to her. *Sign*, he'd said, *and then we'll chat, yes?* Floss had been there too, as sleek and ageless as a rook, and stooped from a long-ago fever and the cane it left him dependent on.

They had given her a moment to realize she was looking at the Official Secrets Act, enacted to fight espionage in the years before the Great War, and bolstered not long thereafter: *Be it enacted by the King's most Excellent Majesty*, it began. She had paused over that and the dire tone of the rest of it, and Sir Reginald had watched her hesitate and smiled quietly. *You're right to think it through*, he'd said, as she'd read it again. *Everything you'll do with us will be strictly confidential. You'll report to Corbett, but not a word to anyone else—that would be treason and handled accordingly.* She had considered the Rubicon she was about to cross, and what it would mean. She had always told Alec everything, and now that would be different. But she had known as well that signing the Act was what would let her do her part for King and Country. And so she had taken a breath, excited and a little scared, and signed her name. *Attwell*, Floss had asked her then, grinning like a fox, *do you remember when I showed you the Vigenère cipher back in your second year?*

In October Floss takes her to an old manor house in Bedfordshire, where a cluster of mathematicians and engineers show her how best to sweep the dial of a wireless machine and pick even the tiniest sounds out of the emptiness of silent frequencies. She learns about ionospheres and frequencies, and how to change the tubes in the back of the wireless—wherever she's going, Floss tells her, she may need to fill more than one role. So she absorbs everything they teach her, and before long her rudimentary skills at the wireless blossom into an aptitude for telegraphy and plain-language intercepts.

As autumn deepens, June goes back to London, where she's staying with Ainsley Finch-Martin, a friend from Oxford, although it often feels as though she spends more time at the commandeered girls' school in suburban Mill Hill. Her days are full of Morse code and increasingly convoluted discussions in German. Almost everyone she works with comes from a background in maths because, as Floss explains, the newer codes need more lateral thinking than language thinking. The night after he tells her this, June lies awake, remembering how much time he had spent at Oxford guiding her into taking German and more theoretical mathematics. From this distance she can see the skeleton of what must have been his plan all along—how long had he known there would be another war? How long ago had he decided to insert himself into her life with the aim of bringing her into his corner of this strange secret world?

Even as June begins to understand how important this work will be, she strives to be the best at all the exams and drills. Everyone there is more than capable of sending or receiving a message in Morse code, but the goal is something much more challenging. June is pleased when she cracks twenty words a minute of taking down an incoming message, but that's still not fast enough—her instructors press her until she can take in whole swaths of information all at once, words and phrases instead of a letter at a time. When she's comfortable at thirty words a minute, with a zero percent error rating, one of the senior radiomen pauses by her station with a muttered *Well done, Attwell.*

In Bedfordshire again that winter Floss shows her a series of Japanese codes, and she finds that she can see the patterns there as well. Excited by the flurry of new information, June digs into the language texts she's given. For weeks afterward, even when she's back in London, the only words she speaks or reads with her trainers are Japanese, and all she reads are reports of the crisis in Manchuria or intelligence documents about the endless build-up of the Emperor's forces. She's never been so tired in her life, but it's a good, purposeful tired, kanji pictographs parading across the backs of her eyelids when she's drifting off to sleep.

Early in the new year, Floss shifts her duties again, this time setting her up at a wireless interception station on the outskirts of London. Suddenly everything she's done seems real—the crackle of the radio means something else now, and the first time she hears a German radio operator's voice her mouth goes dry with trepidation and excitement. Before long, she can identify a few German telegraph operators; they each have a unique signature of sorts in how they tap out the messages. It makes the war more personal, suddenly, more like a genteel game of chess over the radio waves, but now with fatal consequences when checkmate is called.

Through all her training, letters come from Alec, and with each response June has to parse for herself what she can or cannot say. She can't share her exhilaration about the work or what she's learned, and so the letters she sends to him grow ever more anodyne and repetitive—the London weather, reassurances about her safety despite the constant German bombing, a few vague words about how glad she is to be doing her part. She builds the idea of herself as just another girl in an office with a pencil and paper, writing down numbers or taking notes in meetings. The only time she feels honest is when she tells him how much she misses him, and asks him to stay safe. Somewhere out there are Germans taking down RAF messages, and June can only hope they are not as good at their work as she is.

1940, *RAF Manston*

The middle of August, and hell raining down upon them. Messerschmitts, their windows mirrored with morning light, the scream of engine and machine gun, and everywhere the puffs of bullets slamming into earth. The incandescent glow of a Spitfire laced by a German gunner, and men screaming.

Alec presses his face to the earth in a ditch beneath what's left of an apple tree, his heart thundering in his chest. Manston is too close to the coast, too close to the Thames estuary. The Me 109s, when they turn back for home, have to dump their bombs somewhere—a lighter, swifter plane is better when you're trying to get back to the Continent. And Manston is an incredible target—all those planes on the airfield, runways pocked with craters from other, earlier raids, a few score airmen and their ground support, and all of them scared. They pretend that the fear makes them stronger, and maybe that's true, although it sometimes seems to Alec quite the opposite, in moments like this, when the sound of shelling sends them into ditches. But mostly the fear holds them in place, clinging to their duty as if it might save their lives. Alec has never asked why the RAF keep the station open—all the men know it's too close, too dangerous, but Whitehall want them there. Scapegoats, one man says. A diversion, says another.

He has been with No. 600 Squadron since the war started, straight out of the University Squadron at Cambridge. It's a reserve unit, all volunteer in theory, but *reserve* and *volunteer* mean something different now than they did when the war was new. Conscription is now a fact of life, and he'd rather be here than in the army. Flying is an endless source of amazement—the sounds and smells, the banging of the engine into the night and the scrape of wind across his propellers . . . Flight is the best thing that's ever happened to him, except for June. For so long he'd thought he might go back and join Roger in the Guides, but this . . . He belongs in the air, and in any case the cavalry is changing—a recent letter from Roger laments the shift from proper horses to tanks and lorries. Alec can't imagine going to war in something like that, not when he can be up here where the air courses like a river around his plane. Every day he thinks about what his life will be like after the war, about staying in the RAF and making a career of it. Perhaps finding his way to the bases at Peshawar or Agra, and flying over India. And every day he wonders what June would think of a life at the Frontier. Likely enough she knows already what flying means to him, how it makes the sinews of his chest thrum. She has always been the smart one. The smart one, the beautiful one, the best one. He knows how lucky he is.

Another Messerschmitt buzzes overhead, much too close, and Alec tries to make himself smaller and less visible. What he wants most is to leap into his plane and wield the power to drive the Germans away from Manston. Instead, he lies as still as he can, stranded like a fledgling on the ground, breathing in the cordite and sweat.

No. 600 Squadron shares the broken runway with a squadron of Spitfires. Their own Bristol Blenheims are faster than they look, but crowded, the fuselage cramped with three of them in there. He can't always see what he's doing when he comes in for a landing. Too, the Blenheims are unwieldy in the daytime, and most of their missions are night fighter engagements now. At night the sounds of engine and gun seem to echo back from the moon and stars, though he knows it isn't true.

Alec loves being part of something larger, the reciprocal reliance each pilot has on his crew and on the other pilots. He loves his squadron, despite its inherently transient nature and the endless grief that they never have time to process. The men who were here when he joined it have mostly shifted or transferred or died. Even their leaders are changing. Jimmy Wells was his first CO, and he's been gone since early summer, when a training accident killed him. Nothing is ever the same; nobody is ever the same. The men who don't vanish aren't the same either, especially after two months of Manston, under constant fire. Alec sleeps when he can, plays card games like whist and clagg in the mess with the other airmen, all of them always ready to scramble into the gloaming.

A round him, bullets whine and skip. The ditch feels like a long stripe of target carved out of the earth, but he's not sure anywhere else would be better. They have learned these last weeks that there is not much in the way of shelter at Manston. The endless raids have taught them that much.

A plane banks in the sky, and he tilts his head, listening to the pull of metal and flaps against gravity. He glances up—one of the German planes is hit, spiraling into the fields a mile or so hence, and the rest seem to be retreating, a group of Spitfires at their heels. *Good*, he thinks. If the Germans are clearing off, that's one more attack he's survived, which feels like one step closer to being with June again.

He remembers her face when he told her he'd joined the reserves, the way pride and worry had filled her eyes. And again, on that last day before they'd parted, that Sunday in London, nearly a year ago. Everyone knew war would be declared; Hitler had refused all entreaties; it was only a matter of time. And so Alec had gone to London, where

June was spending a weekend with a girl she'd known at university. Ainsley Finch-Martin's people had money and titles, though Ainsley herself was taking nurse's training at Great Ormond, and Alec had felt just a bit shabby.

The three of them had sat quietly and listened to Chamberlain on the wireless. So that was it, then. War. Nothing was different, and everything. An air raid siren ripped through the morning, and he could nearly feel the tension all over London of people looking at the sky, already tired of waiting. Ainsley made tea, and then they listened to the King's speech.

After, June pulled him round the corner of the kitchen and kissed his cheek, and they went out into the sunny midday, watching crews of men struggle to get barrage balloons aloft. At Russell Square they sat close together on a bench, watching pigeons. He remembered the way the pigeons had flung themselves into the sky when a troupe of children passed, lined up two by two in a crocodile on their way to Euston or King's Cross. So quiet, and yet a vibration of panic underneath, all over the city, showing in the cautious evacuations of children, the careful low voices of couples. How many of the pairs he saw were having the same conversation he was having with June?

In the crucible of RAF Manston, he holds tight to the knowledge, as sure as breath, that she is his, and he hers. At the end of that day in London there had been the press of time, and the press of greed for June's touch. It would be months before they saw each other again, perhaps longer. After their tea he had taken her back to the house in Bloomsbury, both of them knowing that he would be back in his airplane the next day. Both of them knowing the war was not going to be over by Christmas, whatever the optimists and idealists said. So she had led him into her room and quietly closed the door, and they had let the hunger speak for them.

Months later, and it feels like the war will never end. Alec lifts his

head; the Germans have gone, for now. They'll be back in a day or two.
Or tomorrow. Or that evening. Or never.

Somewhere a man is crying, his sobs like the lowing of a cow.

A letter comes from June—a friend of her father's has recommended
her to the Foreign Office, and she is excited to be doing her part
at last, spurred on like so many others by Dunkirk, which feels equally
like catastrophe and miracle. Alec's chest fills with ice; London is a
target, and much less safe than the Fens. He writes back and tells her
to be careful; he is more afraid of losing June than he is of the Germans. There is so much more he wants to say, but he doesn't know how,
and he can't bear the idea of being clumsy with her when they are so
far apart, a war and what sometimes seems like half the world between
them. So he tells her he loves her. He tells her to come back to him.
Once upon a time there was a river, he writes, emptying his heart onto
the page, *and on that river lived a bear* . . . It is the best he can do, and
the least.

The squadron moves from base to base. In the nights, settled into
the tight pilot's seat of the Blenheim, Alec narrows his eyes against
the horizon, scanning for the blurry shadows and tracer fire that signify
enemy aircraft. He flies his sorties over the Channel and the North
Sea, his mouth watering with a confused, queasy, iron-flavored triumph when he shoots down his first German plane. Later he'll dream
of that night, of climbing out of the clouds and finding himself in the
middle of a squadron of Luftwaffe planes, the inventive cursing of his
gunner, the German rounds screaming past his small windscreen, the

howling of his guns. Back at base the ground crew paint a tiny swastika on the nose of the Blenheim to mark the kill. Another night, bolstered by the new Mk III radar, he and his crew shoot down a Dornier bomber in tandem with another Blenheim. He watches the bomber plunge into the darkness below, smoke boiling out of the fuselage. Another kill mark goes up on the nose.

When they're not flying, they're still together. Three men, one airplane, one crew. Alec wishes the war would end, but he loves these men. He and Tim Yates, his bombardier and navigator, and Cobber Willis, his gunner, are as close as any other crew—and lucky, besides, to still be together. Lucky not to have to replace one man with someone new—even though every set of men stops being individuals at some point and becomes the mission. They drink together, catch sleep when they can, scramble when the alarm sends them to the sky. They look for German planes, shoot at them, try not to be shot at themselves.

He doesn't realize how far into his routine he's settled until a new pilot joins the squadron—Sanjay Kichlu, one of a score of Indian Air Force veterans who have come to England to join the RAF and fight the Germans. It's not long before Alec discovers that Sanjay, only a year or two older than he is, has been to many of the same parts of Kashmir and the hill country. When they're not in the air, they talk about tigers and snow, drinking too much of the strong milky tea in the station's canteen.

The war in the air rages into the autumn. Alec doesn't know until later how outnumbered the RAF pilots were, how heavily stacked against them it all was. He's glad, when he finds out, that he hadn't known. Doing the impossible is easier when you don't know. But with

Hitler's efforts to quash the RAF and commence with invasion thwarted, the focus shifts. The Luftwaffe is bombing cities now and shows no signs of stopping. Dispatches from London are weirdly calm, describing unthinkable chaos, bombs and ordnance raining down every night, rumors of Londoners sleeping in Tube stations. Often, in the half-awake dimness of waiting, he daydreams of going to the city and taking June away to somewhere as beautiful and safe as the summer meadows of Kashmir.

Meanwhile, 600 Squadron flies south and engages Stukas and German bombers over farmland that used to be quiet. It's still busy with cows; England is always England. Once, flying too low over a pasture, Alec looks out and sees a boy waving to him, what looks like a map trailing out of his hand. He must be a spotter, official or otherwise. When he was a boy, if a Blenheim or Spitfire had cruised overhead, he would have stopped in his tracks too, to wave at the pilot.

In early October he and his crew take the Blenheim out from Yorkshire over the North Sea. It's foggy and dank on the ground, and worse in the air. He wants to climb through the clouds and into the open night. Look for the dark spaces where the stars don't show—the negative space of an enemy plane. The stars are still what's true, just as they were aboard the RMS *Jaipur*. Every man who flies at night knows this, but nobody trusts it like Alec. The other airmen call him Cosmo because he's always cataloging stars.

This time the clouds don't end when he thinks they're going to. He emerges into the clear of night, and as he registers the dark blotch ahead of him as a plane, that pilot sees him as well and the darkness erupts into the noise and light of battle.

He doesn't know how bad it is until he realizes Cobber has stopped swearing. There's too much wind in the fuselage. Tim is crying. Alec tries to see over his shoulder, but all he can make out is his bombardier's outline in the cockpit lights.

"Jerry's having his way with me," Tim says, the words bitten off with pain. "Can you land us?"

Alec has no idea. He needs his navigator to creep farther back into the plane and see what's happened, what he's working with. But there's no time, and Tim is wounded. He's reasonably certain Cobber is dead. And if he can't bring the plane in right, he and Tim will be, too. The Blenheim is fighting him, the Germans are still shooting at him, and he can't shoot back.

"Perhaps!" Alec bellows through the noise of the wind shrieking through the fuselage. He wishes he sounded more confident.

Tim, still crying, makes something like a laugh. "Well, Cosmo, try not to cock it up."

Alec clings to the yoke all the way down, but the plane comes in too hard, the landing strip screaming past at the wrong angle. His thoughts and his heart race, a chorus of fear almost beyond words. Some part of his mind notes how long each second lasts, time slowing as the crash speeds up. *I'm sorry, June*, he thinks. *I'm so sorry*. It's impossible to know what is earth and what is sky until a blur of shadow crisps into the corona of a massive old oak. Then there is the rending of metal as his Blenheim shears branches into nothing. And finally the fearful miasma of smoke and petrol, the plane crushing sidelong against an old stone wall.

Something is wrong in his belly, where the twist of the plane has jammed him into the useless yoke. He pries himself loose, breathless with pain in his front, everywhere, blood seeping into his eyes. His left arm hangs crooked, but he makes himself focus and turns to examine the wreckage. He's right about Cobber, caught in the chest with a German round and slumped into his harness. It's not his fault, he knows that, but still a wave of guilt-laced despair surges over him. Then Tim groans, and Alec pulls himself together. He leans into the ruined cockpit and helps Tim out, dragging him one-armed away from the chaos, trying not to make worse the piece of shrapnel lodged in Tim's thigh. In the near distance, an ambulance races across the fields with its lights and bells on, coming for them. Alec closes his eyes.

They keep him in the infirmary until he stops pissing blood and his ribs and shoulder start to heal, although he's not nearly ready yet to be airborne again. He's lucky, more or less, although it will be a while before the bruising goes away. Tim is healing, too—it's the kind of wound that during a quieter time could get a man sent home, but not here, and not now.

Alec waits anxiously to be cleared. After they let him out of the infirmary, he stares at the sky, plucking at his sling, longing to be airborne. When Sanjay isn't flying, they play cards and talk about Kashmir, and when he is, Alec haunts the Ops Room. He likes it there, the sunken floor in the center the microcosm of their world. Everything has its place in here, from the Perspex situation boards to the heavy doors that lead out toward the mess and the barracks. Even when they scramble, their CO keeps the Ops Room orderly.

One afternoon at the end of November, finally cleared for flight, the world outside full of sleet and an icy fog, Alec's standing in the Ops Room with Sanjay, waiting for the CO to finish up a briefing so he can ask for a flight assignment, wondering if the old man's going to make him beg, when the door bangs open and a half-familiar voice interrupts, "Beg pardon, gents, I'm looking for Squadron Leader Maxwell."

Everyone in the room turns to look at the newcomer, wondering what kind of man makes a point of such an entrance. But Alec, trying to pin down the combination of tone and carriage echoing in his memory, already knows—he'd thought he'd never see any of the boys from the RMS *Jaipur* again, but here is Charlie, taking charge just as he always had.

By the end of the week, Flight Lieutenant Charlie Pascoe has made himself entirely at home with the squadron. He's an ace already, and his Beaufighter, a faster, heavier plane that has already replaced the Blenheims of other squadrons, is scarred and battered. He and Alec pick up more or less where they left off. But Alec was eight then; the age difference between them is no longer a matter of awe for him. It's not long before Alec knows that if he's looking for Charlie, he's probably standing out on the airfield running his hands along the fuselage of his plane, climbing up and down the wings like he used to climb the massive shipping crates in the cargo hold.

Wiltshire, spring. The squadron has moved to RAF Colerne, and Alec wants to be thinking about the new grasses on the Downs, the curl of moss and liverworts on coppice stools. He wants to have a picnic with June, someplace quiet where it's just the two of them. He wants to kiss her until he's dizzy. Until they both are. Sometimes, if he's not careful, he can get lost in thinking of kissing her, of the way her mouth is so gentle it makes him want to cry. She is so capable and so strong, but her tenderness nests in the lining of his heart and won't let go.

But the Germans take most of his attention, flying massive raids every night. From the Downs nearby they can see the bombing of Bristol, and the fluid silver-white trails the dogfights paint in the sky. The news from London, Coventry . . . anywhere, really. Buckingham Palace has been hit, St. Paul's nearly destroyed again and again by fire, cities everywhere in ruins, uncountable dead.

The barracks at the base are worse even than Manston, but once a week a Bedford truck takes them into Bath. Alec looks forward to the brass railing under his palm, leading him smoothly into the sunken bath and the hot water. A brass rail means another week of staying whole. They have twenty-four-hour passes sometimes too, leave to go into Bath and have a drink, sit back with Sanjay or Tim and watch Charlie talk to girls, be something other than a man trying not to think of the odds.

Along with the base, the planes have changed. He hasn't been in a Blenheim since the crash landing in Yorkshire. He'd been lucky not to kill them all; the loss of Cobber was a heavy enough weight on him. But a crate is a crate, and crashing one has not made him fear them. When he's assigned one of the new Beaufighters and takes her up, he finds that flying, at least, has not changed. He loves the air, loves the sway and pull of thermals against the wings and rudder, and the chatter of the Beau's engines.

I n the tail end of spring, a letter comes from June—can he meet her in London? Alec's heart actually leaps—he can feel it ricocheting off his ribs. It's been too long since he's seen her, too long since her voice has soothed him. She is a better correspondent than he is, her letters arriving relatively often, and the request for a rendezvous sends a frisson of delight through him—their leaves have not coincided, and so he has seen her only once in the nearly two years of war. But presumably June is as lonely as he is. He clears a day with the group captain and writes her back, his hand shaking almost too much to get the information down. *Yes, of course, yes, a thousand times yes.*

Two days later he's sitting beneath the wing of his Beaufighter, turning his mother's ring in his fingers, when Charlie finds him.

"Nice, that," Charlie says, gesturing at the ring. "You making a plan for your girl?"

Alec nods, his nerves sparking like flints with anticipation and anxiety. But at least the tension of waiting for a courier to fetch the ring from Fenbourne, where Alec's most prized belongings wait for him in his upstairs bedroom, has passed. "You think she'll like it?"

Charlie chuckles. "May I?" He reaches down at Alec's quiet yes and carefully takes the ring, holding it up to the soft morning light. The diamond flashes out pale yellow, and Alec blinks, taken back for a moment to watching his mother's hands sparkle in the thick Indian sunlight a lifetime ago.

"Not as heavy as it looks," Charlie says. "And I rather like that claw thing holding the stone. Reminds me of a lion, or a leopard." He tilts the bright gold to look at the inside of the band. Alec watches the bounce of light. He's memorized the jeweler's marks long ago—the crown insignia, the 18, the tiny worn swirl of his mother's initials.

"I've known June nearly my whole life," Alec says, taking the ring back and slipping it into the breast pocket of his shirt. "I want her in the rest of it as well."

Charlie tilts his head in acknowledgment; he's heard more stories of June than anyone. "I daresay she'll like it," he says. "Lovely old piece like that."

Alec smiles. He always has the dull ache of missing June juxtaposed against the bright shimmer of loving her, and today is no different. The ring and the aspirations it contains add a layer of feeling, but the foundation—the wanting, the shivery memory of her touch, the quiet knowledge of having a place—is no different at all.

He looks up at Charlie. "This time tomorrow she will have said one way or another."

"You'll do fine," Charlie says. He puts out a hand and Alec takes it and Charlie hauls him to his feet. "You'll do fine."

. . .

The next day finds him on an early-morning train to Paddington. He can't stop patting his pocket to check on the ring. He fidgets all the way to London, trying to read the paper and failing. All he can think about is June. Will it be different, being engaged as opposed to merely having an understanding? He knows they are meant for each other, that their union is inevitable, but the idea of her wearing his mother's ring, of the way her hand will feel against his cheek with that ring on it, tolls like the bells of St. Anne's for Christmas services in Fenbourne. The idea feels like home.

1941, *Y Service*

Like the rest of London, the greenery of St. James's Park has not been spared by the war. Even in the height of spring some trees remain bare, but sparrows jostle in the branches, feathers puffed and plush against the chill of morning. It's a sunny day in London, rare this year, and June waits for Alec on a bench not far from Whitehall. As far as he knows, that is where she still works. But keeping Alec away from Ainsley's flat in Bloomsbury is necessary, now that June's belongings are packed and ready to go, and Whitehall seems like the second most logical place for them to meet.

At least the worst of it has passed, although it's not as though the Germans have stopped their raids altogether. The sky still darkens with Heinkels and Dormiers dropping their bombs across the city, and neighborhoods are still crumbling away into chasms. Every day is rife with the constant tension of waiting for the next raid and the determined way all of London just goes about its business. There is an excitement in being part of it, as grueling and awful as it can be. Still, though, June will be glad enough to leave London and move on to her new assignment.

She checks her watch. Ten o'clock—he should be here soon, if his train was on time. June shifts on the bench, smooths her skirt, watches the sparrows. It's been an age since she's seen Alec, and the realization that they are going to be reunited, even for a day, is exhilarating. If only her enthusiasm could be pure, not tinged by her growing secrets. He will come to her here with his heart on his sleeve and have no idea that she is leaving London tomorrow, bound for Scarborough to break coded German messages for the wireless service outpost there.

And of course she hasn't said a word—can't say a word—to him about any of it. Her first day with Sir Reginald there had been a moment—a few seconds, perhaps, if that—when she had considered not signing the Official Secrets Act. When the idea of the secrets she might be asked to keep and the logistics of never telling anyone—and how could she not tell Alec, as close as they have always been?—had seemed too large.

It had seemed so weighted, but the whole of it had been blanketed in the idea of doing something useful. Something noble. And in the end, of course, she had taken the pen and signed her name. Until now, it has been a wondrous swirl of codes and ciphers, months of fitting text to idea and passing the notes to the other girls in whatever office she found herself. It was real work, just barely close enough to the clerical work she'd told her parents and Alec she was doing. Nothing to tell, no harm done. But all that changes tomorrow when she boards the train north.

She amends that when she sees Alec come around the corner. All of it changes *now*, when she says nothing.

"Alec!" Putting her misgivings about the secrets aside, she meets Alec on the path and puts her arms around him, warming into his hug.

"God, I've missed you," he says. He steps back, regards her with an almost giddy smile, and squeezes her hand.

"It's been far too long," June says, basking in his happiness. "I'm so pleased you could get the day."

"Feels a bit dodgy to be away from base, honestly, even with everything in order." Alec laces his fingers through hers. "I wish it were longer, but a few hours with you is a damn sight better than none at all."

"I've been dying to see you, too," June says. Alec nods, still smiling down at her, and June goes on, faltering for a moment when he takes back his hand and slips it into his pocket distractedly. "I thought we might go over to the National Gallery. All the regular collections have been evacuated, but there are smaller exhibitions, and most days there's a bit of a concert over lunch."

"That sounds like just the thing." He regards the sky, then turns that ridiculous happy grin to her again. "Lovely day for a stroll, too."

They fall into step, chatting and catching up, and before long they emerge from the tree-lined path along the Mall and cross into Trafalgar Square. Alec pauses and regards their surroundings. "Bloody hell."

June nods. "There have been several raids around here." She gestures at the roadway just south of the square. "There was a dreadful direct hit on the tube station there last October."

"I heard about that. Terrible," Alec says, looking up at the buildings around the square. "Do they just keep fixing the windows again and again?"

"Sometimes," June says. "But now and again people will just decide to cover over them and make do."

"I always thought you'd be safe in London." Alec shakes his head.

"I've been all right." She smiles, hoping to reassure him, but inside she feels off-kilter. He might feel better if he knew today would be her last day in London, but she can't tell him, and he gets neither the comfort nor the truth as a result.

He drifts over to one of the bronze lions and pats it. "Knew a chap at school who used to nick a bottle of gin and climb these during holidays." He smiles nostalgically. "He'd come from India as well, so I always suspected he pretended they were tigers."

"Perhaps they gave him an anchor." June smiles a little, wondering if Alec had ever pretended that himself.

Alec's eyes rove the square as if he's looking for something, and then he turns his gaze back to June. "What helped me," he says, "was knowing that eventually I would come home from school and you would be there."

She reaches for his hand again. "It was like that for me at St. Swithun's, as well."

"The thing is . . ." He pauses, and June can see that he's moving toward something. "The thing is, June, I love you, and I have for such a long time. Most of my life. And I can't imagine a life without you in it." He takes a deep breath. "There is nothing in the world that would make me happier than to have you with me forever." He slides a hand into the breast pocket of his uniform jacket, and after a moment it emerges with a flash of yellow in the sun.

June's heart speeds up—she had known this moment was coming for years, and yet it feels completely out of the blue. It's as though time has split into two streams around them—one sped up and blurry, the afternoon full of the chaos of people and traffic in Trafalgar Square, and the other a pocket of perfect stillness in which she stands with Alec by the lion.

"I know you'll be here when I come back after the war, but I want to know you'll be there always. I want to share my life with you." Alec goes to one knee, and June puts a hand to her mouth as he holds up a ring in the sunlight, a yellow diamond gleaming against gold. His voice rough with emotion, Alec says, "June, will you do me the great honor of being my wife?"

Her pulse thunders. "Yes, Alec. Yes."

Alec's whole face lights up, and he slips the ring onto her finger. June stares down at the dazzling warm glow of the gold and the blaze of the diamond. She can't, won't, think about Scarborough or the codes or anything but Alec. Everything else will come later, and she will have to work it out, but for now it is just the two of them in the center of the universe, the way it's always been.

He gets to his feet and embraces her again, trembling slightly, and

June smiles against the rough wool of his uniform jacket. Alec bends to kiss her, but the day is split by the shriek of an air raid siren. Alec looks up as if he's checking for planes.

"Bugger," Alec mutters. He glances around the square and takes her hand again. Together they hurry to the shelter at the square's north end, along with a cluster of other men and women. It's crowded and dark, with a dank, bricky smell, and June wishes they'd gone to the Underground station, although when she thinks about the calamity there last autumn, she's not so sure.

Alec shifts so he's got his back to a wall and pulls her closer to him. "So much for lunchtime concerts," he whispers, and she chuckles. Some part of her listens for the all-clear alert to sound, but she has been in so many shelters, for so many air raids, that this is just a matter of routine now, but for the usual small throb of adrenaline.

"Don't go having air raids with any other lads," Alec says, his voice soft against her ear. He smiles and tightens his arms around her.

"I shan't," she whispers back. She leans close, relishing the clean, familiar smell of him.

In the back of the shelter, someone starts to sing an old army marching song, and here and there people join in. After a bit, Alec makes a cushion from his greatcoat, and they settle in close together against the wall. It's not long before he's talking airplanes with a pair of grocer's assistants too young to enlist, and June smiles at him. She has always loved watching him enjoy the people around him, and even in this environment he is still himself, the gregarious, handsome boy she's always loved. Someone else puts on a Noël Coward record, and one of the grocer's boys opens a packet of sandwiches and offers them to his neighbors.

June strokes the curve of the ring, the glad golden weight of it, like the weight of Alec's love, the solid fact of his attention. Of course she wants to marry him—she loves him with all her heart and cannot begin to imagine a life without him in it. She has known from the start that he might not survive the next crash, or the one after that. It was an unbearable idea, the loss of him, and of all she loves about him—the idea that she might never again see the knob of his wrist, or hear the sentimental, off-key songs he sings to himself when he thinks she isn't listening. All the wonders she never would have noticed without him, down to the spark of color in a horse's mane or the arc of constellations in the night. But all that stacks up awkwardly against the fact of her nascent career and the passion she feels for that, too. Later, she will have to make sure he understands how she feels about her work, about the need she has to be useful. And she will have to find a way to balance the reality of her life with Alec, which the war has left feeling sometimes so ephemeral, with the reality she inhabits with the codes.

B y the time the all clear sounds much later, it seems as if Alec has made friends with half of London. The shelter's occupants file back out into Trafalgar Square, everyone's eyes scanning the horizon for errant bombers. One of the grocer's boys points off to the northeast, where thin columns of smoke rise into the sky. Alec's face tilts up, his eyes narrowing, and June can see in Alec's face the desire to be in his plane, fighting the war. She wishes she could tell him how much she understands.

"I expect we're clear until tomorrow," June says.

Alec nods. With a wry smile he says, "An air raid wasn't part of my plan." He takes her hand and grins, rubbing the ring with his thumb. "It was my mother's, you know. And now it's yours." He kisses her fingertips, his eyes gleaming. "I love you, June."

She studies the way her hand fits into his. It's reassuring, as if his touch will help her find her way through the confusion. "I love you, too."

He beams at her and glances at his watch. "Oh, hell. I'm meant to be on a train not too long from now. Bloody Germans stole our time."

"Well," she says, "perhaps we ought to get ourselves to Paddington, have a cup of tea while we wait?"

He gives her a rakish grin. "Be like being in a film, rather, when you see me off. Dashing flight officer and his beautiful fiancée, and all that?"

June laughs and puts her arm through the elbow he offers, and together they set off for Paddington Station, the ring on her left hand shimmering beneath the afternoon sun.

A fortnight after her arrival, June takes advantage of a rare morning away from the Y station and leaves her tiny bedsit to walk the sea-scrubbed town. Years of war, but Scarborough holds fast. The shops struggle along despite rationing, and Scarborough Castle looms protectively over the town. The scoop of harbor, the fishing boats dotted across the dark water, the capricious speckling of foam on the waves when the wind picks up . . . They speak to her of a world so much bigger than the Fenlands, bigger than London, even, that she can scarcely imagine it. A gull struggles against a slap of wind, and June turns her face to the water. It doesn't feel like summer, not with weather like this, although on the moor there are lambs and flowering gorse.

The red and blue shutters of the houses that ring the water remind her of Alec too, although she's not sure why. It feels like yesterday that she saw him in London, and also as if it has been months ago. Time in Scarborough is elastic—there is the time of now, of the codes coming through and the messages going out, of the urgent clatter of the wireless and the scratch of pencils. And there is the time of everything else, mobile and confusing.

She wishes every day that she could tell Alec the truth, but every day there is more truth to tell, more truth not told. Even among her colleagues, speaking of the Official Secrets Act, acknowledging that there are clandestine works that they are part of, is taboo. Telling Alec is completely out of the question. She believes he would wholly understand—they are both, after all, doing their part for King and Country. But now the thing that was not exactly a lie is explicitly not true: Alec knew she was in London, and now he thinks she still is.

He is such a good man, and it's so easy to drift into missing him, remembering the lightness of his fingers against her ribs, the thistling of hair cut shorter than she likes up the back of his skull. Too easy. She shifts so she's closer to the seawall, not quite so much in the wind. The idea of his proposal had seemed so inevitable for so long, and yet, when he had pulled out the ring, it had been a surprise, a weird click in her chest as things fell into place.

And of course she had said yes. That had been inevitable, too. But now, alone in the lee of the castle, she wonders. Increasingly there is the question of whether they want the same future, and that is a conversation they have not ever had. He had asked her to marry him, and she had said yes, and after the air raid, when they'd gone to Paddington to wait for his train and have a cup of tea together, he had talked about a life after the war, and his plan to stay in the RAF. He had said any number of things about the future—their future—and she had told him how grand it sounded. But she had also suggested that they would talk after the war and find their way together, and who knows how he had heard that. She has never been sold on the idea of a house full of children and herself at the helm—shouldn't Alec know that already?— just as she knows how much he wants exactly that. And now she has a career, a purpose and goals that have nothing to do with motherhood, goals that loom broader even than the life she wants with Alec.

The worst of it is not knowing exactly the moment at which those ideas of the future had changed—at which point *she* had changed. That day with Sir Reginald, her future with the FO had seemed exciting but temporary. But now, with the war happening all around her, people's lives held in the balance of the work she's doing, it feels quite different. Still exciting, but no longer transient. This clandestine life has become something she can't imagine giving up.

As the summer deepens, June and her colleagues at Sandybed Lane work clustered around the wireless radios, headsets clamped against their ears, civilians like June side by side with women who've enlisted in the Women's Royal Navy Service. Many of these Wrens, competent and businesslike in their tidy uniforms, serve as wireless techs, charged with fixing the machines when they break. The station can't afford the pauses that come when one of the wireless sets blows a fuse or loses its bearings; every pause is a leg up for the Germans.

But even in summer, the rain can come in fierce off the North Sea, strafing across the rooftops and then off across the moors. In that weather, the signals break up, caught in the fists of wind and water, and June and the other girls must wrestle the messages out of what's left. One team writes down the codes as they come through the headsets, and the other group translates them onto separate pages, comparing their work against one another's to make sure they've got it right. All of it gets packed into waterproof pouches for the team of Wrens who ride the courier routes from the wireless stations—Y stations for short—to HQ. Now and again, if information seems especially precious, it goes to the station chief for transmission directly to Station X.

June spends many of her shifts at the rickety table in the wireless room's alcove, where she translates the listeners' messages into English.

One night that summer, the whole place seems to glow with the tension of how close they are to a solution. To an answer. June raises her head, looks around the room. Engrossed, all of them, caught up in the tangle of what often seems like nonsense, until one learns how to see through it. The codes run in her blood, fill her dreams. She has always found patterns nobody else could understand, but now her gift has purpose. She has meaning, or her mind does.

And then something clicks—a phrase repeated once too often by a radio operator, a sequence of taps blossoming into something larger— and she falls into the moment that she knows is waiting around the corner of every message, when the layers of code fall together. The sequences of numbers and letters take on a new shape, as clear as day. June pulls back, looks at her notes, and hands the papers across the table to Wendy Fairchild.

"I say," June says, "take a look?"

Wendy nods, running her fingers across June's decoding while she scans the original messages. June takes advantage of the pause to stand and stretch.

"My God," Wendy says.

"It's the real thing, then," June says. She knew it, but hearing the urgency in Wendy's voice changes what it means.

Wendy turns and flags down one of the wireless men from the Royal Navy as he comes back from a break with a cup of tea. "Fetch the chief, will you?" The sailor puts down his cup and runs for the office at the far end of their compound.

Minutes later the station chief bursts into the room. "Attwell?"

June hands him her notes. "It's the *Lohengrin*, sir. They've shown their hand."

He looks up. "You've identified their coordinates?"

June nods. "Yes."

The chief says, "Bloody good show, Attwell," and rushes back out.

Wendy lights a cigarette. "That'll teach them to talk to Berlin."

June chuckles. "I should think we would want them to keep doing it, if we hope to keep stopping them."

Wendy laughs, tilts her head up toward the tiny slit of window, and blows a stream of smoke. "Rather."

June says, "So now we wait?" She's fidgety with the need to keep going, to scratch the messages onto paper and turn them into something that makes sense, but at the same time it feels correct to acknowledge the moments like this, when everything comes together just so.

Her friend shrugs. "That's our war."

And so it is. The *Lohengrin* is a new German battleship, sleek and dangerous, for all intents and purposes invisible in the North Sea as she slips through the waves and sinks British ships. And the war is going badly enough without this—they have lost Crete, and Rommel is waltzing across North Africa, seemingly impossible to stop. So many nights are spent watching the Wrens note down the double-bar sign of a U-boat, or the dispiriting moment when German Control radios back to a ship with a confirmation code—every message the Germans receive that the Y station hasn't captured . . . Sinking the *Lohengrin*, or even just stopping her, would be an incredible boost.

It's two days later, June back at her desk with her pencils and thin sheets of paper, when the message comes from London—the *Lohengrin* is scuttled, and the prime minister offers his personal thanks to the men and women of the Y station on Sandybed Lane.

"Jesus," Wendy says, when the station chief has finished relaying the message. She smiles at June. "What miracle will you manage next?"

June ducks her head, embarrassed. The *Lohengrin* is hardly the first

German ship they've seen to; Y stations all over Britain send urgent messages to HQ every day. But this one does feel special, and the message from Churchill looms large. It seems so unlikely, and yet somehow perfect, that a collection of scribbled notes could lead to a triumph like this (and, a voice in her hindbrain reminds her, not quite sure how to feel, the loss of thousands of enemy sailors). Then, beyond the word from Churchill, the chief has a message solely for her as well. June follows him back to his office, her heart thumping—*it can't be Alec, please don't let it be Alec.*

"They're transferring you," the chief says bluntly, his shoulders sloping unhappily.

"Oh," June says. "I see." She hasn't been here very long at all, despite the elasticity, and the quick friendship with Wendy, but it has felt right for her since the beginning. At the same time, the moves so far have meant learning more new skills and developing her talents. They could be sending her back to London, for all she knows.

"Whitehall will send a car for you," he says. "I'm afraid I can't say more." He shrugs, and June wonders if he disapproves of the use of petrol and the car it will take to get her wherever it is they're sending her.

"I imagine it's too many changes by rail," she says. Even Scarborough to London is two changes at best, and if they're sending her somewhere more distant than that, it could be four or six. For a second she's distracted by the ticking of railway schedules in her head, and she shakes it off. "I've liked it here, sir," she says.

"You did good work," the chief says. "It's no surprise they want you somewhere else."

"Thank you," June says. She looks at the map on the chief's wall, the corners of it curling away from the pushpins holding it in place, the abandoned pewter tea tray on the edge of his desk, the pipe tipped into a dish on the windowsill. Though it's only been a handful of months, sometimes it feels like she has known Sandybed Lane, and this office, for years.

T he next morning she leaves the Y station and finds Floss waiting.
"June, darling," he says, clasping her hand.

"Hello, Floss," she says. "I'm glad to see you."

He chuckles. "You may be the only one left who feels like that." He leads her slowly, his stick tapping against the stones as he makes his way to a waiting car, blocky and black, the driver leaning on the bonnet and smoking a cigarette.

The driver takes her valise and tucks it away in the boot. Floss makes sure she's settled and slides in next to her. The driver throws the butt of his cigarette into the gutter and gets in, and the engine curls to life. Floss props his cane in the corner and turns to face June across the wide seat, his analytical eyes running over her. June doesn't mind—she is long since used to the way he looks at her, as if she's an aggregation of data, not a woman.

"So tell me," he says, pressing the button that raises the partition between the driver and the back of the car, an excited gleam building in his pale gray eyes, "what do you know about Bletchley Park?"

I t's the middle of the afternoon when the car makes its way into the Buckinghamshire village of Bletchley, and June's mouth goes dry. Here, then, is her future—she has known the work she's done in the Y stations goes to a place known only as Station X, but everything beyond that has been fuzzy at best. Does it bode well, the glossy light starting to go golden around the edges even in this old brick factory town? The car winds through the village, and Floss points out the newsagent and the greengrocer and the butcher, the various small shops she will need once she's settled. And then there are the heavy gates, and young soldiers guarding them. Floss shows the soldiers a card, and they step sharply into salutes, then pull the gates open for the car.

The manor itself appears out of the parkland like a vision, but the vision, June thinks, of someone who had never seen a proper country mansion and was putting it together based on a child's description.

Floss follows her gaze and laughs. "Hideous, isn't it? But it suits our needs." He gestures out the window. "And the lake is rather nice."

June has an unwelcome buzz of anxiety, thinking about this lake that Alec will never be able to skate on. And then they're at the door, and she follows Floss inside.

Hours later she emerges into the twilight. She has a chit for a billet in town, a ration book, and a vague sense of what she'll be doing, but for the most part she is feeling unmoored in a way she usually doesn't. The afternoon has been swallowed by the intricacies of her new post, including another lecture about the Official Secrets Act and its application to the work at Bletchley Park. An officer has told her that violations of the Act are treasonous and will lead to prison, at least. It's largely the same message she'd had already from Sir Reginald, but with a hint more melodrama—as he'd paced the room, this man's hand had crept to the holstered revolver at his belt, and June had shuddered at the grim tone he'd given that *at least*.

She sits on the edge of the steps, waiting for Floss to collect her again. Her new colleagues come and go around her as she considers the surprising path that has brought her here. All those months learning the rudiments of her new trade, and now here she is right in the humming heart of it all.

The Japanese codes move like water around rocks, intricate and alchemical, and June takes to them right away. Her colleagues in Hut 7 love the puzzles as much as she does, and sometimes it's almost like a game, despite the grind of urgency that lies beneath everything they do. There are nearly infinite variations and nuances, and the new imperative of containing all the variables is exhilarating. This is nothing like traditional Morse code, or like the basic ciphers she made up in school, dots and dashes standing in for letters, just a new alphabet. Most of the cryptanalysts have done Greek at school; new alphabets and grammars are easily absorbed. What makes the Japanese codes so astonishing is the blur of the pictographs and characters, and the speedy transfiguration of those characters in and out of Morse. And then, the ciphering and the meteorological codes on top of that . . . June has never felt more vital or alive.

Bletchley Park feels like home, and she thrives in the company of her peers. Now and again over the summer the powers that be send her back to Bedford or one of the other outposts, but for the most part she is a girl billeted in the tired old village of Bletchley. She and the other girls who board in the old brick house tell the elderly owners that they're clerks at the radio factory Bletchley Park is pretending to be. When the couple's son is invalided home from France that October, June moves into the old Abbey building on the manor grounds with the Wrens.

She makes friends, all of them bound by the pressures of their work and of secrecy. She misses Alec, but she would rather miss Alec from the bewilderingly ugly old manor than anywhere else. And he seems happy enough with his airplanes and his mates, no matter her fears for him. Life expectancy for pilots is so low, and she worries he is not careful enough. Although: Can he be? Is there an enough?

In the nights that autumn, lying awake in the room she shares with a host of Wrens, she looks at the ring he gave her that spring, and her heart larrups against the walls of her chest. They have seen each other once since then, in August, a tangled visit in London, where he still thinks she lives.

Such an odd day, that. The chaos of London, Alec trembling when he pulled her into a kiss. Lunch at a café near the British Museum, and Alec's long hands looped around a porcelain mug chipped in a bombing earlier that summer or reaching across the table to play with her fingers. Alec's smile, full of promise and lit with hope. The subterfuge for even a single day had exhausted her.

Too, though, he had brought her one of his stories, a quiet balm of normality in their upside-down world. They had been back at the train station, sitting close together on a bench near the platform, and he had sighed and whispered, *Once upon a time there was a river.* And she had answered as if it were a sacred moment of call and response at church, *And on that river lived a bear.* Something had flashed bright and happy in his face, and then he had gone on.

The bear lived in an old stone house in the shadow of the Tower, and in the afternoons he liked to look upriver toward the sunset, watching the light filter through the caissons and abutments of the bridges. The house belonged to a princess, who had come to London to establish an alliance in the spice trade.

It was February, and a fog had crept along the river from the sea. The bear had not seen the sunset in days, just the low glint of sun and moon through the icy haze, but he was happy, curled up before the blaze the princess's manservant had laid in the cavernous marble fireplace. The house was cold, and the princess had fallen into the habit of sitting with her bear by the fire.

One night, the fog left the city in the hours before dawn, replaced by a deadly cold. The river began to close, floes shuddering together into a great expanse of ice between Blackfriars and London Bridge that filled with adventurers and shopkeepers. A fair sprung up. Hawkers and pickpockets strolled the ice. Baiting pits and brothels appeared overnight, penny coins disappearing into pockets and purses, or sometimes into the tiny fissures in the ice.

It was the coldest winter in memory, but the princess took the bear's ears in her hands, warming them both, and led him out onto the ice. He walked between the bookstalls and mummers, the princess crouched on his shoulders like a jockey, the tiger stripes of her hooded cloak bright against the bear's tobacco-colored fur.

The story had had no end; they never did. Instead Alec had stopped and taken her hands in his, kissing her palms and fingertips. Later June had sat in the compartment of the train back to Bletchley, thinking about her future with Alec. In the rhythm of train on track she had heard the bear and his princess, the whisper of skates on ice.

I n November, a letter comes: Alec and his navigator, Tim Yates, are being temporarily reassigned to train Royal Canadian Air Force pilots in Ontario. June stares at the letter, relieved that she will not have to make excuses or pretend to live in London, and then feels guilty for the relief. She can't tell from the way he's written whether he's excited—shouldn't he be? Isn't it a mark of favor that they think he is that good a pilot?

When she writes back, she tells him how proud she is of him. How much she loves him. How much she hopes he will continue to write, no matter where he is. She fills pages with words she knows are true, trying to ignore the prickling feeling of everything she's not saying.

When Japan strikes at the United States that December, Hut 7 goes into overdrive. The Emperor must be stopped. But despite everything June and her cohort do, despite the sudden long, aching nights of taking apart the codes, Japan continues to march across the Pacific. In February, Singapore falls, and hundreds of British citizens, civilian and military, are swept into POW camps. The war is global now, and there are days when June hardly thinks of Alec, or Fenbourne, or anything but the swirl of ciphers she's been given to solve. The heel of her hand takes on a dark sheen from the endless rub of thin paper and the thick black pencils they use. Information trickles in about troop movements or the shift of a Japanese carrier from one part of the Pacific to another. At Bletchley Park they benefit from the lack of co-operation between Japan's army and navy, from the Emperor's arrogance about the West's inability to understand the Japanese language, and from the ornate, flowery tone the signal operators layer into the messages—each honorific adds a bit more to the codebreakers' roster of understanding.

The lake freezes, and frost bristles on the windowpanes. Some of the girls organize skating parties, and one morning at the edge of the woods a herd of deer appears, hoofing gently at the frozen ground to shift what's left of the grasses. In the vast great hall of the manor, the codebreakers and analysts and secretaries put on sometimes-ribald panto shows. Some of the men have come to Bletchley from careers as musicians or actors, and June is astonished by the caliber of their entertainments. She is less astonished by the way her colleagues seem to pair off, and by how much it makes her miss Alec. When his letters come, his handwriting often drifting into illustrations of the sky or trees or something else that's caught his eye, she keeps them close.

Winter deepens, and she takes to doing her work with her hands half-warmed in fingerless gloves, a muffler tight around her throat. June spends most of the winter with her haversacks of messages on A4 paper, painstakingly crafting the paraphrases designed to confuse the Japanese if, God forbid, the British codebreaking work should fall into enemy hands. The Axis nations cannot know that the Allies have cracked their codes. Thus, "Troops of 19th Division will attack April 15" becomes "Expect attack from east mid-April, probably division nineteen." Place names are replaced with code words or left out entirely, numbers written out, dates blurred into rough timeframes. The paraphrases she slips into a customized pair of envelopes—an inner envelope with one coded address, an external one with another. Those, in turn, vanish with the dispatch riders, out of sight and out of mind. It is more tedious work than the loops of the codebreaking itself, but she finds a quiet satisfaction in the process of information moving through the channels Britain has created so laboriously.

Still, the conflict in the Pacific spreads as Japanese forces conquer territory. June and her colleagues have to break codes and transcribe messages faster than ever—there are at least twenty different code and cipher systems the Japanese are using, perhaps more. Her cryptanalysis relies on a working knowledge of the transliteration of the kanji pictograms and kana phonetic symbols into a Romanized alphabet. The Japanese have built a new version of Morse, quite unlike the international code June has known since childhood—this version has twice as many signs, one set for the kana syllables and another for the Romaji letters. And throughout both sets of signs are the honorifics and epithets of the Emperor's hierarchy. For June, the paired signs make a beautiful, imposing litany.

Most of the messages come through in sets of two-kana groups that stand in for phrases and four-kana groups that mean a particular word or number. And, as she grows more familiar with the basic pattern in which most Japanese radio operators transmit information, the better she internalizes the kana she sees most often. Even when the Japanese change their code books every fortnight or so, June's turns at the wireless have taught her the idiosyncratic touches of different operators, and there are a handful of planes whose messages she can identify whether or not they change their call signs.

When the world thaws and the parklands around the manor blossom green and gold again, relief escapes the buildings like water over a dam. June and her friends bicycle out into the countryside, despite the lingering damp. The geese take back their spots on the lake and hiss and honk at anyone foolhardy enough to row out too close.

At the end of April, when June has been at Bletchley Park not quite a full year, she finds herself traipsing down to the lake with a group of girls, carrying a canvas shoulder bag and an old plaid blanket. The spring sun is low in her face and it's a bit chilly yet, but breathing something that doesn't taste like smoke and pencil nubs feels good. There are four of them, a determined group of picnickers brought together by Portia Wallace and Sybil de Cler, a pair of Hut 4 girls from families with the wherewithal to make sure they have the best cigarettes, a decent claret, even nylons. June likes Sybil well enough, but Portia can be tiring—she's being courted by an army man from HQ, and rarely misses a chance to mention him. Sarah Crossley is a clerk's daughter from Yorkshire, a brilliant Wren from a poor family, come to Bletchley Park to work with the enormous Bombe machines that break the codes in Hut 11. They have found one another time and again over the last year, and at this point June knows the friendships are as much a respite for the other girls as they are for her. With these girls, she can be normal, more or less—they're all too clever by half, aren't they? And better for it?

They settle onto the blanket, keeping an eye out for the terrible geese. Sybil kicks off her shoes and rolls up her trouser legs, stretching her toes into the cool grass.

"God," Portia says, "look at you, rolling about."

Sybil smiles. "Practically indecent," she says wryly. "Not my fault my skin calls for air."

"It smells like home, nearly," Sarah says. She sits on the corner of the blanket, her arms wrapped around her knees, eyeing the picnic basket that Portia has casually settled among them.

Sybil sits up again, her attention shifting to the basket also. "What riches, Wallace?"

"Watercress sandwiches," Portia says. She throws back the basket's lid and shuffles through the contents. "Egg mayonnaise on toast as well. Chicken and leek pies. Potted eel. A bit of trifle." She lifts out each item and lays it on the blanket with a showy wave of her hands.

"Anything to drink in there?" Sybil peers into the basket.

"Not my department," Portia says, smiling.

"As it happens," June says, "I've brought this." She reaches into her shoulder bag and pulls out a bottle of Champagne from before the war.

"God bless the Honorable Alastair Corbett," Portia says.

Sarah says, "He makes me nervous, a bit."

"He makes us all nervous," Portia says. She tilts her head. "Well. Not June."

June laughs. "I've known him longer."

"Are you and he . . . ," Sarah trails off, blushing.

"Attwell is hardly his type," Sybil says. "I was in town a few months ago and saw him coming out of a theater with a girl who looked rather cheap, if you take my meaning."

"An actress?" Portia shrugs.

"Actress," Sybil says, chuckling. "If that's what you'd like to call a girl like that."

"You never know," Sarah says.

"In any event," June says, eager to stop talking about Floss and his personal life before Sybil says anything more damning, "it seemed like a good day to open this."

"It's always a good day for bubbles," Sybil says.

Portia smiles and hands around the sandwiches on thin porcelain plates. "When John and I marry, we'll have ever so much Champagne."

Sarah says, "And dancing?"

"Oh, yes," Portia says. She accepts a glass and sips. "We'll drink and dance all night. My sister says there's a jazz band she knows. It'll be marvelous."

"I'm not giving this up for anything, least of all a man." Sybil leans forward, gesturing at the lake. "Perhaps I'll feel differently when the war ends, but right now . . ." She shrugs and smiles at Portia. "You and June seem to have it all worked out, though."

Portia nods, but June looks up, alarmed. She had never thought of herself as being like Portia, and the idea that Portia's path is hers . . . How can that be? She's engaged, but until now she hasn't really understood how that affects how people see her. That even someone like Sybil looks past the codebreaker, past the triumphs of math and patterns and logic, and instead sees someone's future wife and someone else's mother.

She wants to say something—but what? And to what purpose?

Difficult enough that she will have to have that conversation with Alec, but must she really defend herself against this from Sybil as well? More than ever she realizes the necessity of making Alec understand, truly understand, what she means by that *yes* she gave him. He knows her better than anyone, miles better, but what if he sees her as Sybil does? Could she blame him if he can't see the shift in who she is now from who she was before the war?

Six weeks later, she's summoned to the chief's office, where Floss is waiting—they're moving her again. She smiles, eager to continue the work wherever they need her most, but she'll miss Bletchley Park. She has friends here. She fits. Where? she asks. Back to Scarborough? Back to London? Floss shakes his head, his eyes glinting wolfish in the noonday sun where it pushes through the half-pulled blackout curtains. The Far East Combined Bureau, he tells her. Colombo. She stares at him, speechless first with shock and delight, and then with the worry about what this would mean to Alec.

That night she sits in Hut 7 and works until dawn, listening to the wireless and writing down clusters of kana syllables. She focuses on the encryptions harder than ever; if she is busy enough she may not have to consider the layers of worry tugging at her about Colombo. It has been almost two years of the lie, but at least the lie has been roughly the same—not clerical, not really, but close. All these months, all those nights in the hut, the stubs of pencils chewed by the glow of the too-bright overhead lights, walking back to her lodgings and trying not to step on the frogs that creep out of the lake and infest the walkways . . . This has been her life, and she has found her footing in sending letters to Alec that tell him she's okay, and feeling useful, without really saying anything at all about where she is or what she's doing.

So she packs her valise and says goodbye to her friends, and in the early part of the summer she finds herself back at the Thames, boarding a ship that will take her to India, where she will transfer to a series of trains and ferries to Colombo. Not telling Alec where she is when she's in Britain has been hard enough—but to keep from him that she will be in Ceylon, in the very shadow of India? It is impossible, and she wants more than ever to tell him, knowing that he would feel in his chest the tightening of their overlapping lives, as she does. But she can't, no matter how hurtful she finds the responsibility of keeping the truth to herself.

During the weeks at sea, she practices her Japanese and walks the perimeter of the ship every evening. During her walks, she watches the water carve away from the prow of the ship, drinks weak gin and tonics with the cluster of Wrens she's sailing with. Increasingly, she wonders whether that is a path she should consider—the responsibilities and privileges of the uniform pull at her. She is part of something immeasurably important now, but what would it be like to be official, to expand her service from civilian life to the Wrens? But how then to reconcile that idea with marriage to Alec? If he is expecting a wife who will dedicate herself to the management of home and hearth, is that someone she can be? For that matter, if she were to become a Wren and he is a pilot in the RAF, would a marriage even be possible? Separate paths and separate postings, trying to match up their leaves and furloughs until one of them sees fit to retire from service?

She pushes the idea away—right now those questions cannot be her prime concern. Her country needs her; her king is sending her to lead other young women in the war against Japan. She is a civilian, nominally attached to the Admiralty, and she knows that if her ship, or her person, falls into Japanese hands, none of that will protect her. Since the fall of Singapore, there have been rumors of what it's like in the Japanese POW camps, but she can't quite think about that possibility head-on. Worse, though, is the knowledge that she carries secrets like other women carry virtue. It is imperative that she remains free—if she is captured, there is the risk that the Japanese will learn about the work being done against them at Bletchley Park, Hut 7's success with Purple and JN25 and the other codes, the systemic work creeping along to dismantle the Emperor's secrets. If she is captured, it is best for King and Country if she is not taken alive.

And if she is? Who will tell Alec? Who will tell her parents? What will they think, if they hear that she has been captured in the waters off Ceylon? If Burma or India fall to Japan, and she is taken to one of the nightmare camps in Sumatra? Is it really possible that they will never know where she is unless she dies? What damage would it do to her parents, or to Alec? It is unbearable to consider.

1942, *the East*

J une's days aboard the transport ship are full of sun and the angling of birds overhead, the scent of old rope and steel railings in
the summery Mediterranean light.

At dusk, she stands on the deck of the ship, amazed by how different the night sky is as they move farther south. Perhaps Alec could tell
her how to adjust to find the familiar constellations, but he is thousands of miles away, on an entirely different continent. It's been almost
a year since she's seen him, since she's felt his skin close to hers. When
they are apart, it is much easier to not think about what she's not telling
him. It is baffling to her that she can leave the country—board a ship
that will take her to the other side of the world—and yet not tell the
man she's going to marry. Especially when the other side of the world
is, as far as their relationship and his life are concerned, his. Not hers.

The perils of the journey help distract her. The Mediterranean is
infested with mines and U-boats, and the waters along the Arabian
Peninsula are not much better. Twice now she has put pen to paper and
written out her fears, which have added to the list of things she will
never be able to tell Alec. And twice she has lit those papers from a
candle and let them burn. Every day it feels like luck to make it to
sunset—does Alec feel the same, when his days come to a close? She
wants to believe that training other pilots is safer, but there are always
stories about random mishaps. The margin for survival in the RAF

does not seem wide enough. At least he's flying with Tim Yates and not a stranger in the air.

She lies in her bunk at night listening to the ship, to the other girls in her cabin and down the corridor. They murmur together or pray, play endless hands of cards, talk about their dreams and about the men they hope to marry after the war. They have made it through the day, and now they must make it through the night, when the fear of being sunk is compounded by the crawling horrors of the ship's infestations. Some nights it feels more like a vigil, listening to the susurrus of water against the groaning steel of the ship. But then the patterns—all those maps and codes and ciphers June holds in her marrow—invariably slip back into place, and her heart steadies.

When at last they reach Bombay, June stands on deck, trying without success to reconcile what feels increasingly like two separate lives—the commitments to Alec and to her work. Confronted with the reality of India, she understands differently the scale of what she is not telling Alec. She's known, of course, what this would mean to him, but now . . . It feels bigger, more of a problem.

June wonders if Alec sailed from Bombay from this same pier. He was so small then, and her recollection is weighted by the tenderness she's felt for him since she first saw that shock of pale hair above wide brown eyes, his face lost and sad in the vicarage drawing room. She wants to see the things he loved the most, but those will not be here in Bombay— here is chaos, and Alec's India is birds and elephants and the mountains in summer. June glances to the north, although she knows she can't possibly see the Himalayas. But even that adds to the guilt; whatever she sees, whether he would have missed it, she will never be able to bring it to him. That connection is sundered before it can even begin.

He has been her boy as long as she's known him—and yet in crossing the world for her work, the dots and dashes of her vocation stacking
against everything she's ever known, it seems impossible to proceed
into any kind of future without somehow breaking his heart.

It's just as well that their arrival is so distractingly chaotic. The massive Gateway of India stands vigil over the harbor, the stones luminous
as the early sun glints pink through the morning haze. The heat is
bombastic and wet, and the press of Wrens trying to disembark and
make their way to the train station is almost unbearable. The ship had
been crowded, but now they are packed into an even smaller area, in
this inescapable heat. June grips her valise, tries to ignore the slick of
perspiration down her spine. The pier swarms with Wrens and sailors,
a mad crush of people trying to make their way to wherever they're
going next. Most of the Wrens will go with her, to Madras, and then on
to Colombo from there, but others will disperse to Delhi or Calcutta or
any number of other places. A pack of Australian nurses slips past her,
and June shivers despite the heat. What is it like for these girls, knowing how many of their sisterhood have been detained by the Japanese?
How do the nurses left behind carry on in the face of all that?

June steps back from the crowd as well as she can, sizing up the
situation. The heat feels like a layer of damp, itchy cloth pressed against
her by a flatiron. It's madness to be out in it, even early. She doesn't
envy the Wrens their blue wool uniforms. She glances at her watch—
only out of England a few weeks, and already her forearm bears the
imprint of the sun. Half nine, which leaves her with hours before she's
meant to board the train to Madras. For comfort, she runs the recently
memorized list of stations in her head, building a map of the foresee-
able future. It's hard to imagine a trip of this length: Bombay to Madras
is more than twice the distance of London to Inverness, and nowhere
near the extent of India. And even once they've made it to Madras,
overnight and most of the next day on the train, there are two days of

travel still ahead of them before they reach Colombo. And June, impatient and full of purpose, can't wait to get to Ceylon and take up her pencil again.

Years ago Alec had complained about the crush and racket of London, holding Bombay as a quieter metropolis, but how? She will never be able to ask him. The clamor batters her from all directions—Wrens and other new arrivals hailing their friends, vendors hawking shawls and wooden toys, porters and bearers and engines and gulls. She doesn't know where to look first—there is too much movement, too much color, too many people. It's madness, but it's a glory, too.

Just as well she doesn't have to navigate this cacophony alone. Her cabinmate Pamela Glynn, another civilian attached to the Admiralty, has been processed off the ship now too, and joins June by the gangplank. "Bit much, all this."

June nods, relieved to see her. "Makes you miss the air on deck, doesn't it?"

"God yes," Pamela says. They are bonded by their various shipboard travails and all those nights of cards and gin. Pamela's fiancé is posted in Bombay with the army, and June has spent the last weeks hearing every detail of Pamela's plan to leave the Foreign Office the very moment the war is over and she can be demobbed back into her regular life.

Of course, she also wants to be somewhere "civilized," as she kept saying, and June, looking around at the pariah dogs sidling along the edges of the crowd, can't help but think that Bombay is probably not high on Pamela's list. But how exciting, though, to be here, experiencing something that is not England.

Pamela squeals. "Dennis!"

A lanky man, perhaps a bit older than Pamela and clad in the khaki shorts and shirt of a British Army officer, raises his hand. Pamela waves frantically, and he smiles at her, moving genially through the crowd.

"Hullo, Pammy." He kisses her cheek and takes her hand, then turns to June, lifting his peaked cap. "You must be June. I'm Dennis Ruthven, Royal Fusiliers."

"It's good to meet you," June says, shaking his hand. "Pamela has told me so much about you."

His smile widens. "Only good things, I hope."

"I'm glad you're coming with us for lunch," Pamela says to June. "Apparently you're an acceptable chaperone."

Dennis nods. "Had quite the time with the Wren Officer in Charge, trying to convince her I wasn't unsavory." He grins at June. "You're not even Wrens, but she seems rather attached to the two of you."

June smiles. "I should think they'll hardly miss us." She looks at her watch again. It's too early for lunch in the regular course of things, but a half day in Bombay on her way to Ceylon seems well out of the regular course of things, too. And although Pamela can be tiring, June is hungry, it turns out, and the idea of being off the docks has considerable appeal. She glances back around her, watching the sunlight scream off the grimy low waves as they curl against the piers in the shadow of the Gateway.

Pamela pulls at her sleeve, and June clutches her valise and follows Pamela and Dennis out to the street. The sun is even harsher here, an inescapable glow that lends a vertiginous shine to everything. No wonder Alec complained about being cold all the time, if this was the kind of climate he thought correct. The walls that line the street are flecked with red, and she has a disquieting moment thinking it's blood. But beneath her reflexive alarm there is a surge of curiosity, too. After a lifetime of aching toward faraway places on the globe, she has finally reached one of them.

Dennis notes her gaze and smiles. "Betel nuts," he says. "They spit the juice. Bit dramatic to look at, but nothing to worry about."

A turbaned young officer, a Sikh, stands at attention at the side of an official car with Union Jacks fluttering at the corners. He holds the door and they each climb in, June sliding to the far end of the wide cushioned seat.

The long black car nudges its way through the bustling streets, and June watches Bombay pass through the open windows, dazed by the dense enormity of the sheer human presence. There is a part of her that wishes she could have gone looking for Alec's past, but why? To what end, if she can never tell him where she is?

The car is low-slung and wide, and everywhere they turn it seems to June that they are in danger of pushing up too close to people or buildings or, God help them, cows. The driver never stops; at intersections he creeps forward and the masses of people part for them.

June peers out her window, trying to ignore Pamela and Dennis, cooing together on their end of the bench. There is so much to look at outside the car—she's never seen colors like this. On a more prosperous block, flowers cascade from balconies. A trill of jasmine floats in, but it's not enough to mask an underlayer of filth and rot.

"Hanging Gardens," Dennis says. He gestures at a park as they pass it, trees and greenery bursting with flowers, climbing up into a low hillside. "Lovely place, best view of the city from the top of Malabar Hill, but the Parsi leave their dead in the open air." He grimaces.

June looks up at the birds circling. "Are those vultures?"

Pamela says, "It's dreadful."

"It's their custom," Dennis says mildly. "Very philosophical chaps, the Parsi."

June watches the vultures recede. She has heard of suttee, Hindu widows of the higher castes throwing themselves into their husbands' pyres in a ghastly ritual, but this is new. She has an unwanted flash of Alec's parents—his whole household—laid out for the scavengers, although she knows full well they were cremated because of the cholera. The car slows to pass a cart pulled by a bent old man, and June's eyes fall on a gilded statue of a goddess with arms weaving like the eddies of a stream. What would her parents make of this, bound as they are to their stern, dogged Church of England?

"Surely the city could make them change," Pamela says.

Dennis shrugs. "Millions of people out here. It's not England. And the joss sticks help."

"It's remarkable," June says. She tries to accept the layers of scent, though she's almost relieved when Dennis lights a cigarette. He reminds her a little of Alec—tall, fair-haired, good-natured, with a touch of something far away in his face. "Have you been here long?"

"Grew up here," Dennis says. "Parents shipped me to England for school, but . . . Damn glad to be posted back in India." That's what it is, that faraway look—it's the same way Alec's face lightens when he talks about India, some combination of homesickness and memory.

"June's fiancé is from here, too," Pamela offers up. It's been over a year since Alec's proposal, but June still jolts at the word *fiancé*. Dennis looks as though he's waiting for her to elaborate.

"He was a boy here in Bombay," June says hesitantly. She doesn't want to hear from Pamela about how happy they'll be when the war ends. But she has to say something. "He was sent to England when he was small. His parents died."

"I'm sorry," Dennis says.

"He's a pilot now," Pamela says to Dennis.

"Ah," Dennis says. "Bloody rough life." He seems to realize how he sounds, and smiles. "But those chaps know what they're doing." He leans forward to the driver. "Singh, run us by the canteen, that's a good lad."

The driver ducks his head and muscles the car around another corner.

The day passes in a blur—first the canteen, where Dennis buys them sandwiches and tea, and then a street bazaar. Peddlers stand

behind tables sagging and overloaded with all kinds of goods and sou-
venirs, shoes and bolts of shimmering cloth at one booth, lacquered
brass kettles and lamps at another. Men in long tunic-like shirts throng
the marketplace, and it's a moment before June realizes that many of
them have very English umbrellas tucked under their arms. At the base
of a stairway, an elephant-headed deity watches them all benevolently,
incense wafting up from a tray placed square atop his lotus-folded legs.
Some of the peddlers squat along the edges, clearly not as well-off as
the men with tables, but their wares are displayed just as carefully on
worn blankets on the ground.

June's mind is overwhelmed with color and smell, the scent of food
cooking at the innumerable small restaurants and roadside stalls, vats
of richly colored sauces flecked with herbs, the heaviness of spice in
the air, the unfathomable wealth of fresh fruits, most of which she has
never seen before, the crush and reek of incense and bodies—there's so
much she doesn't recognize. So much to learn yet. Cows appear on the
roadside, sometimes laden with necklaces of flowers, and twice now a
monkey has screamed at her from a tree. She's glad to board the train
that evening with Pamela, and gladder still when they make their way
along the car to the compartment they're sharing with two Wrens.

The wrack and clatter of the train is relentless. There are no connecting platforms between the cars, and so they must climb down
from the carriage to the platform during station stops to move along the
train. June makes her way to the buffet car with a Wren from Northern
Ireland who has been to India before. By the time they return to their
compartment, June is replete with new scents and flavors. So many new
words; the language fills her like another kind of code. Ghee, samosa,
vindaloo, masala. Her eyes won't stop watering from the chilies, and her

fingertips are stained a greasy umber. She's brought a couple of samosas back with her, wrapped in a bit of newsprint. Pamela eyes them dubiously, chewing delicately at the tired sandwiches she saved from the canteen that afternoon, but June feels right, somehow. Not all the foods are wholly new—Alec has talked of curries, and at the vicarage Cook had learned to make mulligatawny for him, but even the flavors she has encountered in some form before strike her completely new here.

June pulls a light sweater from her valise and folds it into a tidy pillow. She doesn't think she can actually sleep—the noise is impossible; the windows are open and slatted without glass—but the semblance of rest will do her good. It may also help her tune out Pamela, who is still rhapsodizing about Dennis and the horde of babies she will have with him after the war.

So many of the girls are like this that she wonders if there is something wrong with her. More, though, she wonders how they can make space in their minds for the basic contradiction of these relationships— the violation of trust that some of their jobs require. How can you have a relationship with someone if you can't even tell him what you're doing or where you've been?

It's difficult too, to sit with these women who are on her side, who have joined the same fight, and not be sure what to say about the task that lies ahead. The Wrens are wireless techs or radio mechanics, operators or signalers, and there is no way to know who has signed the Act and who will be part of her team, writing down codes and turning them into information. Some of the Wrens may well have been at Bletchley Park; there are a couple who look vaguely familiar. But there is no way to know without asking, and even that may constitute a violation of the Act.

For a moment her mind fills with an alarming image: the Emperor Hirohito hovering overhead, clogging the wireless lines and sending his kamikaze pilots after the codebreakers. After her. She swallows the fear. There is nothing to be done about it, and once she reaches HMS Anderson she can concentrate on the work—breaking codes, saving lives. Like so many women at home—even the royal princesses—June needs to be of service more than she needs to be safe. This is who she is now.

The train sways through the night, dropping south and east across the subcontinent. June and the other girls in her compartment drift in and out of sleep, rarely more than a light doze. Each time the train stops, its whistles and the screel of brakes chase sleep away. Moths batter themselves against the window slats. Just after dawn, June wakes to the sound of an elephant trumpeting. She presses her face to the window—there it is, smaller than she would have thought, ankle deep in a river, a teenage boy clinging to its shoulders with his knees. The elephant's ears beat, ragged and dignified, against insects. The boy leans down, his torso flat against the elephant's massive brow, and strokes the trunk it reaches to him. Something in June's chest opens, and she fumbles through her valise for Alec's latest letter, a single page from Canada in the weeks before she'd left Britain. She has to squint to read it, even held up to the faint light coming in through the slats, but that's all right. She has committed this, and his other letters, to memory.

Darling June,

Spring has come at last to the tundra, and I am beside myself with relief. Perhaps I will not perish of cold after all! There are any number of plants I've not encountered before. Even their names sound unlike what we would have at home! There are tulips, but also columbine, firewood, Labrador tea, Jack Pye weed, and a host of others.

Were I to tell you a story, the bear would be a creature of the flatlands. There are the Rockies far to the west, and the mountains of

Quebec not quite as far to the east, but nothing here, where it is as flat as wilted napkins at a midsummer luncheon. Beautiful country, to be sure, but quite unlike any part of England I know.

The men here are in high spirits—eager and fresh, and most of them well-suited to the grind of the pilot's life and the challenge of flight. They'll make fine officers. I continue not to understand why the powers that be thought to send Tim and me to Canada of all places, but now I'm halfway through my sojourn I'm glad we've come.

The worst part of it—of everything—is missing you. I think about the scent of your hair, or how it puddles against your collarbones, and become weak with it. There is nothing about you that I fail to miss—nothing. Even the sure knowledge that you are struggling now with wanting to correct my "tundra," above . . . Even that adds to the sureness in my heart.

Consider the maps in your head, my darling, and draw your lovely finger along the latitude closest to those we share—not quite 50 degrees, both of us, but I promise you I shall feel that tracing to my marrow.

Another half a year and I'll be home, reunited with you and ready to rejoin my squadron while I wait to see where His Majesty and Mr. Churchill send me next. I would wait a lifetime for you—another six months is nothing.

All my love,
Your Alec
F/Lt Alec St. John Oswin
RCAF Station Ottawa

The letter stabs at her—there is guilt, of course, in wondering if this is the right path, particularly when she lets herself be confronted by his certainty. By the raw need that boils out of him. By everything. The fact is she loves him more deeply than she can explain even to herself, but even so . . .

She closes her eyes and lets the map grow in her mind—there is Ottawa, on the other side of the world, more than seven thousand miles away, and here is Bombay. Ottawa and London are six degrees of latitude apart; Alec is right that a single thumb could cover both in a single line. Before she left Bletchley Park, she could follow his instructions and make it work. But Bombay is at the 19th parallel, and Colombo even farther south. She quails away from the weight of Alec's belief.

Perhaps they are not the golden boy and girl of her adolescent reveries after all. And from this distance, with the layers of confusion and evasion, there is no way to tell. Perhaps marriage isn't for her. Perhaps she should let Alec go, let him find someone who can love him better and be the kind of woman he wishes she could be.

But the idea of giving Alec up makes her heart hurt. Despite their feelings, isn't it possible that the very closeness that has, from the beginning, tethered them into the unit they have become is exactly what might now tear them apart? If she met someone else later, she could be vague about the war. But this is Alec, and every day she feels it more, the way her choices and duties are pulling at the fabric of them.

1943, *RAF Blida*

January, and the world smells of orange blossom from the thousands of trees in the groves surrounding Blida. The town is an oasis of sorts, old and French and Mohammedan at the base of the mountains. It is nothing like India, and yet. There is something about the scent of oranges, and the chatter of the urchins who line the roads and sell fruit to the airmen, something about the dust storms that fill their planes with grit, that calls to Alec. On their leaves, he goes with Charlie and Sanjay into Algiers and drinks Pernod in some cafés and mint tea in others. The drive in the borrowed Jeep feels reckless at times, as if they're waiting for a German plane to lean across the sky and strafe them into oblivion, but getting away from the dusty airfield and the stench of jet fuel for a handful of hours is a gift. But, like most gifts, it has its complications.

There are corners of Algiers in which the war doesn't exist, in which a man can forget for a few hours. Where Alec can find men who remind him of the Mohammedans in the markets of Bombay and Srinagar, although their Arabic is not enough like the languages of his childhood to help him. The scent of braziers and spicy Merguez pulls at him from the chaos of the souk and makes him wonder if he will ever get back to India. Occasional letters from Roger make the connection between this life here and that life there even stronger; the letters are nostalgic more often than not, as Roger, stationed for the moment in Egypt, misses the mountains where he's made his life.

Across the Mediterranean from Algiers is Marseille, and talking of Marseille with Charlie leads to talk of their days aboard the RMS *Jaipur*, and the boys who roamed the ship with them. And they talk of India too, sometimes; these men are some of the only people he's ever met who understand how hard the landscape of his childhood can tug at him. Sanjay, in particular, seems caught between two worlds here.

Alec longs for June all the time, her absence tugging at him as well, although at this point he is almost used to being without her. Years of going away to school have turned out to be a kind of practice for whatever this is, with him in North Africa and getting farther away all the time. He writes to her as often as he can, although her own letters are coming less frequently. Sometimes they look as though they've been opened and inspected, the London postmark blurred with wear and weather, but perhaps that's what comes of working for the Foreign Office, even as a secretary. She is incredibly precise with her details— nothing that might be censored, nothing too personal.

But it's never enough. He misses the feeling of her skin under his palms, the way her eyes flash when something catches her attention, the bare hint of the Fens in her voice when she's tired. He misses the way her fingers wrap around his wrist to catch his attention when they're walking together. He misses everything.

A lec almost can't remember before the war. He's been flying for nearly four years now, and he can hardly imagine a life based mainly on the ground. Most of his days are a broken rhythm of waiting for alarms or soaring into the sky. Even when he can get away from it, clear himself out of the base, the war and its routines are always there. In the beginning he joined the University Squadron because he thought it would be an adventure, and he left school to be part of the fight because he knew it was important. Germany had to be beaten back; the stakes were too high for him to choose otherwise. And still too, it was a lark. He has turned out to be good at it, and, perhaps more important, he hasn't yet died of it.

But the war is a grind, and if he lets himself think of what it actually means, what his squadron and the other Allied forces are actually doing here in Algeria, or wherever they're sent next, it seems it will never end. And what is the point, really? Someone will surrender, and treaties will be brandished. There will be blame and recriminations, and the endless fields of the dead with their lonely white crosses. And one day there will be another war, another cohort of boys sent off to their deaths. There are days when the war is confusingly remote, except when he flies out into it, over the Mediterranean, or dips his wings over the desert-creased carcasses of tanks and trucks abandoned by the German retreat.

The war is most evident in the gaps left behind by the men who vanish—wounded, missing, or dead—or in the stories new squaddies tell of things they've seen or done. There are men who want the war to end so they can go home to the girls they left behind and forget all this, and men who want it to go on forever because they have the scent of blood in their souls now, and this is who they are.

Sometimes he wakes in the night with a queasy, confused feeling about June. For years he had mostly felt the worry as a quiet fret— is she all right, is she well out of the bombing—but now it's been far too long since he's seen her, and the absence hurts. He had hoped to see her last autumn, in the days between his return from Canada and rejoining the squadron in Algeria. But his efforts at a visit had been disastrous. He had gone to the town house in Bloomsbury with a single bright rose, the best he'd been able to scrape up on short notice in a bomb-scarred London, but June had not been there. Ainsley Finch-Martin had been home, though. The look on Ainsley's face—that flash of surprise—had left a dank feeling in Alec's chest. He had asked to see June, and Ainsley had told him she wasn't there just then, that June was traveling for work and had not said when she might be back.

But she had done him the kindness of writing out Floss Corbett's telephone number on a bit of newsprint, and so Alec had gone to a call box and rung the man up. The conversation, such as it was, had been far from satisfactory—Corbett had told him only that June was out of town for the Foreign Office and no, he was not at liberty to tell Alec where. He had sounded smug and oily, and wholly infuriating.

That had been months ago, and still Alec regrets not calling Corbett out. His arrogance has never sat well with Alec, but what could he do? All that time, and still no clarity—why couldn't Corbett just tell him where June was? Days when he is in the air are better; they keep him from thinking so much about June and the things he doesn't understand. She's never said exactly where she'd gone, although he's asked her twice now when he's written to her. At least her last letter had responded to the question in some way—*I'm so sorry I missed you, Alec. I'd thought there would be more time before you were home from Canada.* He has no idea what to make of that.

Days like today . . . those are more challenging. Alec sits on the chock wedged under his plane's landing gear, leaning back against the metal. He thinks of Corbett's cane and the twist of a limp when he walks, and grimaces. Alec spits bitterly to the dusty ground. He won't strike a cripple, no matter how big an ass he is. Not even Floss Corbett.

He looks up when he hears footsteps—Sanjay is coming across the tarmac, flapping an envelope against his palm. Alec stands, hopeful, his eyes on the envelope, but Sanjay shakes his head.

"Sorry, Cosmo," he says. "This one's mine."

Alec shrugs, aiming for nonchalance without much success. "Perhaps the next bag."

"That may be," Sanjay says. "It takes too long for post to come from home."

"That's all very well for you," Alec says crossly, "you've got your damned letter."

"She'll write," Sanjay says.

Alec looks at the ground, watches the dust eddy across his shoes in what's passing for a breeze today. Sweat pools in the small of his back. "What if she doesn't?"

Charlie, on his way across the tarmac, pauses to listen, and laughs. "Some old gaffer's got her busy typing memos and buying black-market stockings for his wife, I'll wager."

"Perhaps your mail is going to Canada," Sanjay says. "That would seem more likely."

Despite his worries, Alec laughs. They're probably right. It's never been easy to imagine his brilliant girl as a secretary, and the picture Charlie brings to mind seems most unlikely. But he knows June, and if that's what the war effort and that prat Corbett need from her, she'll do it better than anyone.

I f not for the gnawing absence of June, and the ongoing press of war and flying sorties over the Mediterranean, Alec would be happy in Algeria. The sky here seems taller, somehow, and a wholly different kind of blue, a brilliant canvas on which he paints the triumph of hunting Germans and earning his ace. He loves the blur of language around Blida, the intersect of Berber and Arab and a host of other cultures and tongues, the elaborate Moorish gates around the city, the squalor and chaos and grandeur of the labyrinthine nest of streets and alleys. The food in Blida is better than the food in England, olives and lamb and spices. Orange trees by the side of the road. The idea of food growing in the fields outside the city, or in the Atlas foothills that shimmer in the near distance, makes everything feel more immediate, more tangible. Even when the sand whirls into a haboob, and dust and grime coat the world and block his view of the mountains, he knows how to interpret the landscape, how to work with the people.

Not far from base there is a railroad crossing, and an old woman there will fry up a slab of bread and an egg with a thick orange yolk for a couple of coins. There are urchins selling fruit and eggs and bacon by the roadside, and while many of the men avoid this fare because they don't trust the freshness or the vendors, Alec welcomes it. Like everything else, buying something to eat from a clamorous boy by the side of the road reminds him of India. This would be glory enough after the years in England, but on the heels of all those months in Canada it feels like paradise—the terrain, the action, the clamor, the food all feel nearly bespoke for him.

The early-spring clouds float like schools of thin white fish against the cobalt sky. It's so peaceful that Alec can almost forget he's at war, looking for the enemy. The Blue and Green sections of A Flight have been sent aloft on a rare daylight mission to find and interfere with a German convoy reportedly making its way from Livorno to Bizerta. The three Green planes have vanished along the southern scoop of the sea to find the ships, while Charlie leads Blue a hair more north and east, hunting the fighter escorts with Alec and Sanjay at his flanks.

The sun blooms in prisms off the wings of each plane, the engines throbbing against the sky. It's a beautiful day for flying, so perfectly clear that when the first Messerschmitts appear, they seem unreal and almost imaginary.

Alec's radio clicks to life, Charlie's voice rattling through. "Trust you see the bandits, lads?"

"Off to port," Sanjay confirms.

"Got 'em," Alec adds.

The radio is silent for a moment, then, "Engage at will," Charlie says.

Alec glances over his shoulder, gets the thumbs-up from Tim, nods.

The horizon crackles with the light of muzzle flashes as the German guns thunder. There are planes coming from above and behind, from everywhere. The Beaufighter's fuselage shudders, rocked by the punch of German guns finding their mark—there are planes coming from behind them now, from everywhere, Charlie and Sanjay yelling on the radio, then silent as another shot shatters Alec's aerial.

Alec's throat goes dry, and the Beaufighter angles dizzily toward the sea.

Above, a waft of clouds.

Below, the rush of low waves on the Mediterranean, a rocky coastline, a vineyard.

Alec's plane spins against the sky until the coastline lies above him, heaven and earth inverted.

There is too much smoke to see behind him the dozen feet or so to the navigator's compartment, but Alec can feel the stillness and knows Tim is dead already in the rear of the plane, like Cobber before him.

Alec squints into the distance, to where the horizon used to be. His breath comes ragged, the sound of it all wrong as he struggles for air. There's no time, but he has to do something. And if he cannot steady himself, perhaps he can steady the plane.

He clenches his teeth until his jaw aches, pulling at the wheel until the Beaufighter has rolled back nearly upright. The fuselage creeps down the sky, leaking fuel in a pungent rain. An emergency landing will be impossible; his Beau is stiff enough landing on a proper runway; the choppy waves of the sea will kill him. He slips a hand into the breast pocket of his flight jacket, fingering the St. Christopher medallion Constance sent him the year before, and a much-folded letter from June tucked around it.

Gravity wants to hold him in the fatal embrace of the canopy, but he pushes sludgily through the pressure and the stink of burning oil and pulls his parachute off the wall mounting, strapping it to his harness over the life vest. The smoke is getting worse, making him queasy and slow.

He flattens his seat, flips the latch that opens the hole in the floor. His gloves are too thick and unwieldy, and he casts them aside so he can open the hatch. Thank God they'd loosed their torpedoes already or his exit would be blocked. The hatch hangs open, and he knows from his training that there is a spot of dead air—less than a second to get his bearings, but better than nothing.

He looks down through the opening, pats the sides of the old crate as if it were a horse or a dog, the seconds hurtling past on the screaming wind beneath him. If he doesn't jump now it will be too late, his chute won't open in time.

Alec takes a breath and drops into the wide-open air, falling like a stone, the plane too close. He tries to aim himself like a javelin, like a bolt of lightning thrown by a god, like anything that will angle him away from this doomed trajectory.

The Messerschmitt has turned its guns on Charlie's plane, and Alec is helpless to stop any of this, dropping too fast, hardly able to breathe, flinching against the sound of German shells shredding through the carapace of Charlie's Beaufighter. Alec pulls his chute, braces himself for the terrible jolt against his chest and underarms when the parachute billows into the sky above him. His plummet sways into a controlled fall, almost lazy by contrast, holding him in the palm of the sky to watch the Messerschmitts vanish into the distance, their mission of carnage complete.

A hundred yards away, Charlie's plane curls into a spiral, black smoke billowing from the tail, the engines, the cockpit. It fans out into the evening, a pyre in the air.

"Godspeed, Charlie," Alec whispers. He can't see what's happened to Sanjay. God willing, he has pulled away safely.

The airplanes fall screaming into the rocks.

He can still smell the smoke when he hits the water, scrambling to free himself from the drag of the parachute. Somehow his hands have tangled in the cords, his fingers awry at angles his mind won't grasp, and for a moment he is full of a blistering panic that he won't get loose, that the chute that should have saved him will be the instrument of his death. Then at last—freedom. The ropes and his frantic efforts to extricate himself from them have left his hands broken and bleeding, but the shore is not far, and if he's careful, or lucky, perhaps his descent has gone unnoticed. Perhaps there are Allied ships nearby. Perhaps something.

But the boat, when it comes gliding silently over the low waves, is neither civilian nor Allied. It's a wallowing cutter, a battered donkey in the Italian navy. The sailors on board haul him from the sea and cut away the life vest and the jumble of harnesses. They bandage his hands, give him a blanket and a cup of coffee, and lock him in a tiny cabin far belowdecks. And there he stays. His hands are an agony, and he can't hold the coffee. It grows cold while he waits to see what will happen next.

By the time he reaches shore, he has provided the barest information he can to a series of officers. He is officially a prisoner of war.

There are days of fever. There is a beautiful nurse with soft, brisk fingers, who tends his bandages. She coos like a mourning dove when she looks at his hands. She has almost no English, and Alec speaks no Italian at all, but in the fever he believes they can understand each other. *Le mani sono rovinate*, she whispers. He hears: *Soon you will go home. Soon you will go back to the sky whence you came. Soon the war will end.* When the fever breaks, he knows—his hands are ruined.

On a packed transport train a few days later, British officers from North Africa and Gibraltar are shoved in like steerage passengers as the Italians take them to a prisoner of war camp. He looks for Charlie, but Charlie is never there, and the nights are full of the whine of the Beaufighter slapping into the rocks. And June—his whole future, his life—feels further away than ever.

1943, *Campo 78*

ampo 78 sits not quite two thousand feet above the Adriatic in the Apennines, surrounded by olive and persimmon trees just outside the village of Sulmona. The camp is a cluster of brick barracks, yellow and red, hundreds or thousands of officers and enlisted pulled out of the sea or out of the desert. All these men, lost. Most of them British or from somewhere in the Commonwealth. Some of them beset with night terrors and worse. There's one man in Alec's barracks who cries when the sun sets, and again when it rises.

There are rumors about German camps, and for the most part the inmates of Campo 78 agree that their camp is probably a sight better. They have a small library, a newspaper, sometimes a band. They have football and ready access to their Red Cross parcels, which make for unexpected luxuries; men who have been in the German camps say the deliveries are inconsistent there at best. And the guards, most of them anxious to avoid the front, are greedy for cigarettes. Alec keeps a handful of the cigarettes that come from the Red Cross so he can smell them; lighting them is almost beyond him with his hands gnarled into these scarred objects to which he feels almost no connection. They remind him of the branches of the olive trees that arc across the walls. But he welcomes the scent of the tobacco, and now only a few cigarettes last him a long time. The rest he trades to the guards for wine.

He is glad to have missed the winter. The camp is near the highest point of the Apennines, and he hears stories of the way the wind screamed through the barracks. Now, in the tail end of spring, the trees that crest the hillsides outside the camp have begun to blossom, and when the wind is right the flowers drift over the camp like particularly wistful snowflakes. In the depths of winter, the snow would have been less charming, and the ice lacing up the road to the annex at Campo 78/1 potentially lethal.

Some of the ANZAC officers have batmen among the NCOs and enlisted at Campo 78/1, doing hard labor in the quarry between the camps. Alec wants to feel bad for the enlisted men who have it so much worse than he does, but his main feeling these days is a sort of bitter finality. Sometimes he's ashamed of his anger—once the war is over, he will be reunited with June. A lot of the other men aren't going to have that—the camp is full of men who have had letters from home turning them loose and breaking their hearts. He looks at his hands, experimentally flexing his fingers, or trying to.

His hands are not completely useless, even tangled and flamed with pain as they are. The fingers and bones of his right hand took the brunt of the damage and have only the barest fine motor ability. But on his weaker hand he has reasonable function in his thumb and the first two fingers, and he is learning to use them more effectively. Matches are quite beyond him, and holding a pen, but he can shave and button his trousers, however slowly. Perhaps by the time the war ends he'll feel less like some kind of clawed, scar-ridden creature. Perhaps by then he will have learned how to use his new hands, such as they are.

At Campo 78, the prisoners have cleared a field bordered by ragged oak trees for exercise. Sometimes there's cricket. Alec misses the feel of a cricket bat in his hands, but he can't grip the handle. Instead he sits on the sidelines, listening to the crack of the bat against the ball.

If he closes his eyes he can pretend he's about to hit a century. At Cambridge he had batted for Clare College, and then for the university Firsts; had the war not come, he would have taken a blue for it. As long ago as India he had lain in bed at night, his cricket bat just within reach, dreaming of glory on the pitch. His father had played every summer with his regiment, and Alec had loved to sit with his mother in the shade of the striped pavilions and watch the matches unfold for hours. He and Sanjay had sat talking about those days, about matches they'd seen in India, and the particular sound of the bat and ball in the amphitheater of foothills. How is it possible that his days with the bat are over? That he likely will never again lay that splendid slab of willow across his shoulder after a great whacking hit, the world smelling of linseed and grass, and look up to see June watching him?

He's lying in the sun and listening to a match one day at the end of July, his head badly cradled by the pillow of his jacket on the ragged grass, dragonflies shimmering through the afternoon, when a man stops in front of him. An American, unless his flight jacket is stolen. Alec sits up. Behind the stranger, the sun has laced itself along the mountainside. Alec looks at the golden gossamer of fig trees and rocks, and waits.

The American has come to Campo 78 from North Africa, a chaplain en route from one base to another, separated from the rest of the men in his transport. He talks like a man who has almost forgotten the sound of his own voice, information lurching out of him in an order Alec doesn't understand. He wants to know how to play cricket, and if it's true that sometimes a test match can go for days, but mostly he wants to know if Alec is going to be okay.

Alec regards him carefully. The other man is older, perhaps as much as ten years Alec's senior—he pauses, his mind almost emptying as he realizes it's almost his birthday; he's going to be twenty-four in a week? Time is confusing, and he doesn't track it the way some of the men do. Everything is measured in chunks—*when I was with June, when I was at Clare College, when I was not here, when my hands worked*. But sometimes thinking of when he wasn't at Campo 78 makes it worse—if he dares believe that he will eventually go home, what if he's wrong? Or what if he's right, but home is gone? Although, the truth is, June, not Fenbourne, is home.

The American sits beside him. "Did they do that to your hands?"

Alec flinches. The British in the camp have noted his hands and gone on without questions. There was an American pilot in Algeria, and he too had had questions about everything. Perhaps it's an American problem.

"No," Alec says, unsure who he means by *they*.

The chaplain waits a long time, but Alec has nothing else to say.

They get into the habit of taking their meals together. The chaplain's name is Bart Smialowicz, and the handful of men who talk to him call him Padre until the day he finally steps out onto the ragged, not quite green of the athletic field, hefts a cricket bat experimentally, and slams the first ball bowled to him into the mountainside. After, they call him Smasher. Smasher talks incessantly. At first Alec thinks Smasher believes that the endless anecdotes and details will somehow shield him from the war. Later he understands that Smasher is filling him with stories to distract him from his hands, and from the war. The chaplain feels guilty about the rest of the men in his convoy, and about his mother in Minnesota. About his parish, also waiting, and their fears that he might not return. He feels guilty about the cousins in Poland he's never met, whose fates he doesn't know.

Alec listens. Sometimes he tries to say something he thinks will help, but most of the time he feels as though Smasher is just trying to get out all the words before it's too late. As if either of them knows what *too late* means. But it's something he can do, easy enough to sit quietly beside Smasher while they eat the scant bowls of pasta with watered-down tomato paste and cheese, or the fresh figs and fruit harvested by the enlisted men at Campo 78/1 throughout the summer.

Most nights Alec dreams of Charlie's plane. He continues to hope that Sanjay escaped, that he survived and made it back to base. Now and again he dreams of the sea, of sinking into the Mediterranean with the tangle of his parachute, but as a boy, slipping from the deck of the RMS *Jaipur* and sliding silently beneath the waves in a wash of canvas and cord. He wakes missing the shipboard stars, disconsolate that he will never fly again.

I t's the end of August before he tells Smasher about June. He hasn't talked to anyone about her until now, except Charlie and Sanjay. But Smasher has started to be talked out, at last, and his ramblings have begun to sound more like questions. And he is a priest, a chaplain as well as a friend; he is required to keep Alec's secrets. At first the story comes out haltingly, Alec trying to decide where their tale begins. When he was eight and arrived in Fenbourne? Earlier, even, before he'd ever heard of June Attwell, when his lungs were still raw with the smoke of Bombay? Later, the first time he took her hand, the first time he kissed her? When he understood how well his palm fit in the small of her back?

When Alec closes his eyes, he remembers the yellow blouse June wore that day in London when he proposed. He remembers the light in June's eyes when he took his mother's ring from his pocket, the lion like hope behind her, and the quiet, clear *yes* that he felt all the way through him. When he looks at his hands, he's almost glad he hasn't seen her in so long. But it's impossible to ignore the ache in him that only her touch has ever been able to soothe. And impossible as well to describe the ache to Smasher.

Smasher helps him write postcards to Roger and Constance, a step up from the Red Cross notice they would have received when his captivity became official. Then they tackle the much harder task: writing to June. The last letter he had from her may as well have been a hundred years ago. And a letter is not nearly what he wants or needs. He had hoped they might have a leave together while he was still in England, but the war, or Floss Corbett, had thwarted him. A day would be nowhere near enough time to bury his face in her hair and feel her hands cool and strong against the curve of his elbow, anchoring him against the war and the loneliness, but it would have been better than no days. But now there have been months of not wanting to share his heart with the guards, too proud to ask another British officer for help, and not being able to write a letter himself. But now he has Smasher to help him.

It's a short letter, more empty than full, he thinks. Even with Smasher he doesn't say everything he needs to say, and so the letter is too short, a sparrow when he would have liked to send a goshawk. A dinghy lost on the ocean of missing her. If she gets it—*when*, he reminds himself, always *when*, never *if*—she will know where he is.

1944, *HMS Anderson*

There is always something in the roof, moving through the palm leaves. Sometimes it's the rain, pounding so violently against the thatching that it brings to mind the thud of the ack-ack guns at home. Even when it's not raining, the rattle of the leaves never stops. Tonight, during a break in the showers, it's no different. A snake, then, or one of the spiders June keeps seeing, bigger than her hand and bristling with hair. If it's a spider, she can ignore it, almost, as she does the enormous mantises that sit on the wireless tables and watch them work. But the snakes . . .

It's worse when she's on the wireless, taking a shift for a Wren. Those eight-hour shifts are usually an exercise in solitude, broken up by navy men on hourly patrols, the inconsistent arrival of other girls to offer a break for the loo or just a chance to stand and move around for a bit. And being unable to get away from the sound of slithering, or the chitter of various creatures on the floor or walls, can be hard. Nights like this, when she's breaking codes, she can look up or shift around now and again, although she spends most of the time hunched over a table with her pencils and stacks of paper, turning the columns of numbers into something usable to send via teleprinter to Melbourne or Kilindini.

They've had a boon lately—a captured steel chest of Japanese code books that let them translate some of the codes nearly instantly. One of them is obsolete already, so frequently do the Japanese change their practices, but June has made a point of translating the information it contains into English so she can develop an even stronger familiarity with the shape of the messages, and where to expect which kind of information. It helps, on a practical level, but the expansion of her knowledge is exciting, too.

She turns, stretching her arms until her shoulders creak, and glances over her shoulder to see if their mongoose is around. Not theirs, really, but all the girls talk about him that way. In town, the Sinhalese tell her that the mongoose is a pest, like the minks at home in England, but in the wireless hut nobody cares what their mongoose does when he's not with them. They call him Box, and give him the run of the station, the mess, even the loo. June loves his bristling swagger, not to mention the way he reminds her of Kipling and Alec. When not knowing how Alec is faring feels darkest and most terrifying, she clings to the idea that Box in some way stands in for him. It's ridiculous, she knows, superstitious claptrap. And yet.

The rustling comes again, and she looks up. It's not in the roof—and it's not Box. Now that she's paying more attention, she recognizes the sound as the rattle of cards being shuffled in the corridor outside. June smiles. One of the facts of this life is the seemingly random nature of assignments, and the way a person you liked is often someone you might never see again. In this case, it is happily the opposite—the powers that be have sent Wendy Fairchild to Colombo. Wendy is a Wren now, one of the wireless operators, and she carries a deck of cards with her everywhere she goes. She says the shuffling helps her focus, which June can't argue with. They all have their tricks in those inevitable moments when the clicks and buzzes of the wireless run together into a hypnotic murmur.

June looks at her watch—shift change, so Wendy and her cards must be coming off her watch, relieved by one of the other Wrens. It's no time at all before Wendy bursts into the room. Becoming a Wren has not made her any more decorous.

"Good evening," June says.

"Hallo, Attwell," Wendy says, grinning at her. "Sink any ships tonight?"

June smiles, although she wishes Wendy would not bring up the past. Even acknowledging that they were stationed together at Scarborough feels as though it skirts the parameters of the Official Secrets Act, despite her own gladness at their reunion.

"No," she says. She glances down at her papers. So far tonight they have divulged only vague notions of troop movements, information that June has already passed along.

Wendy sits on the edge of the desk and leans closer with a conspiratorial whisper. "Truffit put her mug down on the table just now without looking and it moved." She shudders cheerfully. "She'd put it on something's back, can you believe it? Whole ruddy thing would have walked right off the table if she hadn't stopped it."

"She trapped a mantis in a cup the other day," June says. Merrill Truffit minds the insects less than most of them, which is good, as she seems to attract them.

"As long as they're creeping to her and not me, that's all very well." Wendy laughs, shuffling her cards against her thigh. "Seen Box around?"

June eyes her warily. After two years, she is somewhat accustomed to most of the more alarming fauna that inhabit the station and her barracks in Colombo, but sometimes one of the girls will report an insect so large or grotesque that June can hardly stand to hear about it. And Wendy, as much as June likes her, has a predilection for spreading word of these egregious creatures.

"He was here a little while ago," June says.

"Wish that mongoose would go after the crawlies more often," Wendy grumbles. She gets to her feet. "Are you coming along to the beach to-morrow?"

"Yes," she says. She gestures at the papers before her. "I'll clear this tonight." Thinking of the beach at Mount Lavinia, where she's gone to swim as often as she can since arriving in Ceylon, is distracting, but it feels good to hold a reward out for herself on her days off. She wants to sit in the sand and watch the warm, clear waves cresting in off the green and blue water, and the cormorants and, most of all, the fisher-men, who remind her somehow of the old men at home in the Fens, weaving their wicker basket nets for eels.

"Then I'll leave you to it," Wendy says.

"Yes," June says. "I'll see you tomorrow."

The beach makes a grand respite from the war, but does nothing for her endless fears about Alec. They gnaw at her, cheating her of sleep, which she can't afford, but it's been like this since the end of November, when a months-old letter had come from her parents. Those letters are always a mixed blessing, as June can read between the lines and see that they would rather know where she is, that vague state-ments about the Foreign Office are not enough information for them. June understands—if she were in their shoes, she would struggle, too. For the most part, their letters are roll calls of the village, comments here and there about christenings in families she knows, the comings and goings of men on leave, holidays at the vicarage. But in that one there had been something new—a message relayed from Constance Fane, who had had a series of telegrams. Alec had been shot down over the Mediterranean, picked up by the Italians before a British ship could reach him.

June has never quite steadied herself from Alec's first time shot down, and during the little time she'd been able to spend with him when they were both still in England he had not much wanted to talk about it. She knows almost nothing about what happened, or if there were other incidents about which she hasn't any idea. If she thinks about it too closely, it sends a shuddering, echoing fear through her. She loves him; she does not want to lose him. And there are times when the juxtaposition of her affection for him and her desire to have a future built on career and a life of the mind is too chaotic a collision. There is no right answer, no way to solve it without breaking someone's heart. So to hear that he had been shot down again and taken prisoner . . .

But an Italian camp is better than dead or missing, better than most of the alternatives, and so she clings to that. One of the effects of being on this side of the world has been the breaking of time. The narrative of the people she loves happens out of order with her own story, because it takes a long time for her letters to reach home, routed through the Foreign Office couriers back to London for the subterfuge of postmarking and the censor's stringent gaze, and longer still for anything from Fenbourne to reach Colombo. This is magnified by Alec's captivity— two months ago she received a letter from him, routed for almost a year through innumerable channels, stamped and prodded by the censors on both sides. But that letter had come from Italy, and she knows from her sources in the Admiralty that Campo 78 closed when Italy surrendered in September, its prisoners escaped into the mountainsides or loaded into trains for German POW camps. Alec did not escape; as far as she can gather, he followed the order to stay in place and await the Allies. And now, like most of the other men who obeyed, he is in one of those German camps.

June carries that letter in her pocket, a simple folded card with someone else's plain printing utterly unlike Alec's exuberant scrawl. A few sentences about the Italians taking good care of them, a comment about olive trees in the mountains. Nothing about what's happened to him that has made it necessary for another man to write his letters for him, except a single throwaway line—*banged up my hands rather in the last shaky do.* She wrote to Floss in the hopes of learning more, but it's been weeks now, and she has heard nothing.

It's possible there are other letters in this confounding handwriting waiting for her somewhere. The post at Anderson has been regular enough, but there are girls whose letters came while they were temporarily elsewhere. Mail forwarded or lost and never seen again. Even Pamela, whose fiancé is still only as far away as India, is subject to the maddening tides of communication. It's likely enough the same has happened to her, that Alec's letters are caught in the system somewhere. She gathers from things she's heard from her mother, or from the Wrens, that the post is equally inconsistent the other direction, but nevertheless she writes to Alec once a month—it's not often enough, and she feels sick over it, but it feels less bad than more letters compounding the deception. The more often she writes him, the worse she feels, sending half-truths to this man who loves her with all his heart, going through God knows what in Germany.

But sending off these letters is the least she can do. Perhaps there is a middle ground of sorts between the kind of woman she is and the kind of wife she does not want to be. Given what she knows of the German camps he may need more than she knows how to give. Duty means something new now. And so, perhaps, does love.

The roof rustles again, and June tries to relax. Probably it's Box, hunting. It helps that the mongoose is so good at being a mongoose; it helps her keep the fears at bay. Box has been with them since spring, killing kraits and chasing the larger insects, and one of the other girls swears she saw him hypnotize a cobra. June is reasonably sure this is not strictly true, but it doesn't matter. Wherever Box wants to go in their compound, he is welcome, although she wishes he would stay close.

So far they have been lucky; except for the kraits that Box tackled, and one scare with a viper, all the Wrens have avoided the snakes. Not that there's time to think about them—the signals come in fast, and the work of either transcribing or decrypting them is endless and precise. Most of the time it's Wrens capturing the signals, then sending them around the corner to June or the other codebreaker. The Japanese meteorological codes are beautifully ordered, intricate columns of numbers that June must unravel until they turn to messages.

But often as not June is happy to do the Wrens' work—they face the same risks, and the lines between who is a Wren and who is not seem sometimes to have collapsed. The night before she had taken Lucy Kent's shift, because Lucy, who is barely twenty, wanted to go to the Silver Fawn with an officer she'd met the day before. And everyone knows that June will take all the shifts she can—ask Attwell, they say.

Time passes because she forces it to pass, or so it seems. Ceylon is both Shangri-La and Purgatory. When she arrived, there was a skeleton crew of codebreakers and wireless operators; most of the Far East Combined Bureau had gone to Kilindini or Delhi by then. Set up in an old whitewashed building that had once been a school for the sons of landowners, politicians, and prosperous merchants, June and her colleagues had operated more as a way station than a proper outpost for a long while. That had changed last September, when FEBC had come back to Colombo. It's better now, with the Wrens. Before, it had been so lonely, no matter how deep she had sunk herself in the work. Now, though, it's more like Scarborough, or even Bletchley Park.

For the most part, June would rather be here, listening to the scratch of her pencils or the static-blurred world beyond Ceylon. If only the weather would cooperate. Monsoon season is mostly past, and in theory it is the best time of year throughout Ceylon. Often there is rain despite the change of seasons, and thunder too, crackling through the headset until her head hurts. But worse than the deafening interference from nearby power lines and the local airfield or the rain is knowing that they may be missing codes—a transposed digit, a dot noted in place of a dash, can mean life or death. There is no margin for error. Even when their shifts change at the wireless, there is an elaborate dance of headset and pencil so someone is always listening, someone is always writing. They cannot pause, ever.

But tonight, beyond the weather, there's a low whine, like a dog or an old lorry. It's not one of the usual night sounds, and she's never heard it before over the headset, either. She stands and goes to the wireless room, where Lucy Kent is now back on duty after her night off. June stands next to her, trying to place the sound, which is now getting louder and more insistent. And then it crystallizes for her—it's an airplane, too low and too close, and it reminds her of London in the Blitz.

One of the navy men bursts through the door. "Shelter now, ladies! Zeroes incoming!"

Lucy glances out into the night, still listening to the headset. "Can't," she says. "Too much message traffic."

"I'll take it over," June says.

"Sorry, miss," the sailor says to June, his breath coming too fast, "orders are to get civilians to safety!" He hovers behind Lucy. "You too, Kent."

They all flinch as the plane rumbles overhead, the guttural throb of the engine filling the room. The angry pocking of the guns follows, and the sailor and June crouch low until it passes. Lucy hunches closer to the wireless, her face gone pale. Outside, someone is screaming.

Lucy stands, the headset in her hand, Japanese messages still trickling through the static and out into the room. June reaches for it, but Lucy doesn't let go. The three of them are still standing like that, viscous black smoke rolling into the room, when the plane passes again. Bullets from its guns lace through the palm leaves and send fragments blasting into the room. One bayonets the sailor in the base of his throat, and he drops, blood welling like spilled milk.

"The shelter!" June shouts. Time is moving wrong, and she can't shake the sound of the plane. She can barely see through the smoke, just enough to see Lucy still hesitating. And another plane, the engine protesting.

Then the roar of engine vanishes in the shriek of metal twisting into trees and concrete. Lucy drops to her knees, screaming, and in the instant before the plane explodes, June dives to cover her. *We should have gone to the shelter*, she thinks. Then the sound of the explosion rolls over her, deafening her, and the wall shudders against the blast. Fragments of tree and metal and glass explode around them. The world goes dark.

S he wakes in the infirmary two days later, dizzy and weak. A scattering of small shrapnel wounds itch as they heal, and her arm is in a sling, a separated shoulder jammed back into place. Her knees, her face, the side of her head . . . everything hurts. Doctors and medical staff hover, check her chart, examine the wounds, vanish again, the tide of them ebbing and flowing according to some schedule June can't identify.

Another set of days pass, and Wendy comes to visit her, her face drawn. "You saved that girl's life," she says without preamble.

June looks down at her counterpane. Lucy is bruised but back at work in the wireless hut, according to one of the medics, but June keeps thinking of how she hadn't managed to save the sailor. "She was awfully brave, staying with the wireless like that. If it were up to me she'd be in for a promotion."

RAFE POSEY

Wendy smiles. "Braver than I would have expected. She'll go far, I should think. But so could you." She shrugs and pulls a sealed packet from her bag. "In any event, these came for you while you were . . . out." She pats June's good shoulder and leaves the packet on her lap.

"Can I ask you something?" June tries to sit up straighter, though the effort sends a thrum of pain through her. They are close enough that she knows there are Fairchild parents in the Midlands somewhere, but she and Wendy, like almost everyone else in their world of make-believe, have never delved much deeper into each other's lives.

"Of course," Wendy says, her face creasing with concern.

"I wondered," June says, and pauses, unsure how to continue. There is the Act to avoid, and while their covert careers have had a fair amount of overlap, they have diverged quite a lot as well. "I wondered what you tell your people." She gestures at the packet Wendy has handed her. "Being laid up like this has brought it home, rather, not ever being able to say a word."

Wendy studies her hands while she considers her answer. "Not the same for me, I suppose," she says at last. "I don't have anyone waiting for me like you do, except my parents. Of course, they lost the plot years ago. Told them I was off to the Wrens and bob's your uncle."

June nods, pondering Wendy's response. It makes sense that as a Wren her friend has more options, or at least more cover. A Wren could at least tell her people she is stationed overseas and leave it at that. "Thank you," she says after a moment. "That helps." Though it doesn't, really, not at all.

"You're quite welcome," Wendy says. "And, Attwell—good show, the other day. Not a lot of us would have had the wherewithal to pull that off." And with that she lets herself out.

June turns her attention to the packet. There's not much there, but the battered card from Alec hits her like a punch in the gut. She has wondered before if they will both make it through the war, but this is the first time, confined to her bed, she has ever wondered if somehow he will survive and she will not. She turns the card over. It's cheap stock, postmarked from Germany six months earlier, routed through the usual channels. *Am safe. Prisoner at Stalag Luft I in Germany. I hope you will write via the Red Cross. Love to everyone.* God, it sounds nothing like him at all, and the handwriting is still not his. The math of it doesn't make sense—when he was still in Italy he had said his hands were banged up, but that was so long ago. What has happened to him, to his hands, that would leave him still unable to write to her?

At least she knows where he is now. Or where he was, six months earlier, which will have to suffice. She pauses over *I hope you will write.* Likely the systems are failing once again. No matter—this is progress, of a sort. Six months ago, he was alive. She looks in the pouch again, and finds a note from Floss:

I'm sorry to hear that Oswin is in one of the German camps. We hear of unspeakable conditions, and while they are not as savage as the Japanese camps they are hardly fit, some of them, for our men. I do hope he's well enough, when the war ends, to come home. I'll keep my ear to the ground, but I shouldn't hold my breath if I were you. No news is better than bad news, as they say.

More to follow—F.

She puts Floss's note aside and holds Alec's card to her chest, and for the first time since she was a very small child, she thinks about praying. But the deity of her childhood seems as unreal as ever, and instead she writes back to Floss, thanking him for his note and hoping he can find out more. And she writes to Alec as well, telling him to hold steady. She doesn't mention the Zero to either man—Floss likely already knows, and Alec never can.

After another week in the infirmary, the doctors take the stitches out of the back of her head, where a piece of shrapnel had left a cut like the bite of a large bird. When they order her to take ten days of leave, she protests—she has already been out of the codes for more than a fortnight and the business of stopping the Japanese feels more urgent than ever. She takes her convalescence in the hill country, where it's cool and the trees are full of birds and animals so lush she is half-convinced she's imagining them. She spends the first day in Kandy, exploring the ancient city and its temples, wondering what Alec would think of them and then shying away from those wholly futile questions. From Kandy she makes her way up to the plantation the officers use as a getaway lodge, complete with golf and dressing for dinner. Local boys shear the tops from coconuts for her, and an old Tamil woman in a dark red sari, gold rings in her nose and ears, brings her tea every morning in a quiet room looking out over the shaded green fields. The food at Anderson is good—there is always strong coffee and fresh fruit, always enough to eat—but here it's another level up. She has fruit and hoppers at breakfast every day, letting the yolks of the eggs run across the crisp edges of the thin sourdough bread, lacing all of it with a spicy pol sambol. In the evenings, she avoids the dinner crowd and stays in her room, and the old woman brings her coconut shredded into greens and dishes of fish curry laden with coriander sprigs and redolent of tamarind and lime. There are so many fireflies at night that sometimes she struggles to find the stars; the whole dark sky is laced with life.

Too, the days of luxury have filled her with a new kind of guilt—she has felt bad for a while now about the food at Anderson, given the privations her parents, let alone Alec, must be facing. To sit on a verandah and watch thrushes and bulbuls flit through the afternoon light makes her feel like Marie Antoinette, or worse. She has never been anywhere so peaceful as this, surrounded by birdsong, and there is no guidebook or care instructions to tell her how to feel when purple-faced monkeys leap through the trees, their strange barking calls echoing off the lodge. But Alec is in a German prison camp, and the war is still on, and she needs more than ever for this to end.

After the war she'll have to find her way back into a normal life again, and all of this will be a scar of sorts, hidden quietly beneath her skin as if a companion to the pale V-shaped line beneath her hair. She will never be able to reveal these scars to anyone, least of all Alec.

And throughout her recovery, the question of what her future is meant to hold nags at her. There might have been a point at which she could have chosen a path that severed her from Alec and gave her the Wrens or the Foreign Office instead. But now that moment, whenever it was, seems hazy at best. And, in the larger picture, it has become irrelevant. Alec is a captive now, and keeping her promise to him is how she can save him, if there is anything left of him to be saved. Before the POW camps, perhaps she would have found a way to keep following this path of numbers and logic. Perhaps, even in the volcano of heartbreak that would have resulted, they would have been all right. But now it seems unlikely that Alec would heal from such an event. On the contrary, he will probably need her more than ever. A decent woman would honor her commitment to a man like Alec.

1945, *Stalag Luft I*

At Stalag Luft I, the Baltic Sea is not even a mile distant, and the same grim January wind that curls the snow across the frozen shore slices down through the camp like a bayonet. The camp is L-shaped, with a forest to one side and fields to the other, all of it surrounded with miles of barbed wire and guards who are as ready for the war to end as the men they're watching. There is not much hope, and never enough food.

The men—Kriegsgefangene to their German captors, but kriegies among themselves—huddle in their barracks, pulling ragged blankets and what's left of their clothes close for whatever warmth they can offer. But they've been wearing the same two uniforms day in and day out since the Red Cross issued them last summer, and what's left is threadbare and filthy, the ragged seams singed in places from the men's efforts to burn out lice and fleas. Alec is lucky—Smasher is in the better of the two North compounds, and sometimes the men there have enough running water or fragments of soap that they can perform a sort of rudimentary laundry. In West, where Alec shares his room with eight other officers, the lot of them crowded into three-tiered bunks with shoddy mattresses filled with wood chips, they're glad just to have indoor lavatories.

Until October, it had not been so bad. The food had been dreadful, but it had been just enough, combined with their weekly Red Cross parcels, to sustain them. A man could live on a bit of bread and margarine to start the day and a handful of potatoes and cabbage boiled with a small hunk of horsemeat later on. Sometimes there was a dab of marmalade, or a cup of barley soup. But in October, everything had changed. Until the end of last month they had been down to half a parcel each week, and at the same time their German rations had winnowed away to almost nothing—a potato most days, the heel of an old loaf, weak broth with a parsnip or a chunk of beet.

In Campo 78, the men had been glad not to be in a German camp, and now Alec knows they were right. His progression from there to the interrogation camp at Dulag Luft and then north to this barren strip of Pomerania, with its washed-out sky, had felt like a descent into a new kind of horror. In Italy there had been certain comforts their captors had arranged, and while those had not dampened the sting of captivity, they had made a way to mark the time. Some of the same comforts exist here, but they feel rather different. Grimmer. There is a library of sorts, football on some of the grassless yards outside the barracks. There are concerts sometimes, men performing pieces from *Peer Gynt* or thundering sections of Tchaikovsky, on instruments borrowed from the Germans or built from the leftover slats of broken bed frames. In the autumn, when the weather was less unforgiving, he had found ways to join Smasher for a walk around the fences, the two men talking of the lives they hoped to resume—or start fresh—if the war ever ended. But the heart of winter, and new edicts from the camp's commandants, had ended that.

At Christmas, an artistic Cornish lad called Fred, one of Alec's bunkmates, drew up a menu with traces of holly and mistletoe laced around the edges. Alec has no idea what Fred had had to trade to the Germans to get colored pencils, or if they were remnants of the crayons that had once come in Red Cross parcels. But it had made Christmas feel nearly like a celebration, or at least like there might be a reason to celebrate sometime in the future—reading the words *plum pudding with white sauce* or *deviled ham entree* took them out of the truth of it, just for a moment. The miserable kriegie bread, underbaked on their rudimentary stoves and often a bit soggy until a man could find a way to toast it, and topped with potted meat and a dribble of Klim, could stand in for a Welsh rarebit if he tried hard enough. And sometimes it was easier to try.

There are cats in the camp too, half-wild creatures that have, some of them, taken a shine to a man here or there and been given names or ranks. Some are too wild to name, and those are unaccountably called roof rabbits by the commandant. In Alec's barracks there's a broad-shouldered gray-and-white tom who curls up on his bunk now and again, nestling down into the thin, infested blanket. The men in his room call the cat Jack because he's big enough to take on a giant, and they jockey for a turn trying to get him to sleep at their feet.

While it's sometimes possible to move between the compounds, so that the Americans in the northernmost compounds and the British in the rest are not completely segregated, the capricious nature of some of their captors makes access to Smasher and the other Yanks unpredictable at best. Smasher is Alec's friend and confidant as well as his scribe, and without him, Alec feels lost. So he keeps to himself, the slight progress he'd made with his hands now erased by cold and privation. Alec stays in his bunk most of the time, his back to the wall, trying to read the books the Red Cross workers bring in and stroking Jack's stripes.

When spring finally comes, it's a nightmare, despite the beginnings of primroses in the courtyard of the German officers' barracks. The primroses are too pale, as if this place has sucked the life from them as well as from the men. The wind has not died with the winter, and sometimes the cold from the sea is unbearable. And after six years of war, there are now too many rumors, each of which builds hope even while the world in which Alec finds himself destroys it. The Russians are coming, or the Americans. The war in Europe is winding down at last. The Germans are going to kill them all, or they're not. Nobody knows.

And they are all so hungry. It's not long before there is nowhere near enough food to go around, January's uptick in rations having proved all too brief. They've been combining their meager Red Cross parcels for months, but even so, it's not remotely enough. The men are all sick, even at the best of times, their insides tormented and angry. In their badly ventilated barracks, men's lungs fester, and often as not the latrines flood. There are rats and vermin in the walls now, and no way to fight them. For a long time, the cats had kept the worst of it at bay, but now the cats of Stalag Luft I are gone.

Alec hates what they have made him, from his hands to the broken ache of his gut. He hates them. To be reduced from an officer to a creature who will eat a man's cat to keep himself from starving . . . And as the details of death camps and wholesale slaughter come in across the hidden radio, the hatred sits harder and steadier in his chest.

Even without the hunger and trauma, morale is lower than it's been in the year and a half that Alec has been here. Access to the libraries or the recreation yards, such as they are, has been more sporadic than ever, and the post, already irregular at best, has nearly stopped. The letters that do come from home creep in five or six months beyond their postmarks, often closer to a year. Usually they are warm missives, the kind of thing a man tucks into his shirt and keeps close. Words of love and encouragement, confusing reminders of the mundane life to which they are all so desperate to return. But dotted throughout, like stars extinguished in the night sky, there are letters that bring heartbreaking news—women who had said they would wait and changed their minds or their hearts, parents who hadn't lived long enough to see their sons come home. Alec would rather have nothing from June than those. He suspects those men, so eager to open the tattered envelopes, would have waited longer if they had known the contents.

I n the end of March, beneath a pale sky, Alec goes out to the ersatz football pitch in the hopes of catching a few minutes of the elusive sunlight. He has largely given up on being warm, ever, but on a day like this, when the sky is not the empty gray it has been for months, he has at least the hope of a few minutes of brightness on his face. He's sitting in the dusty remnants of grass when a scuffle breaks out at one of the nearby fences, not far from the base of a guard tower. He shades his eyes with his hands, squints at the chaos. They're all worn out and tired of being here, guards and captives alike, and tempers are frayed; it seems inevitable that the slow end of the terrible winter is signaled by squabbles. When he realizes that the man at the center of the skirmish is Smasher, Alec scrambles to his feet and goes to see what's wrong.

Smasher is standing too close to the tower, blood oozing slowly from a cut on his cheekbone. One of the other Americans, a turret gunner named Mike, is tugging his arm and trying to lead him back away from the fence, away from the tower, away from the guard prodding at him with the muzzle of his rifle. But Smasher is refusing, and keeps pushing close again. As Alec comes up alongside him, Smasher shoves at the guard.

"I said, let me walk!" Smasher bellows. The guard reels backward, trying to keep his balance.

Alec, glancing at the guard, steps in front of Smasher. "What's happened?"

Smasher focuses on Alec, his eyes narrowing. "Apparently an act of kindness is now some kind of threat to their precious Prussian honor." He throws his arms out in a wide gesture Alec assumes is meant to encompass the guards, or the camp, or possibly all of Germany.

"He was already pissed off, and then he gave his bread to someone else," Mike says, "and this son of a bitch"—he points at the German—"is giving him a hard time about it." He takes Smasher's arm. "Smasher, c'mon, we gotta go."

Smasher shakes him off. This is the first time in weeks Alec has had the energy to go out into the camp, and he hasn't seen Smasher in a while. He isn't prepared for how gaunt his friend is, or how angry. He reaches out, meaning to join Mike in leading Smasher back to the Americans' barracks, or at least away from here. The guards won't pursue them into the barracks, usually, and most of them don't care what the men do, as long as it won't come back and get any of the Germans in trouble. But Smasher is immovable.

The German soldier stalks up and shoves Alec out of his way, going face-to-face with Smasher. "*Ich sagte jetzt!*" He raises his rifle. "Now!"

Smasher pauses, trembling with rage. He steps back, his eyes resting on Alec and Mike, and he shakes his head. Very slowly, he bends and unlaces his boots.

"These should fit you," he says to Mike, who takes them with his brow furrowed.

Alec says, "What are you doing, old son?"

Smasher says, "Here," and pulls a stubby scrap of pencil and a small, ragged Bible from his pocket, handing them to Alec.

Alec looks down at them, trying to make his hands clutch them better. "I don't understand."

"Just practice," Smasher says. He puts his hand over Alec's, pressing the pencil against Alec's palm.

The soldier elbows Alec away again, yelling at Smasher in German, and Smasher pushes back at him. By now there are guards and prisoners standing in a circle around the two men, all of them tired and dispirited. Everyone has taken a side, but hardly anyone cares any longer what happens to them. The hell of Stalag Luft I has taken its toll.

A German officer with a colonel's braid and pips on his epaulets pushes through the crowd, slaps the soldier's hands down, and murmurs something to him. The soldier flushes dark red, salutes, and takes a step back. Smasher pauses, and there is a moment in which Alec feels time stretching in all directions. Here, now, is when everything else will spool out into infinity. He steps forward again, raising a hand to quiet Smasher.

The colonel looks Alec up and down as if he is something he has found on the bottom of his boot. He smiles and pulls out his Luger, polishing the barrel on his sleeve. And then he slips off the safety and puts the Luger to Smasher's head. Alec, his chest iced with horror, cries out, and a German soldier lunges at him, shoving him into silence with the hard rifle stock.

Still smiling, the colonel pulls the trigger.

"There," he says, his English lightly accented. "Now that is done."

The Germans walk away, and Alec and the Americans stand over what's left of their friend, the shot echoing in their ears. Mike kneels and murmurs a prayer over Smasher's body, brushing Smasher's staring eyes closed beneath the perfect smoky circle of the bullet hole. Two German soldiers break through the knot of prisoners, and slowly the men disperse. The Americans go one direction, Alec the other, his chest numb as he struggles to breathe. He can't tell whether he might weep or if what he's feeling is more rage than grief, or some maelstrom of both. That night, curled into his infested blanket with his knees jammed against his chest, he tries to let himself cry, but there's nothing there. One dense sob escapes him, but there is no release there, no mourning.

. . .

The ice that rimes the shore of their blunted peninsula has melted away by the middle of April, when news comes to the camp of the death of Franklin Roosevelt. The Americans gather together, shocked and mournful, pressing the guards for more news. Alec is stunned too—they have all tracked the Allied progress across Europe with considerable interest, even sometimes with hope, and it's hard to reconcile the waiting with the loss. The kriegies have a radio hidden in the walls in the West compound, cobbled together from spare parts by a pair of RAF boys; sometimes Alec thinks about the radio and the rest of it, everything the Yanks and Brits have pulled together to fight back, and he knows how it sounds. Secret radios and newspapers? Milk tins with false bottoms and wristwatches with no insides but a rolled-up transcript? It sounds like the sort of thing he would have admired at the cinema a lifetime ago, entirely invented.

Rumors of the end of hostilities continue to swirl, and sometimes the men stand at the fences, looking out across the miles of barbed wire and guard posts, wondering when their liberators will find them, and who they will be. The dark pine forest to the west is full of crows the Germans shoot at when they get bored. Alec can't hear the crack of rifle fire without thinking of Smasher, and sometimes he thumbs through the Bible Smasher gave him and tries to make sense of the verses. He has never been a man of faith, exactly, and the loss of first Cobber, Tim, and Charlie, and now Smasher has only made that more clear.

On the rare occasions that the world around them is quiet, Alec can almost hear the sea off to the north and east. But he can hear the whispers too, accounts of atrocities and genocide trickling through the rumor mill as the Americans and Russians converge on Berlin. The whispers say millions dead, and camps full of living skeletons and industrialized murder. It is beyond him that the world has let this happen. And when he has a telegram from his aunt's solicitor in Fenbourne telling him that Constance has been killed in a bombing along with June's parents, and the vicarage largely destroyed, his faith dwindles further. He carefully tucks Smasher's Bible away with his letters in the rucksack the Germans issued him when they took him out of Italy. He struggles with how to understand what's happened—without Constance he would not have had a home. And that home would not have been the same without Cyrus and Imogene Attwell, who had shared their household so generously. The loss leaves him numb, especially the idea of all of them gone in an instant. And when he thinks of June, he feels even worse. What must it have been like for June to learn that her parents were gone, her family erased in the space of a moment? He can only imagine her shock, the bafflement of grief. It aches at him that she would have had to endure the funeral alone, unless Roger had been able to get leave to go. He doesn't even know where Roger is, if he's safe.

It feels like the world is spinning along without him. He should be with June, keeping her close and helping her work through the sundering of her heart. How is it possible June is an orphan now, too?

He wants to go home, but he doesn't know what that means anymore. Fenbourne? Anywhere in England? Wherever June is, if she can still want him like this. He thinks of going back to India, where he hasn't been since he was eight years old. But he can't go there with the RAF now. He can't go anywhere with them. And in any event there are rumors about India too, that the British Raj will clear out soon and leave the country to the locals. He doesn't know what to think of that.

The sound of waves reminds him of the RMS *Jaipur*, but also of the year he was seven, when they went to Kashmir. He waits for the Russians, or the Americans, and thinks of the houseboats and chinar trees on the Dal Lake in Srinagar, and the turbaned Sikhs selling scarves and textiles in the markets in the city. He thinks of his mother and the stories she used to tell him, or the way Kipling's tales sounded when she read to him, each character taking on a voice of his own as she read. In the trenches in the first war, men had recited Tennyson and Keats back and forth, trying to stay whole and sane. In Germany, without Smasher to help him, Alec finds himself lost in "The Ballad of East and West." He hadn't known he'd remembered it, but now, digging deep into the wells of his memory to find his way through this nightmare, Kipling's cadence comes back to him like the hoof-drumming of the dainty red mare at the poem's heart. It's an anchor, the same way June is, the poem holding him fast to those days in India with his parents, or in Fenbourne with Roger and his mare Noor. He has had two letters from Roger, and Alec hopes the anchor will hold Roger safe too, as the conflict wanes.

And then, at the beginning of May, when the camp is ruffled with a new set of rumors, he has a letter from June dated almost a year ago. It's too short, and it makes him feel the lack of her in ways he's afraid to acknowledge, but she tells him she loves him, and she tells him they will be together again after the war. Something in him loosens, like the weeds that used to tangle into willow branches along the River Lark. As of last summer, she hasn't forgotten him. She hasn't given up or let go—their tether is intact.

So he turns his face to the horizon and waits. Someone will come soon. It's time to go home.

BOOK THREE

1945, *Fenbourne*

June hikes across the esker, pausing at its highest point. The village and the countryside around it unfold almost as she'd imagined. How many times has she drawn it, the cluster of precise asterisks and squares to indicate buildings and rubble, the sheep she can hear nearby. Her eyes seek out the old monastery, the ruin of stones on the distant opposite hillside. In the bottom of the valley, where the stream has wound down out of the mountains on its way to find the sea, she knows there will be a small stucco cottage, shadowed by a copse of myrtle trees and what's left of the monastery's broken church. She's seen the cottage in aerial photographs, nearly invisible even with the jeweler's loupe she's carried in her pocket since Bletchley Park. All those months of knowing there must be something here.

She's looked so long. How can it feel sudden to have found the valley? How can it feel so unexpected?

She wakes before she finds him, the dream shattering as it always does. She has dreamed so often of going to Italy, even Germany, to bring Alec home, but now there is more urgency, awake or asleep. Now she doesn't know where she would even go to find him.

I n the morning June struggles to pull herself together, shaken by the dream, but real life is not much clearer. Without the vicarage, she is unmoored. She has a room for the moment in the Rose and Crown. Fenbourne has gone back to the low hum of activity she remembers from half a decade ago, but its scars are enormous. The ruins of the vicarage, all that broken stone angling up to nowhere, the mullioned windows shattered and dangling from the skeleton of the conservatory . . . Her childhood home destroyed. Once she had known every thread of carpet, every knot in the wooden floors and banisters. It is impossible that all of it has been erased.

Worse, though, is the dizzying, endless loop of realization that the wreckage is also where her parents died. Try as she may to stop thinking about it, she can't help imagining what it must have been like—a quiet evening in the drawing room, the two of them sitting with Constance, their conversation interrupted by the sudden hiss and shriek of the German bomb. Thunder and fury, and then silence.

The void created by her parents' absence is unfillable. They had been more than just June's mother and father, or the vicar and his wife. Cyrus and Imogene Attwell had been part of every facet of Fenbourne society—her father the shepherd at its helm, her mother a force of nature, coordinating volunteers and bringing aid wherever she could. Now the village is full of places where they can no longer be found. June had not been ready to see St. Anne's standing alone and nearly unscathed alongside the ruins, not ready to stand in the churchyard and see their names on the raw slab of marble. Not ready for any of it.

If Alec were here, she would not feel so alone in her grief. But he's not. She doesn't understand that, either. It seems impossible that he is not back—the war in Europe has been over since May, and thousands of men have been repatriated. She had followed that news as well as she could in Ceylon; she had expected to find him here upon her return. Even through the fretting about what she would tell him about where she'd been—the idea of having to make something up, create even more layers of deception, had burned in her chest—she had wanted nothing more than to come home and find him. They would have mourned together, just as they had done everything for so long.

She's been back in Fenbourne not quite two days, and she has spent half that time upstairs in this room she doesn't know, the eaves low over her window, trying to adjust to the strange new angles of her life.

B reakfast is a tired affair with too-damp oatmeal cladded with milky skin, a far cry from the lush fruits of Colombo, but at least she's had weeks to make her transition back to the real world and start to acclimate. Mrs. Bixby, who has run the Rose and Crown for as long as June can remember, hovers and clucks like an old hen. June, accustomed now to the odd blend of autonomy and order that the war provided, has no idea how to talk to her.

Afterward, she pedals a borrowed bicycle through the village. She nods to the grocer and the butcher's boy. Everything is the same, as long as she avoids the church and the devastation that surrounds it. The postmistress stops her to offer condolences, and June struggles to respond, especially when she sees the curiosity, and the questions she'll have to dodge, flickering in the postmistress's eyes. After so many years of only seeing colleagues who knew what she was doing, who were part of her work, she lacks a frame of reference to talk to others. She carries too many secrets within herself now. There are too many questions she must guard against.

T he village falls behind June as she pedals out past the garage where the smith used to be, past the poplar-lined turn that leads to the Ely road, past the low, squat bungalow where Mrs. Hubbox lives. Something has kept June from visiting her, an anxious, uncomfortable echo she can't quite identify. Cook has retired to a village in Kent with her daughter's family, but June doesn't know what the Attwells' former housekeeper is doing now, and she knows without question that her parents would want her to look out for Mary Hubbox, a fixture for June's whole life. It's enough to know for now that Mrs. Hubbox had survived the bombing, that she had been at market that day. But she wishes her parents and Alec's aunt had been at market, too. Or in the unscathed church. Or anywhere, really, except where they'd been.

Out on the lanes, the world opens up, and for the first time she feels like she can breathe. Off to the west the spires of the cathedral at Ely break the horizon; in every other direction, the world is made of dikes and hedgerows. She knows this world as well as she ever has—the Highland cattle, the redpolls and bramblings, the avocets she can hear in the distance, the lanes as straight as curtain rods. The sameness of the autumn landscape is a comfort, despite the bewilderment that swarms like hornets—her family is gone, Alec is missing. Nothing is as it should be.

She pulls her bicycle off to the side of the lane to let a man with a team of oxen come through. At the crossroads, she'll turn right and then right again, and make her way to the familiar old cottage at the north end of Fenbourne. Another destination to dread, certainly, but Mrs. Bixby had seemed unsure whether anyone was taking care of it. So this morning she took it upon herself to call on the elderly Mr. Swift, who had been her parents' solicitor as well as Constance's. He has known June her whole life, and it is easier than she hopes to per-suade him that her engagement to Alec, who is nominally the owner of the cottage, is enough of a tie to give her the key. Now at the very least she can stop by and take a look.

Alec's last missive, a thin Red Cross form sent from the German

POW camp a year ago last spring, is in her pocket, folded carefully away. She doesn't have to open it to know what it says. It's the same solid printing as his notes from Italy, not his own hand. The man who wrote for him in Italy must have been transferred to Germany as well. And, like his Italian notes, it mostly doesn't sound like him—it's too stilted, almost aloof, a collection of comments about weather and passing the time as well as he can. But this message ends differently from the others—there's a line asking her to remember the princess and the bear for him. Every time she has read the letter since its arrival she has had the same electric lurch in her chest that she had the first time. How is she meant to parse it? Is he giving up, or holding out hope? The message and its effects are disjointed and jarring.

She can't get over the feeling of dislocation—they were so close, when they were both still in England—and then the trajectories of their wars diverged. There has been nothing from him for so long, and she doesn't know whether she should be more afraid that he has stopped writing because he's given her up or that he is longing to tell her where he is, and can't. The other possibilities are too terrible to consider.

The house is silent when she steps off the bicycle and wheels it through the stone wall's front gate, which she latches carefully behind her. A turtledove regards her from the edge of a battered wheelbarrow, its mate swaggering along the ground beneath.

June has only been inside for a moment when she realizes how unprepared she is for this responsibility. Constance has been dead since January, and the house is dark and vacant, as cold and musty as a mausoleum. June has no idea where to begin—the house isn't dirty, exactly, beyond a layer of dust coating every surface, but the feeling of emptiness is oppressive. The worst is the sense of a life left midway: the kettle on the hob, a set of linens folded on the end of the bed, the careful stacks of mail on Constance's desk. How can she ready the cottage for Alec if she can hardly bear to be here? It is nearly beyond her, reminding her both of Constance and of her parents. She has sat in these rooms, walked these halls, a thousand times. Now she paces through the house, wishing she knew what to do.

The longer she stays in the cottage, the more her disquiet grows, but so has her resolution. She bicycles back into the village. By the end of the afternoon she has made arrangements to become a caretaker of sorts for the cottage until Alec's return. While she waits, Mr. Swift has his clerk make the necessary calls to see that the utilities are available for use, and then the plan is set. She takes the bicycle back to the Rose and Crown and calls Fenbourne's one taxi to drive her and her handful of belongings to the cottage.

That night, June hardly sleeps. She's taken the bedroom that Alec's uncle used when his leaves and furloughs brought him to visit. It's odd to find herself here, but she feels a bit less like an intruder now than she had. She spends much of the night making lists, setting her plans for the cottage into neat categories and subcategories. Having so much space to herself is confusing; at the barracks in Colombo she had had a tiny square room with a basin in it, with slatted windows to keep out the weather and mosquito nets to do what they could about the insects.

In any case, here she is, setting things in motion. She has a world to remake.

The next day June takes the 10:15 to King's Cross. On the train, June writes a letter to Roger, letting him know that she is readying the house for Alec, wherever he is. Roger, who finished out the war in Burma, probably knows as little about Alec's whereabouts as she does, but she asks anyway. Then she draws maps of Alec's locations for the past six years, as far as she knows them. His absence is a puzzle, but puzzles have solutions. She cannot bring back her parents, or Constance, but she still has hope for Alec, and in London there are people who can help her.

Her first stop is a Red Cross office in Westminster. But the man she talks to there is overwhelmed with displaced persons and refugees and knows only that most of the men in German camps were repatriated within days of liberation. Even when June persuades him to look into the particular camp, he is only able to tell her that Alec's name is not on the rolls as one of the men flown back to Le Havre by Allied planes. He doesn't know what that suggests, although it is possible that his name was missed, or that he returned some other way, or that he stayed on the Continent. But June is not interested in vague possibilities. She wants proper information, data she can put into an equation of sorts to find her answers.

Outside, London is the same confounding blur it was after the Blitz, though there is a new measure of order threaded through it now that the war is over. She had taken a taxi from the station to Westminster, and the scarring of the city has left her shaken. She was there for some of it, during the Blitz, none of this is new, but it feels different somehow. The checkering of bombs is hard to comprehend—so much of the city is unscathed, and then around a corner the next block is gone entirely, single structures left standing like an old woman's teeth. Children play on the precarious edges where houses used to be, unmindful of the dangers of shifting rubble or unexploded ordnance.

In Westminster, the endless to and fro of people on the sidewalks pulls her eye away from the destruction. She stops in the shadow of the Abbey, tempted to go inside, but she worries she will feel more out of place than ever. It reminds her that her parents would have prayed for Alec's safe return, although they might have hedged their bets by appealing for human aid as well. But June has never been able to reconcile faith and reason the way her father could, and in this instance it is no different—she does not believe that God could bring Alec back, but perhaps her connections at Whitehall can.

The enormous Italianate building that houses the Foreign Office on King Charles Street has always struck her as a bit over the top, gone a bit tatty at the edges despite the once-magnificent décor inside. No matter—she is here to find Floss, not to critique the architecture. With the war over, there are fewer gatekeepers than there had been, but still it takes nearly an hour for her to work her way into the outer chambers of Floss's dominion. He has had the same secretary—Mrs. Copeland, with her cat-eye glasses and beady eyes—guarding his doors as long as June can remember. She greets June politely, but without any particular favor, just as she always has, and asks June to wait.

Floss emerges after only a few minutes, the base of his cane thumping on the thick carpet. "June! What a lovely surprise."

June stands. "I don't mean to disturb you."

"I am, as ever, your servant," Floss says, smiling and guiding June into his inner sanctum.

June tries to smile back, but her face feels brittle with impatience. "Alec's not back. He's missing." She gestures eastward. "The German POW camps were liberated in May, most of them, and the men largely repatriated the next month. But Alec wasn't among them."

"I'm sorry to hear that." He sits and regards her steadily, his good leg jiggling a bit. "I'm sure you know most of our men came home, but lot of good chaps died, and nobody ever wrote it down in all the confusion. And some of them were taken back to Russia, rather than being sent home properly. Happened quite a bit in some of the German camps close to Poland and whatnot."

June hesitates, trying to collect her feelings before she pushes on through Floss's brusque response. "I would have thought the Russians would follow the rule of war. Even the Germans mainly hewed to

Geneva and the Red Cross. In any case, if we're not at war with them, they can't very well have prisoners of war."

"Stalin is not a great believer in Churchill or Truman, and many at Whitehall think he's using our boys as bargaining chips." He shrugs, brushing invisible dust from his trouser legs. "Seems he'd been mowing down the Russians we liberated when we sent them back, as if he felt their capture indicated some kind of weakness. So we stopped sending them back."

"Can you find out if they have him?" She stands. "I've known you to find deeper secrets than this, Floss."

"I will do what I can for you." Floss stops fussing with his suit and looks up at her, his face serious. "But you'd be wise to prepare for the possibility he won't come home at all. Or, if he does . . . They may have broken him, June. He may be very different now."

"Please just find out what you can," she says. She has no way to convey to Floss what Alec is to her.

"He may not even be where I can find him. And if he is, it's a new world now. A new war. The old methods of making things happen no longer work. But of course I'll make what inquiries I can." He gets up and goes to the window, looking out toward St. James's Park across the street for a moment before he turns back to her and continues, as if everything he's saying is perfectly reasonable. "As a separate issue, I'll be opening a new station in Berlin, once they've done with carving it up. Think about the work you could do there. Be so much better for you than waiting around like this."

June bites her tongue. Does he have any idea of what an ass he sounds?

"Don't look at me like that," he says. "I know you're worried about Oswin. He's a good lad, and he's served his country. But so have you, and, well, I hate to seem unkind, under the circumstances, but you're not out of it. You're what we need. Not more wives and babies."

June shakes her head, her whole body strung tight with wanting to shout at him, even as she tries not to wonder what exactly it is he's offering. She stands and goes to the door. When she turns back to him, her voice is rough. "Just find him."

She is halfway to the stairs when a better solution clicks into place. Floss may not be able to help her, whatever his contacts in the intelligence community, even if he wants to. Perhaps his old methods won't work, but he is not the only man in Whitehall to whom she can take her query.

As June strides along the corridors and ornate staircases that separate her father's friend Sir Reginald Cooper-Byatt's domain from Floss's, she practices asking him for help. He is not Floss; they are not friends. He is a benefactor, nothing more. But if taking the problem to him will help her find Alec, she will do it.

Sir Reginald comes around his desk to greet her, clasping both her hands in his. "I was very sorry to hear about your parents," he says quietly. He leads her to the seating area facing his vast window, and sits facing her.

"Thank you," June says. Some of the wind goes out of her sails— keeping her focus on Alec has helped her avoid the cold, raw place of mourning her parents.

"What a thing to come back to," Sir Reginald says. He frowns. "Are you home for good, then? And quite recovered?"

"Yes." She pauses, wondering if he too is going to try to recruit her for some new effort with new enemies. "Thank you for seeing me today."

"Of course," he says. "How can I help you?"

"It's my fiancé," she says. "He's missing." As she explains about Alec's captivity and what Floss has told her, Sir Reginald's heavy brows sink into a worried glower.

When she finishes, he shakes his head. "Ah. Yes, Corbett is quite right that we're having a bit of a sticky spot with the Russians. That said, I may have a man in Moscow who can tell me if your lad is there. I'll see if I can reach him first thing tomorrow."

When the phone rings a few days later, the clarion of it takes June by surprise despite the vigilance with which she's been waiting for Sir Reginald's call. She steels herself and picks up the handset with the steadiest greeting she can manage.

"He's in Odessa," Sir Reginald says without preamble. "A guest, they're calling it." His sigh crackles through the phone lines. "There is good news—he is not in hospital, not in some type of camp. Red Cross and Crescent are doing what they can, and the British attaché in Moscow has access now and again, and they report that conditions are fair enough."

A sob of relief rises in her chest, and she pushes it down before the sound emerges. "What can I do?" Her hands tighten on the handset, but with determination, not nerves.

"Nothing just now," he says. "Having a spot of difficulty with their government, but he's an officer with a fine record, and we may be able to find a way through this. At the very least, we can try to keep him from being sent to the Gulag."

June feels numb. It was one thing when Floss had brought up the terrible possibility of the Gulag, quite another to hear Sir Reginald dismiss it as an option. She hadn't realized how afraid she had been of losing Alec to Siberia forever until it was no longer a worry. "Thank you, Sir Reginald."

"This office owes you a great debt, Miss Attwell. Let's see if we can bring your young fellow home."

June's bedroom in the cottage looks out to the east, and on a clear morning the sun comes in and mottles the uneven wooden floorboards like water waiting to be swabbed away. June has brought the globe in here, despite the pangs it gives her. In some ways, it's a comfort, a means of connecting herself with the past that hurts less now she knows that Alec is alive, and where he is. Too, the part of her mind that was so busy during the war, now frustrated by the relegation to household inventories, has begun to speculate on the more engaging problem of map-making. So many of these countries no longer exist—there are changes on nearly every continent as empires rise and fall, ceding or grasping new territory. Thrace, German East Africa, the Ottoman Empire . . . All folded into somewhere else or renamed by new governments. Sometimes, almost guiltily, she looks at Berlin, imagining the fresh partitions between East and West.

Each morning when she gets up she lays a fingertip atop Odessa. It seems that if she can find Alec on the globe, perhaps he will know she is waiting for him—an irrational thought to be sure, but it feels solid enough, a worthy talisman. June has spent untold hours scouring railway timetables and maps of Eastern Europe and the Black Sea, memorizing every route by land or sea from Odessa to London. As the crow flies, it's not so far, but when that distance is compounded by the Soviet shadow that has fallen across the eastern half of Europe, hope is hard to come by.

And always, there are lists—lists for the cottage, lists for Alec, lists to remind her to push through the mourning when it crests against her in waves of dizzying sorrow. Sometimes memories creep in unbidden—her father reading by the fire in the drawing room, the triumphant smile her mother tried to contain when she won a trick at bridge, the three of them on the coast of France during a school holiday, so many small moments bundled into a set of lives—and each time she has to remind herself to keep breathing. She has almost nothing left of her parents but memories. Is this how Alec felt, when he first came to Fenbourne? His parents and hers—gone suddenly, randomly, in a rain of chaos and fire. Even in their orphanings there are lines of connection to bind them.

When she finds herself stacking her pencils the way her father did, she pushes the memories away. But there are echoes everywhere—sometimes the crescent moon reminds her of the tiny scar left on her mother's forearm by a twist of wire in the garden. Sometimes a bicycle catches the light like her father's glasses had. And always the absence of them. Somehow, though, she must organize the cottage, to the extent she can. While cleaning and cooking give her something to focus on that is more immediate and less abstract than Alec or the future, neither truly holds her attention. A few months ago she was part of the war effort; lives and histories were in her grasp and often under her control. Polishing a banister or boiling an egg . . . They are no substitute for the columns of codes that occupied her life for all those years, nor for the bond she had had with her team of Wrens and Admiralty civilians in Ceylon. Sometimes, in the rare moments at night when the birds go quiet and the geckering foxes have all found other ditches in which to hunt, she would give anything to have the silence broken by the flap and clatter of Wendy Fairchild and her deck of cards. But

Wendy is in America, stationed at the British embassy in Washington, and often as not, thinking of her only leads to thoughts of the past, or of Floss. And now, despite herself, Berlin.

She rings Sir Reginald once a week, torn always between decorum and determination. She ponders seeking out the men who had been in Germany with Alec; she has gone to London a dozen times to press the Red Cross for information, but his camp had held more than a thousand Britons, and there is no way to know whether they even knew him. Instead she pores through newspapers, slowly building a lexicon of Russian names and words, the occasional clusters of Cyrillic letters blossoming like ciphers. She makes lists and charts—everything from the routes of troopships that might bring him back to the names of anyone she has ever done a favor, and how they might help. She writes to friends in the Wrens and the Admiralty. And she watches the stars in the low night sky, hoping Alec can see them, too.

When she needs a respite, she walks into Fenbourne, or farther out along the sluice road, depending on whether she can stand the idea of seeing the ruins, or talking to the well-intentioned villagers from whom she feels so disconnected. Determined to make herself useful in the village, she stops in at the teas Melody Keswick holds to discuss the issue of helping Jewish refugees fleeing the horrors of the Continent.

But whether or not she chooses to visit the village, the lanes are a balm, stretching out to the horizon as they always have. By November, the light has changed—it comes in flatter across the fields now, making its way to the sharp, clear gleam of winter. The nights are cold and full of the promise of ice riming along the edges of the Lark, but today is relatively balmy, and the sound of insects and birds echoes through the afternoon. Above her, a host of watery clouds scud petulantly across a

Wedgwood blue sky. The canal flows with brackish water, swifts careening just above the surface to eat invisible insects. Willows and black oaks line the opposite bank, shading the field just to the other side, where a herd of Black Herefords grazes, the red calves nudging one another and their dams.

She pauses at the crossroads, trying to decide whether she wants to go into the village. Sometimes there is comfort in the fact that the village, despite its scars, is still more or less the Fenbourne she remembers from her childhood. The Lark is the same. The sky over the canals rings with the cries of ospreys and thrushes, and at St. Anne's the massive old trees are full of rooks, just as ever.

As June turns toward the village, a boy comes around the curve of the hedgerow, a brace of hares slung over his shoulder. He stops dead when he sees her, his sharp adolescent face going pink as he grins.

"Blimey, if it isn't Miss Attwell," he says, his accent unexpectedly pure London.

June's eyes widen. "George Cowan?"

"That's right." George glances down at the road, then back at her. "I'm so sorry, Miss. They were good to me, your parents. Awful, what happened to them."

"Thank you," she says. "I hadn't realized you were still in Fenbourne."

Something changes in his face, and it's a moment before June recognizes it as something she has seen in her own eyes lately. So many orphans, she thinks. First Alec, and then she herself, and now George.

"Mrs. Hubbox took me in," he says, subdued.

"I'm glad you're all right," June says. She ponders him for a moment, thinking again of Mrs. Hubbox, who must also be in mourning; the vicarage had been her home as well. "And, George?"

"Yes, Miss?" George tilts his head at her like a sparrow.

"Will you ask Mrs. Hubbox to call on me, when she has time? I'd like to ask her advice about some things around the house." She smiles. "I would be very grateful."

George grins at her. "Happy to, Miss." He glances at the hares. "I'd best be home, now."

"Yes indeed," she says, realizing belatedly that the hares are probably poached.

George ducks his head and resumes his trek along the hedgerow. June watches him go, pleased to have encountered him, but also relieved—if Mrs. Hubbox is available, her help with the cottage will be invaluable.

Two weeks later, a miracle. A boy skitters into the cottage's front garden on a battered bicycle, his bell ringing. June, roused from her perusal of a map of shipping patterns in the Black Sea, opens the door just as he knocks. He pulls a telegram from his messenger bag, and she takes the thin paper and fishes a handful of coins from her pocket to tip him. As he races away again, she opens it, nerves skating like eels beneath her skin. And then, the relief and adrenaline too much to contain, she lets herself cry—Alec is coming home on a British troopship, part of an exchange of prisoners in the next few weeks, actual date to follow.

That afternoon, June writes to Sir Reginald to thank him, and then she renews her focus. She traces routes across the globe, folds and refolds maps to show the most likely paths of Alec's return. As the days grow shorter, she visits her parents' grave more often, although she has still not crossed the threshold of the church. Attending a service would be beyond her just now—the idea of some other man in her father's place, leading the congregation, leaves a great cavity in her chest.

Perhaps as time passes she will feel otherwise. It helps when she makes complicated housing charts for Melody Keswick, trying to help with the refugees, whose losses she can't begin to comprehend. Meanwhile, Mrs. Hubbox comes now three mornings a week, and George appears to help with smaller tasks when he's not in school. Often as not, June comes back from the village to find him sweeping the porch or pulling years of debris from the bedraggled and overgrown garden behind the cottage.

At last, well into January, word comes from Sir Reginald: Alec's ship will dock in London three days hence. June stares at the telegram that brings her the news, then folds it with shaking hands to put away. That night she sits out on the front steps and watches the sky. The future, whatever it holds, is here.

1946, *Fenbourne*

She hardly sleeps the night before his ship is due, trying to come to terms with what she will tell him when he asks how she's spent the last few years. She knows she looks different, not least because of the sun her pale skin couldn't avoid in the tropics regardless of her efforts. She knows she *is* different, after so many years of war and absence. But he must be different too, after everything. Finally she gives up altogether and takes an early train into London. She would rather wait at the docks than wring her hands anywhere else.

The crush of sailors and dockworkers reminds her of her own travels, and she can't help but hope that the troopship bringing Alec to London is less infested than the one that took her to India. She straightens the cuffs of her jumper, running her fingers around the ring he gave her all those lifetimes ago. She remembers Alec's face when he proposed, and his hand pressed against the small of her back, the bright London sun, the warmth of him coursing through the yellow silk blouse she'd been wearing, the softness of his mouth when he kissed her afterward in the darkness of the shelter.

When the ship docks, the thud of the hull against the dock echoes in June's heart, and she can hardly breathe. She had sent a telegram to the port in Gibraltar, hoping to tell Alec she would be here, but there's no way to know if he received it, and that adds a layer of unease to her excitement. There is a flurry of activity, and then at last the gangway lowers, and men begin to come off the ship. They're all so thin, and while a few have tilted their hats to jaunty angles, they all look out of place somehow, relieved and wary all at once.

Just as she steps closer, hardly able to bear the waiting, Alec appears at the top of the gangway. He's wearing a too-large coat hanging open and a flat blue cap, with a worn rucksack slung over one shoulder. He looks like part of a crew of some kind of tramp steamer, not a pilot. June nearly doesn't recognize him—he looks cold and alone, not at all like the Alec she used to know.

He steps onto the gangway, treading hesitantly down to solid ground, and June moves forward to meet him as he reaches the end. His eyes widen as he spots her.

"Alec," she whispers. His eyes have locked onto hers. His cheekbones are too sharp. All of him is. Alec is emaciated, perhaps only ten stone now. How has this happened to him? She tries to take him all in, tries to see all of him at once, but he's got his hands behind his back, and he's still just looking at her the way he would regard a ghost.

A moment of panic—what if he no longer wants her? What if the war has broken what they had? Her heart quails away from the idea that after everything, they might be over. How can they take apart something that lit them both like the sun? But then, at last, his face opens, and she can see that boy again in his face.

"June," he says, his voice ragged.

"Yes, Alec," she says. "Yes."

He comes to her then, his arms tight around her, his face pressed to her shoulder like an animal looking for its burrow, trembling.

June had thought they might stop in London, find lunch or a cup of tea, but Alec is skittish and pale, hewing close to her even while he seems almost to inhabit another world entirely. When she asks him if he's hungry, he shakes his head, his face uncertain. "Not just yet."

"All right," she responds, although she can only imagine he must be ravenous. But he's likely overwhelmed—perhaps once things are calmer and he is less absorbed by the urban maelstrom surrounding them he will want something. She had hoped for a more triumphant return, which seems unfair now that she has seen him. And forcing him to sit in a crowded café, with all its noise and humanity, seems more complicated, and more fraught, than she would have guessed, and so instead she hails a cab and directs the driver to King's Cross. She had tried to be prepared for scars, visible or otherwise, and for the immutable changes that a POW camp might wreak on a man, let alone one camp after another.

In the taxi, she turns toward him, meaning to say something about Fenbourne, but then she sees his hands, bundled on his lap, and something creaks in her heart. His right hand, especially, bears the marks of whatever has been done to him, and it has curled into itself like a paw. The left is better, but still mottled with scars, two of the fingers crooked and gnarled. How can this be? Those lovely long hands, broken now. She can only imagine the pain and misery he must have gone through. She was ready for so much, or thought she was. But she had not girded herself against the sound that comes from her at the sight of his hands, or for his face, crestfallen and defensive, when he hears her.

She reaches for his hands. When he flinches, she feels it all the way through her. But then he lets her cradle them in her palms. She wants to hold them to her lips. She wants to heal them with her touch. It's another thing she has no idea how to navigate. And underneath her sorrow for him, an ache of confusion—how could she not have known? She goes cold when she thinks of his letters from Italy and Germany, and that unfamiliar penmanship, and wants to strangle him—*banged up my hands* is all he had had to say?

At the station, Alec shrinks into himself, his face closed and wary. June takes his arm, keeping him close to her. When last they had walked like this, her hand had tucked neatly into the crease of his elbow, and now her fingers vanish into the folds of his outsized topcoat as if his arm is not even there. Her Alec, that sweet boy with stars in his eyes . . . How could this have happened to him?

"I'm sorry," Alec says. "All the people, and the trains . . ." His shoulders jerk in a shrug.

"I'm right here," June says. She squeezes his arm. "I won't let go."

He nods, but he's shaking all over, the effort he's putting into following her almost visible. As gently as she can, she shepherds him onto the platform, then onto the train, holding her breath when he freezes midway through stepping into the carriage. Every moment brings something that makes him flinch—the metallic thud of a compartment door closing, the rattle of chains between the carriages, the shriek of the whistle. When the train rumbles into life, Alec shudders, his jaw clenched so tightly she imagines she can hear his teeth grinding together.

"We'll be home soon," she says as the train emerges onto the rails outside the station.

Alec turns to her, his eyes searching her face. "I don't . . ." He pauses.

"I've been staying at your aunt's cottage," June says softly. "Getting it ready for you. Mrs. Hubbox has been helping me. So we'll go home, and then we'll see if we can suss out what comes next, all right?"

His gaze clouds when she mentions Constance, and June takes his hands gently into hers, sitting as tight against him as she can. "I've got you now, Alec. I'm here."

Alec nods, his shoulders loosening. "All right."

He's quiet then, watching her when he's not eyeing the landscape rolling past outside. When the train emerges into the countryside, he relaxes a bit more.

"Quite a thing, having a compartment to ourselves," he says. His leg jitters nervously, and he goes back to looking out the window.

It's not much later that an older woman appears in the doorway with a trolley laden with hot beverages, pastries, and sandwiches. Alec regards the trolley hungrily, and June's heart pangs for him. "Would you like something?"

"I don't know," he says helplessly, and after a moment June realizes he doesn't know how to choose.

"Ah, he's moithered, the poor lad," the old woman says to June in a lilting Welsh accent. "What about a cup of tea, then?"

"That would be lovely," Alec says, his voice soft with relief.

"Righto," she says. She bustles about to get them each their tea.

"A couple of sandwiches also," June says. "Do you have the cress today?"

"Gosh," Alec says. "I haven't had a proper sandwich . . . I don't know when."

"Two cress," the trolley attendant says, nodding, and hands the two paper-wrapped sandwiches to June, followed by the cups of tea. She pauses to regard Alec, her lips pursed. "Would you like something sweet as well?" She points to the simple pastries that occupy the top tier of the trolley. "The sticky buns I do like, but the seedcakes are rather better."

"Caraway," June says to Alec, setting the china teacups and their saucers on the small table that juts out just beneath the window. His eyes light up, and she smiles and asks the woman for two of those as well, thanking her for the recommendation.

"Glad I am to do it," the woman says, beaming. "Just a small little thing can help a day."

"Indeed it can," Alec says.

June thanks her again when she pays for the food. When she's gone, June sits down across from Alec and lays out the food like a picnic, arranging the sandwiches and cakes. At her elbow, the spoons rattle in the saucers as the train moves along the track. Alec stares at the sandwiches, and her brow furrows. Hoping to encourage him, she picks up the egg and cress sandwich and unwraps it to find better bread than she would have expected, and more butter. "Go on," she says to Alec with a smile. He pauses and reaches with his left hand, awkwardly clutching the sandwich in the rough vise of his thumb and first two fingers. His right hand stays in his lap like something he's left behind.

His eyes close when he bites into it, and for a moment June thinks he's in pain. But then he swallows and opens his eyes, and she realizes he is swamped with emotion.

"They're good, aren't they?" She takes a bite and has a drink of tea.

Alec nods reverently, eating his sandwich in a series of bites so precise, nearly delicate, that June wonders if he's trying to keep himself from swallowing it all at one go. It's only when he turns his focus to the seedcake and the sweet, murky tea that June sees he needs both hands to hold his cup. She understands now how severe the damage to his hands must be—how tangled and scarred his fingers really were. When she notes the furrow between his eyes as he concentrates on his grip, and how steadfastly he seems to be refusing to look at her, she can't help but wonder if he's embarrassed or ashamed. Wanting to give him a moment as best she can, June nearly fumbles her own sandwich, and turns her gaze out the window.

Alec says almost nothing else for the rest of the trip, as if he's exhausted his store of conversation for now, and June stays mostly quiet too, trying not to overwhelm him further. She doesn't want to prattle at him, but every few minutes she tells him something about the village— a new baby for the grocer's daughter, an enormous eel found in a basket in a tributary of the Lark, Frank Burleigh taking over the smithy and expanding it into a proper garage. Little details to give him anchorage.

When they arrive in Fenbourne, she leads him out of the station, trying to avoid the curious eyes of the village even as she knows the task is hopeless.

"Shall I call the taxi?"

Alec looks down at her, then shakes his head. "Would you mind if we walked?"

"Not at all," she says. In fact it is a relief; perhaps the even lines of horizon and dike will work on him as they have worked on her, orienting her to the familiar landscape. He nods and shoulders the battered rucksack again, and they set off, falling into step just as they used to before the war.

She had meant to walk the longer way around, following the curve of the Lark to their bridge, and then up the sluice road to the cottage, but Alec sets their course. Before she's ready, they reach St. Anne's and the shell of the vicarage.

Alec stops abruptly in the shadow of St. Anne's, staring at the ruin.

June takes his arm again, and he shifts a step closer to her.

"I knew," he says, glancing at her, "but I didn't really. Not until now."

"Yes," June says. "It's rather . . . I am still getting used to it myself. Sometimes I come around the corner and I'm thinking of something else and then it's just . . . It's just there, waiting for me."

He frowns down at her, his eyes sad. "I'm sorry, June. I . . ." He trails off. "Well, I know it wasn't my fault I wasn't here, but I feel I ought to have been."

"You mustn't feel that way," she says urgently, looking up at him, and squeezes his arm again.

He pulls away gently, moving to lay his hand against the oval of stones that still rings the front garden of the shattered building. "Sometimes I thought I'd never see Fenbourne again," he says. "Or you, June. Everything is . . . It feels very unreal."

June catches herself wanting to say something about the POWs she helped process at Anderson, liberated from Japanese camps. She knows their stories better than she knows Alec's, which seems wrong on any number of levels. But of course there is no way to tell him any of this. Instead she says, "I expect so," which feels inadequate, at best.

Alec looks at her and smiles, but the smile doesn't come off quite right. Perhaps he feels the insufficiency of her words as much as she does.

By the time they reach the cottage, Alec seems more disoriented than ever. He had startled at the raucous calls of crows, looking at the sky as if it were too broad for him, or too low. June hangs his coat on the stag-headed iron coat rack in the front hall. Without it, he looks both taller and thinner, and it jars her. He prowls the parlor and the kitchen, drifting out into the garden and back again, and June follows quietly, trying to understand what he reminds her of. It's not until he goes up the stairs, awkward and a little off-balance, that she realizes he's all points and angles. Alec, but somehow not. Just like what's left of the vicarage.

She listens to him pacing upstairs, wonders if he needs anything. Or if space is what he wants. Then the clunking, throttled sound of the bathtub tap and the old water heater. June relaxes, or tries to, turning to a crossword for distraction, willing herself not to invade him with her listening.

He comes back after a while, settles finally into the overstuffed sofa, still awkward, his hair damp and uncombed. "I didn't mean to just disappear. When I saw the tub . . . It's been so long." The good fingers of his left hand stroke the scars on his right. June can't tell if he knows he's doing that, or if it's some kind of check that has become habit.

June sits beside him, trying to stay close without hovering. "Would you like tea? Or something more to eat?"

Alec stares past her, his eyes roving about the room. "I . . ." He turns back, focuses. "I'm sorry. I feel very off-kilter. Like I can't quite tell if this is a dream."

"I know," she says. How to tell him that she too has come back from an entirely different world to find Fenbourne shifted and wrecked in ways she cannot ever quite grasp? Reality has become as slippery as the darting of a swallow under the eaves, and she is alone in the vastness of trying to manage her own confusion. June sighs. She can share her mourning with Alec without sharing her story. She will have to. For the rest of their lives, she will have to.

They talk into the evening, Alec halting and slow. He is clearly not ready to tell her what has happened to him in the camps, and of course she can't tell him about her war, either. When he tries to ask her about the bombing, June freezes. He undoubtedly believes she was in England when it happened, that she would have been home for the funerals, and even considering the infinite extra layers left behind by her clandestine life is exhausting. She tells him the closest she can to the truth—she had not been back in Fenbourne yet when the vicarage was bombed.

"Ah," he says. "Foreign Office kept you busy, then?"

"Rather," she says, trying to see ahead in the conversation so she can steer as needed.

He nods. "Fellow in Germany had a girl at home, a Wren, off at the Isle of Wight." He shrugs. "Glad you were safe in London." His brow furrows. "More or less, in any event."

She's relieved when he doesn't pursue it, relieved when she doesn't have to obfuscate or make up stories. But it stings, just a bit. It rankles that he thinks she was here in England, a flower to be protected, her work not even worth asking about. As soon as she thinks it, though, she's angry with herself—he is just back from nearly three years as a prisoner, and already she is expecting him to be his old self. When clearly he no longer is.

If only he didn't look so haunted, it would be easier to let him chew his secrets at his own pace. But June can see it all gnawing at him. She pauses, trying to feel her way through the conversation.

"I'm grateful you were able to get word to me," June says.

"I wish I could have managed more often." He glances down at his hands. "And I wish I'd been able to write you myself."

"But we all did as well as we could, didn't we?" She pauses, trying not to drift too close to topics she mustn't broach. "In any case," she says brightly, "it was just always such a relief to hear from you."

He almost smiles, but then his face closes off. "There was a priest, a chaplain. An American. Smasher, we called him. He was the fellow who helped me." The ghost of the smile is gone, and when he looks up again, his gaze goes straight through her.

"Perhaps we can talk about him another time," she says carefully. "If you like."

"Perhaps," Alec says. He focuses on her for just a moment before he gets to his feet and goes back to scrutinizing the room.

One step forward, two back, it seems. June stands, thinking to embrace him. She loops her fingers around his too-bony wrists. She can feel something between them, perhaps more memory than want, but something. A current. When their eyes meet, she feels their past as a jolt in her belly, and something in his face says he feels it, too. For a moment, the world seems to shift back into place. But then Alec looks down at his hands, sighs, and gently pulls away.

"I think I might need a bit of time to myself," he says. "I don't know how . . ." He makes a gesture that seems to include her, the cottage, perhaps all of England. "I'm sorry."

"All right," she says, working to keep her voice even. "There's no rush, Alec."

"Thank you," he says. His shoulders sag a bit. "Good night, June."

He goes up the stairs, stumbling a bit on the uneven carpet that he used to step over without a second thought, and June is left alone on the sofa. She can hear him moving upstairs, his boots treading heavily across the boards, and the creak of springs as he settles onto the bed. She doesn't know if he's going to sleep—it seems early, although she supposes he must be feeling as though it's later, and the dark has come sooner than she's used to. Perhaps he's just sitting quietly by himself in his old room. She doesn't know quite what she had expected for this first day together, but now she realizes it was far too much.

She stands, looks around. They can make a life here, for now, although there is not much holding either of them in Fenbourne as far as she knows. Not any longer. But first there is the matter of helping him be here, helping him recover, as much as that's possible, from whatever his captors did to create that distance in his eyes and between the two of them.

She doesn't know what to call it, even for herself. It's not merely that he is more changed than she expected, more damaged. She feels as though there has been a shattering, a sundering of sorts, in what they had, and now they are in the dawn of rebuilding something new. What that new life is, she can't quite say. His bedroom door is shut when she goes upstairs, and she tries not to feel it as a slap. Instead she lays her fingertips against the heavy wood and whispers a quick good-night to him.

By the time June falls asleep, her room lit by a waxing moon and the low fenland stars, her door slightly ajar in case he needs her in the night, she has convinced herself that she can fix this. Everything is different, but they are together now. She must believe that they are still them, although their configuration has shifted. But that is a puzzle she can solve. She believes that the boy she knew is still in there, cloaked in the layers of captivity and war, and that somewhere in those layers is a man who still loves her with his whole heart. The pressing thing now is that he needs her. She knows enough, and the rest will come.

1946, *Fenbourne*

The clock ticks away the night; outside, the moon has risen in a clear sky. Alec sits on the edge of his bed trying to work through everything he's feeling—bewilderment, to be sure, and the same disorientation that has plagued him since that terrible day over the Mediterranean. And June . . . He had not expected to see her at the docks, had not known how to talk to her, except in those confusing, awkward bursts like some other version of himself. He had not known how to reach out with these dreadful appendages and bring himself back to her. She must be hurt by the distance between them, but what is he meant to do? So much has changed since last he was in this room, on this bed, that it's hard to understand how the room has not changed like everything else. How many places has he slept since he last slept here? Twenty? More? And with each transition, something else vanished or was left behind, although never the ghosts of the friends he's lost. Those follow him as loyally as hounds.

And to find himself living here, in Constance's cottage, with June . . . He has dreamed his whole life of being with her, of a life like this, but now that he has it, he has no idea how to navigate the reality. And how is it that his aunt is dead? It hadn't felt quite real before, but now her absence is everywhere. It would have been dreadful to be here without June, knocking around the house by himself. What would it feel like to be alone? How claustrophobic might all that empty space become? Even this single room is nearly too big for him. But he doesn't know how to ask June if she's staying, if this is how they live now. If this is the first in a series of moments he can count as real, as the beginning of their life.

In Odessa, he had shared his quarters with three other men. There had been clothes and bedding, and the Russians had made an effort to combat sickness and infestation. They had had plumbing and cheap calico towels, rations heavy on root vegetables and light on grains and decent meat. They had been prisoners still, despite the end of the war, and the relative comfort had been balanced always by the fear that at any moment one of them could vanish onto a train to the Gulag. But. Better than Germany. He tries not to think about the men still there, waiting to be sent home, or the officers who had acted as their keepers. The Red Navy fellow in charge of him had been so serious, though he'd seemed so young. In the end he had turned out to be older than Alec, but his relative innocence had blurred everything. Alec had liked him, but now, with weeks on the sea and most of a continent between them, he can't help but wonder how much of that fondness had been a misplaced gratitude.

The light beneath his door shivers as June comes upstairs and pauses just outside on her way to the room beside his. He feels so far away. In Odessa there had been music at night, winging its way down the corridors from the lush quarters of their Soviet captors, and sometimes the music had slipped into his fetid dreams and left him dizzy and confused. Here there is no music, but the sounds of the fens are better, though perhaps equally confusing. A fox barks at the night, and somewhere far off in the distance the defensive double-noted call of a tawny owl answers. He goes to the window, looks out in case he can see anything alive out there. Beneath the moon, the black peat expanses stretch out as silver as a badger.

And, standing, he feels that pull again toward June. He feels so powerless—he is right here, she is right there—but he is helpless to bridge the gap. There is too much space between the way she looked at him tonight, with love and hope, and his fear that she will not want him. That the way he sleeps, or doesn't, will frighten her; that his hands are too rough and broken for her skin; that whatever he has become after all the years of war and captivity is not the man she deserves.

Alec wakes at dawn to the rich songs of siskins and mistle thrushes. The realization that he has finally escaped the horrors and come home brings a thick, blasted fire of guilt with it, and he has to lie still until it goes away. What little sleep he'd managed had been full of the cats of Stalag Luft I, and the host of dead who travel through his dreams and infest his sleep—Cobber, Tim, Charlie, Smasher . . . All the men who died while he survived. The men whose fates he doesn't know prey on his dreams as well—is Sanjay one of the lost? In Odessa, the Russians had been generous with their vodka, and it had sometimes helped him care less about the dreams. He had never liked the stuff, but it had been a damn sight better than the lethal booze some of the men had distilled from God only knew what in Germany. He had never been sure whether drinking that had been intended to help them forget their circumstances or just kill them outright.

He gets to his feet, rubs and tugs at his hands to ease the stiffness that comes with sleep, and goes to the window, trying to orient himself to the view of the winter-burned fields out the window. Alec has wanted to be back in Fenbourne with June for as long as he can remember, and now that he is . . . Well. Before the war, he had mostly come to feel at home in the Fenlands. He knew the people of the village, and their dogs, and sometimes their cows. He had overheard Cook gossiping with Miss Laflin, the postmistress, over the back fence at the vicarage a thousand times, or the teachers at school whispering about the headmaster, Mr. Shotley. In the ten years between Alec's arrival in Fenbourne and the morning he'd sauntered off to Cambridge and Clare College, he had come to terms with its habits and mores, finding his place.

And before that, India. Bombay and Srinagar and the rest, places that felt as much like home to him as England ever had. Could a man ever really let go of the colors and landscapes that had meant home from the beginning? June has shown him so much here in Fenbourne, but even she had never been able to make Fenbourne quite replace that other life she had never known, full of elephants and temples.

The truth is, war has peeled away all sense of home from anywhere, even here.

Alec knows he should be grateful. He is alive and reunited with the woman he's loved his whole life. He is going to have to try harder than he had last night, if he hopes to make it right with her.

"One step at a time," he mutters to himself. He picks up his towel and a change of clothes and goes to the bath. The night before he had bathed in water nearly too hot for him, scalding away the thick, stale film of ship and stress. During the passage from Odessa to London he had washed himself as well as he could, standing in his cramped cabin with a rough cloth, a crust of bad soap, and a basin of cold water. It had hardly been enough, but compared to the miserable shared tap of Odessa, and the horrors of Germany, it had been adequate. But now . . . The extravagance of being able to settle himself into the deep tub here, letting it warm his hands and the rest of him, is an immeasurable glory. He had nearly wept, but he had been so self-conscious, aware that June would be downstairs wondering what he was doing. But there will be other baths, as many of them as he and the ancient water heater can stand. He can be clean all the time now. His hands tremble as he fumbles with the tap, and again he nearly cries.

. . .

Downstairs, June is sitting at the kitchen table with a cup of coffee and the telephone directory. He had smelled the coffee from upstairs, his senses lighting up with want, but the directory throws him. For a moment, he wonders if she means to memorize it, the way she has always memorized everything.

She looks up and smiles. "Good morning, Alec."

"Good morning," he replies. His hands drift behind him and out of sight, but he forces himself to let them hang at his sides. Perhaps if he can pretend well enough that he is not ashamed of them, it will become true.

She stands. "Would you like some coffee?"

Alec lets himself wallow in the idea. When was the last time he had good coffee? Algeria? And whatever it is that she has brewed, it does not have that watery character that he had seen on bases and in cafés during the war.

"Please, yes," he says. He takes the chair across from her place, makes himself meet her eyes. "It smells marvelous."

At the sink she runs the water until it's hot, fills a mug, and lets it warm for a moment as if she too finds the cottage a bit too cold. Alec's chest flutters. He is having his morning coffee with June, an idea that only a few weeks ago seemed like a distant and improbable future. The idea echoes: *I am having coffee with June. I am here, with June. June is here.*

When she sets the mug in front of him, he presses his left palm to it, letting the heat push into the sore spots in his bones. His right hand he settles in his lap, out of sight. Trying to be less self-conscious is a process, it seems, though he feels as if his inconsistency will only make things worse. The coffee is not the oil-black concoction he remembers from Algeria, but it's unlike anything he's had in ages, the aroma so dense he can almost touch it. He lifts the mug and sips carefully.

God, he thinks, hoping June won't see the emotions welling up. "This . . . I haven't had anything like this in years, June. I would have thought with rationing . . ."

"I know," she says. "I'm lucky to have the good stuff. It was a gift from Floss Corbett."

Alec looks away, trying not to let his reflexive irritation about Corbett color how the coffee feels. How that next sip tastes. He makes himself smile. "Lucky, that."

"If you'd like cream or sugar . . ." She gestures at the two small jars in the center of the table.

He hasn't seen proper cream in years, and his mouth waters. How is it that such luxuries are just there, right before him? He's always taken his coffee black, but turning down real sugar and rich cream now feels tantamount to turning down a meal. After years of Klim and worse, such a notion is nearly beyond his ken.

"Might be nice, a spot of cream," June says quietly. "Sometimes you just want that bit of extra."

Alec settles his mug in front of him and reaches for the cream with the rough pincer of his left hand, then goes back for the sugar.

When he's finished, the coffee is nearly dun, and he's almost embarrassed. When he sips it, it's too milky, and too sweet, but the wash of it into his throat and his belly is incredible. Yet that beautiful rich coffee is all but lost in it. It never crossed his mind that something as simple as a coffee on a cold morning could be so confounding.

He looks up sheepishly. "I've made it too sweet."

"Think of it as a treat, then," she says. "There's more in the pot if you'd like a fresh cup. You can have it however you like."

"Second chances," he says before he considers his words.

"Indeed," June says, regarding him warmly. "I wondered if you might like to take a walk with me." She looks down into her nearly empty mug. "I know you saw a bit of Fenbourne yesterday, but . . ." Her brow knits. "I thought it might anchor you, a bit? The familiar?"

The image of the shattered vicarage surfaces. He takes a long swallow of coffee to buy himself a moment before he has to answer. His stomach tightens. "Perhaps?"

She nods. "All right. It might be good for you." She shrugs, her smile quivering just a bit. "And I would like it very much myself."

When she stands, lifting her mug for one last sip before she takes it to the sink, the ring on her left hand flashes in the morning light, and Alec's heart speeds up accordingly. In the bustle of the day before he hadn't noticed the ring, but now it seems part of the larger domestic tableau they're inhabiting. He wants to take it as a sign.

"June?"

She turns back to him, a look on her face he doesn't know how to interpret. Wary, perhaps? His chest hurts, thinking this is how he has made her feel.

"You're right." He rubs his hands together, trying to center himself and corral everything he's feeling. "That does sound like a good idea. Let's."

"Grand. Thank you." Her eyes shine. "I was going to make myself a bit of toast and some eggs—would you like some?"

He is always hungry, even when his stomach hurts. And his stomach almost always hurts. Too, it's hard to navigate the new landscape of being in this cottage with her and trying to figure out what they are now. Who he is now. He blinks, tries to stop himself from overthinking all of this.

"Thank you," he says. His stomach growls, although he can't tell whether it's with hunger or nerves. "I would love some."

. . .

When they head out, the sun is as high over the hedgerows as it's likely to get. Alec had forgotten how short the days were here in January. But God, the air feels good. It's too cold, sinking into his lungs like a stone, but the relief of another day away from the tired, metallic air of his cabin on the troopship is immeasurable. When he falls into step with June, she smiles; she seems as relieved as he is that this works. He feels like he should be talking, but what can he say? He's surprised when she loops around the long way, instead of following the sluice road straight into Fenbourne. At least they're together, doing something that feels relatively normal, as if she understands that he is going to need some time to get his feet back under him again. The clarity of the air is such a gift, but after a certain point, when the chill has gone bone-deep, the bitter wet of the Fens and the terrible searing cold of the German camps are not so different. He jams his hands deeper into his pockets, but the cold is inescapable.

In the village, it seems as though all roads lead to the vicarage. Alec stares up at the emptiness, trying to take in the enormity of the destruction. They stand together for a moment. He has an ocean of things he wants to say to her, but with the ruins looming over him it's so hard to begin. Finally he says, "You must miss them awfully."

"I do," June says. She slips her hand around his elbow.

He holds perfectly still, his heart banging away at the feeling of her touch. His mind races, trying to find the right thing to say. "It won't always be quite this raw."

June gazes at him, and he stares back, captivated by the impossible color of her eyes, the dark wing of brow on fair skin, although she is perhaps not as fair as she once was. But time has passed for them both, and God knows he doesn't look the same anymore, either.

"Thank you," she says at last. "That helps more than you know."

They resume their walk. As they pass the solicitor's office, June reminds him that eventually he'll have to stop in and handle the various legal issues of probate and inheritance, and he's grateful when she doesn't suggest he do it now. Instead she leads him through the lanes, and gradually he finds himself not as disoriented and lost. For the most part, the village seems much the same. He's been away for what feels like half his life, but perhaps Fenbourne is the kind of place where time runs more slowly, and things change much less.

When they reach the bridge over the River Lark, June stops, her arm tightening on his.

"Oh," he says, his chest full of feeling again. "Oh, June."

"I thought you might want to see it," she says, her voice low but strained, as if she's trying to make it sound light. "One of the best parts of Fenbourne, as far as I'm concerned."

How to tell her how often he thought of this bridge, and those stars, while he was in the camps? How much time he used up in meticulous reveries of drifting on the river with the girl he loved more than anything? He pulls her closer, feeling her hand against his ribs through his coat and layers. Can she feel his heart, how it beats for her?

When they reach the cottage, Alec stops in the lane outside the stone wall and faces June. "Thank you."

She blinks. "For what, Alec?"

He gestures at the landscape, the cottage, everything. "For making it so I didn't have to do this alone. And for bearing with me."

She looks up at him with a crooked, sad smile. "I know things are . . . confusing, but I want to help you."

"June . . ." He pauses. "I missed you terribly. All the years I was flying, I just wanted to see you again. And in the camps . . . Thinking of you was how I bore the worst of it."

Her eyes well up with tears, and she steps closer. "Oh, Alec . . . You sweet boy. I am just so very glad you're home. That we're home."

Alec nods wordlessly. The tide of his anxiety has not turned, but: *Home*, he thinks. Perhaps there is hope after all.

That night when he goes upstairs, the clock still too early despite the low black quilt of night overhead, he tries to sound less abrupt when he says good night. Every time he thinks he might be able to take another step closer, presume upon her for the things they used to share, he remembers his hands. Tonight she stood when he did, and before he came upstairs she stepped closer, paused, and hugged him. He had frozen, a dreadful moment of panic, and then somehow he had managed to put his arms around her, and they had stood like that for a second or two before he felt so confused and awkward that he'd stepped away. And he'd wanted to kick himself, but there was too much he didn't know—where to put his hands when the hug ended, for one thing, and what to do with the dizzying blur of her hair against his face, when to let go or not. The uncertainty derails him—he knows she still loves him, or at least that she still feels some kind of connection to him. But how could he touch her with hands like this? Would she even want him to? Surely she can't want them on her. So, another night alone, but this one less of a disaster than the last. She had said *home*, earlier; they share that want. Then he will keep working to make it so.

June continues her work with Melody Keswick and the displaced persons, telling Alec while they eat or sit before the fire in the evening about the day's meetings or the news that trickles into Fenbourne about the rest of the world. With each day that passes, Alec feels more at home in the cottage and in Fenbourne. When he walks through the village by himself, he tries not to avoid people, tries to focus on the moments of beauty that call at him, whether a hare watching him from the side of the road or a sow thistle prickling against his palm. He wishes it were easier to shove his hands into gloves, so that he could stop relying on pockets for both warmth and disguise. And each night he tries to push himself to act on his feelings, and each night he fails. The gap between what he wants and what he can do feels wholly insurmountable, even while he can sense June's growing uncertainty. The hugs become a bit less awkward, but there is always that moment when his hands fall to her waist like they did so long ago and he panics. He always pulls away, feeling the pang of knowing that before, he would have left his hands in place and pulled her close to kiss her. And now he looks down into her face and wonders if that is what she wants, and how he is meant to know. It used to be that kissing her was one of the best things he knew, and now it is just another way he can't remember how to be.

While June comes and goes, Alec struggles to reorient himself. He shuffles through newspapers and magazines, coming to terms with the new state of the world, teaching himself how to turn the pages again. He practices pages with Smasher's Bible too, scrawling out verses he recognizes on a sheet of rough paper with a stub of pencil. His efforts to write have been disastrous so far, but he keeps at it. And for now June has offered to help him with letters to the families of the friends he lost, as well as requests for information he will send to the RAF in the hopes of finding out what happened to Sanjay and the others.

Every time he walks through Fenbourne he pauses at the office of his solicitor, Mr. Swift, then goes on. It seems too final, somehow, no matter how clearly Alec understands the task will need to be done. It seems easier to spend his time instead looking through the pages of adverts and seeing if anyone is hiring for whatever it is he can do. Although that is a question itself, isn't it? There are days when the queries for men who can lift or write or operate a machine overwhelm him, and those days he is most likely to strike out as far as he can into the fens until he is alone with the sky and his hands don't matter as much.

With the RAF he had had a future, not to mention a plan for himself, and for June. Money is not the main concern—he has his parents' estate and the small sum that had come to him at Constance's death, but he has always thought of those as something to set aside for the future. In the present he needs to work, to be productive. Despite his ruined hands, there must be something, mustn't there? A way to find his way back to the sense of purpose he'd had as a pilot?

Midway through the first week, Mrs. Hubbox comes, along with a boy called George, who appears to belong to her despite his East End accent. It's hard to think of the housekeeper as Mrs. Hubbox, when he knew her for so long as Mary, the Attwells' maid. How has she become this middle-aged woman with a cheerful Cockney son? Later, June tells him that George had been one of their evacuees, and that Mrs. Hubbox had claimed him after his mother's death in a Whitechapel bombing. He tucks away that information, trying to rid himself of the sense that Fenbourne has become a bewildering orphanage.

A few days later, June returns from one of her meetings with a basket. Alec stands to greet her, distracted by the basket but also by the excited glow in June's face. The basket shifts in his arms as she hands it to him, and a low whimper escapes it. He sits and opens the lid, and a small brown puppy pops up, all eyes and ears and tail.

"June?" He glances at her, but most of his attention is held by the puppy. He lays a palm across the top of her head, and her tail flutters. When he lifts her out of the basket, she wiggles against him, licking at his face and fingers.

"I thought you might enjoy the company," June says quietly, her eyes still gleaming. "You know Melody's retrievers, yes? One got loose, and apparently there was a tryst with a spaniel from one of those farms on the Ely road."

"I see," Alec says, but he's only half listening. The puppy is soft and so warm, her belly against his forearm like a compress. He looks up at June. "She's lovely."

June beams at him. "At any rate, she needed a home."

The puppy nips at his fingers, and Alec cradles her against his chest. For a moment he can almost believe his hands are fine. Here is something he can hold without wishing for his hands to be as they once were. He sets the puppy on the floor, and she winds herself around his legs, tail wagging ecstatically before she sets to chewing at his boot-laces. "She's a beauty. And look at those paws!"

"Yes," June says, stepping closer and eyeing the puppy. "I expect she'll be a good-sized dog, Alec."

"I imagine so," he says. He reaches out with his left hand and brushes it across the back of June's hand, his stomach knotting when he doesn't know what to do next. The puppy barks, and Alec stands. When he goes to the door, the puppy follows, and he grins at her.

"There's a bit of rope in the kitchen, if that would be useful," June says.

"I'll get her a proper lead tomorrow," Alec says. He bends and strokes the puppy's back. "Come on, little girl." The puppy barks again, and he scoops her up and carries her outside.

It's a clear night, early enough that the moon is just rising off to the east. Alec makes sure the gate is closed and sets the puppy carefully down on the tired, frost-gray grass. She looks at him, barks again, and sets off to explore, looping back to him every few minutes. Alec watches her, hardly aware of the cold, his heart beating so hard for June and this little tobacco-colored animal that he can hardly stand it.

Overhead, the stars pepper the sky, and when he looks up to find his bearings the way he always has, his breath catches. For the first time in years, he remembers his mother telling him how to follow the stars from Ursa Major to the North Star at the tip of the smaller bear's tail. He looks back toward the house, where June is leaning in the open doorway, watching him. He smiles.

The puppy completes another loop, pouncing at Alec's feet and grabbing his laces again. He crouches to fuss her ears, then glances back up into the night. How many times had he sat in the velvet dark with his mother and listened to her tell him stories about the stars? All those swans and dragons, princesses lost and found. The star bears shimmer overhead, the most constant thing he has ever known, the stories and the stars his guide and solace.

"Ursa," he says. He looks back at June. "What would you think if I called her Ursa?"

June's face lights up, and she glances at the sky. She smiles at him. "Ursa is perfect."

1946, *Fenbourne*

A Sunday in early February, and the six bells of St. Anne's peal into low-slung clouds. June sits at the kitchen table, coffee at her elbow, working the crossword in the Sunday *Times*. It still feels like a bit of a luxury to have it fresh on Sunday mornings, rather than waiting for a bundle of them to arrive by ship at Anderson. But today's puzzle is less of a solace than it usually is—the weather has muffled the world, and so she is too aware of the church bells. The changes ringing out over the fens from St. Anne's belfry had always meant home, and the complicated course of a plain bob minor had been one of the first codes she'd ever understood. They have sounded the same her whole life—from the bawling tenor of Great Tom to the clear treble silvering out over the fens from Little John. The apostle bell, her father had called that.

Nothing feels quite right this morning, least of all the weather. She's been back from Ceylon for months now, and she has still not gotten used to the cold. No wonder Alec used to complain so, when he first came to Fenbourne. The cold feels deeper today, damper. Although she tends to wake fast and clear, she feels a little foggy and on edge. The chill doesn't help, despite the fire she built in the drawing room when she first got up.

She's relieved when Alec and Ursa clatter down the stairs. For the most part he seems more comfortable than he had upon his return from Odessa, and she knows Ursa has a lot to do with that.

"I'd come with you, if I weren't so cold," she says, watching him drape himself in coat and muffler.

He pauses, one boot on and one off. "Later, then," he says, smiling. He leans down and rumples Ursa's ears, then turns back to June. "Back in a tick."

She nods and goes to the stove so there will be coffee ready for him when he returns. She measures carefully, feeling as always mildly guilty for having it at all. So many things are still scarce in the Fenlands, even with the war behind them. She would have thought life would be getting back to normal, but Labour seem to think they all need to be kept in hand somehow. Maddening, really. Can they keep people living out of ration books indefinitely? She and Alec have a better situation than most, with two ration books and her connections in the Foreign Office. It's not black market, at least, although she will grant it's not quite cricket, either.

It helps also that now and again Mrs. Hubbox and George bring over jars of preserves or a pie or a bit of potted hare. Having some meat in a pie is more than welcome, something that's not eel, a bit of gravy that tastes like something other than turnips. June is confident about the cottage's garden and what she can grow there when spring comes— greens, potatoes, beets, whatever George can help her plant.

While Alec and Ursa are out, June turns her attention to solving some of the cold. She goes upstairs and puts on a warmer jumper, then adds more wood to the fire, the crackle of kindling soothing while she waits for their return.

When the kitchen door creaks open, June goes to greet them. "Did you go far?"

"Far enough that this happened." He gestures at wet, mud-layered Ursa, smiling, and puts his palms against the puppy's face, murmuring to her. "Dreadful muddy creature."

Ursa wags her tail so hard she nearly falls. Alec has trained her to wait in the kitchen until he can get a cloth for her paws, so she stands quivering on the mat just inside the door while Alec steps out of his Wellies and into the pair of hard-soled slippers he's left by the stove.

"Ursa," Alec says, his voice going higher as he turns back to the dog, "you're doing a good job waiting. Such a good job. Now let's have those feet, please."

He stations Ursa on her towel, clumsily wiping off her paws and brushing the mud out of her feathery tail. He's become more adept at wrangling her, but today the task is made much more difficult by the fact that she won't stop wagging. June smiles as Alec tries to corral the puppy's tail again.

"If you don't hold it still, I can't possibly make it clean," he says, his voice playful. Ursa licks his nose. "I can't. Not possibly." To June he says, "God help us if it gets much wetter out there."

She laughs. "I should think we'll have another freeze. That should help. Or snow. I imagine she'd like that."

Ursa drums her forepaws excitedly on his leg, and he laughs and takes one of her ears in his left hand, tugging it gently. "Oh, don't look at me like that, you silly baby." She follows him, barking, as he scoops a cup of her food into her bowl. June's heart swells, watching him wait patiently for Ursa to sit quietly before he sets down the bowl before her.

June shakes her head. "She's so good. You've done wonders with her already."

Alec grins. "She's a dream to teach." To Ursa he says, "Much smarter than I am, aren't you?" Ursa wriggles.

June laughs. She loves this new tone in his voice when he talks to the puppy. It's always unexpected, though it reminds her of the animated way he used to tell her stories when they were younger. Again she has that pang of wanting to be closer, and not knowing how to make it happen.

"It's warmer in the drawing room," June says. "Would you rather have your coffee there, by the fire?"

"Warmer sounds ideal," Alec says, and leaves the kitchen, Ursa at his heel.

She pours a mug of coffee for him, picks up her Biro and the unfinished puzzle, and follows them into the drawing room. There, Alec has settled himself on the sofa, close to the fire with the newspaper, Ursa sprawled on her cushion nearby. June sets Alec's mug on the coffee table and pauses, eyeing the wing chair on the other side of the fireplace, her usual spot these days. This routine they've settled into, while companionable enough, is not what she wanted—is not, as far as she knows, what either of them wanted. Alec has been home nearly a fortnight, and dithering will not solve a thing. She turns her back on the wing chair and takes a seat on the sofa instead. Alec looks up and smiles at her before going back to his paper, and June lets the smile settle over her as she resumes the crossword.

"Christ." Alec fumbles with the newspaper. "The parliamentary delegation is leaving India."

"Yes," June says. "But it was only meant to be a short visit. Matter of weeks, really, to see how best to move forward."

He frowns at the article. "Yes . . . But end the Raj?"

"Well," June says, "I would imagine that the cost of the war has something to do with it. We haven't the coffers to finance an empire any longer, nor the manpower."

"This Richardson fellow says, 'India has attained political manhood,' among other things. What a phrase."

"It's inevitable," June says. "Even Ireland has self-rule now. And India won't have dominion as Australia and Canada have. They want true independence."

"But India is not Ireland or Australia," Alec says. "It's quite different.

You don't understand. Half the civil service is Indian. We've trained them and shown them how to rule."

June shrugs. "Yes, and now they have that. There's nothing more we can do there. Even if Britain had the resources."

"Look here," he says, "my family have been there for generations. My mother loved India more than you can imagine. Father used to hunt with princes in Kashmir."

"I understand all that," June says, picking her words carefully. "But every time they vote they elect people who want us to leave. It would have happened after the Great War, but for a few holdouts in their Congress. Independence will have its cost, but I can't help but think staying would be far worse."

"Most of them love us," he says impatiently. "You don't know what it's like over there."

June bites her tongue, wanting to avoid both an argument and anything that strays too close to her secrets. In Ceylon there had been a mutiny, native troops wanting to turn over the Cocos Islands to the Japanese when it looked as though they might win the war. The mutiny had ended with executions and protests, and the next year there had been a general strike. She wants to tell Alec that not all the King's subjects love him, but that path seems perilous in every way. Instead she says, "Be that as it may, at this point, we can leave gracefully or we can be thrown out, yes?"

Alec frowns. "It's just . . . Everything changes too bloody fast. There was a Hindu chap in my squadron, one of the best pilots I ever met, and he kept telling us the end of the Raj was bound to happen sooner or later, but hearing that is quite different from seeing it unfold right before us."

June pauses, caught up in the echo of his assumptions. She had quite forgotten how maddening he could be when he'd made up his mind about something. Perhaps she should ask about the squadron, divert him somehow. But it had gone badly when she'd asked him about the chaplain in the camps, and she still feels the same sick regret about the look on his face as he struggled with how to answer.

Agitated, Alec reaches for his coffee, letting the newspaper fall to the sofa between them.

"No, you're right, those are rather different," June says at last, hoping to make peace, but as she's working through the rest of her response, a log pops loudly in the fireplace.

Alec spins away from the sound, and his mug flies out of his hand, shattering against the edge of the table with a crash. He curls into himself, pushing back into the corner of the sofa as he claps his hands over his ears with a low whimper. Ursa rushes to him, nuzzling his knees and whining.

"Alec?" June moves closer and puts a hand to his forearm. There are often gunshots in the fens as people chase off vermin or shoot birds to fill the pot in their winter-sparse kitchens, and while she's seen him startle and flinch a few times when he's heard them, this is quite different.

"I'm here," June says softly. "We're all right."

Alec turns and looks at her, his eyes pained. "I've splashed you," he says, his voice low and shaky.

June puts a hand to her face. Now that she's noticed it, there's the sting of the hot coffee on her skin. She wipes it off impatiently and moves her hand to his shoulder. "How can I help you, Alec?"

He gets clumsily to his feet, his face changing. June can't tell if it's embarrassment or resentment or something in between.

"Excuse me," he says, barely audible, and then he walks away, moving as though his legs have gone weak beneath him. Ursa follows so close he nearly steps on her, and together they go upstairs.

June goes to the bottom of the stairs, then stops. When she was very young there were men in Fenbourne who had come home from the Great War with shell shock, and sometimes Alec reminds her a bit of them. Her parents had sat with those men and tried to help them, and she wishes there were a way to ask them what to do for Alec.

When he goes out later with Ursa, she offers to join him. He stands for a moment in the kitchen, pulling his coat close around him. "It's awfully cold," he says at last. "You stay warm. We'll be back in a while." And then he and Ursa are gone.

It stings, a bit, but she shrugs it off. If he needs some time, so be it. She sinks into the sofa. The fire leaps up, poplar bark peeling with a hiss from the kindling while an oak log settles in the grate. June arranges herself so that the heat brushes over her shoulders, and settles in to read *Brideshead Revisited*, which Wendy, in her letters from America, has insisted she will love. So far it reflects an Oxford quite different from the place she remembers, but perhaps that is part of its charm.

But it's difficult to focus on the book when she's worried about Alec, especially as the afternoon keeps passing without their return. By the time they've been gone nearly two hours, it's falling dark outside. June stands and goes to turn on lights, her emotions flickering from concern to anger and back again. They've gone for long walks before, but this time, after the episode with the fireplace, it feels more concerning.

As she's putting up the kettle for a cup of tea, the kitchen door thumps open and Alec comes in, not quite steady on his feet. With him is George, carrying a heavy ceramic casserole. Ursa and a lean gray dog of uncertain provenance follow them.

"Look who I've found outside," Alec says too loudly. June steps back.

"Evening, Miss," George says.

"Good evening, George," June replies.

Ursa pauses on her mat and waits, but the other dog comes straight in, tracking wet paw prints across the floor.

"Your new friend is not very mannerly," Alec says to Ursa in an exaggerated whisper. She thumps her tail against the door.

George laughs and whistles his dog back to his side. "Sorry about Skip. He's more an outdoors type."

"Happens," Alec says, grinning.

"Herself sent me along with this," George says to June, holding out the casserole.

"Oh, lovely," June says. She sets the dish on the table and lifts the lid—a dark, heavy stew, redolent even cold of thyme and the gamey scent of hare. Perfect for the weather. And, she thinks, eyeing Alec, perfect for after a drink.

"He waylaid me on my path home," Alec says, shrugging dramatically.

George gives her a cheeky grin. "I'd best get back, Miss."

"Thank you," June says. "And please tell Mrs. Hubbox how grateful I am."

"Righto," George says. He whistles again, and Skip follows him out the door and into the evening.

When he's gone, June takes a moment to gather herself, setting some of the stew to warm on the stove. Alec drops into a chair at the kitchen table. June glances at him over her shoulder. Perhaps an argument would break them from their routine, but when she thinks of his face that morning, the fearful quiver of his hands against the sides of his head, pushing him is beyond her. Instead she asks him if he's hungry and lets herself replace the frustration with gratitude when he quietly nods. Further upset won't do Alec any good, but a cup of tea and a bowl of stew might.

That night June hears him pacing his room until the pacing is interrupted by the now-familiar sound of the tub being filled. Does he feel as alone as she does? Perhaps if she slept close against him it would heal him somehow. But what if it made everything worse? Instead she waits—for what, she's not sure—and listens to the wind screaming outside as if it's following the dikes out toward the Wash and the North Sea.

At least his nights seem somewhat better since Ursa's arrival, although "better" is a relative term. Even with the dog sleeping in a basket, soon to be outgrown, by the side of his bed, it seems as though he still struggles to fall asleep at all. But it had been worse, those first few nights after he'd come home . . . more frightening. God. His bed is just on the other side of the wall from her own, and often she had woken in the night to hear him crying out unintelligibly. God knows there are memories lodged in her that come back in the middle of the night, playing out again and again without respite—lepers begging on the streets in Colombo and Madras, the sailor bleeding out after the Zero attack, a POW who'd come through Anderson with a gangrenous foot that one of their medics had had to remove, and once the fearful screaming through her headset of a German radio operator trying to call for help as his ship burned.

But whatever Alec finds in his dreams is undoubtedly worse; she hesitates even to speculate on what it might be, after years of active duty and so much time in the camps. What he must have seen and gone through. Perhaps if he would talk about it, if she could find the means to draw him out. Although if she's honest with herself, she must admit that the guilt she feels over the secrets she carries is easier if Alec holds his own so close.

Fenhall, the Keswick country estate, is elegant and dignified, but every time June goes to one of Melody's meetings she finds herself longing for the chaotic visage of Bletchley Park. Sometimes she wonders whether what she's really missing is the war, but that concern is not sustainable. She can't afford to miss that life. Better to pretend it never happened, to admire the Regency-era bricks and planters and formal gardens of Fenhall, and let the past go. It helps that she can see the immediate benefit of the work she does with Melody—they are reuniting families, or trying to, and looking for homes for the Continent's innumerable displaced persons and refugees. It's disquietingly necessary work. And June is pleased to be of service again, even on the days when her efforts feel pointless, as if they will never succeed in helping enough people.

But today's meeting has been more good news than bad: one of the Polish families Melody is sponsoring has found permanent housing and decent prospects in Norwich's small Jewish community. When June drives back to the cottage late that afternoon, she smiles to herself, pleased by their small success. Anything she can do to lessen the Reich's unfathomable stain feels like a triumph.

Alec is in the drawing room when she gets back, Ursa at his feet while he brushes her, a Debussy suite playing low on the wireless. The fire is just embers in the grate despite the chill. He's been edgy around the fire since the episode that Sunday, and June is not sure how exactly to work through that. At least it's not as cold as it has been, and the lack of a fire seems more manageable than it might have on another day.

He looks up when she comes in. "You look cheerful—must have been a good meeting." He smiles. "I daresay Melody couldn't do a thing without you."

"I'm sure she'd do fine," June says. They've talked about her work with Melody before, but he hasn't made such a point of complimenting her. Perhaps he's trying to make up for Sunday, although by the end of the evening she had felt as though they were all right again, albeit still stuck in their mutual limbo.

He gives Ursa a final sweep with the brush and releases her. The puppy pads genially over to her cushion, where she settles with a contented grunt.

On the wireless, the announcer introduces the next piece, a selection from Wagner's *Rienzi*.

"Christ," he says through clenched teeth.

She turns in confusion. "Alec?"

"Could you turn that off?" He gestures at the wireless, and as quickly as she can June moves from the sofa to turn it off before returning close by Alec's side.

"I'm sorry," he says at last, his voice low and raspy. "The Germans . . . Now and again they'd play something for the whole camp to listen to—supposed to inspire us, or something." He gestures with his chin at the wireless. "A lot of Wagner."

June puts her arms around him and girds herself for the inevitable distancing, but it doesn't come; instead he stays where he is, his breath gradually evening out. If only he would put his arms around her, and they could hold each other . . . But his hands stay tucked in his lap. As softly as she can, she breathes in the clean smell of him at the back of his neck, and then, before she quite knows that she means to do it, she kisses his nape. Alec's breath hitches, but he doesn't move away.

All instinct, her lips move to his ear. His hands rise, then fall back to his lap. June pulls away, just a bit, and he lifts his head. She's moving so slowly, afraid that if she goes too fast Alec will bolt. And then she's kissing him, one hand on his forearm and the other draped light against the faintly stubbled line of his jaw. He makes a sound, almost a moan.

June's heart is too fast, too loud. She's half-afraid of the thunder of it, but the only thing that drowns it out is kissing Alec. When his left hand comes up against her waist, trembling just below her ribs, she almost forgets to breathe. Slowly, she unbuttons her blouse, takes Alec's hand as carefully as she can, and presses it softly to her breast. He makes that sound again, his palm gentle against her. She fumbles with the buttons of Alec's shirt, and the plaid fabric pools away from her fingers. When she dips her face to the hollow of his clavicle, his other hand settles itself at the small of her back, pressing her closer.

June looks into Alec's eyes, coffee-dark and as urgent now as the throb of her pulse. She can feel him quickening against her, and for a moment she thinks recklessly of slipping her fingers below the waist of his trousers, of giving in right there on the sofa. She smiles and leans closer, and Alec's twisted fingers trace across her skin, then pause. "Upstairs," he says hoarsely. He gestures at the windows. June nods. Anywhere, she thinks. Anywhere.

After, they lie together in Alec's bed. She feels as if a curtain has been pulled and the sun let in, even while she's not sure what's next or how to proceed. But perhaps for the moment the larger picture doesn't matter. Perhaps she can leave it to one side, for a bit. So much of Alec's return has been so difficult, and right now she just wants to bask in what's happened.

Alec breathes slowly against her collarbone. His fingers have found a place at her hipbone that seems to fit them just so, and June wants to bask in that, too. When his breathing evens out, she kisses the top of his head and lies as quietly as she can, making a map of him in her mind.

The end of February is snowy and frigid, and more often than not Alec and Ursa return from their treks wet and rimed with half-frozen mud. June is always chilly, and having Alec to curl up against in the night is a boon. When they sit together by the fire in the evenings, tangled together while they read or listen to the wireless, she keeps a hand on him, or leans shoulder to shoulder with him. June knows she is the ballast that keeps him steady. In many ways the new routine is the same as the old, but June loves the ways in which it is different—the feeling of being part of something, of belonging with Alec again. Of being together. She continues her work with Melody, and Alec spends most of his time with Ursa or poring through newspapers, looking for a job and sometimes trying to find the men he'd flown with.

But even with many of the same trappings, their life in the cottage is not the same as it was. The constancy of touch, of curling together in the night . . . Alec had warned her early on that he would be a bad bedmate, that the dark places he occupies in the night might cost her sleep. And it is true that there are nights when his dreams echo out of him like the spray of lake from a collapsing dam and he wakes wordlessly, sweating and reeking of fear. June tries to be his ballast then, too.

March brings more snow and a leaden cold that settles across the Fenlands. Most mornings Alec is downstairs first, letting Ursa out into the brisk air. Sometimes, though, June's sleep ends even earlier than Alec's, and on those mornings June finds the tracks of rabbits and shrews outside the kitchen door. It will be spring in a few weeks, and beneath the snow there are early shoots waiting to flourish.

But with the longer days come more of Alec's bad memories. An early primrose on the lip of a ditch can be fine one day during an afternoon walk, and anathema the next. It's impossible to know where the strains will come. He has begun to fret out loud about whether he will ever find work, and if not, how he will be able to support her when they marry, and his tension adds a new stress to their relationship. June worries over it—surely there are innumerable things he can do, even if they are not the things he would have done before. And surely he will not let his pride get in the way of this partnership they both want so much. Especially when the stress he feels over living together before they're married only adds to his other anxieties.

In April, Roger comes to visit, and June keeps him back to catch up while Alec is out with Ursa. She and Roger had corresponded the year before, while June had been occupied with trying to find Alec; Roger had made his own efforts through the echelons of the British Army. With Alec finally home, Roger had put in for leave, but in the postwar chaos it had taken this long for him to be approved and shipped back. It's the first time Roger has seen his nephew in three years, since they'd both been in Algeria, and June, unsure what Alec had told him about his hands or anything else, had braced herself for the shock she was worried Roger would feel.

But it had been better than she'd expected. Roger had seen worse and wasn't afraid to say so. And when June had had a chance to talk to him alone, she had told him of Alec's fears. All those dashed hopes, roosting like vultures. Roger had sat up with Alec late into the night, the two men talking quietly. The next morning, Alec had seemed lighter, somehow. More determined and less troubled, as if he had found a way through the maze of his efforts.

A few weeks later Alec bursts out of the house and into the garden, calling June's name. A startled skylark flits away, its song interrupted, and June straightens up from the vegetable plot, which she's been clearing of the debris of a sudden spring squall. For a moment she thinks he's hurt, and she starts toward him.

"Look," he crows, brandishing a letter as he crosses the garden. As he approaches she can see that his eyes are bright with tears. "It's Sanjay! He made it!"

June regards both Alec and the letter with pleasure. Of all the men to find . . . They had been more than just pilots together; Alec and Sanjay had been friends.

"Another chap got my address to him," Alec says, his voice breaking. "He's in Scotland."

June steps closer, more relieved than she can say. "He's well, I hope?"

"Very much so," he says, his eyes racing over the letter again. "He always said he'd head to Edinburgh after the war . . . I believe there was a woman there his family wanted him to marry. In any event, he's working for a shipbuilding company . . ." He glances back at June. Something is ticking behind his eyes while he thinks it through, and June goes still, waiting. He looks so alive, and she doesn't want to startle it out of him.

"He wants to know if I'd like him to put in a word with the foreman," Alec says at last. "And I think we ought to talk about that, June."

She blinks. "About moving to Edinburgh?" She tilts her head. "He's quite sure you could find work?"

Alec nods. "Place called Livingstone and Gray. Apparently they've brought on rather a lot of former airmen and whatnot . . . Sanjay says they want men who know their way around a plane, or a ship . . ." He regards her quietly for a moment and puts his arms around her. She leans gratefully into his embrace, loving the feel of him, the warm clean scent of his skin.

"Shall we marry, June? Start over together, somewhere new? If Sanjay can get me a line on something . . . I'll never find anything here, but perhaps in Scotland it would be different."

She hugs him closer. Perhaps somewhere else there will be fewer ghosts, and she and Alec can strive to become something new, not a different iteration of what they were before. "Yes," she says. "Let's."

Fieldfares whistle in the hedgerow, and the scent of mud and water rises fecund from the ground. If they go, she will miss the Fenlands, but in a village where the church bells ring out all they have lost, everything is full of echoing reminders. Very well, she thinks, the maps already coming together in her head in a hopeful shimmer. Onward.

BOOK FOUR

1948, *Edinburgh*

The house on Shakespeare Close is frenzied with tulips, rocketing out of the soil at Alec every time he comes up the front walk. The riot of late-spring color, all those reds and yellows, and the way the stones of the oldest lanes hold together in the Old Town and the castle remind him of Srinagar, a bit. Morningside, in particular, feels sometimes more like a small town than part of a bustling city, and he likes it that way. Edinburgh Castle and Arthur's Seat loom in the northeast, but he and June are largely free of the flurry of activity that the city proper carries through summer.

On a day like this, the May sun streams through the tulips and lights up in filigree the veiny leaves of the pear tree craning upward where the front garden meets the street. The whole of early evening is a balmy weight on the back of Alec's neck, and Edinburgh seems like the best idea anyone has ever had. He pauses to dig for his latchkey on the front stoop of the old villa, its yellowing Georgian bricks reassuringly solid and dappled with the crisp shadow of the rhododendron.

This part always takes a moment—despite the work he's done on his hands over the last two years and all the improvement that has come with that work, there are still these pauses like the skipping of a note in a song. Fetching out his keys bedevils Alec endlessly, though he's experimented with a variety of systems: larger key fobs that are easier to grasp, a strap built into his attaché case to make the keys quicker to find, a loop from his belt into his pocket . . . but nothing has ever quite solved it. *Per ardua ad astra*, he thinks. Through adversity to the stars. The RAF's motto, and now his own. He grips the key at last and smiles. The struggles have been worth it. The struggles have brought him to Edinburgh, to a job he likes with Sanjay at Livingstone & Gray in Leith, to a new closeness with June. To this lovely old house on the oversize lot, his and June's, bought by the pair of them with their combined inheritances and the proceeds from selling Constance's cottage. A long series of confusing days and weeks, getting them out of Fenbourne, but look where they had ended up. It's the perfect place for starting over, or for a young married couple looking to start a family. Ad astra indeed.

Inside, Ursa greets him with a quivering tail and the mincing smile she sometimes wears when she has spent her day on the sofa, where she knows very well she is not meant to be. Alec lays his hands against the sides of her jaws and shakes her head gently; the waft of her tail increases. She follows him to the kitchen, where June has left him a note: She is at the university, working on her research into algebraic varieties, and will be back before supper. Alec smiles; he has always known how brilliant June is, but watching her bask in the work, the way she looks when she talks about zeta functions and a thousand other things he doesn't understand, gets into his chest and lights him up with pride. He taps his fingers on the note, then heads upstairs to change into something better suited for a ramble up to Blackford Pond. Ursa follows him.

The sun won't be down for hours yet, and the angle of the light through the bedroom window, broken into piecework by the thick leaves of the magnolia outside, catches at the pale scars on his thighs. He hardly remembers how they got there—which disaster marked him. His hands, his legs, a knotty tangle at the base of his spine, some of the hearing in his left ear. The trains on which he had been shifted across the Continent had sometimes come under fire. British, American,

Russian . . . perhaps the Germans themselves, if they had known what manner of train it was.

When he's dressed, he lets Ursa lead him back down the stairs, where she goes straight to the front door and sits, her eyes fixed on her collar and lead.

"Silly baby," Alec says. Ursa's tail speeds up, but her gaze doesn't falter. He slips the collar over her head, running his thumb up the smooth slope of her forehead, and clips the lead on. He checks his trouser pocket for the house key, and then they're off.

Ursa stops to smell the rhododendrons, sniffing for mice or moles, then moves on, uttering a low, excited whine to lead him down the walk to the gate. Rachel Murray, a young mother who lives round the way, is out on a walk as well, with her son, Ian, in his pushchair.

"Good afternoon, Mr. Oswin," says Rachel. She smiles at Ursa.

"Afternoon," Alec says. "Fine day, isn't it?"

"'Tis" Rachel says. "Everything all bright and growing."

Ian, not quite two, wriggles, reaching for Ursa. She sits, quivering, and stares at him.

Alec says, "Ursa, would you like to say hello to Ian?"

Ursa takes a step closer, sits again, and delicately raises her right front paw so Ian can reach it. He grabs her paw and squeezes ecstatically. "Doggie."

"She likes you very much," Alec says to the baby. He's glad, watching Ursa lick Ian's fingers, that Rachel is not the kind of mother easily overwhelmed by a fear of dogs or their theoretical germs.

"She's nae the only one," Rachel says.

Alec nods. The bond between the two has been clear since the first time Ursa and Ian saw each other, not long after the Murrays moved in last summer. It can be difficult, sometimes, to navigate the confusion of watching Ursa with a small child—sometimes it's hard to push away the fact that he had hoped for a baby of his own by now. June has her reasons, certainly, and they make sense—she is in the midst of her program at school, her focus almost entirely on the intricate dance of equations that make up her particular cosmos, and dealing as well with the stressors of being one of very few women in the university's graduate courses.

And of course there are his hands. They do well enough now for the quotidian details of maintaining a house and garden, and at the shipyards he has adapted tasks as much as he can. But being a father . . . That strikes him as a wholly separate list of challenges. Could he even hold a baby with these rough, knobby hands? Surely he will find his way through it, when the time comes.

After a few more pleasantries, Alec and Ursa continue down the Close to Mortonhall Road. He weaves Ursa's lead from hand to hand, practicing his grip as the doctor has instructed him. June had set herself to finding him help almost from the very first moment of their life in Edinburgh, and Captain Carnaby at the Royal Infirmary, for all his unorthodox ideas, has in fact helped him considerably. Alec had been afraid that Carnaby would fixate on his mental state or soothe him with snake oil, but he has turned out to be a sensible chap. It's no small credit to him that Alec's left hand has grown stronger and more functional, or that the right has regained a small measure of its old mobility and grip. The exercises Carnaby demands are grueling, but even on his worst days, Alec must agree that June's searching has paid a considerable dividend.

Ursa pauses to nose around the head of the path to the Jordan Burn. Most seasons, it's hardly a trickle even before it vanishes under the willows beyond Glenisla Gardens, but the sound of it is always a delight. Part of what drew them to this part of Edinburgh, already desirable with its detached houses and the proximity to the King's Buildings at the university, was the greenery.

He tugs the lead gently, impatient to get to the pond and the trails that curl away from it. "Come along, Ursa."

There are swans at the pond, a cob and pen drifting with a clutch of cygnets trailing after them. Ursa eyes them, and Alec taps her softly on the forehead with his knuckle. She looks up at him, tongue lolling free, then back at the swans. He knows she won't chase them; an encounter with a farm goose before they left Fenbourne has left her permanently wary of large birds.

Watching the swans sets currents moving in his chest, reminders that although he is happier in Edinburgh with June than he's been perhaps ever, there are still those gaps. Perhaps it's the cygnets, the family the swans have made. Too, there is an energy in June that he doesn't understand. He's seen her sit as still as the ice that rimed the fens sometimes in the dark of winter when she's working her equations or solving a puzzle, and he's admired the grand long stride she has when they go for their walks. But this new hum feels like both at once, and he doesn't know how to name it or what it means. Sometimes he finds her looking out the window at something too abstract to see, rather as if there is something hailing her, a clarion call that only she can hear. He feels in his bones that June's longing for something more is not less than it was when they were children. In those moments, he can almost see a shadow surrounding her, the pent-up vibrations of a girl who has not yet found what she's looking for.

And that shadow worries him—it makes him wonder about her work, about the delays, no matter how reasonable, in growing their family. Love is meant to be all eggs in one basket, isn't it? He knows he wants her forever, and she wants him, too. He believes this despite the lingering guilt, the idea that he has somehow trapped her, despite the ways the war changed them both. That feeling he had the first time he met her, of being with someone who could see who he really was, or was meant to be, has left him feeling as if his life is both more real and more perilous. He has so much more to lose now.

An hour or so later finds him back at home, a set of schematics spread out across the dining table before him. It's a new tugboat, which he hopes to sell to one of his connections at the port in Aberdeen. He's eyed the bones of it in its berth at Livingstone & Gray, and now, studying the clear blue and black lines before him, he can see how it will look. All those years running his eyes over horses, cars, planes . . . Selling ships was not what he had ever expected to do, but he loves the deep joy that comes from being able to imagine the sweep of the hull, or the exact circumference of a smokestack, and find confirmation when he looks at the plans. One day he hopes to be part of the design team in their crowded, fuggy offices overlooking the mad glory of the yard, and if that dream is to come true, he must teach his hands to draw again. He lays a sheet of onionskin paper over the blueprint, licks the tip of the pencil clenched in his left hand, and begins to trace the tugboat's lines.

His hand has just started to tremble from the effort of following the lines so precisely when the jackdaws who nest behind the chimney call out their chuffing alarm. Ursa looks up, her tail wagging and her ears shifting forward as a car purrs to a halt outside. Alec glances at the door, puzzled. June walks to the university most days, not quite a mile from Shakespeare Close to the mathematics department. But as the engine idles, he recognizes the pantherine throb of it—Floss Corbett's sleek Bentley. Alec goes to the window and regards the blue-and-gold MK VI crossly, trying not to admire its lines.

"Beautiful machine, even if Corbett is insufferable," he says to Ursa. It's hard to say why exactly Corbett bothers him so much—their interactions have been few and far between, and he's never been less than correct with June. Alec just has a vague sense that Corbett views him increasingly as a nuisance. And that sense pushes up against the doubts he carries on his own and makes them that much worse.

Ursa nudges at him as if she can tell he is starting to fret at himself. Alec drops his palm to the sleek crown of the dog's head, tells himself not to be an ass, and goes to the door to greet June as the car slides back into motion.

She embraces him as she comes in, and hands him her school bag, since he's standing closer to the rack. "Don't get too close," she says belatedly, "I'm head to toe chalk dust. Honestly, I'm quite sure I'm breathing it by now."

Alec chuckles. "Only you would be more worried about that than your exams. They're what, a fortnight from now?"

"Yes." June smiles and lays her hand against his cheek. "Has Mrs. Nesbit left supper for us? I'm ravenous."

"Cold meat and a jam roly-poly," he says. He'd worried, when they started looking for someone to do for them, that they'd never be able to replace Mrs. Hubbox, who had gone to care for her elderly father in Ely, taking George with her, rather than following them to Edinburgh. But while Mrs. Nesbit has not quite replaced Mrs. Hubbox in their hearts, she has been a boon. Alec likes the days Mrs. Nesbit comes, because she is a much better cook than June, whom he suspects of exaggerating her lack of skill so they have a reason to keep Mrs. Nesbit on. Too, June's program at the university requires so much of her attention that finding time for more domestic pursuits seems unlikely. Perhaps that will change when she finishes her degree. Or when a baby comes.

"I've got to change," June says. She pauses in the foyer, glancing in at the papers he's strewn across the dining table. "Will you be a darling and set things out for us?"

"Gladly," Alec says, and goes to the kitchen.

After, they settle in the drawing room with the wireless, June stretched out the long way on the sofa to read with her feet in Alec's lap.

"I'm glad you're home," he says.

"I am, too." She smiles at him. "We were talking today about the Weil conjectures. Rather a lot to think about. Brilliant man." She lowers her book to her chest. "Are you and Sanjay still thinking of going down to Nottingham for the First Test next month? You'll be gone a week?"

"I think so," Alec says. Australia have come to England for the Ashes series, and it's been years since either he or Sanjay has seen any proper cricket. It's confusing, of course, because it reminds him of dreams long past, and of Smasher, dead in Germany. But it's cricket, and perhaps adding new memories will help soothe some of the old ones. It would be fine to watch Norman Yardley bat a century instead of having to read about it in the paper a day later. "We probably should have found a way to that two-day match in Yorkshire, instead."

June reaches for his hand where it rests atop the back of the sofa. "This will be good, though. You and Sanjay will have fun."

"Yes." He kisses her palm. "Although it's not certain he'll manage the whole run. Parvati is expecting again, and although it's still quite early on, Sanjay's a bundle of nerves."

June, as if she can hear the longing he tries to contain, sits up, tucking her feet underneath her. She nods, looking down at her hands as if she wants to say something. Whatever it is, Alec is not sure in that moment that he wants to hear it. He knows why they have not begun a family of their own yet, and she knows that he is looking forward to the day they do. It's a tired argument at best. Only the day before they had been at it again; after years together they are still not quite on page with what their family should look like.

"In any event, they've got all their aunties and Parvati's mother and lots of people," he says, "so I expect we'll still go."

"I hope you can," she says, piercing him with those eyes of hers. "It will be good for you."

That night Alec can't sleep. There's just enough light from the street-lamp at the corner to lend a glow to the tobacco-dark of June's hair on the pillow. He knows she would prefer to have even less light while she sleeps, but full dark is too much like the dank, filthy, lightless sheds the Germans would put the kriegies in for the slightest infraction. Full dark is too much. He leans closer, trying to distract himself from the grim memories by recalling newer, better things—the moon-light and the sea and the two of them on their honeymoon. It will have been two years in July, but his heart still quickens when he thinks of it. Her skin in the summer moonlight, the soft pale expanse of her dotted with blue and gold and red from a bit of stained glass in a hotel window in Wales. The swell of emotions in the brief ceremony at a registry of-fice in London, Sanjay and Ainsley Finch-Martin standing up for the two of them, Roger sending his blessing from Kandahar.

He leaves a kiss on June's shoulder and goes to the tiny square bed-room he uses as a workshop and study. Ursa follows, yawning, and stretches out on her cushion in the corner. There's a sturdy table set up alongside the window, which looks out over the road and catches the soft golden light at the end of day. In jars on the table sit the tools Captain

Carnaby has assigned. In Germany there were men in the infirmary, or more often in barracks, with damage that the doctors there had treated with exercises, and he had expected Carnaby to recommend something along those lines. But while work of that kind is part of his therapy, he has also found himself confronted with paintbrushes and clay, fragments of thin wood that he's meant to be making into something else, pots of gruel-like paste that remind him of the flyers slapped up through London in the Blitz. Handling these items, turning them over in his hands, trying to make his fingers work, is hard, often painful, and in the beginning, it was nearly beyond him.

After that first afternoon consult with Captain Carnaby, he had come back to the house with his hands feeling as battered and sore as they had in years. But June had helped him then, has always helped him. A day later she had brought him a jar of paint, a sheaf of paper, and a tin of hair-tipped brushes. He had struggled to hold a brush, or to control its path through the thin layer of the vermillion paint she'd poured into a saucer. It had been well-nigh impossible, but she had wrapped her hand around his and guided him across the flimsy paper. *You need to be able to write*, she'd said. *I'm here, and I'll help as you like, but you need to build your hands up again. Painting will help with that.*

He seats himself on the high stool at the table and reaches for a scrap of sandpaper. He makes his fingers grasp it, forcing his right hand to perform, and then he concentrates on smoothing the edges of the structure he's been working on. Such minuscule work, so painstaking, but one notion has stuck with Alec—the idea that if he is using these paints and pastes to craft something that matters to him, he will progress faster. And so he is building a house. But it's not just any house— not a house one might find in the Fenlands or Edinburgh.

He looks at his work. It is nowhere near done, but it has begun to take shape, the thick walls he's formed of clay to look like the heat-defying walls of his home in Bombay, timber laced with rushes and held together with dung and soil, whitewashed until on the hottest days it looked like a mirage. If he were to build rooms, or the compound, he would have to build the room in which his mother died, the stable yard in which he learned to sit a horse, and the servants' quarters. So he is building a shell, a memory.

His hands ache against the smoothing of another layer of clay, but it's a good ache. It reminds him a little of the way his shoulders would pull when his Blenheim wanted to carve the sky with a particular arc and he had to fight the yoke.

When he reaches a stopping point, he wipes the bulk of the clay from his hands with the rough towel he keeps ready on his desk. The house is so quiet. In winter the boiler groans like ghosts. But in May, especially a lush, rainy May such as this one has been, the radiators are silent, and the trees are whole and green. The froggy trill of a nightjar comes in through the open window.

He should try to sleep. June will want him to have slept. But here he is, awake on another of his endless night missions. The moonlight glows indistinct and prickly through the trees, and Alec looks up at the sky and counts the stars.

1950, *Edinburgh*

Almost Christmas, the world glowing gray and white outside the kitchen, and snow dusted over the frozen ground. The sun will be down far too soon, and the coming close of day throws lavender shadows as the trees lengthen into the afternoon. It's the coldest winter in Scotland for more than sixty years, and June is more than happy to sit by the fire while she works her crossword. She's layered herself in jumpers, her back to the hearth while the flames hiss and gallop. Ursa lies nearby, her paws quivering in her sleep. June regards the puzzle, confronting a clue about maths, which seems like a happy omen on a cold afternoon, especially one on which she has spent the morning honing the details of the latest draft of her dissertation. She smiles and pens the letters into the boxes.

Alec comes back from the kitchen with a heavy mug of tea cradled between his palms.

"Bloody cold," he says, settling into the warm spot beside her on the floor. "You know what it reminds me of?"

June sets the puzzle on the hearth and turns her attention to Alec— sometimes the cold reminds him of the brittle world of the German camp and all the stories he hasn't told her. What he *has* told her is ghastly.

"Once upon a time, there was a river," Alec says, "and on that river lived a bear." June lets out her breath, relieved and pleased, and follows him gladly into the world of the bear and his princess, the story swirling with enchanted stones and the gleam of Himalayan snow. When he trails off, she lays her fingers against Alec's shoulder, and he leans into her touch. He has always been rawboned and lean, but now, almost five years after his return from Odessa, some of those hard planes of bone have finally layered with flesh, and the feel of him under her palm blooms a warm sense of well-being in her. She wants the rest of the story—will Alec ever not stop before he gets to the end? Long ago she had given up asking him to finish; if he wanted to, he would. But it has seemed sometimes as if he leaves them incomplete on purpose, like the girl in the thousand and one nights, or Penelope with her weaving.

June has loved the bear stories for most of her life, ever since she gave Alec a map she had drawn of Fenbourne, the path from the vicarage to the cottage on the sluice road marked out one precise black *x* after another. He had looked at the map, tracing the roads, his fingers lingering where she had marked the bridge over the Lark, the overgrown yew bush behind the postmistress's cottage. The next day he had appeared at the vicarage with one of his father's old uniform buttons, taken from the small metal box of treasures he'd brought from India.

"Second Lancers," he had said, offering the button to her as they sat on a bench in the conservatory. "I had two, and I thought it might be best if you had one and I the other."

June had thanked him, and she's sure she must have said more, if nothing else to ask him about the Lancers, or about his father, but all she remembers now is the way the button had sat in the palm of her hand, a small brass nub that meant more than she could say. The button is upstairs now, huddled with other treasures in a small ivory box her father had brought back from the Boer War before June was even born—one of the few relics she has of the vicarage. But she and Alec are the same, in some ways, the small things writ large, handed back and forth like a canteen in the desert.

. . .

L ater that evening, she and Alec are due at Sanjay's home at half past
six for dinner. She likes Sanjay and Parvati, although it can be hard
work, pretending to be more ignorant of India and the topics they raise
than she truly is, until the result is that she feels more distanced than
she would have if she'd never seen India at all. Too, there are the babies.
There are three of them now, a four-year-old girl and twin boys who
have only just turned two. June wants to look at them and feel the rush
of heat to her heart, that longing to nurture, that she knows Alec feels.

"I'm looking forward to seeing Sanjay," Alec says, smiling.

"I should think so," June says fondly. Alec's job has changed somewhat as they've given him more responsibility—he functions now more
as a liaison between design and sales than he had before, with a secretary dedicated to interpreting his cramped, dreadful handwriting. Both
men have become increasingly integral to Livingstone & Gray, but the
trade-off has been that they're in different offices now and see each
other much less frequently. And it's good for Alec to see Sanjay, to have
that extra bit of connection to India and his time in the RAF. To be
reminded, among other things, that a man can leave the RAF and find
a new career without it being a loss.

A lec always takes the same route, up through Bruntsfield, and June
watches the city pass outside her window. Edinburgh is laced in
ice, a winter filigree adding a festive sense to the night where it glitters
on windows. Ahead of them, the castle crouches above the city like a
giant stone animal, watching and protecting. June has always loved the
way it glows at night, lit by countless lanterns and the moon.

The Kichlu household occupies a tidy Georgian town house a stone's throw from the narrow, jagged lanes and alleys of the Old Town. Parvati's family has lived there for nearly a hundred years, their ancient Punjabi heritage blended into the Scots traditions they've lived among for so long. Sometimes June envies them the long history they have in this place; she doesn't feel nearly so connected to anywhere.

Parvati welcomes them into her home with a kiss on each cheek, her accent more Edinburgh than Lahore, completely at odds with the rich red and gold fabrics of her outfit. The four of them exchange pleasantries, Sanjay and Alec chatting away about sports and slapping each other's shoulders companionably. Parvati watches them with an affectionate smile. "Look at them," she says, "blethering like old aunties." June laughs, but she's right—most of what the two men ever talk about is their coworkers at the shipyards or their heroes on the cricket and football pitches.

Sanjay's mother is waiting with the children in the drawing room, where Parvati has set out pistachios and a bowl of roasted chickpeas that remind June of Anderson. Sanjay pours drinks, and June takes her gin and tonic gratefully. Shivani, the four-year-old, clings to the tail of her grandmother's dupatta. The twin boys, Ronit and Rakshan, are less reticent, and when they swarm Alec, June hangs back. She has no idea how to talk to a two-year-old, much less a pair of them. Alec, though, has no such issues, and it's only a moment before he's sitting on the floor with the boys climbing him. When he pulls sweets from his jacket's inside pocket, the boys crow with delight. Shivani drifts closer, considering.

There's a pair of lavishly upholstered ebony footstools not far from Alec, and June sits gently on one. She watches Alec coax Shivani closer, losing track of what the boys are doing until their wrestling bounces them off the inlaid center table between the footstools. It's an old, sturdy table, the base of it an intricate carving of a banyan tree surrounded by jackals and birds, and Rakshan lets out a wail, clutching his elbow.

Parvati bundles him close to her, examining his arm with exaggerated care until she's tickling him. He chortles happily, elbow forgotten, and his brother joins him on Parvati's lap.

"Let's get you all upstairs," Parvati says, hugging them. She stands and puts her hand out for Shivani. The children say their good nights as Sanjay swoops them into hugs. Alec shakes each child's hand, and even Shivani giggles at him. Then Parvati and her mother-in-law usher the children out and up the stairs.

"They're so big," Alec says to Sanjay.

"My little warriors. Their sister is the smart one, I think." He laughs. "You need some of your own, Cosmo."

Alec glances up at June. "We'll get there."

June smiles, but her face feels tight. "Something smells awfully good," she says instead of responding directly.

"I have been kept out of the kitchen all day while she's worked on our dinner," Sanjay says, his face lighting up as Parvati comes back into the room.

Parvati regards him indulgently. "It's a surprise." As they move from the drawing room to the dining room, she leans close to June with a conspiratorial grin. "He is so easy to keep happy." She shrugs encouragingly. "Your Alec is not so different. And, June . . . He is a canny touch with the little ones. He'll make a fine father, that one."

June forces a smile. Parvati is quite right.

All through dinner they talk about the Partition of India and Pakistan. Sanjay's family has been split by the new border, and he's hoping to bring more of his relatives to Edinburgh to join his mother in this household. June has never been as far north as Punjab or Kashmir, so it's a relief not to have to pretend at not knowing. But as the conversation shifts from the northern mountains of India to a hill station both men remember closer to Bombay, her discomfort grows. June hasn't been there, either, but she remembers Bombay itself, and the mountains all green and hazy in the distance. And even more than that she remembers Kandy and the hill station where she recovered from the attack on HMS Anderson.

The food itself only makes it worse. Part of June's effort to build a wall between her secrets and Alec was to pretend that the spices and flavors of Indian food were completely new to her. Since the beginning, she has let herself "develop" a palate that is closer to her actual preferences. But sometimes the lingering effects of the earlier pretense catch up with her, and that can be galling, as it is tonight, when Parvati sets a simmering dark cauldron of dhaba-style chicken curry on the table. Sanjay plasters his hands over his heart with feeling. June's mouth waters at the scent of it, the way the cardamom and masala sweep the room, and she wants nothing more than to take a bit of roti and scoop the curry into her mouth.

"I should warn you, it's a bit spicy," Parvati says, with an apologetic glance at June. She gestures at a second serving dish, a rich butter paneer. "But the paneer is quite mild."

"Thank you," June says. "They both look lovely."

Parvati beams proudly, arranging the ceramic bowls so everyone will be able to reach the food. June reaches for the dish of chutney, adding some to her plate. She dips her spoon into it and takes just a bit into her mouth. The burst of mango and tamarind grabs at her, and she pauses as the memories rush in. Parvati leans in, heaping a plate with curry, roti, and chutney, and June smiles. Her pleasure fades when Parvati hands the plate to Sanjay, who rubs his hands together gleefully. While the others are talking about boating on the Dal Lake in Srinagar, she serves herself some of the curry and scoops a bit onto a piece of roti. The curry and the chilies it contains are hot enough to make her eyes well up, but God, the wealth of flavor. She closes her eyes, savoring the heat and richness.

When she opens them again, Alec is eyeing her indulgently. "Sure that's not too hot for you?"

"Not at all," she says. "It's delicious." Alec nods and asks Sanjay to pass along the curry.

"Funny, rather," Alec says, "but when I was there, we mostly ate English food. And now here I am in Scotland eating curry."

Parvati chuckles. "There have been curry houses here for a hundred years or more."

"Rather a catchall term, though, isn't it?" Alec carefully sets down the serving plate.

"It comes from a Tamil word," June says. "Kari. It can be translated as 'relish for rice,' generally."

Sanjay raises an eyebrow. "That's right—good job!"

"June's a whiz at crosswords," Alec says to Sanjay. He grins at her, then turns back to Sanjay. "I can hardly understand a word of her dissertation—she's brilliant, really. Quite a girl."

June looks away. The pretending is hard enough on an average day, but this is all exhausting, the colors and smells and tastes taking her back to places she cannot say she's ever been, and often misses. It's been a long time since she felt so alone with the secrets.

After dinner, Parvati goes to check on the children and see if her mother-in-law, who has remained upstairs, needs anything. June stays with Alec and Sanjay, who retire to the drawing room, nattering on about airplanes and tugboats. She's not sure that's where she's meant to be, but certainly Alec doesn't expect her to join Parvati to look in on the children. It's confusing, though, to parse what Alec believes their future holds. When Parvati returns, bringing in a tray of coffee and small sweets from the kitchen and setting it on the old teak sideboard, June finds herself watching the other woman's meticulous attention to fixing a cup of coffee and a plate of sweets for Sanjay. Her own mother had been like that, fussing over June's father's tea until it was perfect. June stares down into her own coffee, missing her parents and trying again to identify where she should be, which role she should assume. How much of her own dreams she will be expected to give up to support Alec in his.

They're quiet in the car on the way home, June ruminating on the waves of emotion, the food, the possible blight on her future.

Alec sighs happily. "They're a grand bunch. The little ones are delightful, aren't they?"

She almost flinches. What is there to say to that? *Yes, of course? No, please stop asking about children?* At last she says, "They're certainly a handful."

Alec glances at her. "I know three at a time is a lot for you to consider," he says quietly, "but imagine how grand it will be when our children can play with theirs. They'll be like cousins, nearly."

June has neither siblings nor cousins, and, having found Alec when they were so young, she has never felt as though she needed them. "I suppose so," she says at last. She's starting to have a headache. "When it's time. We have our whole future ahead of us, Alec."

"Well." He frowns. "Your degree will be finished this spring. And, if you'll forgive me saying so, we're in our thirties now. We don't have all the time in the world."

"I know," she says.

"It's been years, June. Years."

"I know," she says again, tersely, and leans her face to the window, hoping the cold will soothe the dull ache coming up between her eyes.

When they get home, he whistles Ursa to his side, clips on her lead, and goes out into the night.

Left alone, June pulls her arms tight around herself, as if she can pull herself away from the endless argument. Because it *is* endless, Alec pushing with various degrees of subtlety, and her responses never what he wants. Endless because she has known all along what he wants, what he believes family looks like. She may have agreed to marry him, to start a family with him, but he can't expect her to become one of those women whose lives revolve around their husbands and children, can he? He knows very well what kind of woman she is. They can't both win.

Perhaps Floss was right, all those years ago, before Alec came home, when he said she was meant for more than making babies. But how can it be that she and Alec can be so far apart on this issue, even after years of talking about—or at least around—it? They have been Alec and June, June and Alec, for a score of years and more. Despite her doubts in the darkest years of the war, when he was lost and she was not sure what there would be for either of them if he came home, they have ended up as a pair, a nearly matched set. And Edinburgh, for the most part, has supported that. They have found their way together, have they not, just the two of them?

That first year, they had been so busy, what with Alec starting at the shipyard and working with Captain Carnaby, and her own time filled with the thrilling crush of mathematics and schoolwork. They had not seen each other enough, but the time they'd carved out had felt so immediate and important. And now, with that hard year firmly in their past and both job and doctorate resolved, she almost wishes it back. When they'd become more established, there had been different pleasures—the ability to take time now and again to explore Scotland, even a summer fortnight, once, delving into the dark green world around Inverness, all that water and mystery. The tall, ragged stones of Culloden Moor, redolent of grief and a fierce, devastating hope. Alec had been too quiet there, and for a while she had wondered if it had been a mistake to visit the old battlefield with him at all. But that night in their room in an inn looking out over the loch, starlight creeping up along the water into their bed, he had opened himself to her at last, finally beginning the process of telling her about his war.

When Alec comes back, he pours himself a whisky and joins her in the drawing room. She can hardly look at him. Nothing has happened; she has done nothing wrong, exactly. But these waves of feeling have her feeling unmoored and reactive. She needs time to think, but what, really, is there to think about? She is here, with Alec, the man she loves and wants to spend her life with. Sooner or later, she will give him the baby he wants so much. Sooner or later that will happen, despite her quiet efforts to prevent it thus far, and then, she imagines, Whitehall and the rest will be lost to her.

God. She has never meant to hurt him. What he wants must seem so simple to him—a matter of love and biology, but even more than that, tradition. Family. And, because he doesn't know the truth about her war, that makes sense. He has no idea what she stands to lose or what she's already given up. He will not give up because he doesn't know why he should.

He has loved her so hard, since almost before she can remember. She longs again for the days when things were more immediate and less complicated. "Do you remember the stars?"

He looks up, startled, with a slow smile. "Under the bridge? Of course."

"I was just thinking about them," she says.

"I should make stars here in Edinburgh," he says.

Through the pang in her chest, June smiles. "I like that idea."

"Perhaps I'll paint them in the nursery," Alec says quietly. He regards her a bit diffidently, as if he's wondering how she'll react.

June takes a breath, quells the panic. "Perhaps so."

1957, *Edinburgh*

Over the years, the ride to Leith and back has gelled into an agreeable bookend on Alec's workday—the bus out, the city hazed with mist and the bustle of shops opening, Alec just another man on his way to work; the bus back, everyone considering the tasks completed or left undone, the shadows long in the streets. The tide of husbands returning to shore, as it were, as regular as the surge of flotsam that drives up against the shipyard docks.

He loves the familiar patch from the bus stop to Shakespeare Close, the newsagents and shopkeepers who know him by sight, the stripes of spring sunlight through the butcher's awning. But what he loves most is the last bit, the last few steps that bring him home. Edinburgh has felt like home since the beginning, but since the birth of his daughter, Penny, four years ago in January, the house on Shakespeare Close has been numinous with the way his heart beats. His steps quicken as he turns the corner, especially on this Friday, the threshold of his too-quick weekends with his girls.

Penny is playing in the garden with Ursa, the pair of them digging in the soil while Mrs. Nesbit watches. Ursa hears Alec coming and pauses in her close observation of the little girl's work, wagging her tail at Alec with a volley of barking. Alec joins Mrs. Nesbit, smiling. He loves watching the way Ursa shadows Penny. His affection for Mrs. Nesbit is a bit more ambivalent; although he's damn grateful for her, there are days when her presence in his house, or, as today, in his back garden, reminds him too much of what—or who—is missing.

Penny looks up. "Daddy!"

"Hullo, princess," Alec says. He bends and opens his arms to catch her, and she runs to him, flinging her tiny arms around his neck. Ursa trots companionably behind her.

"Daddy, Ursa ate flowers," Penny says, wrinkling her nose as Alec picks her up.

Alec grins at her and looks down at the dog with her tail waving happily back and forth. "Did she really?"

Penny nods. "That one." She points to a somewhat trampled patch of gerbera daisies.

"I see," Alec says. He leans down, dipping Penny ostentatiously as she squeals and clings to him. "I can't imagine why she thought that was a good idea."

Mrs. Nesbit chuckles. "I don't believe it was the dog's idea, exactly."

Alec laughs. "Yes, I expect not." He sets Penny back on her feet and shakes Ursa's jaws in his hand the way he has since she was a puppy. She's eleven now, the first spread of gray and white starting to salt her muzzle and toes. Sometimes in just the right light Alec can see where the white will continue to spread into rings around her eyes, and at those times he has to steel himself against the inevitable loss. But now, in the bright spring evening, she looks much as she always has, mahogany and chestnut gleaming through her coat.

"Good dog," Penny says, thumping Ursa's side with the palm of her hand. "No flowers."

"Yes," Alec says to both of them, "no flowers." Penny giggles, and she and Ursa go back to the patch of soil where they'd been "gardening" before.

"Mrs. Oswin rang," Mrs. Nesbit says. "She said she'd be back by Penny's bedtime, but to go on and eat without her."

Alec tries to keep his smile steady. "I see." His shoulders sag, just a bit. He had hoped to talk to June sooner rather than later about his ideas for a summer holiday. He's done the work already of coaxing June into taking time away from the university—it'll be summer, after all, no students to manage, and surely whatever she'll be working on by then will be able to spare a few days. There are innumerable holiday parks within a few hours' drive of Shakespeare Close, but putting his finger on just the right one is proving more complex than he had anticipated. Part of the problem, of course, is that there is part of him that will never quite understand why he's not taking Penny and June on holiday to Kerala or Srinagar. It's an odd incomprehension—the logical part of him understands it perfectly, and yet there is something in the back of his mind that doesn't quite grasp the reality. His own summer holidays when he was Penny's age seem magical in his memory, his parents young and healthy, lit by the Indian sun against a backdrop of mountains or ocean or sweeping green hillsides.

There is nothing like that here, of course. If there were more time he would take June and Penny to Portugal or even Corsica, from which Mr. Livingstone has recently returned with his face taut and pink with sun. So Blackpool or Skegness, probably, or perhaps a holiday camp in the north of Wales.

Mrs. Nesbit smiles gently. "Would you like me to fetch you anything before dinner?"

"Thank you, no." What he really wants, Mrs. Nesbit can't get for him—June here, present, watching their child grow from a baby into a little girl. Penny is blond like him, but she has June's marvelous eyes, and the older she gets, the more that same intelligence shines forth. He adores her, adores the way his heart stretches when he sees her, the way she likes to trace her stubby fingers along the loops and whorls of the carved doors of the cabinet in his office. He has loved her since before she was real.

Penny fills his heart; it is that simple. He had thought by now there would be another baby, but it had taken a long time for Penny to come. And now the years keep passing, and it seems ever more likely that Penny, like him, like June, will be an only child. There are days he feels as if something is being held back from his life, just beyond his reach.

Upstairs, Alec changes and sits on the edge of the bed, considering the evening. He had hoped to have a few more minutes in the garden with Penny and Ursa, given the weather, which has been quite mild for March in Scotland. But he's spent his week clambering awkwardly around the frame of a nascent ship, up and down ladders or perched on a scaffold, and it's left his hands tired and sore. Perhaps tonight he'll soak them in Epsom salts, before he spends his weekend doing garden work outside.

The sun catches the stained glass and casts dapples like poppies through the room. Poppies for Remembrance, not that he needs any aid in remembering the Great War, let alone his own war. Nobody does— in some neighborhoods in London and Birmingham, or throughout most of Coventry, there are still ruins standing. Sometimes when they're rebuilt or repaired the new construction seems more like a scar than a home—he has heard from George Cowan that work has finally begun on rebuilding the vicarage, which Alec can't quite imagine.

He frowns, considering the village—there's a holiday camp on the beach at Skegness, affordable, lots of activities, and only an hour or so from Fenbourne. They could go to the seaside, the three of them, and then show Penny where her parents had grown up. She's not even five years old, but it would be good, wouldn't it, for them to start to build a sense of history for her?

He stands and goes to the window as if staring out into the evening will conjure June home. It doesn't work; it never does. It seems as if she's at the university more often than not, although most likely that is not objectively the case. But he feels her absence all the way through him, just as he always has. The distance that wells up between them, fed by her work and his confusion, is a wound he doesn't know how to heal. There will always be more work for June, more pressure to create a proof or move up the professorial ladder. It had been jarring, but not really a surprise, when she had moved seamlessly from writing her dissertation to accepting a fellowship in the maths department as Dr. June Oswin.

He sighs, steps away from the window. They can talk later that evening; the extra hour or so won't make a difference in their planning. It's just that he likes the idea of the three of them at the table together, eating and sharing their days. It's important to him that Penny knows she's part of a unit. Part of a family.

As expected, June is not back for dinner, but Alec had hoped she'd be home in time for Penny's bath. Alec sits on the low wooden stool by the tub while Penny sails a small wooden tugboat in circles around her. The boat is a scale model of one of the boats he thinks of as his at Livingstone & Gray. Sanjay's children have toy boats from the shipyard as well, Alec reflects, although he rather doubts Sanjay has ever had much to do with his children's baths. Of course, Sanjay has a wife who holds their family as her entire focus.

Once Penny's clean, Alec slings her onto his back like a monkey, galloping obligingly through the upstairs while Ursa bounds alongside, barking. He tucks her in with her worn stuffed bear, mildly relieved that she doesn't ask where her mother is.

"What story would you like, darling?"

"The bear and the rani, please," Penny says.

Alec grins at her. "Not the one about the elephant and his trunk?"

"No," Penny says. "Not tonight." She smiles up at him sleepily.

"Yes, all right," he says. "Then we will save our Kipling for another night."

Penny snuggles close to him and hugs the worn mohair bear.

"Once upon a time there was a river," Alec says, "and on that river lived a bear." He pauses. "Perhaps one day you'll see where the black bears live in the Himalayas."

"But I want to do that now," Penny says. She shifts impatiently. "Tell me about the princess, Daddy."

He laughs. "Very well."

The bear had been at his princess's side for as long as he could remember. When she laid her fingers against his ears, the world would quiet away from them. You are my bear now, she said, and I will never let go.

When the thaw came, and her frigate could groan away out of the ice and out to the open sea, the maharani asked him to choose— north, to the aurora and the mythic white ice bears, or south, to the unmapped oceans that, as far as any of her sailors knew, were full of dragons. The bear chose south.

It wasn't long before the estuaries and islands were left behind. The days lengthened; on the tenth day, a pod of whales surfaced alongside the frigate, their powerful flukes casting an imposing shadow across the deck. When the whales began to sing to their calves, the bear leaned closer to the princess, letting her tears fall into the soft fur behind his ears, his heart beating much too fast.

Penny is almost asleep, Ursa snoring lightly on the rug beside her bed, when Alec looks up to find June standing in the doorway watching them, her face awash with emotion. He smiles at her, glad to see her despite the small bristle lodged in him over her absence.

"You're from India, too," Penny murmurs. "Like in the story."

"Yes," Alec says. "And my mother used to tell me these stories just as I tell them to you. They're part of our family."

Penny nods, struggling awake as June comes in.

"Hush," June says gently. "You sleep, darling girl. I love you." She leans close and kisses Penny's forehead. Alec hugs Penny and tells her he loves her, then follows June out into the hallway, pulling the door mostly closed behind them.

"I'm sorry I was so late," June says quietly, as they descend the stairs.

Alec nods and steps into the kitchen to start the kettle for their evening cup of tea.

Following him, June continues. "We were working on a piece about Euler's number and probability, and it all got rather away from us." She brightens. "I'm glad I got back for saying good night, though. And for the story." Her face fills with feeling again. "She loves that bear."

"Of course she does," Alec says. He smiles. "Speaking of animals, I thought I saw a polecat in the garden the other night."

June nods. "George's last letter said they've been having trouble with one getting into the chickens."

"Spring in the Fens," Alec says, shrugging philosophically. "In any event, I thought we might talk a bit about our holiday."

"Our . . . Ah, right. This summer."

"It will do us all good to get away, get some sea air."

June points roughly eastward. "The sea is just there."

"You know what I mean. The open ocean. Waves and sand and whatnot."

"I suppose," she says. She steps around him, getting out two teacups and the sugar.

"I wish I could take the pair of you to India," Alec says, the story still on his mind. "Take a proper holiday with a warm beach. Palm trees and coconuts."

"Well." She pauses, staring down into the beveled glass jar that holds the sugar. "That seems a bit extravagant. I don't see how it could possibly be an option."

"Are you quite all right?" Alec turns so he's looking right at her, holding her gaze. "You seem a bit . . . not here."

She shakes her head briskly, her lips tight. "No, I'm fine. Thank you. Just preoccupied with the Euler."

"I see," he says. While he works on the tea, June settles herself at the kitchen table, reaching for the deck of cards and the cribbage board they keep by the breadbox. Despite her frequent absences and her endless preoccupation with mathematical formulae he can't begin to understand, the two of them have managed to build their routines. And one of them is a cup of tea and a game of cribbage every night before bed.

"I thought perhaps Skegness," he says.

June looks up from the cribbage board and its pegs. "Lincolnshire? You want to take our holiday at the Wash?"

"It's not the Wash," he says.

June stares into the distance, mapping it in her head. "It's hardly fifty miles. I'd call that close enough."

"Fine," he says, "but Cornwall and Cardiff are too far, and if we went to Skegness, there's a grand holiday camp there, and then I thought we could take Penny to Fenbourne after." He pours the boiling water into the teapot and sets it and the cups down on the table. "We could start her building memories about the family."

"But, Alec, what will we tell her? How do we explain when she asks where our families are? She's awfully young for learning about the war, never mind understanding any of it."

"I don't know exactly," Alec says, taking his seat.

June regards him for a moment. "I expect there are parents all over Europe trying to explain those things to children."

"Undoubtedly," Alec says quietly. It's a daunting task, trying to wrap his head around all the losses, when she lays it out like that. How to explain, even to a four-year-old, the set of stones with the same final year for June's parents and his aunt? The dreadful fate of his own parents? At least there's Roger still alive, out in Kenya, who has visited just frequently enough that Penny has grown attached to him.

"At any rate," June says, pouring the tea, "we can do Skegness, if you like. But next year perhaps London or York, take Penny to a museum."

"Perhaps. We'll talk about it more," Alec says. "Hardly writ in stone."

"All right. Now. Once more unto the breach, hmm?" June turns her attention back to the cards, shuffling the deck before setting it face-down beside the board. "Come cut for dealer."

I n the middle of August, they load up the Morris and make the slow trek down the coast to Skegness. It's a long day's drive in the best of conditions, but made much longer by the unseasonable weather—it's been cold and wet all month, the afternoons peppered with thunderstorms, and now there are gales coming in off the North Sea, rain welling up underneath the car and vanishing the tarmac as Alec creeps along. The world outside the car is a blur of green and gray and yellow, towns and fields alike invisible in the rain. But despite the weather, and despite his vague concerns about June, who is distracted by her need to prepare for the incoming batch of students in the autumn, Alec is excited. Mrs. Nesbit and Ursa will watch the house for the near-fortnight of absence, and perhaps a change of scenery will do him and June some good.

· · ·

Penny is dazzled by the holiday camp from the very first moment, when they are greeted in the chaos by a young man in a green-and-white-striped blazer. He introduces himself as Arthur and whisks them away in a cart to a pale blue chalet. There is so much noise, so many people clamoring at one another, and somewhere a baby crying, and the rattling small engine sound of the carts. Penny is wide-eyed, clinging to Alec's hand even as she pulls to the end of his reach, trying to see everything.

Arthur leaps to the porch and opens the chalet's door, then goes back to the cart to collect their valises while Alec and June stand in the cozy front room with Penny, looking over the space. When he's brought in everything, the boy hands Alec a key with a flat tab made of Perspex, the chalet's number embossed upon it.

"That's everything, then," Arthur says cheerily. He points to a toggle switch by the door. "If there's anything else at all, you can ask anyone in a blazer to look me up, or you can flip that. It lets the switchboard know we're needed."

"Brilliant," Alec says, and tips the boy a crown. June thanks Arthur, who nods and smiles, telling Penny he'll see her later.

"Well," June says, her tone a bit dubious, looking around and stepping into the slightly larger of the two bedrooms. "This is pleasant enough. Awfully noisy out there, though."

Penny says, "Daddy, what about me?"

"Your room is just here," he says, leading her to the second bedroom. Penny climbs up on the single bed. "Mummy?"

"Yes, love?" June meets Penny's serious gaze. Alec smiles, watching them.

"Did you see the horses going 'round?"

June puts her head to one side. "Horses?"

"The carousel," Alec says.

"Ah," June says. "I did, yes. Aren't they lovely?"

Penny nods as if this is the answer she'd expected. "Daddy, can we go on them?"

"I should think so," he says. "Plenty of time. We have the whole week here, before we go to Fenbourne." Penny accepts his answer, and yawns. Alec realizes with a pang how exhausted she must be even after dozing half the ride down.

"You were brilliant in the car," he says. "Let's have a bit of a rest, shall we? And then we can see what else is here."

Penny nods. "Lie down, Daddy." She pats the pillow next to her.

"Very well, darling," he says, obeying. Penny lies down next to him, her thumb slipping into her mouth.

June regards them with a smile. "Okay, sleepyheads. You rest. I'm going to get a walk, stretch my legs a bit, if I can find somewhere at all quiet." She leans down and kisses Penny's forehead, then Alec's, a strand of her hair falling against his cheek.

"We'll see you soon," he says. She nods and lets herself out, and Alec lies still, listening as Penny's breathing evens out and she drifts into her nap.

For most of the week, time at the camp passes in a blur of dodgem cars and carousel rides, Penny perched on her wooden palomino's withers and clinging to the pole in front of Alec. Despite the sporadic rain, they let Arthur guide them through the innumerable entertainments the camp offers, from the crowded lunch tables to the rickety carts like mining cars shimmying along the rails. Sometimes in the evenings, they leave Penny in the chalet to sleep, despite Alec's vague concerns about the so-called Nurse Patrol, and go to the vast, hangar-like halls for the cabarets and dances. It's been a long time since he's seen June in a frock like this, or since he's had to remember how to dance.

One day, Alec impetuously enters and then wins a ridiculous knobbly knees contest, his trousers rolled up to his thighs. Penny is beside herself, convulsed with giggles. But June's bemused expression is rather less than Alec had hoped for. When Alec and Penny sign up for another round of follies, June begs off with the start of a headache. But for the most part, he and Penny and June are almost always together, like a planet with two suns, but right there, within grasp.

Friday morning Alec wakes up to a slow fog coming in off the sea. It seems like the kind of ground-heavy mist that will burn off with the sun, so he agrees when Arthur comes to find him at breakfast and suggests they go to the beach once conditions have cleared. Penny has heard from an older child at the playground that there are donkeys at the beach, and has been tugging at him for days about going to see them.

The North Sea is laid out before them, gulls and terns spinning on the breeze, waves grooming the horizon. Penny leads Alec and June over to the paddock where the donkeys are standing together, their ears back against the wind.

"I like that one," she crows, pointing to one wearing a band across its brow that reads WINNIE. Alec eyes Winnie dubiously, but once he's paid the fee and Penny has been lifted into the small, worn saddle, he feels more certain. Winnie is plodding and deliberate, and he and June walk her up and down the strip for a bit, Penny perched proudly atop the donkey.

"Such a princess," Alec says, "with your noble steed." Penny beams.

By the end of their afternoon with Winnie, their shoes are full of sand and Alec's jacket pockets bulge with collected shells.

Alec has been happy here, the three of them together. It has been grand, despite the chaos, and he's not eager to leave, though it's clear that June's interest has waned. The next morning, Saturday, they'll continue the trek to Fenbourne. He has no idea how to feel about that and is glad not to have to suss it out in the next few hours. Penny is exhausted after the sea air and the excitement, and falls into a deep sleep almost immediately. June lightly brushes Penny's pale hair away from her face, smiling, and goes to the sitting room, where she drops onto the sofa and pulls the low coffee table closer.

She's brought two decks of cards in with her, and starts laying out a game of patience. Alec likes a game himself, but his are simpler affairs, with a single deck and a reasonable chance of success. June's version is something she learned from Floss Corbett, who claims to have been taught it in a wartime bunker under Downing Street by its inventor, Winston Churchill. And even June, as brilliant as she is, wins only one hand in every four or five.

"I thought I might get a drink," Alec says. "If you wanted to come along." He glances at the cards. "I mean, before you really get started."

June looks up from setting down the Devil's Row, six cards that must be played in a particular order and can't be used anywhere else in the game. "Oh, I thought we were in for the night."

Alec frowns. "It's just that it's our last evening, and I'd hate to miss anything."

Her shoulders tense. "I could do with half a moment without all those people, Alec. It's been nonstop all week."

"I thought you were having fun," he says.

"Alec, all the balloon races and posing for photographs with strangers . . ." She sighs and turns away. "I've really tried to be a good sport about it all."

"I hadn't realized it was such a trial," he says, a bit defensive, and startled by the intensity of her feelings.

She regards him sadly, her face tight. "I'm sorry. It's not really my cup of tea, and I'm knackered."

Alec studies her, startled and dismayed. "I suppose I thought this would be grand for the family."

"It was a lovely idea." She sets down the cards. "But why must there be a parade for the Home Counties? What does it matter if this set of people come from Kent and that set come from Bucks? Why must we all be forced to be friends for a week?"

"I don't know," he says, deflated. "I thought the idea was to make the best of it, get away from our regular lives for a bit."

"Well, we've succeeded," June snaps. She rubs her forehead and picks up her cards again.

He blinks, stung. "I suppose you'd rather have stayed at work."

She looks back up at him, opens her mouth to speak, and falters. In her hesitation Alec hears her answer. For a long, silent moment neither of them says a word. The distant sound of revelers drifts in, the noise only enhancing the silence between them. And then, without another word, Alec crosses to the door and leaves the chalet, the door clicking firmly shut behind him.

1957, *Fenbourne*

It has rained in the Fenlands too, and the landscape is thick with the clotty stink of mud and reeds. Bulrushes line the high-water ditches, their bristle brush heads crowned with dragonflies and buntings. The roads run as straight and flat as they ever have, and as the landmarks and miles tick away in her head June steels herself for the moment the lane becomes the high street and the village surrounds them. The drive from Skegness was only a couple of hours, and she wishes it had been longer.

She is still unraveling Skegness itself, the exhausting suburban rites of forced entertainments. She had been glad enough to try; she doesn't begrudge Alec her time away from the university, exactly. And it had been good for Penny—so good, and June has loved watching her daughter make her way through the complicated world of the holiday camp. She thinks of Penny on the donkey at the seaside, the broken scallop shells Penny had collected to decorate a sagging castle, the sand slipping back toward the tide or lifted on the wind.

But the camp itself . . . The endless games, poor insipid Arthur . . . She had hated it, and she had tried so hard not to. But now that the week of Skegness is behind her, June can feel relief uncoiling in her belly even despite the tightness wrapped around her heart after her argument with Alec. He has hardly spoken to her since. She had been so tired, and the last thing she had wanted in the world was to go back out into the evening. Such a small request, really, and yet it had slid right through her reserves like a blade. She had snapped, and now here she is, redolent of the guilt of that dreadful moment as they drive through the afternoon.

Fenbourne is a set of shapes in the distance, the spires of St. Anne's shimmering in the August sunlight like a mirage. June has such mixed feelings about her return. Homecoming is meant to be a joy, isn't it? But she feels something else—there is no home in Fenbourne to welcome her. Perhaps it's the idea of coming back to a village where every memory is tinged with grief—even the wondrous moments have that curtain of loss behind them now—or the way it feels almost like going backward to return to this haunted place.

She wants to make things right with Alec, and perhaps being back in Fenbourne will help them through it. It's their home, after all, not just hers. Or it was, for all those years, even in the confusing shadows of India and Alec's life and losses there. All those summers with their birthdays one after the other, Cook making a Victoria sandwich for Alec, the games of hide-and-seek in the hedgerows or the dark upstairs of the vicarage.

"Mummy?"

June turns in her seat and looks back at Penny. "Yes, love?"

"How much longer until we get there?"

"Only a bit longer," she says.

Penny scratches her nose. "But how do you know?"

"Well," June says, "I grew up in Fenbourne, so I know more or less how long it takes to get there, but also, I've looked at the map, so I know the best route between the two places."

"I want to look at the map and see, too," Penny says, putting out her hand imperiously.

In the driver's seat, Alec chuckles. "Apple doesn't fall far, does it?"

June looks over. This is the first thing he's said in a while, and it feels good. She smiles and opens the glove box to pull out the Bartholomew guides in their worn case. She flips through until she finds the sheet for this part of the country. They're part of the half-inch series, and she's always liked the way the linen backing helps them keep their shape.

"Here," she says. She opens the map and points to the tiny dot of the village. "That's Fenbourne." She moves her finger east a bit, closer to the curve of the Wash. "And this is where we are right now."

Penny takes the map, frowning attentively. The sight of her daughter peering at a map gives June a lurch of pride, though she knows full well Penny is far too young to actually understand it, let alone read the names of villages, market towns, and tributaries. Still, she likes the idea of the two of them looking at maps together, perhaps tracing railway timetables across the paper country.

"Daddy," Penny says sternly, "don't get lost."

He doesn't get lost, of course. June watches him drive, his hands confident on the wheel despite the scars and whorls of the old injuries. Sometimes she wonders if this is what he was like in the air, his palms deceptively languid on the yoke, his whole attention on the horizon, the wiry muscles of his forearms tight when he makes a turn. June wonders if he is feeling the same tensions she is about their return. She pauses, then reaches out and squeezes his shoulder.

"Almost there," he says. His voice is terse, but he doesn't pull away, so June leaves her hand where it is.

"Oh, yes, I see," Penny says. She shakes the map authoritatively, for all the world like a cartoon banker with his newspaper.

"Thank you for your help with navigating," Alec says, grinning at her in the rearview mirror.

Without warning, the haze of village in the distance resolves into Fenbourne itself, just as June remembers. Well. Nearly. There are more cars, more people, more everything. The yew behind the postmistress's house is gone—and who knows if it's even still her house. The chemist's next door is now a car wash. The Morris rumbles down the high street, and Alec's shoulder tenses beneath June's hand. As they drive past the train station with the village's name in dark gold paint on the swinging wooden sign, June has a flash of sitting in her father's lap, a too-straight fringe across her forehead, reading the timetable for the express train to London. She smiles, but it falters in the swirl of conflicting feelings. Her parents would have loved Penny.

The Black Dragon sits on the banks of the River Lark, an old travelers' stop in Fenbourne, sparrows nesting beneath its old Tudor eaves. They have never stayed here, but the Rose and Crown is yet another place laden with too many memories, especially those of her return to Fenbourne after the war with her parents dead and the vicarage destroyed. She has sat in the pub here and had a drink with Alec a handful of times, watching the boats on the Lark, but those are not the kinds of memories she wants to avoid.

Alec pulls the Morris into the car park behind the inn, and the three of them tumble out eagerly, as if they'd been driving for days. He shakes out his hands, grinning at Penny. "Here we are, then. Our old stomping grounds."

June stands still, taking in the burr of sound from the front of the building—cars and people, mostly, a bicycle bell, the sharp bark of what sounds like a small dog. "It's been so long," she says.

Alec looks over and smiles, just a bit, and her whole body relaxes.

"Ages." He stretches, craning his neck to stare at the familiar sky.

"Can I look at the river?" Penny asks.

"Of course," Alec says. "Your mother and I used to spend rather a lot of time by the river. I'll be awfully glad to show it to you." He puts out a hand, and then the two of them round the building and cross to the riverbank, June following close behind.

The village has built a low wall along the riverbank here, and Alec lifts Penny and settles her on his shoulders.

June gazes at the river. Their river, out of all the rivers in the world. Their Lark, and their bridge not half a mile upstream. The dark green water flows smoothly, interrupted when it eddies around the bright blues and reds of small boats tied up here and there at the river's edge. How many times had they stood here together, dropping stones into the water to watch the ripples? Looking for fish or flood debris?

Alec glances at her with a faint smile as if he too feels the pull of the river. "Do you remember that winter we were, what, eleven? Twelve? And you poured that cup of tea into the river to see what the hot water would sound like when it hit the cold?"

June laughs. "Of course," she says.

A swan cruises past, followed by a cygnet. Alec tugs Penny's ankle and points with his elbow at the swan. "Look, princess."

"Oh!" Penny says, "Is that a baby swan?"

"It is indeed," Alec says. The sound of a motor putters up to them from around the bend, cushioning the cries of gulls.

"I wonder where the nest is," June says.

"Can we go see?"

June looks up at Penny and smiles. "No, darling. We mustn't bother the wild things."

Alec says, "Your mother is quite right."

"Daddy?"

"Yes, princess?"

"Once upon a time there was a river," Penny says.

"Oh, there was, was there?" Alec's eyes widen with delight. "And then what?"

"A bear!" Penny chortles and pats his temples and points at the water. "Does this river have a bear?"

"Not that I'm aware of," Alec says. He tilts his head just a little, staring upstream. "Well. Perhaps it has, sometime."

Penny shifts on his shoulders. "Down, please."

"We should get checked in," June says. "And eat something."

Alec lowers Penny to the ground. "Yes," he says. He looks around as if he's trying to take in everything about Fenbourne, both old and new, and shakes his head. "Did you see the car wash?"

"I did," June says. "Imagine."

He shakes his head again with a wry smile. "I can't."

June doesn't sleep well that night, and at breakfast the next morning she is grainy and overtired. She tries to focus on watching Alec and Penny with their toast and jam. It's been a while since rationing ended, but real bread still seems miraculous, and she knows Alec feels it, too. She catches his eye and smiles at him, and this time he smiles back. She looks away to try to hide the rush of feelings she has from his smile, from watching him eat without wariness. It took such a long time for his insides to heal, and even then it was years before he stopped tensing up if anyone left even a morsel of food behind on a plate. June knows she will never really understand what happened to him in the POW camps, particularly in Germany; the few stories he's told her are impossible, with nothing she can recognize to anchor herself against the horror. Catastrophic.

After breakfast they strike out on foot. June is in no hurry, and it seems easier to focus on the details of the walk—the dab-and-wattle facade of the Rose and Crown, the jumble of homes and shops that surround the Black Dragon, the new post office, all the children and dogs she's never seen and doesn't know. Alec is loose and relaxed as well, ambling along the cobblestones and narrating the sights in a silly voice that makes Penny giggle, lifting her to his shoulders again when she asks him to.

At the turnoff to Melody Keswick's old home, Fenhall, June stops and points to the mansion almost out of sight around the curve of the drive. "That's where Ursa used to live, before she came to live with Mummy and Daddy."

Penny peers up the drive with interest. "When she was a baby?"

Alec says, "She was so small she was nearly like an apple."

Penny laughs. "No, Daddy. She's a dog."

"Quite right," he says, "not an apple. Rather more like a coconut with legs."

June smiles, and he crosses his eyes at her the way he did when they were children, trying to make her laugh. It works, makes her feel lighter. She steps closer and bumps up against his arm with her shoulder. And then they continue on their way until they reach St. Anne's. June lays her palm against the humble stones. At least the church is more or less the same, the windows replaced or rebuilt since the bombing all those years ago. It doesn't make up for the loss of the vicarage, or the modern brick monstrosity going up in its place across the churchyard. They had had a letter last Christmas from George Cowan, who had mentioned that he'd heard they were rebuilding the vicarage, but June hadn't really understood what that would feel like until now. Her old home is gone, erased by the war and time and progress.

She looks at Alec helplessly, and he catches her eye. He lowers Penny to the ground and puts his arm around June's shoulders. The weight of his arm feels like safety, and she leans into him, away from the ugly new building.

Alec rests his cheek against her head, just for a moment. She squeezes his hand gently, relieved that they seem to be doing better.

Then they walk together to the churchyard, Penny at their side. June sighs. The graves will be hard, but better than the bricks.

The churchyard is full of drifted leaves, blasted out of the sycamores and poplars by the gales that have filled this August, and burnished in the late-morning sun. Everything is green and gray—leaves, headstones, the church. A wind comes up off the fens; it smells of black, fecund mud. Like flooding. She can almost hear the bells tolling the warning.

Nearby, the slab of Barnack stone that marks Constance's grave no longer sits flush. It's been pushed up by the roots of a white willow pollard, tilted like a drunken signpost. Alec stares down at the stone, then leans closer and thumbs away a layer of winter-left rime from the words carved there. *Constance Tennant Fane*, it reads. *Beloved Wife, Devoted Sister and Aunt, 1888–1945, In God's Care.* Her husband, Anthony, is buried next to her; when June and Alec were very young, his aunt would take them to the churchyard every Remembrance Day to lay a poppy on Anthony's grave, and on his birthday a bouquet of harebells.

The churchyard feels different, tangled with the new and unknown. Even the summertime shadows are different, with the old vicarage gone. She's afraid to know what else has changed—what's happened to the cottage on the sluice road, or if there's anything left at all of the stars beneath the bridge over the River Lark.

June lays her hand on her parents' angel marker, not praying exactly, but wishing them well. Even while she knows they would counsel her to turn her heart to her family and shake off the opportunities Floss dangles for her now and again—posts in Berlin, Hong Kong, even Washington—she also knows they, especially her father, would be proud, if they knew what she were capable of. What she'd done in the war. What she could now, given half a chance.

When she looks up again, Alec is sitting on the old stone wall with Penny, nodding solemnly.

"They're all gone?" Penny asks. She looks more curious than worried.

June joins them on the wall. "Yes, love. My mother and father and Daddy's mother and father are gone now."

"Oh," Penny says. She clambers down from the wall and goes to look up at the angel.

Alec and June exchange a look, waiting for the questions they're still not sure how to answer. Penny stares at the angel for a few minutes, then seems to come to some conclusion and walks back to them.

She puts her hands on Alec's knees, looking up at both parents. "Are you sad they're gone?"

It takes June a moment to collect herself, but the answer is simple. "Yes. Very much."

Alec nods, laying his hands atop Penny's. "I would have loved for all of them to have met you. And they would have thought you were the very best, princess." He stands and scoops her up, holding her over his head, her arms out to the side while she laughs. "The very cat's pajamas."

"Cats don't wear pajamas," Penny says, as he sets her back on the ground.

"Well, not regular cats," Alec says. He widens his eyes dramatically and whispers, "Not the ones we can see, anyway." Penny giggles.

June gets to her feet, grateful that he's distracted Penny from harder questions. It's so effortless for him, the clowning and affection. As a boy, he spent much of his life without a father, but somehow the ideas he's cobbled together from dreams or memories or vague imaginings of his life before England have made him into someone for whom fatherhood is as natural as the curve of the earth. Sometimes it can be hard to distinguish the blurry line between envy and admiration.

Everything used to be so simple—she was June Attwell, and he was Alec Oswin. They belonged to each other from the beginning, until the war came and changed them both. Changed the world around them too, and left less room for a love like that. It is intolerable, all of it. Floss and the university will move along without her, given the slightest opportunity, and Alec and Penny will love her as hard as they can, but they won't give her the sense of purpose that her work has provided.

Try as she may, June has no way to reconcile her obligations to her family with her obligations to her work. She loves Alec and Penny with all her heart. But increasingly it seems Floss was right. That he'd always been right. She is not one of those women who was glad to have the war behind her, who feels the tug of children and nurturing. She's tried so hard to do both, to manage the widening gap between motherhood and vocation. But it's endless, feeling always as though she's giving short shrift to one or the other.

Penny says, "Once upon a time there was a cat," and points at a ginger cat sunning itself in the lane.

Alec says, "That's right, princess. And what was it doing?"

"It was in the road," Penny says. She frowns, concentrating, then beams happily. "Wearing pajamas."

Alec stops in his tracks, his face alight with love and joy as he looks down at her. "Oh, that's lovely," he says. "What color pajamas?"

They walk away ahead of June, Penny still talking about the cat, and for just an instant June almost cannot breathe. She loves them so much, and yet. They are a pair, Alec and Penny, a unit. And more and more she feels that she is not part of it. The tether connecting her husband and her daughter does not quite extend to her, and she feels its absence as if it were the sword of Damocles suspended overhead.

"Wait for me," she calls, and when they stop, the two of them hand in hand, both of them golden-haired in the sun, telling stories as if it's a language only they can speak, June thinks her heart might break.

1959, *Halifax*

The aurora paints the night more often than not, greens and magentas curtaining down from the heavens. Alec spends most of his time on the forecastle, watching the sun sink into the great basin of the sea before the ship, the pink foam of cloud hovering overhead. He's midway through the crossing from Leith by way of Liverpool, and the world is all ocean. Pods of porpoise cleave the ship's wake, throwing sunlight like pennies against the hull. The RMS *Highlander* is Livingstone & Gray's first ocean liner, and Alec loves every inch of her—the clean white lines and perfect crimson of the stacks, the fin of the bow slicing through the water, they all work on him like a spell. For years now he has watched her come together in the shipyard, always thinking that if he were to board her, take her out into the world, it would be like sailing again on the RMS *Jaipur*.

It's not, though. Not at all. Even when the whole sky is broken open with stars, the constellations anchored in the darkness, this crossing is not that crossing. And now, halfway through, he no longer wants it to be. It's a relief to have it be neither the bewildering voyage from Bombay to London nor the very different return from Odessa. Both sailings had been fraught with not knowing what would come next, ships and crossings as clear as hinges linking one part of his life to the next. His life had changed so much between the first crossing and the second, and since his return from the war there have been other enormous shifts—chief among them his reunion with June and the eventual arrival of Penny.

He misses them more than he can say, his brilliant girls, and being away from them pulls at him in ways he doesn't like. But it helps that the ship is his domain. His floating kingdom. He knows every paisley in the carpet, every whorl in the oak of the banisters. He knows that the pulleys on the fourth starboard lifeboat are inclined to squeak when the wind comes straight from the north.

Livingstone & Gray have not been in the habit of ocean liners—tugs and dredgers have been their bread and butter for a generation, and the *Highlander* is a departure from their history. And she is his. This grand ship has been his since Roland Livingstone himself called Alec into his cluttered office and asked him to try his hand at a design after all those years of his informal apprenticeship to the design team. And Alec had thought of every ship he'd ever laid his hands on, every boat whose hull he'd patted. And somewhere at the intersection of those memories, midwifed by the design group, the *Highlander* had been born. She's small for a liner, a kestrel skimming the sea where the newest Cunard ships are more like eagles. When she hits the waves broadside, she balances like a frigate on the water.

He's standing on the deck one night, still dressed for dinner and watching the moon lay a track on the waves, when one of the junior navigation officers comes up alongside him.

"Good evening, Mr. Tremayne," Alec says. He gestures out at the water. "Lot of ice."

"Yes, sir," Tremayne says. "Thought we'd miss them with the southern route, even this time of year, but . . ."

Alec nods. They had wanted the ship to skim across the Atlantic like a skipped stone, three days from Liverpool to Halifax. But icebergs have slowed their progress, calving off the coast of Greenland like monstrous sharks, and if Alec is honest with himself, this way is better. He's never seen anything like the looming crowns of blue and green and white or the underwater reefs the helmsman works to avoid.

Tremayne says, "You were in the war, sir?"

"I was," Alec says. "Flew planes for a bit." An incomplete truth, but what else is there to say? He looks at his hands, left resting atop the right on the railing. He still sometimes yearns for that feeling of being aloft in his crate.

Tremayne nods. "Navy." He points off to the north. "Sunk a U-boat off the Faroes on a night like this."

"Good man," Alec says, impressed. "That was a bloody hard show."

"Chow is a lot better this time across," Tremayne says, and laughs. "But you know how it is, you're out with your mates, you and them against the enemy . . ."

"I do," Alec says. But there is only so much thinking of those days before he comes up short against the memory of Charlie's plane shattering against the rocks, or Smasher dead in the German mud. He tries to concentrate instead on what Tremayne said about food—best to think on the vol-au-vent and Charlotte royale he'd eaten earlier that evening, on the dot of jam Penny had by her nose when he'd hugged her goodbye last week.

"Well," Tremayne says, "best get back to rounds. Have a good night, sir." He touches the brim of his cap and sets off around the curve of the forecastle. Alec watches him go, glad both for the moment of connection and the quiet that follows it, and then turns his gaze back to the sea.

There is nothing he would have liked more than to bring his girls with him for the *Highlander*'s maiden voyage, and when Livingstone & Gray had first proposed that he make the crossing, Alec had started to daydream of ways to make it happen. But then the trip had changed, a two-day pause in Halifax blossoming into almost three months taking the measure of the Livingstone & Gray offices there with the aim of finding a new project. Alec had hesitated—it was a long time to be away from his home, away from Penny and June and Ursa, away from everything . . . But the RMS *Highlander* was his ship, and he had worked for the company for more than a decade now, building himself a place there. And really, ten weeks is not such a long stretch in the great scheme of things. Penny is in school, and Mrs. Nesbit will run the household as competently as ever, whether Alec's there or not.

A lec is waiting to disembark in Halifax, looking out over the barely ordered chaos of passengers unloading and the swirl of dark water, gulls swooping and screaming overhead, when Tremayne finds him and hands him a slim oilskin packet of letters.

"Came by air mail," Tremayne says. "Anyone meeting you, once you're through customs?"

"No," Alec says, thinking of the way it had felt to see June waiting for him on the dock when he'd come back from Odessa, her face open and hopeful. He had not dared expect her, and yet, there she'd been. He looks down at the gangplank, wishing she and Penny were at the other end of it.

"Well," Tremayne says, tapping the brim of his hat, "I wish you a good stay in Halifax."

"Thank you," Alec says. He pats the railing fondly, tucks the packet of letters into his inside breast pocket, and moves toward the gangplank with a last wave at Tremayne.

. . .

It feels like no time at all before a taxi deposits Alec at his lodgings, a yellow-brick house across the street from Point Pleasant Park in Halifax's South End. He raises the brass bull's head that acts as a knocker and lets it fall against the door.

An older woman answers the door almost immediately, her eyes a cloudy green behind glasses. "You must be Mr. Oswin. I'm Mrs. Carter."

"Yes, Alec Oswin. Very nice to meet you."

"The harbormaster's boy let us know your ship had docked. I'm pleased you found your way here. Do come in." Her voice is round with just the hint of an Irish lilt. "May I take your coat?"

"Grand, thanks," Alec says. He glances around the foyer, a tidy, welcoming space with pictures of the Pope and Queen Elizabeth on the wall. Ahead of him the foyer opens up into a sitting room, where he can just see the ornate mantelpiece of the fireplace and the gleaming brass candlesticks centered there, and more of the rich blue-and-gold carpet that sinks beneath his feet. "You have a beautiful home, Mrs. Carter."

"Oh, thank you." She clasps her hands. "Well, I'm glad enough to be taking another man from Livingstone and Gray as a boarder. We were sorry to lose Mr. Lurie back to Scotland."

Alec says, "He couldn't say enough good things about boarding here."

"I'm so very glad to hear that," she says. "Now then, you can leave your suitcase here for the moment, all right?"

Alec sets down his valise and follows Mrs. Carter. In the sitting room, French doors opposite the fireplace lead to a wide patio that stretches out into the garden beyond.

"Oh, that's awfully nice," Alec says, "having the park out one door and your garden out the other."

Mrs. Carter's face lights up. "Just wait until we start having more blooms, Mr. Oswin. We've had our daffodils, you can just see them, there," she says, gesturing outside, "and the snowdrops, of course, but we're right on the edge with so many others."

"I'll look forward to that." And he will, although it won't be his own garden, which will be gangbusters in the Edinburgh spring any day now.

Mrs. Carter nods and leads him to the dining room, pointing out the kitchen as they make their way back to the foyer. "My daughter-in-law, Maeve, prepares most of our meals. She's an excellent cook."

"Wonderful," Alec says. After a week of the fancy food aboard the *Highlander*, something homey sounds like just the ticket. He follows her up the stairs, where she pauses in front of a wall hung with pictures. She points to a photo of a young family standing in front of the fireplace downstairs: the young man with curly dark hair, his arm around a fair-haired girl holding an infant. "That's Maeve and my grandson Cullen," she says. "He's ten now. And that was my son Desmond, God rest him."

God, she's lost a son. "I am so awfully sorry." Alec regards the photo again, a pang in his chest—they look so happy.

"Thank you." Her hand comes up to touch the cross she wears on a long chain as she gathers herself. "In any event, your room is just here. The bath is down the hall."

"This will do very nicely," Alec says. He takes in the tidy room with its pale, rosy wallpaper, and smiles at Mrs. Carter.

"Very good," she says. "Dinner is at seven thirty, in the dining room. Breakfast is somewhat less formal. I ask that if you're going to miss a meal you let me know so that we may plan accordingly. Also, we lock the front door at eleven, so do please be back by then if you go out in the evening. And I ask that you do not bring guests back with you. I like to keep a quiet home, especially with my grandson here."

"I quite understand. I have a little girl myself, back in Edinburgh. Penny."

"What a sweet name," Mrs. Carter says. "You must miss her."

"I do, yes," Alec says. "Awfully. She's only just six."

"Such a lovely age," she says. "Well, I'll leave you to settle in. Please let either Maeve or myself know if you need anything at all."

Alec says, "I shall. Thank you."

She closes the door behind her, and Alec looks at his watch—just past five now, plenty of time to settle in and wash up before the evening meal. He puts away his few belongings and sits down with the oilskin packet in the wooden chair at the writing desk under the window. Across the street, the low stone wall that borders the park has a gap in it, and he can just see the trail leading down into the trees. A stand of pines towers over the wall, a small red squirrel chittering in a high branch. It's so bucolic, but somewhere not too far away, he can hear the particular curl of a freight train's bellowing horn. For an unsettling moment his pulse races, his memory filling with the train that took him from Italy to Germany and the stench of too many frightened men wedged into a single car. He closes his eyes and counts to ten, then counts roses on the wallpaper until present prevails over past.

He unwinds the waxed laces holding the packet together and puts aside the thick envelope with his name on it in June's precise writing, saving the best for last. There's a letter from Roger, now retired to a horse farm in Kenya and hoping to come to Edinburgh next year. Alec's pleased—he hasn't seen his uncle in years, and it's good to get caught up. On Roger's infrequent visits, it's a delight to watch him with Penny, whom he adores. Then at last he turns to the letter from June.

Dear Alec,

I hope this finds you well, and that you have arrived safely in Nova Scotia. I imagine it must have been an incredible voyage! We miss you—the house is quiet without you, and Ursa doesn't quite seem to know what to do with herself. Penny, in a rather sweet effort to help, has been telling her your bear stories—or, rather, Penny's versions of your bear stories. It's quite charming, as you can imagine, and I believe it's helping both of them.

The garden has started blooming. That crocus border you put in is going to be a glory soon, and Penny has been gathering marsh violets when we take Ursa to the pond. It's a shame you're missing these, but there will be roses when you come home, and likely sweet pea blossom as well. I'll look after the garden as well as I can while you're gone, but I expect your flowers will be pleased to see you home. Still, God knows I've needed the distraction—I've put in for that new Reader position the department has opened for next year, the one we talked about last spring. It would be quite a feather in my cap, but what a tiresome, nerve-wracking process!

We had tea last week with Parvati and the children (Sanjay has not come home from London yet). Did you know that when Penny is with her friends she sounds much more the wee Scot than when she is with us? I suppose you must. It always catches my attention, though, watching her move so easily into their world. She is such a clever child, and so adaptable.

In any event, we hope you had a lovely trip, and that your work in Halifax goes brilliantly.

Stay safe, Alec.

Love,
June

Alec smiles to himself and runs his fingers over the careful printing, marveling as always at June's ability to write in perfectly straight lines on unruled paper. He brings the letter to his nose, wishing he could breathe in the scent of her. There's so much he's missed already, and for just a moment he wishes so fiercely to be home that the sprawl of weeks ahead of him seems impossibly daunting.

After a moment, he opens the second note enclosed in June's letter, and his heart pangs against his ribs at the sight of the smudged, childish scrawl with its careful uppercase letters and the false starts of misspelled words.

Dear Daddy,

Mummy says right now you are on your ship in the North Atlantic. She showed me on a map the way your ship would go, and each day we are going to look at the map and try to mark where you are. Also we are crossing off days on the calendar but there are so many days left! At school we are learning about Robert the Bruce. Mrs. Nesbit told me a spider helped him save Scotland. Are there spiders where you're going?

Love Penny

He sits for a long time looking at his letters, missing June and Penny like air.

In the dining room that evening he finds Mrs. Carter looking through a French textbook with Cullen. A loaf of soda bread waits with butter and a jar of jam on a cutting board at the foot of the table. A covered bowl sits near the table's center. Metal crutches lean into the corner beyond the table.

Mrs. Carter says, "Ah, good evening, Mr. Oswin. This is my grandson Cullen. Cullen, this is Mr. Oswin."

"It's very nice to meet you, Cullen." Alec puts out his hand.

"Likewise," Cullen says. He hesitates briefly before flattening his palm against the uneven landscape of Alec's, and Alec realizes too late that he may be putting Cullen in an awkward position.

Alec smiles and leans close with a conspiratorial smile. "Don't mind the hand—ran into some trouble in the war."

Before Cullen can respond, a young woman steps into the room carrying a ceramic serving dish—Maeve, Cullen's mother. The young widow.

"Oh, Mr. Oswin," Mrs. Carter says, standing and moving the textbook to the sideboard, "this is my daughter-in-law, Maeve."

"It's lovely to meet you," Maeve says, her blue eyes crinkling at the corners when she smiles.

"It's a pleasure," Alec says. "This all looks wonderful." He gestures at the salmon she's brought out, the smells of butter and lemon rising along with the rich scent of the fish, and the fish itself surrounded by new potatoes flecked with parsley.

"It's Friday," Cullen says dourly. "That's why there's fish."

Maeve laughs as she begins plating the food. "Don't fuss. Tomorrow I'll be making you something you like better."

Cullen says, "Well, you could hardly make something I like less," and grins at his mother.

"In that case perhaps I'll be giving it a try," Maeve says wryly.

Alec thanks her as she passes him his plate, and she smiles at him before serving the rest of the table. Then she turns to Cullen. "Will you lead us in a blessing, love?" She folds her hands and bows her head.

Mrs. Carter and Cullen follow suit. Alec hesitates, then bundles his hands in his lap, touched by the easy humor and familiarity woven through their exchanges.

Cullen clears his throat. "Bless us, O Lord, and these Thy gifts, which we are about to receive from Thy bounty. Through Christ our Lord, amen." He pauses. "And bless Dad and Uncle Sean and Granddad too, Lord." He crosses himself.

"My sweet lad." Maeve brushes the dark curls back from her boy's forehead, then turns to Alec. "So, Mr. Oswin, is this your first time in Halifax?"

"Yes," he replies. "So far it seems like a lovely place."

"Oh, 'tis," she agrees, slicing into the soda bread. The crust gives way with a hearty tearing sound. She chooses the thickest slice and slathers it carefully with butter and jam, then slides it onto Cullen's plate. In a soft voice she says to him, "Extra jam for my best boy."

Alec glances down at the table—Cullen is only a bit older than he was when the cholera struck, and the unabashed affection with which Maeve and her son comport themselves tugs at him.

"The fish is delicious," Alec says. "The peas as well. That's mint?"

Maeve dips her head in acknowledgment. "Yes," she says. "It's my mam's way, with mint fresh from the garden. I'm pleased you like it."

"It's awfully good," Alec says. "I don't have much in the way of herbs in my garden at home. Rather feel like I ought to, now."

"Just a set of pots will do you," Maeve says. Alec gives this some thought, asking questions and taking in her answers as they eat, Mrs. Carter chiming in here and there with her own ideas on gardening.

After a while, Cullen speaks up. "Gram says you came by ship, Mr. Oswin. What was it like?"

"It was splendid, crossing the whole of the Atlantic like that." Alec goes on, happy to be telling them the story of his crossing—icebergs and the rough cast of the waves against the ship, the steady soar of an albatross in the Georges Bank.

"It's quite a journey," Maeve says, during a pause. "All that ice. It was like nothing I'd ever dreamed of."

"I wonder if you came by the southern route as well," Alec says.

"I believe so." Maeve's forehead creases. "Beautiful, most of it, except a bit of a storm near the end."

"Just a wee young thing when Des brought you home," Mrs. Carter says affectionately.

"And fat with that one," Maeve says, her eyes gleaming as she looks at Cullen. He blushes, just a bit, and she puts an arm across his shoulders in a quick hug. "Eat your fish, then."

Cullen shakes his head. "I can't. It's looking at me."

Alec chuckles, then reaches over and turns the dish. "There. Now it's watching me instead."

Cullen laughs. Maeve's mouth quirks up at the corner.

"Speaking of watching things, I didn't see very much of the city on the way over," Alec says. "We're fairly close to the harbor here, aren't we?"

Mrs. Carter nods. "When the wind is right we can sometimes hear the tugboat captains talking back and forth with their ships' horns."

"I'm going to have a ship and see the whole world when I grow up," Cullen says. "London and everywhere. Like John Cabot."

Maeve's face lights up as she looks at Cullen. "That's a grand notion."

For dessert Maeve brings out a small cheesecake decorated with strawberries, Mrs. Carter following her with coffee, cream, and sugar on a round silver tray. When Alec tastes the cheesecake, the sweetness melts against his tongue. Mrs. Nesbit leaves a traybake or some other dessert fairly often, but nothing quite so lush as this.

"This is excellent," he says to Maeve. She smiles.

Cullen takes a bite of cheesecake and chews thoughtfully, quiet for a moment. "So, do you work with the boats at Livingstone and Gray?"

"I do indeed. In fact, I worked with the design chaps on the *Highlander*. More physical than it sounds, mind." Alec pauses, remembering the early days of the ship coming together. "To make sure the design is coming together you have to monkey about in its bones, you know? A ship like that, it doesn't have riggings and so on like a pirate ship, something to climb in, exactly, but in the beginning especially you spend a good bit of time dangling from a rope with the shipwright, checking the lines. Make sure it feels right and all that."

"That's amazing," Cullen says, his eyes wide. He pauses. "Did you work with ships in the war, too? Were you in the navy?"

"No," Alec says, "I was a pilot. RAF."

"Well, you're in it now," Maeve says to Alec with a laugh.

"Oh, gosh!" Cullen exclaims. "Did you fly Spitfires?"

Alec warms to Cullen's enthusiasm. "Bristol Beaufighters. Quite a lot bigger than a Spitfire, and two engines rather than the one. And not nearly so nimble."

Cullen's eyes gleam. "Were they single-seaters, too?"

"No, there were three of us to a plane—pilot, gunner, navigator," Alec says. He hesitates. All the glad memories of the camaraderie will never not be confused with the loss. "Got rather crowded."

Maeve says, "Cullen's been mad for planes since we saw a demonstration from the base at Shearwater."

"I was like that about cars when I was his age. And motorbikes. Planes came later." Alec beams at Cullen, thinking of those long-ago afternoons with his uncle, the sounds and smells of the race-warmed cars. The echoes never really go away, do they? And now here they are awakened by this bright-eyed boy in Canada, of all places.

Mrs. Carter says, "I don't know how he keeps them all straight, honestly." She shakes her head fondly at her grandson.

"The show at the base was super," Cullen says. "There were so many kinds of planes—Spitfires and Hurricanes and all, and a lot of bombers, and some planes from the Great War. We saw an aerobatics demonstration, too!"

"Oh, yes, I expect that was quite a show." The echoes keep coming, but there's a lightness in his chest, too. "You have a favorite?"

Cullen tilts his head thoughtfully. "It's all of them," he says at last, "but I liked the fighters better than the bombers. How fast they were."

Alec nods. "The fighter planes make quite a racket, don't they? Especially a whole flight of them at once?"

"It was brilliant," Cullen says happily.

"It was a right shebeen," Maeve says, her voice dry and affectionate. "Now, lad, it's coming up on time to say good night."

"Can I show Mr. Oswin my planes?"

Maeve says, "In the morning, perhaps. I expect he'll be needing some quiet tonight, after his travels."

The boy frowns a bit. "But, Mum . . . I'll be quick."

Maeve stands, her eyes warm as she regards her son. "Cullen, if there is one thing I know for certain, it's that there's no quick with you and your models. Perhaps tomorrow."

"First thing," Alec says. He'd be happy to look at the planes now, but he doesn't want to overstep. "I'd love to see them."

Maeve mouths a thank-you at Alec over Cullen's head, her hand on the boy's shoulder. "It's time we were off, lad," she says to Cullen. He makes a face but doesn't protest as she hands him his crutches.

Mrs. Carter steps around the table to kiss Cullen's forehead. "Sleep well, lovey."

Cullen kisses his grandmother's cheek, then turns, pausing with his elbows angled out from his crutches, his left foot limp beneath the stiff braces. "See you in the morning, Mr. Oswin."

"Good night, Cullen." Alec gets to his feet, moved by Cullen's seeming nonchalance. "I'll see you and your planes tomorrow."

The next morning, it's a moment before he knows where he is, why the room isn't moving with the sea, but then he soon remembers. Sunlight slices through the curtains and sets the pines and maples outside aglow. He stays still, listening to the swell of unfamiliar noises ringing through the morning—the house shifting as it warms, the distant thunk of the boiler in the cellar.

The air is layered with the wafting scent of baking spices, and his belly rumbles with a confusing wash of memory and hunger, of missing Cook and the vicarage and the days when he and June were still so young—before the war and his hands and the rest of it. He lets the feelings settle, and he gets up to begin his day.

Alec performs his morning ablutions, washing and shaving carefully, and wincing when the hot water pipe clangs with use. He dresses quickly and heads for the stairs. In the corridor he stops again at the family photos—in the light of day, the picture of Maeve and Cullen with Desmond plucks at him.

In the outsized kitchen, Maeve is setting down a rasher of bacon and a carton of eggs, two round cakes cooling on a rack on the counter beyond her. Cullen sits at the kitchen table, a newspaper spread out in front of him dotted with paint and glue. He's squinting down at a tin airplane, dabbing paint carefully into the markings on its wings.

"Good morning," Alec says. He smiles at Cullen, taking the seat across from him, eager to resume their conversation about planes. "Fine-looking Spitfire you've got there."

Cullen grins at him, holding up the plane. "It's my newest."

Maeve says, "Would you like some coffee, Mr. Oswin?"

"I would love some," he says. "Thank you. And please call me Alec."

She reaches across to the rack of mugs warming above the Aga and pours him a cup. Alec takes a long swallow, grateful for its warmth. It may be spring, and Halifax may benefit from the mild coastal climate, but that doesn't stop the distinct nip in the air this morning.

Alec lifts his face, basking in the scent of ginger and a bit of citrus. "The cake smells marvelous."

Maeve sips at her own coffee and smiles. "I made one for the bazaar at St. Columba's this afternoon. The other we'll be having for the household."

Alec's mouth waters hopefully, and he eyes the cakes again. All of this reminds him so much of his childhood in Fenbourne. There had been bazaars and jumbles at St. Anne's too, part of the flurry of spring festivals dotted through the Fenlands. One year there had been a troupe of Molly dancers in from Suffolk, and twice he had won a silly trinket for June at the fair. "The bazaar sounds a jolly time. Will there be a coconut shy, things like that?"

"There will be. All manner of craic through the afternoon. All in good fun, though, right, lad?" Maeve tousles Cullen's dark hair, then sets to work with the bacon, humming quietly to herself. It's a tune Alec doesn't recognize, perhaps something from her Irish childhood. He sips his coffee, his mind whirling with quiet questions.

Cullen rolls the Spitfire across the newspaper, adjusting the wheels until they move more smoothly, then holds it up so the light through the kitchen window catches it. "I think this is nearly finished."

Alec says, "You've done well with the markings."

Maeve calls over her shoulder, "What will you be building next, Cullen?"

"I don't know," he says. He flies the Spitfire through the airspace above the table, thinking, then glances at Alec. "I don't have a Beaufighter. Mostly just Spitfires and Hurricanes. And a Lancaster."

Alec considers this. "I suppose Beaus are a bit harder to find."

"I suppose so," Cullen says. "American planes are easy to find. I have a Mustang upstairs."

Alec asks, "You only work with Allied planes?"

Cullen shrugs. "So far. I have a friend at school who has a Messerschmitt and a Stuka and a Zero, and sometimes we have dogfights."

"Very good, as long as you win."

Cullen smiles. "Were you in the Battle of Britain?"

"Yes. Night sorties mostly." He shrugs, trying to cover the shiver that rises in him, thinking about those nights.

Cullen tilts his head, thinking. "But . . . how did you know where you were? Or where the other planes were? If it was dark? Did you have to black out your lights?"

"Well," Alec says, "at first it was quite difficult, of course. But you can steer by the stars, and after a while we had planes with radar, and that changed everything."

"Like a bat," Cullen says.

"Yes, I expect so." Those early nights, flying blind in the dark . . . He's still not sure how to measure the astonishment of flight against the fear.

"Did you ever shoot anyone down?"

"Heavens, Cullen," Maeve says briskly, turning to give him a stern look. "I'm sorry, Mr. Oswin."

Alec shakes his head. "No, quite all right." He looks down at his hands, then meets Cullen's gaze. "Yes. A few German planes." Cullen stares, and Alec continues quietly. "Terrible responsibility, really. I'm glad to be shut of it. But I miss the flying. The sound of a Beaufighter's engines is quite unlike anything else I know."

Cullen ponders this. "I heard Spitfires at Shearwater. They're awfully loud. Wouldn't a Beaufighter be even louder, if there are two engines?"

"Considerably, yes, but the way a Spitfire echoes when it climbs is something else entirely." He looks at the airplane again. How many Spitfires had he seen over the years? There had been a squadron of them at RAF Manston, and he remembers them shredded on the runways by the Luftwaffe's relentless raids just as well as he remembers them airborne over the North Sea, glittering fiercely against the enemy. It's disorienting to think of them—he had known, sailing across the Atlantic to Nova Scotia, that he would miss Penny and June and the overgrown back garden and Ursa and the rest of it. But he had not for a moment expected to find himself missing the airfields of England and Algeria, the gleaming snouts of planes waiting in a row.

Maeve puts a pot of jam on the table. Her voice gentle, almost as if she can feel how unsettled he is, says, "Mr. Oswin, will you take your breakfast now?"

Alec smiles at her gratefully. "That would be grand, please."

She nods and turns her attention to the cooker. A moment later she sets down a plate of bacon and eggs with a thick slice of toast in front of each of them.

"Thank you," Alec says. The bacon is thick and crisp, the scent of it intoxicating, and he tucks in enthusiastically, happy a moment later to emulate Cullen's eager spreading of butter and jam on his toast.

After a few minutes Cullen looks up from his breakfast. "Mr. Oswin? Were you ever . . ." He glances briefly at his mother and lowers his voice a bit. "Did they ever shoot you down?"

Maeve turns, her lips pursed. "Cullen, lad . . ."

"It's fine, really," Alec says, folding his hands together and trying to corral the memories. "Had a couple of bad moments, yes. Inevitable, really, during wartime."

Cullen hesitates, his brows furrowing. "Well. I was wondering about your hands, what you said last night about the war."

Maeve raises her eyes to the ceiling. "Cullen, you're a brilliant boy and my whole heart, but your questions . . ." She shakes her head. "I'm so sorry, Mr. Oswin."

"No, it's quite all right. They're fine questions." He smiles at Cullen. "They got me over the Mediterranean, and I had a bit of a job getting free of the wreck. Never healed quite right, but I'm lucky it wasn't worse."

Cullen says, "Oh, yes, I see." He takes a breath, shifting in his chair. "I had polio. That's why . . ." He gestures at the crutches. "My dad, too."

Ah, Christ. A vague memory snakes in—Bombay, the night clotted with smoke and rot, his own mother's face taut with grief and glassy with fever as she tells him that the cholera has taken his father. He rubs his hand across his face, banishing the memory, and gazes at Cullen and Maeve. His chest aches when he sees the grief's shadow on her face, and the clear light of her love for Cullen. He can't begin to conceive what that must have been like for her, how afraid she must have been. God. "That must have been unspeakably awful for you. For both of you," he adds, meeting Maeve's eyes. "I'm terribly sorry."

Cullen, his voice small, says, "I don't really remember. I was only three."

Maeve offers a sad smile to Alec. She lays her hand across Cullen's. "Your grandmother will be in soon, love. She'll not be wanting to hear about this."

"No, I know." Cullen pushes the Spitfire along the edge of the table toward Alec. "After breakfast do you want to see my other planes?"

"I'd like that very much."

Cullen darts a look at Alec and turns back to his mother. "Can Mr. Oswin come to the bazaar with us?"

Maeve says, "I'm sure he's got any number of other things to do, Cullen."

"No, I'd love to, really," Alec says, smiling. "I haven't been to a bazaar since I was a boy."

Cullen grins happily, and Maeve rumples his hair. "Go on, then, and show Mr. Oswin your airfield."

She hands him the crutches, and he gets to his feet, watching Alec over his shoulder to make sure he's getting up from the table, too.

Maeve watches Cullen go, then turns to Alec, her expression warm. "Perhaps there'll be a bit of extra cake for you later, Mr. Oswin." Her eyes twinkle as she adds, "Alec."

A week into his visit, Alec is more at home in Halifax than he had expected. Most of his time is taken up at Livingstone & Gray, whose offices occupy the upstairs of a cedar-sided block of a building just past the ferry landing, but the routines of the Carter household have enveloped him as well. Ever since that first afternoon and the bazaar at St. Columba's, out in the pale spring light with Cullen and Maeve, Alec has felt completely comfortable with them. Watching Cullen be absorbed into a pack of boys, one of them with a stunted arm that makes Alec wonder whether he too had been stricken with polio, had warmed him; it had seemed like a privilege to be part of the everyday with them. He had not minded keeping pace with Maeve as she moved through the crowd, and although she hadn't talked much, the quiet had been companionable and easy.

That camaraderie grows stronger as the weeks pass, as does his sense of the city. By the end of Alec's fifth week in Halifax, the round front window like a giant eye regarding the shipyard's domain and the staid blue-and-silver L&G sign mark the top of what he thinks of as his Halifax, just as the Carter house and Point Pleasant Park mark the bottom. He has his patch, as it were, the part of the city where he knows the babies by sight and the dogs by name. He knows which greengrocer Maeve is talking about if she asks him to pick something up on his way back from the office, and what the old woman down the road most wants to hear about her rose garden when he passes by every morning.

It's reassuring to have his routines, to know which evenings he will write letters home to his girls and which days he is most likely to get the packet from Edinburgh. Those letters are his tether, despite all those moments he's missing, quotidian though they may be, and each one a thorn in his heart. June's messages bring him news of Penny's spring concert at school and the related May Day revels, a loose tile on the roof, a branch come off the pear tree, the boy down the road sick with measles. When he hears that Mrs. Nesbit has slipped on a loose flagstone in the garden and sprained her ankle, Alec has a wave of guilt, as if his absence from Edinburgh is to blame for everything. And Penny's sporadic notes build in layers in his chest as well—a few lines here and there about Ursa or school, or Penny's fun with her friends. There are also mentions now and then of "Uncle Floss," who confusingly seems never to appear in June's letters. He's told his daughter a bit about Cullen, and twice she mentions him in her responses. And it warms Alec each time as he thinks about a vague fantasy of a friendship for Cullen and Penny, never mind how illogical the idea is, or how implausible.

He misses home. Stopping to have a natter with the stately old Labrador at the chemist's down the road is not really a substitute for Ursa, but every bit helps. Too, he feels his place at the Carter house. There had been that first rush of activity—not even twenty-four hours in and he'd had two meals and that glory of a church bazaar with Cullen and Maeve—and since then he has felt increasingly like this is home too, in a way. He has his breakfast with Cullen every day, the two of them talking about airplanes or dogs or a host of other things, and dines with the family in the evenings. Thrice now he has cut the grass for Mrs. Carter on a weekend morning, because it's one less thing she has to pay a neighborhood boy to do, even for a few weeks. His days are square and secure, the march of time forward sometimes confusing as it moves him deeper into his Halifax visit, deeper into this family and his growing attachment to Cullen and Maeve, and always closer to the day he boards the ship that will take him home.

During the week, he takes the trolleybus to the waterfront and the alcove he shares with a gruff pipe-smoking Quebecois whose blueprints and sketches litter the room like palm leaves. Most days, Alec takes his lunch at the Everard, a shabby little diner not far from the wharf. It's the kind of place that must once have catered to stevedores and shipwrights, now more likely to feed men like him stepping away from the office for an hour in the middle of the day. He finds a certain comfort in the worn banquettes in the booths, and the nicks in the long countertop that runs the length of the building. They remind him of the pubs near the shipyard at Leith, the scores of lunches and pints with Sanjay and the other men from the office, and there is a quiet joy in being somewhere familiar.

Today, though, he and Armand, the draftsman, are meant to be settling the question of Livingstone & Gray's next build, which has been a slow process at best. But now, after weeks of forms carved into paper with a T square and a thick black wax pencil, Armand's fragrant pipe smoke thick in the air, they've found the gem they're looking for: a sloop that will race along the cresting waves like a Thoroughbred.

At lunchtime, Alec makes his way to one of the creaky wooden benches that sit along the docks, waving off the pigeons and gulls hoping for a prize. He regards the birds warily—Maeve has packed him a lunch of leftover meat pasties, their crimped edges a rich brown, all of it flaking away in his hands. If he were a bird he would want this too, but he's made the mistake before of throwing something to the gulls. They'll grant no quarter and make a dreadful racket besides.

As with so much else Maeve has done in the past weeks, the pasties make Alec a bit homesick, if that's the word. It's less missing Edinburgh, or even his family, and more a nostalgic longing for his mother, or for those quiet afternoons with Cook and June at the vicarage. Of wondering what would have been without the war, or without his particular war, without the loss of the vicarage and his and June's families, all of it contained in the way a layer of crust peels away when he bites it. It's a form of magic, really, the conjuring, the spells woven through Maeve's baking, as if she were a wisewoman of old, or a benevolent sorceress.

He finishes his lunch, the gulls swooping and screaming overhead, barking back at the breeze. Alec pauses and looks out over the water, where a seal is bobbing in the light current between two fishing trawlers in their berths. He watches until the seal dives again, and then Alec packs up to go back to the office.

1959, *Edinburgh*

I t's inevitable, really, that Penny should be so enthralled by Wojtek, the famous Syrian bear now living out his "retirement" from the Polish Army at the Edinburgh Zoo. Nearly every weekend this summer, June has taken Penny for her pilgrimage to see Wojtek wave to the crowd and eat biscuits. Penny is convinced the bear is under an enchantment, and so she tells him stories about her family, a patchwork of fact and fiction. All of this June watches with her heart alight, even while it reminds her of the ways that Penny is so much more like Alec than like her.

When Alec had first floated the idea of his being gone for so long, it had alarmed June. And truth told, the first few weeks had been hard. It's embarrassing to admit, even to herself, how much she has come to rely on Alec and Mrs. Nesbit to manage nearly everything about the household. Even when Alec sailed for Canada, she had not filled the vast space he'd left behind as she ought to have done; she had asked more of Mrs. Nesbit. Worst of all, it had taken a calamity to make her see what she was doing—a loose stone in the garden, and Mrs. Nesbit catching her foot on it and taking a tumble. She hadn't been badly injured, thank God, but a sprained ankle was nothing to scoff at, and June, though anxious about taking on the household by herself, had of course told the older woman to stay off her foot and rest at home.

But with Alec in Canada and Mrs. Nesbit with her family in Oxgangs for the past fortnight, June has had more opportunities to spend time with Penny on somewhat different terms than Alec's presence allows for. They've found more small bonds—the strolls through Morningside to the market, the shared excitement when they come to the bookshop halfway between home and the teashop, even the way Penny has started taking just one lump of sugar in her tea, emulating June.

Today, with the midsummer sun still aloft in the late afternoon, and a breeze coming down off the crags and stirring the leaves of the sycamores and rowans that fill the zoo's landscape, June feels as relaxed as she has in a while. Even in summer her work at the university has been more of a trial than usual—after months of rumors, a Reader position had finally opened in the department, and she and her colleagues had fallen headlong into the scrum of competition, scrambling to publish more research, line their ducks in a row . . . Next week the chips will fall as they may, and despite knowing quite well how the department operates, an old boys' club as stolid and conservative as any thickly carpeted, pipe-smoke-clogged gentlemen's establishment in London, June is cautiously optimistic. She has better, deeper research than anyone else in Edinburgh—in Scotland, for that matter—and years of building her reputation in Fourier series expansion and the Basel problem.

"Mummy, can we go and see the lambs next?"

June looks down at her daughter, who beams up at her. "Certainly, if you've had enough time with Wojtek."

Penny turns her jacket pockets inside out, looking a bit put upon. "I don't have any treats for him. And last time Uncle Floss said he would bring me a special biscuit, but then he didn't come today."

"He's very busy," June says. "I'm sure he'll bring some another time." She takes Penny's hand, and together they take their leave of Wojtek.

. . .

Mrs. Nesbit returns on Monday, and June watches Penny fall back into their old routines with a bit of a pang. June has done her best with the house itself, but Mrs. Nesbit looks around and sighs once, gently, before setting after the place with her duster and rags. Even Ursa seems to mind the Hoover less when Mrs. Nesbit is running it. And although June has vague misgivings about whether Mrs. Nesbit should be back on her feet and running full tilt, the housekeeper insists she's right as rain.

On the Tuesday June meets with the maths chair, it isn't until she steps back out into the evening, heartsick and frustrated, that she really understands how much she had pinned all her hopes on the new position. She's been climbing the ladder from her days as a graduate assistant and post-graduate fellow until now—Senior Lecturer at the Department of Mathematics, prominent publications and important research in her dossier, years of commendations and favorable notices filed away carefully with an eye toward this next level. And they should have chosen her for the one Reader post, rewarded her efforts with the freedom to focus more on research than instruction, a passel of graduate students at her beck and call . . . But that door is closed, the whole idea abruptly terminated by a single apologetic sentence from the department chair—*You've got everything we want in a Reader, June, but there's your family to think of.*

So Mark Larimer will be the new Reader. He's a boor even at the best of times, and inclined to use his brilliance lazily, riding other scholars' coattails. They've jostled each other for position for a decade. And now he's won.

She glances at her watch—perhaps she's taking a bit of advantage of Mrs. Nesbit's return, but she's got plans for an early dinner with Floss, and he should be here to collect her any moment now. She had hoped it would be a celebratory dinner, but it's just as well Floss will be the first person to whom she vents her frustration. He will understand without all the other layers that Alec would bring to it, all the years of marriage and the decades before that, his ideas about what kind of family they are or are not meant to be.

A silver-blue Bentley glides gently to the curb, and Floss rolls down his window as if she's conjured him. He's smiling, until he sees her face, and then it's as if he's seen the whole situation writ large. His smile vanishes as he opens the door for her. "You look as though you could use a drink."

"I could," she says, climbing in and settling beside him. "Today has not been all I had hoped."

He nods sympathetically, leaning forward to give the driver an address off Leith Street, close to the New Town. As they drive, the familiar gray-green city unfolding alongside the car, June tells him about her meeting. About the chair's decision, and his rationale, her own argument regarding the work she's done, the efforts she's made, the time she's dedicated to the university. By the time they pull up in front of a café, she's run through the whole story. Floss's frown deepens, but he doesn't respond until they're seated at a table in a shadowed corner not far from the front window. Trust Floss to find a table from which he can see everything happening outside but still remain nearly invisible himself.

"Well," he says at last, after he's ordered his usual bottle of Champagne, "I wish it had gone rather differently. Unfortunate they can't see what they've got in you, but one door closes, another opens, all that."

"I'm not sure there are other doors in Edinburgh, just now." She shakes her head. "I really did think they thought better of me than this."

"It's a shame, truly," Floss says, "but of course one can't deny your chair has a point."

June glances at him sharply, startled and a bit dismayed. Floss is the one person she would have expected to always be on her side.

"I've been telling you for a dog's age what I thought you ought to be doing—could be doing—and you've always told me you can't because of your family. And now someone else tells you the same thing . . ." He takes out his cigarette case, selects one, and taps it on the table. "Honestly, Attwell, what did you think would happen, if you kept to the middle of the road like this? For someone like you, the middle can never quite work. You're meant to be committing to something—that's how you are, not someone happy with half measures."

The words feel like a slap, but the worst of it is knowing that he's right. But to admit that means facing reality and putting away the past she misses. All the roads taken or not, the innumerable impossible futures, may as well be smoke and mirrors.

"June, darling," Floss says, his voice conciliatory, as if he's realized how he must sound to her. He reaches across the table, pats her hand like an ancient uncle. "Come with me to Berlin when I go back. It's just getting better, now the Soviets have stepped up their space program."

The rush of excitement is palpable—past or not, that work has an undeniable claim on her. But it's not possible. "Floss—"

He cuts her off. "We could make it work. What if we were to put you on staff at the embassy, bring the family along . . ." The waiter returns and uncorks the bottle, and June and Floss sit quietly while he pours. When the waiter is out of earshot, Floss says, "We need you out there, and you've got the language background. Berlin, Vienna, wherever you like. I expect we could find something for Oswin to do. Be good for the little girl as well, don't you think? Broaden her world a bit?"

She looks down at the table, at the weave of the damask tablecloth, the perfectly aligned silverware. There are patterns everywhere, and nobody sees them better than she does. She takes a breath. "It seems nearly impossible."

Floss lights his cigarette and shrugs philosophically. "The same was said about many far greater obstacles. And there's always a place for the best. Think about it, will you?"

June nods. It is such a boon to hear, but it hurts too, having what she wants almost within reach like this. Floss grins and raises his glass in a toast. "To your glorious future, whatever it entails."

"Thank you," June says. She clinks her glass to his, and they drink.

"Lovely stuff," he says, eyeing the bubbles. "At any rate, how is Oswin liking Canada?"

"He seems very settled in," June responds. Floss raises an eyebrow, but she doesn't elaborate.

"Speaking of the New World, I expect you remember Wendy Fairchild?"

"Of course," June says, with the usual pang of missing Wendy and the work they did together for so long. She takes refuge in another sip of her drink.

"She's been in Hong Kong for an age," he says, "but she's just been transferred to Buenos Aires, our embassy there. Must keep track of the Peronists and runaway Nazis and whatnot."

With the university feeling much less now like somewhere she might ever belong, the lure of everything Wendy is experiencing—and everything Floss has ever offered June—tugs hard at June's sense of purpose and her need to be *doing* something. "I expect she's brilliant there," she says, trying not to let the new layer of resentment and confusion show.

Floss nods with a smug smile. "Quite."

"I'm glad," she says. She takes another sip. With any luck the evening can be salvaged, and to that end she asks Floss if he's read the latest responses to Kolmogorov's solution to the Hilbert problems. It's a relief when he leans in seamlessly to her change of topic.

June wakes the next morning disoriented and tired, and that overcast feeling sticks with her all day, even when her return to the maths department is less jarring than she had feared. One of the junior lecturers gives her a sympathetic *Hard luck, June*, when she passes his office, but for the most part everyone seems not to even notice. And, while the lack of fuss makes some of this easier, it also makes her wonder how she ever thought they would choose her. When did she start having stars in her eyes and believing in impossible dreams? She misses Alec, misses the familiar, stable hum of him in her world. She knows Alec misses her too, but over the course of his trip his letters have sounded less urgent, in some ways. More focused on the work in Halifax, or on the family he's living with while he's there. But now, with only a few weeks left, and this feeling she has that Edinburgh has turned on her, somehow . . . She misses him more.

By the middle of the next week, just over a fortnight before Alec is due to board the ship that will bring him home, June feels stretched thin by her competing desires to be part of this family and part of Floss's world at the same time. And worse, there is a part of her that resents giving up Berlin, and then feels guilty for that as well.

That Friday brings a letter from Sybil de Cler. June is almost reluctant to open it—it's been years since she's heard from Sybil, and it feels like a bit much that her past insists on remaining front and center. Still, she's curious about what Sybil is up to after all this time.

But the letter is much more than anything she would have expected: Sybil is at Oxford now, teaching at June's old college, where the faculty are looking to bring in a visiting research fellow for the Michaelmas term. *I know this is not much in the way of notice,* Sybil writes, *and I'm terribly sorry, but the post has only just come vacant. When they asked me if I knew anyone who might be suitable, you were the first person I thought of. You've made quite a name for yourself, and anyway, wouldn't it be brilliant to work together again?*

June stares at the letter, trying to take it in. Before she knows quite what she's doing, she's flipped through the pages of her calendar, eyeing the Michaelmas term. Four months at Somerville College, maybe five, building proofs and immersing herself in the life of the mind she's been working toward her whole life. Somerville means more girls like her, girls too clever by half, and Sybil there, someone she could actually talk to sometimes about the old days. She looks at the letter again—all that research, a lecture twice during the term, rooms in the college with a view of the river. Nothing to do but maths. Guilt snakes through her when she thinks of stepping away for those months. But Oxford is hardly Australia; there are trains and motorways, weekend holidays halfway.

She looks up and finds Penny watching her patiently. With a pang, she realizes Penny is waiting to walk with her to the fish and chips shop to pick up their supper. "I'm sorry," June says. "I had a letter from a friend."

"I like getting letters," Penny says. "Like the ones from Daddy. Maybe Ronit and Rakshan will write me letters when they go to India again."

"Quite possibly," June says. Penny is only six, but the way she connects ideas reminds June of herself at the same age. As they walk, Ursa ambling slowly beside them on her lead, Penny chatters about the flowers they pass, or the birds that flit high overhead. June smiles to herself. Penny is so like Alec.

After the fish and chips are gone and Penny has had her bath, June sits at her bedside to read Kipling's "Rikki-Tikki-Tavi," one of Penny's favorite stories. She tucks Penny in with her worn stuffed bear and opens *The Jungle Book*, flipping through the familiar pages to the tale of the valiant mongoose.

"'This is the story,'" June reads, "'of the great war that Rikki-Tikki-Tavi fought single-handed, through the bath-rooms of the big bungalow in Segowlee cantonment.'"

Penny is almost asleep, Ursa snoring lightly on the rug beside her bed, when June pauses in the midst of narrating Rikki-Tikki's triumph over the vicious cobras and his ascension to the coveted post of house-mongoose. When there is no protest, June leans close and kisses Penny's forehead. "Good night, Penny. I love you." She pats Ursa and goes out into the hall, leaving the door slightly ajar behind her.

Downstairs, she sits with Sybil's letter again for a moment, eyeing the phone. Guilt laces through her; her first inclination was to talk to Floss, not Alec. She stands in the hall, looking at the familiar wood-work, the play of moonlight through the windows, and lets herself wonder whether Edinburgh or Oxford, or somewhere else entirely, is where her future lies.

A few days later, she hovers before a shining red pillar box, two letters in her hand. One she has written to Sybil to express interest and ask more about the Somerville post. The other, to Alec, was much harder to write, because she suspects she knows what Alec will think. But Oxford is her chance at redemption—a chance to take her place among scholars in an utterly different way, to light a path that Penny will be able to follow as well. Oxford can change everything, for all of them.

She takes a breath and drops the letters through the slot.

1959, *Halifax*

When the powers that be at Livingstone & Gray stamp the racing sloop with their imprimatur, Alec's job shifts from design to the earliest parts of marketing, and the pressure changes. He has phone calls to make and copy to draft, appointments to book with furnishers and builders, a host of quotidian details to arrange. He misses having his hands on the ships, but it's not time for that now—and the sharpened focus of announcing the new ship is a different type of excitement.

Despite his pleasure in the work, sometimes he feels a measure of discomfort, brought on by something he can't quite name. Of course part of it is his belief that he should be at home. Not here, settled perhaps too cozily into the comforts the Carters provide. He's built Spitfires and worked on homework with Cullen, the two of them finding their patterns and routines winding together more every week. Somewhere in the back of Alec's mind is a layer of guilt over how attached he has let Cullen become; it won't be easy for the boy when it's time for Alec to leave Halifax. Too, he has fallen into the habit of sitting up at night with Maeve, each sharing about their childhoods and their families, India and Fenbourne and a village just outside Dublin. More than once she mentions Cullen's cousins—but Desmond's siblings in Thunder Bay and Edmonton are so far away, and Ireland even farther. And Alec can't help but wonder about Penny, the only child of two only children. Penny loves Roger and loves the ghost stories he tells her that keep her up at night during his very rare visits, but it's hardly the same as family her own age.

But with only a handful of time left, he's still trying to balance the tug of home with the very different anchor he has found here in Halifax.

One night he dreams of frozen crows falling like blocks of obsidian from the sky above Stalag Luft I, and the screaming of kriegies being brought to heel with the crash of rifle butts and bullets. He wakes to find his hands aching and a throb of pressure over his eyes that reminds him of that dark time just after the war when he hardly slept.

The next morning a letter comes from June, and it is not the balm Alec had hoped it might be. She sounds sanguine enough about losing out on the Reader position that she'd hoped for, but still Alec is rankled on her behalf. How can the chair not see how brilliant June is, how hardworking? Even so there is also the small, terse voice in the back of his head arguing that the man has a point; June's family needs her.

The whole thing makes him a bit uneasy, and his disorientation grows as he reads the rest of the letter, puzzled and a little cold. But the point is clear—she's been offered an opportunity at Oxford and feels she would be foolish to pass it up, Penny is getting older and has done well enough with Alec abroad, just the Michaelmas term, back by Christmas. *Imagine me*, she writes, *in the black robes of a don at Somerville*. He reads that sentence again, touched by her obvious excitement, but at the same time the idea sticks in his craw. He can certainly see how a post like that would go a long way to make up for the sting of her situation with the maths people at home. But imagining her away at Oxford . . . Her place is with him and Penny, just as his place is with them. And then the capper: *Floss reminds me not to underestimate the boost this could give my career.*

June has never made a secret of how important her work is to her, no more than he has of his wish for family. Perhaps what he has always wanted has never really been in the cards. And perhaps Corbett's influence is more pernicious even than he thought. He's never felt Corbett wants to replace him as June's husband, but God knows there are other ways the man has held a bit more sway than Alec would like. It's hard to tell from this remove, through all the confusing, half-nostalgic layers of life with the Carters, whether or not there is something else he should do to make the pieces of his life fit more securely.

Can't wait to tell you more, she writes, but that gives him pause as well. She has not presented it as a discussion and it's not quite an edict, but the sentence about Floss Corbett makes it feel as though it may as well be. Damn the man—Corbett has moved with an unsettling efficiency, using every moment of Alec's absence to reorder the world. He stares at the letter as if it contains a map he hasn't deciphered yet, one of those secret messages June used to leave for him when they were children—a cairn, an arrow chalked on a wall, a false alphabet. But nothing rises to the surface beyond his bewilderment.

He doesn't begrudge June her career or her dreams, does he? But her place is with him and Penny. And harder than the confusion about the message itself is not knowing what she's said to Penny about it, if anything, not knowing what's unfurling for his future, his family's future, while he's an ocean away.

That evening, Alec sprawls in one of the stolid rattan chairs on the back terrace, happy and exhausted. Maeve and Cullen had invited him to go to the beach, and after a bit of dithering he had agreed. The pleasure and ease of their company had been exactly what he needed. It was a long afternoon picnicking and watching cormorants and gulls cruise along the breakwater, and he feels more a part of Maeve and Cullen's unit than ever. Settling onto the sandy blanket with them had felt entirely natural, as had carrying Cullen to the low surf and letting him feel the sweep of the water against his legs, and listening to the boy tell him the history of pirates in Nova Scotia.

Sometimes Alec doesn't know what to make of the Carters or how he feels about them; there are moments when it seems as though he's stumbled into another world in which this is his life. Those moments leave him disquieted at best, but he can't help the draw he feels. He could not possibly adore Penny more than he does, but watching Cullen reminds him how much he would have loved to have had a son of his own, and the larger family his sights had been set on for so long. And as the weeks have crept along, he has noticed Maeve more often watching him quietly.

It's not long before Maeve joins him on the terrace with a tumbler of Irish whiskey in each hand and settles into the chair opposite Alec. She's not much of a drinker, but now and again she'll have a dram with Alec after Cullen's gone to bed. Dragonflies and swifts lash through the low lavender sky above them. Inside, the sitting room lights blink on, and Alec can just make out Mrs. Carter taking her seat beside the hearth with her newspaper. She's not chaperoning, exactly. But he's not quite sure she approves of these palavers.

Maeve takes a sip, shudders. "Desmond loved a bit of whiskey, but for the life of me I'm still always ready to be done almost before I've started."

Alec smiles. "Acquired taste, I suppose."

She nods, gesturing out toward the stand of elms just outside the brick wall that borders the garden. "Look, a raven. No—a pair. They mate for life, don't they?"

"I don't know," Alec says. He eyes the ravens, the pair of them sitting thickly on the branch, their feathers dark and soft in the beginnings of twilight.

Maeve nods sagely. "Des used to teach me about birds and the out-doors. All these years and still I want to go and find him when a jay leaves behind a feather, or there's a robin's egg in the grass." She shakes her head. "You're lucky to have your June, Alec."

"I am," he says quietly. But the idea of "his" June makes him just a bit uneasy. The letters from home bring him the details of life on Shakespeare Close, but the undercurrent of June's need to be working has not escaped him. Nor has what that means for the household. Twice now Penny has written happily about how much she likes the fish and chips from the shop down the road, and he has the sense that with Mrs. Nesbit more or less out of commission the family dinners he's always cherished have fallen somewhat out of favor. And this latest letter seems as if the life he'd hoped for will be one step further away.

"She and your Penny are lucky to have you, too."

He lifts his glass to her. "And Cullen, you," he says.

"I'm blessed to have him, and it's my good fortune I'm able to be home for him and not busy with work outside. A mother belongs with her child, sure."

Alec looks down at his drink, then back at Maeve. She would never understand what June is asking—even a handful of days away from Cullen would be too many for Maeve. The thought gives him a thick, unpleasant feeling, as if he's been caught in a disloyal sulk. Instead of responding to Maeve he says, "Very handsome birds, aren't they?"

Maeve tilts her head, watching the ravens mutter and launch them-selves. "Des used to tell Cullen and me the old stories," she says. "Brian Boru and the rest. Lugh and his ravens."

It gives Alec a pang to consider what it must have been like for Cul-len to lose something like that, as he himself had as a boy, especially given how important the bear stories are to Penny. "He sounds like a fine man," he says, shifting himself on the love seat and shying away from the rest of it. "A good father to Cullen, too."

"Oh, that he was." She lets out a small sigh. "When I lost Desmond . . . I lost my way, a bit."

Alec doesn't say anything—she's moving toward something, as clear as stepping out on a wire.

"They called it the Crippler," she says. "The whole of Canada was scared half to death. And at mass every Sunday they would read the names—so many. An adult here and there, but so many children, Alec." She meets his gaze, her eyes full of pain. "Then masses half empty, everyone after keeping their children safe to home."

"It must have been terrifying," he says quietly. "Like the cholera." He grimaces, remembering the smell of fire, and Maeve nods.

"When Desmond got sick, I thought he was tired, sure," she says, her voice almost too low to hear. "And then Cullen . . . I thought the world was coming to an end. Father Mayhew kept coming along and telling me the Lord had a plan. And then Desmond . . . he was hardly alive, Alec, an iron lung breathing for him, and then he was gone." She trails off and takes another sip of whiskey.

"I'm sorry," Alec says. "So very sorry."

"I couldn't even grieve him properly." She gestures with her glass. "Everything I had left went into taking care of Cullen. I was so afraid of losing him, too. And Father Mayhew . . . Well." She makes a little *tsk* sound and shifts in her chair. Alec leans forward so he can hear her, as if the gathering darkness of the evening has made her soft voice even softer. Her smile, when it comes, is a sad one.

"Well," she says again. "He came to the hospital, and there I am with my tiny little boy, and Father Mayhew is on about the Lord and His sparrows, and . . . I don't know what it was that came over me,

Alec. I told that man I couldn't accept the word of his god, not with an island full of dead children and my good man gone, and what did he, with no wife, no children, even know of what we'd lost?"

Quietly, wanting to comfort her somehow through the swelter of feelings rising in him, Alec says, "I can't think how exhausted you must have been. How bloody afraid."

"Like a banshee, I was," she says simply. "Railing at a man of God like that until I ran pure out of words." She takes a last sip of whiskey and sets down the empty glass. "I didn't go back to mass that week, or the next. I was so ashamed."

Alec gazes at her, unable to organize his feelings into words. At last he says, "But you were suffering so very much, Maeve. You can't blame yourself for that. We all do things we regret when the burdens become too heavy."

"I was so angry," she says, shaking her head. "And I wished him ill, Alec. God help me, I wished he would know, somehow, the feel of a loss like that."

"You mustn't be so hard on yourself," he says. "Sometimes we are faced with the unreasonable." He stops, startled when a broad-shouldered gray-and-white cat leaps up to the top of the wall just beyond the terrace and stands there watching them. Alec blinks—the cat looks so much like his old barracks cat Jack, even down to the ragged tips of its ears. Alec falters, trying to quell the sudden shaking in his hands.

Alec is vaguely aware that Maeve is responding, but the cat is on the move, its tail lashing as it prowls. It pauses on the edge of the terrace and lets out a hoarse yowl. Alec turns away, sweat beading down his spine and the back of his neck. He has too many ghosts, but mostly their haunting has slowed. This is something else, though. His stomach drops as the cat comes closer and winds itself around the legs of the table, looking up at him with its green eyes lanterned in the light from the house. Jack used to do that, curl the crooked end of his tail around the legs of Alec's bunk, purring like a racecar. The big cat had been lying there purring on that last day, the last cat left in their barracks, before . . . Alec shakes his head, trying to rid himself of the memory of men crying with hunger and Jack's tatty gray coat gone still, the engine quieted, before one of the other men had taken Jack away to turn him into something else. Not a cat.

"Alec? Are you all right?" Maeve's voice is soft and confused, but he doesn't look at her. Instead he watches the cat, hoping it will just go away, but instead it jumps up on his lap, purring like Jack always had. The weight of it, the soft puff of its fur . . .

"Get it away," he chokes out through the nausea. Maeve stands and shoos the cat away, and as it vanishes into the darkness at the back of the garden Alec forces his trembling hands into stillness. "Thank you," he says at last, when he thinks his voice will be steady enough.

She takes a seat beside him. "I take it you're not keen on cats, then?"

Alec hesitates, trying to find his way through what he wants to say. What he wants her to hear. How much he needs to explain himself to her and offer her something in return for her story. But the words come slowly. "When I was shot down . . . I was a prisoner of war for a long time, in Italy first."

Maeve tilts her head, her eyes searching his face. "First?"

"When Italy surrendered, the Germans took me. Nearly two years in one of their camps, and it was almost the end of me." He takes a breath. "There was no food for months, only a knob of cabbage now and again, our rations not coming . . . We were so hungry." He stops. "I haven't told anyone before." *Not even June.* It feels wrong to say any of this out loud, especially to Maeve, and his next words stick in his throat. "There were cats, though." He tries to meet Maeve's eyes, but his gaze skitters away. "That's all there was."

Maeve's hand goes to her mouth, and Alec's heart sinks. What if he's said too much? But then she leans toward him, her brow furrowing. "You were surviving. Isn't that what God wants for us? To do the best we can and survive?"

Alec looks down at his hands, then away. The last thing he wants to think about is Jack in the barracks licking Klim from his palm before everything went from bad to much, much worse. When he finally looks up again, Maeve is watching him with tears in her eyes. The relief in finding someone so kind, so understanding, to hear his darkest moment, feels like a gift. There is an element of peace in it, perhaps even of absolution. But it nags at him that he's brought Maeve something he has never shared with June.

"You poor man." Slowly, she lays her palm against his cheek, her thumb brushing tenderly against his cheekbone. When she puts her arms around him, he lets her hold him for a moment, too aware of the rawness of it, unsure if he should return the embrace. But there is a comfort here that he didn't expect, though he's seen her with Cullen often enough to know how warm she is. It's disorienting to be so close to this soft bask of affection. He's tried to think of her as Desmond's widow or Cullen's mother, but now she is just Maeve. Not new information, but a new way of realizing something he had refused to notice before.

Her fingers brush the back of his neck, and he shivers. He wants to relax into her care, but with her softness so near him and her scent rising around him like butterflies he knows that is a path best not taken. He can feel her pulse. Or his. He's not sure, and not sure it matters. In his confusion, time stretches out like a willow on the bank of a stream.

Alec pulls back, guilty and confused by the threshold on which he's hovering, but Maeve stays close and still. The whiskey and her embrace have warmed him, and the terrace feels like a pocket out of time or place. It's a dangerous feeling, as if he and Maeve have opened a per-plexing, new liminal space. Agitated, he finishes his tumbler of whis-key. "I should probably turn in."

Maeve's face falls. "Oh, already? Would you not like another wee drop first? It's so early yet."

Alec shakes his head, and Maeve's eyes fill with disappointment. Regretfully he says, "I'd best not."

"I understand," she says quietly. She gets to her feet and takes his glass.

Alec frowns, sorry that he seems to have let her down and unsure how to navigate this confusing new space. He stands, too. "Well. Good night, then."

"Good night, Alec." She moves to the door, where she turns back to face him. "You'll forgive me saying so but . . ." She gives him a small, rueful smile and speaks so softly he strains to hear. "What I wouldn't give to be in June's shoes." And with that she disappears inside.

Alec lets out a whoosh of breath, overcome with feeling. An owl passes overhead, silent on its way to the pines across the way. He watches it go, trying to understand what's just happened.

The last week of his time in Halifax races past, and Alec makes half a dozen fitful starts of a letter to June. He resents having to write it, having to ask her to hold off on a decision until he's home, and he's frustrated that he will likely be on the ship back to Britain by the time she gets the letter he finally composes. He needs to get back to Edin-burgh and try to understand what's happening. Or try to fix it, if there is something that can be fixed. He also struggles with the alarming, tangled threads of his ties to Maeve and Cullen. He can't forget what it felt like to be held, or the words she said before she went inside the house, and the effort to quash his confusion and try to act as if nothing happened is exhausting. And even beyond that, he doesn't know quite how to leave them, especially when he thinks about how much time he's spent with Cullen, how much their routines have intertwined. And he needs to settle himself back into his real life, not this strange existence where he waits for Maeve to smile at him and then feels a rush of shame when she does.

Not that she is smiling as much as she had before that night on the terrace. She's never mentioned it, but sometimes Alec looks up to find her regarding him pensively. He feels as though something has changed in how she talks to him even while he cannot pinpoint exactly what that difference is. Sometimes he feels as if she is avoiding being alone with him too, and he's glad to have so much to do at Livingstone & Gray to tie up the loose ends and ready the project for its next stages; he can't be at the house and see Maeve without his thoughts blurring into disarray.

His last morning in Halifax, the Carters join him in the dining room for a send-off. Cullen has got him a book on the pirates of the Atlantic coast, full of garish, lurid illustrations. And Maeve, who seems to remember everything he likes best, has made him a Victoria sandwich, laden with cream and raspberry jam. Even after all these weeks of Maeve's baking, she can still surprise him, and it lights a discomfiting spark in his chest that he doesn't quite want to extinguish.

"It's not your birthday, of course," she says, "but perhaps it isn't always needing to be?"

"It's perfect," he says, tugged at by memories of Cook's sponges at the vicarage and a thousand other bafflements and memories. "Utterly perfect."

She pinkens gladly, but then her smile fades a bit. Her shoulders square as she takes a breath and pulls one of the flowery index cards she keeps in a tin on the kitchen windowsill from her apron pocket. "Thought I'd send the recipe along. For June."

Alec falters just briefly before he takes the card from her. He understands all in a moment what this is, understands that Maeve is acknowledging—accepting—the way things are, the way they must be. He's touched by her stoicism, and by her kindness. "Thank you," he tells her, even as he knows very well June will never make this cake. "Thank you awfully much," he says again. "For everything."

Maeve ducks her head. "We're going to miss you."

"It's been a pleasure to host you, Mr. Oswin," Mrs. Carter says.

Cullen looks up, his eyes sad. "You were the best one we ever had."

"It has been my honor to know you," Alec says, his voice stiff. There is too much to say to this boy, and he's not sure how to acknowledge the hole saying goodbye to Cullen is going to leave in Alec's world. Or, worse, the hole he's going to leave in Cullen's. "You're a grand lad, and I would not have enjoyed Halifax half as much without you."

"Do you think you might come back?" Cullen's eyes brighten with hope.

"Acushla," Maeve says gently.

Cullen glances at her and looks away again, picking at his cake. "Will you write, at least?"

"Of course," Alec says. "You as well, I hope. And perhaps one day when you're having your adventures I'll see you again, yes?"

The boy nods tightly. Maeve watches her son, her brow furrowing with concern, and reaches along the table to take his hand in hers.

Alec leans back in the chair that's been his for so long now, watching these people for whom he has come to care so deeply. It's time to go home—well past, if June's letter is any indication—but the idea of leaving Maeve and Cullen behind colors the relief of homecoming. He reaches into the inside pocket of his jacket and pulls out a parcel wrapped awkwardly in brown paper, then slides it across to Cullen. "I had hoped this would come sooner, so we could build it together, but . . ."

Cullen reaches for the parcel and pulls out a small plastic-wrapped Beaufighter kit. His eyes widen. "Where did you find it?"

The gladness in Cullen's face warms him, but it does nothing to soothe the ache of leaving. "Took a bit to track it down, certainly. Let me know how it turns out, will you?"

"I will," Cullen says. He turns the model over in his hands, and Alec grins, recognizing the excited glint the boy gets in his eyes when he's planning a build.

Maeve smiles at Alec, her eyes glistening.

Alec puts his palm to the boy's thin shoulder. For a moment he's lost in the memory of Roger squeezing his shoulder this way, a lifetime ago in that stormy night coming from India, the rain lashing into his face. Out front of the house a taxi is sounding its horn. Alec gets reluctantly to his feet. It never would have occurred to him, all those weeks ago, that at the end of his time in Halifax he would feel this way. The pain of goodbye is persistent and unavoidable, and being the one who is leaving feels no better, it transpires, than being the one who's left behind.

1959, *Oxford*

Snow has laced the mullions, and in the quad below her window June can see Potiphar, the illicit tomcat who prowls House as if he owns it, mincing carefully through the dusting that has stuck to the tired winter grass. His feathery fawn tail lashes against the weather as he stops to sniff something—a tiny bit of red in the white—a poppy left fallen from Remembrance Day, perhaps. June brushes idly at her own poppy, still pinned to the woolen folds of her muffler where she's hung it near the gas-flame hearth to dry.

The flower makes her think of Alec more than usual; November 11 has been a hard day for him as long as she's known him, because of his father's service, and more recently because of his own history. Immersed at Oxford and surrounded by students roughly the age Alec was when he went to the RAF, June can't help wondering what he would have become, if the war had not come and scooped him out of university. He had been flying already at Cambridge, but she can imagine him easily out of uniform, a regular undergraduate in the jaunty pullover and cap of a Cambridge sportsman with a full cricket Blue. Perhaps he would have given up the RAF. Or perhaps the skies would have been his home for longer, under his own terms, as the cricket pitch had been.

Alec's particular interruption, infinitely more than her own, feels oppressive sometimes, and grossly unfair. As if any of it is fair to anyone. She looks back out at the cat, who is now emerging from beneath the hedge like a small blue-eyed lion, a perfect example of a life well-lived on one's own terms. June envies him a bit, although she knows his life is rougher around the edges than she would ever wish for herself. Too, Potiphar reminds her of Box, not least when he appears in the evening with a gift for her—a mouse, sometimes, or a vole. Just as well it's winter, or who knows what he might bring in. Potiphar stalks the quad and corridors alike, keeping order according to his nature—no wonder the students and scouts of Somerville College have named him for the captain of Pharaoh's palace guard.

She gives him one last glance, then sits again and turns her attention back to the spread of papers strewn carefully about the table before her. June has spent the Michaelmas term studying Hodge manifolds with an eye toward connecting Kodaira and Calabi. It seems possible, nearly, although a proof for the Calabi conjecture hovers just out of reach. She can almost see it, the unfolding of those elegant lines of Calabi's theory, the way they underpin something greater. But a proof doesn't happen at speed, not unless one is prodigious indeed, and she will have to be patient. Next week she will give a lecture on bilinear forms and the Kähler manifold to whichever of Somerville's girls wish to attend. She expects the audience to be slight, at best. Still, though, it's a luxury to have the time to follow the threads of the proof she hopes to find.

It's six weeks to Christmas, hardly a month until her time at Somerville ends. She will be glad to get back to Edinburgh in time to spend the holidays with Penny and Alec, the quiet traditions they've built over time. Although: this year will be different—it's only the second Christmas in hundreds of years that the day itself will be a public holiday, although nothing like Hogmanay, a week later.

In Fenbourne, when she was small, they had hung holly and bunting round the vicarage, hosted carolers with mulled wine and tiny cakes. And the bells . . . The bells of St Anne's had rung out at midnight every Christmas Eve to call the faithful to the midnight service. June's father had rung the bells until that last Christmas, not long before the lethal bombing. The bells at St. Anne's had been a constant. Every year they had broken the silence of midnight in the Fens on Christmas Eve in a ceremonial refrain she had loved. But that last year in Fenbourne, with Alec missing and her parents dead, the bells had been nearly unbearable.

On Shakespeare Close, as at the vicarage, there will be holly and bunting, a tree and a mound of parcels waiting beneath it, and Mrs. Nesbit, as she has every year, will prepare a Sowans Nicht meal for the family on Christmas Eve. For a moment, June can almost smell the acrid smoke of a rowan branch burning, someone in the neighborhood trying to turn their luck for the better. She almost laughs, though ruefully: perhaps when she gets back she should ask Alec to burn one for them this year.

She has missed them, although the idea of leaving Oxford brings with it a considerable measure of regret. At Oxford she's doing something she loves, with people she likes; she has basked in the respect she's found in this temporary post at Somerville, and all in all it gives her the sense she was right to step away from her post at the University of Edinburgh, however temporarily. Still, she wishes she had handled all of it more smoothly with Alec—she had tried to explain, when he returned from Halifax, to help him see how she was drowning, how the need to change the world around her became overwhelming and urgent. June had felt as though she might lose herself, and perhaps it had been a mistake to say so to Alec, given how he'd looked at her and looked at his hands, as though suggesting that he had suffered losses she could not imagine. When she goes home, she will try to mend the rift she caused between them.

Her choice to leave Alec and Penny in Edinburgh, no matter how necessary Oxford and this time would be to her own survival, has hurt them, Alec perhaps especially. He has sent perfunctory letters, almost entirely narrating Penny's activities and endeavors, leaving his own daily life out of it. On the very rare occasions she's been able to phone them, he has been pleasant enough, but that distance is always there. She had hoped he would come to terms with this better, or sooner. That after all these weeks there would have been a letter that felt right. But no. And soon she will be back in Edinburgh, where she will have to face her choices head-on—and how is it possible to know you made the right decision and still feel the taste of the wrong in the back of your throat?

But no matter her ambivalence about her return to Edinburgh and her increasingly unsatisfying work there, her sojourn in Oxford has given her an anchor for her sense of self. Perhaps that will help her be a better member of her family. Still, it's impossible to look at the proof she's developing and not know how much she will miss this sort of work, the focus on research rather than teaching. It lacks the life-or-death urgency of codebreaking, but there is something about the way the language of algebra unfolds that lights her mind, and her heart, the same way.

If only it were possible to have a real post at Oxford. Sybil has hinted that her own spot may be coming open in the not-distant future—not something she can talk about just now, all very hush-hush—which has served to light a fire in June's imagination. Perhaps Sybil is going back to codes or one of the new, postwar, semi-secret intelligence offices? There's no way to know, given Sybil's discretion, and the curiosity niggles at June. She is intrigued by the idea of filling Sybil's post if it becomes available—it's more teaching than research, more like Edinburgh than this visiting research fellow post at Oxford, but still a continuation of her time at Somerville. Which, despite the occasional sniff of cronyism she feels about her position here, she loves.

Too, it has been a boon to see Sybil nearly every day. She hadn't realized how tired she was of the secrets, and how lonely she'd grown within them, until suddenly she no longer had to keep them. Even if the endless reach of the Official Secrets Act kept them from telling each other what they'd done in the years after Bletchley Park, before the end of the war, it was enough to be able to talk about the work they'd had in common, and the people they'd known. About the ghastly old manor and the geese and all the rest of it. After all the years of quiet, it's been almost too easy to fall into the habit of that connection again. And tonight it will only strengthen, with drinks planned for the evening with Portia Wallace, whom June hasn't seen in nearly two decades. But Sybil and Portia have met up the Friday after Remembrance Day every year since the war ended to toast those they lost to the enemy, and tonight June will join them.

The next time she looks up, Oxford is well into the gloaming. It's after five, and June is going to be late if she doesn't leave soon. Sybil's terraced Victorian house isn't far, just off the Banbury Road, but although it's stopped snowing, neither the temperature nor the slick surfaces are going to make it an easier walk. She makes sure she's got the key to her room and a few pound notes in case of an emergency, then heads out into the cold.

Until Oxford, it had been a long time since June had had much time to herself, and still, after just more than two months, she is not quite accustomed to the raw relief of that freedom. She has no one to leave a note for, nobody who will wait up for her, except Scroggs, the Somerville porter. Nobody interrupts her when she's head down in working through a proof or consolidating her notes. Sometimes she looks up from her papers and wonders, just for a moment, how the house is so quiet—where everyone has gone.

But crossing the lamplit quad, sharing space with undergraduates racing back to their rooms and then the dining hall, brings June a sense of peace. Somewhere out there is Potiphar, making his way through the evening, and against the low, dark sky she can hear the jackdaws that roost in the college's smokestacks and chimney flues. Her joy, still fresh on these Oxford evenings, is a startlement of sorts.

She steps out through the porter's lodge, nodding to Scroggs, and turns onto the Woodstock Road, shuddering at the wind coming down from the north. Ever since Sybil's invitation to join her and Portia this evening, June has been mildly fretful—she and Portia hadn't had all that much in common when they'd known each other at Bletchley Park; Portia had been much more caught up in her fiancé and her eventual return to her wealthy Mayfair lifestyle. Sybil has kept June up to date, over the years, as Portia has been widowed and remarried, her family growing in a postwar life in London, as far from their exciting past as possible.

Not for the first time, June wishes she could talk to either of them about her fracture with Alec, but Sybil has stayed away from domestic life, and Portia is too much in it. Besides, Sybil has already listened patiently to June's screed about Edinburgh and Mark Larimer, the asinine thorn in her side. It would have been galling enough to be Larimer's also-ran, but to be left out of it entirely . . . Well. That had hurt, and so she had asked for and been granted a short sabbatical.

And such a good respite it has been, too. Walking through the cold, letting the rhythm of her footsteps push away the endless annoyance at Larimer and his acolytes, she feels as at home in Oxford as Potiphar, and smiles to herself at the comparison. He is very much Kipling's Cat that walked by himself, and she thinks again of Box, and reading "Rikki-Tikki-Tavi" to Penny.

When she reaches Sybil's house, she climbs the stairs and rings the bell.

Sybil throws open the door a moment later with a cheery "Attwell!"

"Darling June," Portia says, coming up behind Sybil. "It's been an age!" She embraces June, kissing her cheek.

June returns the embrace, handing her coat and muffler to Sybil, and follows them into the drawing room. She hadn't quite realized how much the chill had got to her and settles herself in a chair near the fireplace.

Portia takes a seat on the sofa, neatly crossing her legs. "Tell me everything," she says eagerly. "All about Alec and your daughter. Mine are all boys, of course, but little girls are such a delight."

"Well," June says, already feeling clumsy and insufficient in the face of Portia's interest, and knowing she needs to express an interest of her own. "We live in Edinburgh, the three of us, where I've been at the university for some time."

"Yes of course, Scotland," Portia says, her eyes wide, as if it's as exotic as Rhodesia or the Solomon Islands. "And how old is your daughter? Five?"

"Penny will be seven in January," June says. The idea jolts her—seven sounds so different from six, perhaps because seven is what she herself had been just before Alec's arrival.

"I don't know how you do it," Portia says, shaking her head. "I would absolutely die if I were away from my children for months."

Portia's words sting, although she can't have meant it quite like that. Sybil goes to the bar at the corner, laughing. "Yes, but you're a regular Mrs. Miniver. June's an intellectual."

Portia waves her off. "Even so. I mean, honestly, my eldest is at Eton now, and when I think about sending the others up after him . . ." She continues, and June listens, trying to see the girl she used to know behind this urbane, matronly face. She can't imagine what it must be like to have four sons, but Portia was always good at keeping track of a lot of moving pieces, whether puzzles or people. Perhaps this is just how she has translated her skills from Bletchley Park.

Mixing drinks at the bar in the corner, Sybil says, "Oh, don't let me forget, Mrs. Tisdale left a quiche Lorraine, I'm meant to pop it in the Aga at seven. She promised even I couldn't cock it up, but I expect we'll see."

Portia rolls her eyes. "Darling, you'll manage. I'm here to help."

"As if your cook is any more likely than Mrs. Tisdale to let you in the kitchen," Sybil says with a chuckle. She comes over with their drinks and joins Portia on the sofa. "Gin sours."

"Marvelous," Portia says, sniffing her glass with a smile. She turns to June, her face growing more serious. "I'm awfully glad you could join us this year."

"I am, too," June says. To Sybil she adds, "Thank you so much for asking me."

"Nonsense," Sybil says. "Wouldn't hear of missing an opportunity to reunite Attwell, de Cler, and Wallace, especially tonight."

"And anyway, I've missed you," Portia adds.

June nods, moved and a bit surprised by the depth of feeling the reunion has brought her, and is relieved when Sybil clears her throat solemnly and raises her glass.

"To our dead," she says quietly. "Captain John Fitzwilliam, killed in Rangoon."

They drink, and June bows her head. The sad, reverent look on Portia's face . . . Is that what she would have felt like, decades later, if Alec had been lost? For a moment she misses him terribly, staggered by the relief that he is not among the dead. That he is home and alive.

Portia, her face still tight, says, "First Officer Sarah Crossley, sunk off Madagascar."

June had known Sarah had been killed by a U-boat, but it is different, hearing it like this. As Portia and Sybil offer up other names, June sits quietly with them, realizing how lucky she's been. She's known people killed in the war, just as they have, but she hasn't lost a husband or a close friend to the battlefield. She raises her glass for the sailor who'd been killed at Anderson, and again for Alec's lost friends, Charlie and Smasher. For valiant Lucy Kent, who had survived the Zero that day at Anderson only to die of a fever on the ship home after the war.

When their glasses are empty, Sybil goes to make a second round, her hand a bit heavier with the gin this time. Speaking of their dead has made June want to speak of the living, so she asks after other people they had known at Bletchley Park, and as their reminiscing grows less somber, so does the mood. Portia and Sybil chatter about their mutual past, time swirling around and through the year that June was with them, too. She doesn't know everything the others talk about, but she can't quantify the relief she feels to be able to talk about any of it.

She's pleased to be reunited with Portia, but watching the two of them together she feels a stirring of envy—they had had more time together during the war than June had had with anyone, and more time since, as well. She should have stayed closer herself to the women she knew at Bletchley Park and elsewhere. And she had, for a time, but it had begun to chafe when so many of her old friends had wanted to talk more about their dinner parties and children than anything else, and the rest had gone off to have adventures that had left June feeling isolated and out of sorts. But imagine the relief, if she had been able to make it work, if she saw some of them more often.

They're a few drinks in when June reminds Sybil about the quiche, which leads to the three of them poring over the detailed instructions Sybil's housekeeper had left. Once the quiche is warming, Sybil opens a bottle of chilled Veuve Clicquot and pours it into tiny crystal glasses etched with translucent snowdrops.

They're back in the drawing room, waiting on the quiche, when Portia brings up the entertainments that some of their colleagues put on. June had never been clear whether the goal was purely to keep up morale or if in fact the mostly public school men had set out to create an environment more like their university days. When she brings this up, Portia suggests it's a meaningless distinction.

"Either way," she says, gesturing with her glass, "it kept us distracted and occupied, didn't it? Greased the mental wheels, such as they were."

"All those posh actresses," Sybil says.

June laughs. For such an urgent, staid place, Bletchley Park had had a finely honed sense of whimsy and endless resources—official and otherwise—for recreation. "I remember you flirting with that Randall fellow in the chess club, Sybil."

Sybil snorts. "He turned out to be rather dull, in the end."

"Gosh," Portia says, "I had forgotten all about him. Do you remember when the chess team came here, to Oxford? Might have been after your time, June. It was the most absurd thing."

Nodding earnestly, Sybil leans in. "Beat Oxford's chess club badly, and ever since the boys here have wondered how a tiny village like Bletchley could field a team like that."

June stares at them. "No, you can't possibly be serious. What about the OSA?"

"They came to Oxford as if they were from the village," Portia insists. "Whole article about it in a chess magazine a few months later."

"And didn't they get what for," Sybil says, her tone dreamy. "But they'd won, and not let on who they actually were."

"Astonishing," June says. Such foolhardy behavior from men she'd known best for their caution. But they'd all been caught up in it at Bletchley Park, hadn't they? It had been a world of extremes, the old lines of British society starting to crumble in the service to something grander. What a life it had been.

Across the table, Sybil jumps to her feet. "God, please tell me I haven't burned the quiche. Mrs. Tisdale will positively murder me."

But she has not, and so the three of them cluster together at one end of the dining table. Time becomes fluid, the three of them staying up much too late, drinking and playing cards and talking about the past. When it comes time that June is meant to go back to Somerville, Sybil shushes her goodbyes and asks her to stay the night. June ponders the idea for a moment, but why not? Nothing is calling her back there, and it's cozy by Sybil's fire. By the time she falls asleep, tucked under a soft blanket on Sybil's sofa, she feels almost as if all the years since Bletchley Park had never passed. As if they were still the same girls they'd been that spring with their picnics beside the lake.

It's an afternoon in late November when a student June doesn't know appears at her door, knocking thunderously, and tells her she has a phone call waiting in the porter's lodge. June's heart sinks—there is no way this is good news, not with the expense and effort required to make a trunk call with the new direct system. She follows the girl to the office, takes the phone.

"June," Alec says, his voice scratchy. "It's Ursa."

"Oh, no," June says, her heart sinking as Alec explains that Ursa has died in her sleep during a nap on the hearth that morning. "My God, Alec, I'm so sorry."

He clears his throat. "It was her time, I suppose, and I'm glad she went easily, but it feels awful nonetheless. Penny is beside herself."

June leans against the wall. Bad enough that she's not present when

Alec needs her, but being gone when Penny is going through something like this feels dreadful. She should be there to help them with their grief.

"I wish . . ." She trails off uncertainly. "She was such a grand dog."

Alec makes a small sound, as if he's trying to quash a flood of emotions. Through all the layers of distance she wants to comfort him. After a while she asks if he can put Penny on, and Alec asks her to wait, the phone clunking to the hall table. When he comes back, he sounds even worse. "I'm sorry," he says raggedly. "She's not up for it just now." June closes her eyes against the sting of it. In the background, she hears the wracking sound of her daughter's sobs, and her guilt expands like a spill of wine across a table.

When she hangs up the phone, June lets herself cry. Ursa had been such a good dog for so long, part of their family in ways June had not expected in the beginning. And as the afternoon stretches on after the call, and she can't stop thinking about Alec and Penny sitting in the house in Edinburgh mourning their grand old dog, June feels worse. It was not her fault that she couldn't be there to help him in the war; even in the worst of her guilty feelings, she knows that. But this time? This time the fault is hers, and whatever her absence has meant for them during this sorrowful time can be laid square at her feet. And, to her shame, there is part of her that understands that this will serve to bond Alec and Penny closer still, and in some way she envies them. But she had loved that dog too, ever since she'd first laid eyes upon the litter of tiny brown pups, and she'd been grateful to Ursa for everything she'd done to bring Alec back. When she thinks about how Shakespeare Close will be without Ursa, it's almost impossible to comprehend. Ursa has never not been there.

She stares morosely out the window, hoping for the comforting appearance of Potiphar from beneath the bushes, but the world is quiet of cats. She can't help but think of Alec's unhappy, somewhat resigned response to her news last summer that she wanted to take a leave from the University of Edinburgh and accept this post, however temporary, in Oxford.

Edinburgh seems like another life, in many ways. But unless something happens with that hint Sybil floated weeks ago, June can't stay here. Staying here would mean another wound to Alec and Penny as well, although there would be good schools for Penny, and places Alec might find work he likes as well as Livingstone & Gray. But wondering about how her life will be in the spring is too complicated—there are too many unknowns.

The rest of the month passes too quickly, and suddenly it's December, and time for her to speak before the undergraduates. It's funny, at Edinburgh she had never been nervous, lecturing. But here, wearing the black gown of a don, it's different. She stands at the lectern and looks around the hall, conscious of all the bright young faces of girls who were only children during the war, and behind them, lounging in seats at the rear of the hall, Sybil and Floss. She's known Floss was coming—they'll have dinner after the lecture—but it's been long enough since they've seen each other that he seems more out of place than she's used to. And it's jarring to see Floss and Sybil together; obviously they've known each other for years, but seeing them rubbing shoulders feels new. They've been in different strands of June's world, however connected, and now the warp and weft have brought them together. She has never been more grateful for the peculiar song of algebraic varieties in which she can immerse herself.

After, a cluster of students approaches June. They're bursting with questions about the Calabi conjecture, and June warms to their enthusiasm and confidence. One, to June's bemusement, has brought with her a copy of June's most recent article for the *Journal of Algebraic Inequalities*, and asks, shaking, if June can sign it.

When the girls disperse, Floss makes his way forward, Sybil at his side.

"Hullo, darling," he says, smiling warmly. "Marvelous lecture, that. Love what you're doing with cohomology and all that."

"Thank you," June says. "I'm awfully glad you were able to come up for it."

"Wouldn't have missed it," he says.

"Brilliant talk," Sybil says. "Wish I could stay and join you, but I'm already late for a prior engagement."

"Another time, then, and thank you, Sybil," June says. "This term . . . I've had a wonderful time. And I'll see you Tuesday at the faculty luncheon, yes?"

"Quite," Sybil says. "Perhaps they'll break out the good sherry this time." They laugh and say their goodbyes, and June walks with Floss to his car, waiting with its driver in the mews behind the building.

At dinner, she tells Floss about her term at Oxford. It's gratifying to be able to share with him again, and to let herself warm to his careful listening. It feels right, sitting with him in the controlled chaos of a restaurant, their conversation cloaked by the low racket of people dining, the scent of his gigot of lamb rising between them. When she slows and asks him what he's been up to, he talks about his work in Vienna, in terms more vague than June would like. She doesn't need further reminding that her own tenure in the secret world Floss inhabits has run its course, that most of his life is stamped TOP SECRET, while hers is not. Still, he draws her in, the old city of Floss's half stories coming together in a pointillist haze across the maps of Vienna that June carries in her head.

"What I really need," he says after a while, pushing away his plate, "is someone who can go do actual work in mathematics and education at the British Council, our outreach group. Third secretary of education under the deputy minister of international outreach, or what have you." He laughs. "Obviously I can neither confirm nor deny any stories you may have seen in the press or popular fiction about the clever lads and the messages they bring over from Prague and Budapest, but if they did exist, I would be on the lookout for someone to turn those messages, however imaginary and unconfirmed, into new messages to be sent back to Whitehall."

June nods uncertainly, trying to ignore the frisson between her shoulders. There is no reason on Earth for him to be telling her this. Unless.

"Someone who won't cock it up, or turn traitor, like that piker Burgess."

"No," June says, "I should think not." If Floss is concerned about a new round of treachery on the scale of Guy Burgess and his circle, who had betrayed England for the Russians time and again, no wonder he's talking about needing help. She folds her hands together, the nervous electricity still coursing through her, trying to sort through her questions to find the right one to ask first.

"Just between us," Floss says, leaning close, "I've been eyeing Sybil for the post. Awfully keen, knows her codes . . . Fluent in German, even, but I expect you remember that from before."

June nods, but she's gone cold. Sybil had been one of the smart set at Bletchley Park, educated in Switzerland, vacations in Biarritz and Gstaad, fluent in German and French, which had made her invaluable to the translation work. But Floss can't be telling her she's effectively been replaced, can he?

As if he can read her thoughts, Floss says, "Ideally, of course it would be you. You're bloody June Attwell." He shrugs. "But you've made it clear over the years that your family must come first."

June looks down at her plate, noting every detail of the crest in the silverware, the infinitesimal traces of sauce and parsley left from her fish. What he's talking about, if she can get past this new wrinkle of Sybil, is a return to the meaningful work that had meant so much. Not to mention codes upon codes. Layers upon layers. She can almost see them laid out before her. She does not wish in the slightest to wound Sybil, but her own timer is running out, in more ways than she can count. She is almost through her term at Oxford, and in a few weeks she will go back to Edinburgh, where the chair will continue to take her work for granted. The idea of being passed over again is galling, to say the least. Sybil had suggested she might be leaving her post—is this what she'd meant?

God, the idea of building those messages, working for England again . . . It doesn't matter that Sybil speaks German; June is nearly fluent as well, and in any case the codes will be in Russian, which June has a vague grounding in already. And it certainly isn't harder than the Japanese characters and syntactic puzzles she had had to learn for the Y service. She thinks of Alec and Penny, tries to push away the knot of new guilt already budding in her stomach although she has said nothing, done nothing. There is nothing about this idea Alec will like, but she is already thinking ahead, as if this is a real possibility, starting to structure her argument about the opportunities for Penny, a fresh start for them all.

"Don't count me out," she says softly. Floss looks puzzled, and she continues. "I need to think about it, but . . . I'm not out of it."

His face clears into a delighted grin. "You take the time you need."

. . .

That night, lying awake in her rooms as the stars and moon shift across the firmament, June hears Potiphar meowing in the corridor. When she goes to let him in, he jumps up on the foot of her bed, washes himself, and gradually curls into a sleek tawny block against her hip. She lays her fingers against his shoulders, pets him gently. The future is terrifying still, but in a way she understands—there is a threshold before her, a liminal moment in which she could change her entire world. She can save herself, do her duty for Queen and Country. She doesn't let herself think about the new layer of secrets or wonder what the cover might be for where she goes to work or what she does there. As exciting as this future seems, she is not quite ready yet to face those particular consequences, inevitable though she knows them to be.

She's too restless to sleep, and sits up, trying not to disturb the cat. After a moment she lights the gas fire and flicks on a light, then sits down at the table with a sheet of paper and a pencil, going back to the old childhood tools she'd used to soothe herself, building lists and maps. Her father had bought her an immense atlas of the world, its pages wide and perfectly smooth, the whole world laid out before her. She had been six, perhaps, or seven. Before Alec. She had fallen into it then too, page after colorful page of the loops of road and rail, the legends full of symbols, the pink of Siam and the pale yellow of Argentina. Her mother had regarded the sprawling maps without much comfort, as if she'd wondered even then what such an interest might suggest in her young daughter. But decades later, concentrating on those images is the same balm for June it had always been.

Austria had been a pale blue, and Vienna had sat on a page of its own, a splash of city with the Danube winding across like a ribbon. Another ancient city, wrecked by bombs and the loss of generations of its men, and perhaps, suddenly, astonishingly, a new place in which she can make a difference.

By the time she's ready to fall asleep, the cat curled quietly beside her, she wishes she had some kind of equation to help her find her answers—a map, as it were, for finding her way through the questions. Still and all, she feels a shivery silver hope somewhere deep inside her, and perhaps that is enough.

1960, *Edinburgh*

The new year arrives in a curl of Hogmanay smoke, salt on the sills and bits of holly, rowan, and mistletoe tacked to every sash in the house. Mrs. Nesbit is stolid and true to her Presbyterian roots, but there are other roots that run deeper and, like a good Presbyterian Scot, Mrs. Nesbit is practical enough to appease those gods and spirits as well. Alec admires the way she hedges her bets, but perhaps that's to be expected in a city where pagan rites like saining the house with juniper smoke and first footing the houses of your friends with gifts of fruitcake and whisky had filled the gap left by the centuries-old half-banishment of Christmas.

Alec had not missed Christmas when he and June had first come to Scotland. The absence of Christmas and Boxing Day as holidays had been puzzling, to be sure, but it had helped as well while the two of them had made their transition into this new life, away from Fenbourne. In Fenbourne Christmas had been nearly unbearable after the war—with his aunt gone, the cottage on the sluice road had never come to feel quite the same. And all through the village there were too many ghosts, too much looking over his shoulder for the dead and gone, hearing their lost, familiar voices in the tolling of the bells. There had been no way to attend the Christmas sermons in their beloved St. Anne's, with the remnants of the vicarage looming so close, and the new cleric no match for June's father. And it wasn't as though not going had felt much better, honestly. Hearing the bells across the frozen fens, the rolling notes skating along the ice and the low clouds . . . It had felt like invitation and banishment both.

In every particular, the fire festivals and ritual cleaning of Scotland's solstice had made for a much clearer rebirth for the pair of them. Alec has liked Hogmanay since that first winter here, although he and June had only joined the torchlit masses on their trek through the cobbled streets once, early on. Once had been enough for the half-drunken, wobble-voiced chorus of "Auld Lang Syne" that marked the start of the year. The throngs had bested him—all those people crowded together and making the best of the cold, every breath punctuated by the writhing crackle of bonfires popping through the night . . . It was hardly a German barracks, but the clamor and jostle had hit too close to home. It was still too soon after his return from that vile time in Odessa and Stalag Luft I, and it had left him shuddering with revenant fears, and eager for the celebratory drams on offer across the city. And even when he couldn't hear the fires, the inescapable smoke had reminded him of his last days in India, of Bombay, and the impossible stench of the cleansing flames that had taken his parents from him, smoke rising blackly behind the Gateway as his ship pushed out and away.

But still, despite the echoes, despite all of it, something about Hogmanay and its conflagrations appeal to him. He had tried to explain it to June, but even she, knowing him all the way through, had regarded him, perplexed by the seeming contradiction. Perhaps, in the beginnings of his mother's Tennant blood, there is some ancient Pict or Viking swimming quietly through him, waiting to welcome the lengthening days with fire. Or perhaps the pyres that had cleansed Bombay had left an unexpected mark, a handhold of sorts—the stain of it terrible but familiar.

He feels hopeful, stepping into this new decade, although he can't say why exactly. The household feels marginally more stable since June's return from Oxford, although not quite as steady as he would like. Losing Ursa has created a dreadful void in his days. It would be so much easier if nobody went away, if things could just stay the same for a moment. His hand drops sometimes from the arm of his chair as it always has, but now there is that jarring sense of free fall, as if the engines have stalled out, when there is no sleek dark head to lay his palm against.

And it's not just Ursa's absence that leaves him feeling so unsettled. As long as he's known her, June has withdrawn a bit when she's trying to work something out, and although she's back, although the family feels whole once more, there are days when June seems further away than ever. Sometimes it is a more genial distance—one he recognizes from their early days, when she would lose herself in maps and timetables— and he has no way to know what she is charting behind those ocean-glass eyes. But other times it feels different, more pressing, especially when it comes on the heels of a letter from one of her overseas friends. At Christmas, when he had a letter from Cullen and Maeve, that longing and confusion in his chest had opened up again as he'd fallen into remembering, just for an instant, how close he had felt to them, and that low hum of guilt. And this is June, for God's sake, his lodestar.

Of course when the spring term starts, much too soon, it will gall her to have to work with Larimer again, particularly in the wake of what sounds like a grand Michaelmas term indeed at her old college. Still, she has a place at the university here, support for her research. And she's home, the two of them finding their way back to each other after all those months of separation—when he'd come back from Canada, his head full of model airplanes and fresh-baked pasties and cakes, he'd been angry and hurt, half-choked with the feeling of having been blindsided by that letter of June's. By the time he'd made his way from Liverpool to Edinburgh, he'd chewed so long on the idea of her going to Oxford that it had taken on the immense weight of a line in the sand, a gauntlet thrown.

And yet. When he'd come up the front walk last summer, and Penny had run down the steps to fling herself upon him, he had looked up at the front door and seen June standing there, that small smile gilding her face, and his heart had leapt despite the hurt. He had been so relieved to see his girls again. The next weeks had been hard, to be sure. His confusion and resentment hadn't gone away, and there had been days in her absence when the anger had come back, when he had missed her so much his skin had hurt, when he had taken Penny to the zoo or Loch Lomond and it had felt as though the world was just the pair of them. But his future should have June woven through it, shouldn't it? In the tapestry of his life, she is the golden thread that runs through everything, fundament and fabric at once. Without her, the center cannot hold, and the warp of the loom has nothing to weave.

But today, on a cold Twelfth Night afternoon with a sky the color of newsprint, Alec can almost believe that the bewilderment is behind them. Almost. He hovers in the foyer, feeling rather at loose ends. Livingstone & Gray are closed for the Christmas holidays, and he's anxious to get back into the traces there, continuing the work in Leith that he'd begun with Armand in Halifax.

He moves into the drawing room and fiddles with the wireless, but the Home Service offerings today seem either excessively choral—reasonable for the Feast of the Epiphany, but not what he wants—or melodramatic narratives about nurses and soldiers. This is such a disorienting day, not least because he can remember how Twelfth Night felt at the vicarage when he was a boy, he and June each hoping to find the lucky bean in the special crumbly fruitcake Cook had baked each year. It had always seemed like such a triumph to find the bean and wear the crown, to spend the day with his aunt and the Attwells, and now and again Uncle Roger too, to sit next to June in the front pew of St. Anne's and listen to her father's Epiphany sermon. The church had always had a glossy, gray smell to it despite the incense and smoky, melting candles, as if the Fens had come to listen, too. In the winter there had been the smell of dogs and wet wool as well, and the peat smoke from the fires that warmed so many of the area's homes. It could not be more different here on Shakespeare Close, where today the whole house smells of the scones Mrs. Nesbit is making, a farthing concealed in one to give luck to the finder.

He gives up on the wireless and goes to the sofa with the newest issue of the *Journal of the Royal Horticultural Society*. It's never too early to plan spring planting, and he likes the RHS's tone, which, in addition to avoiding the overbred sound of so many other garden magazines, lauds the gardens as much as the gardeners.

Alec is basking in the scents of Mrs. Nesbit's work and thumbing through the journal's pages when Penny skips into the drawing room with her stuffed bear, humming a tune he doesn't recognize.

"Daddy," she says, stopping and laying a palm against the wireless, "I want to listen to Jim Starling."

Alec lowers the magazine and regards her affectionately. The Jim Starling series is not at all the kind of thing he would have expected a little girl to love, centered as it is on the adventures of a working-class lad and his group of friends in the north of England, but one of Sanjay's boys had showed her the first book, and she'd been off to the races. And now that the BBC have added a six-part Jim Starling radio show to its afternoon programming this week, she's fallen into that, as well. He glances at his watch. "Children's Hour comes on at five. What if I read to you while we wait?"

Penny weighs this carefully. She's already a strong reader, and sometimes the independence asserts itself as a somewhat stubborn pride, even while she is still a little girl who likes to hear a story. She's considering his offer when June comes downstairs.

"I have something for you, Penny," she says, holding out a sheet of graph paper and a worn copy of *The Hundred and One Dalmatians*.

Penny goes to her mother and takes the book and the paper, regarding them curiously. June continues. "I thought I would make you a puzzle."

Penny settles herself onto the sofa beside Alec. "This is my favorite book."

"Yes, that's why I chose it," June says. "I thought it might be rather a lark if we had a way to talk to each other. Our own secret language, if you will."

Alec smiles at her over Penny's head, pleased by the endeavor. It's true that Penny is in many ways very much her father's daughter, but her intellect comes from June. Marvelous, then, that June is looking to build this connection.

Penny regards her doubtfully. "Like a code?"

"More or less," June says. "A code is slightly different, though. This is a cipher."

Hoping to be helpful, Alec says, "How are they different?"

June smiles at him. "A cipher uses one symbol for another," she says. "In this, for example, there's a key word in the book, and once you know that, you can use that word to find out which letter is substituted for which. In a code, it's more . . . conceptual. The word 'osprey' might be a warning that something is going to happen."

Penny says, "What if we called Daddy another name so people wouldn't know who we meant?"

"Yes," June says, beaming at her. "That is a very good example of a code."

Penny's face lights up. June's praise is hard to come by. "I bet Jim Starling and his friends have a code."

"So the key word . . ." Alec trails off.

June raises an eyebrow. "That's half the fun, finding that."

"Oh," Penny says. "That sounds hard."

"Not at all," June says. "Here." She sits on Penny's other side, taking the book in one hand while she points at the paper with her other.

"This one is fairly simple—the key word is the same number of letters as this block here, you see? And you see, here, how the block of letters in our cipher has a letter repeated? So one thing you can do is look through the book and find a word with repeated letters in the same spots."

"Spots," Alec repeats. "Funny, in a book about Dalmatians."

June smiles at him before turning back to Penny, the two of them falling into the puzzle together. Alec sits back and watches them gladly before returning to his newspaper.

When he hears the rattle of the post being delivered, Alec gets to his feet and goes to collect it—bills, mostly, and a circular announcing a flashy new department store opening in Tollcross in the spring, but in with the rest a thick, creamy envelope embossed with the government's golden lion and unicorn, addressed to June. And, in nearly illegible print above the lion's head, a single word: *Corbett*. Alec regards it unhappily.

"Letter for you," he says, taking it in and handing it to June. She takes it, her brow furrowed; he's heartened when she looks as puzzled and wary as he feels. "From Corbett, I gather."

June nods, turning the letter over in her hands. "Yes, he's been in Vienna for some time, I told you that. Cultural attaché at the embassy, something like that."

"I remember," he says, although that's only partway true. He remembers her telling him that Corbett had gone off to do something on the Continent—he'd been glad the man would be farther away than usual—but hadn't really paid enough attention to the details, such as they were. "Couldn't pay me to live in Vienna."

She looks up again. "Whyever not?"

"Live among . . ." He pauses; Penny is paying attention again. "Be hard to adjust to the new language," he says, instead of saying what he'd started with, about living with the enemy. Even thinking of it makes him feel like the walls are closing in, and for just an instant his mind freezes like a broken reel of film on Smasher's last minutes, the soldier yelling at him with those bloody harsh consonants. No. Thank God he's free of all that, and here instead.

Penny says, "Where's Vienna?"

"On the Continent," June says. "It's the capital of Austria."

"Oh," Penny says. "Daddy, is Jim Starling on yet?"

He forces himself to smile. "It will be very soon, darling."

"Okay," she says. She lays the cipher and her book neatly on the end table. "What do you think will happen to Jim and the gang today?"

Alec beams with delight. "I suppose we'll have to wait and find out." He sits beside her, listening while she reminds her bear what had happened in the previous episode. The wireless warms up, and then the familiar notes of the Children's Hour sound.

June stands. "I may go lie down a bit before supper. Penny, love, will you tell me what happened with Jim, later?"

Penny nods, already engrossed in her radio show, and Alec follows June into the hallway. "Everything all right?"

"Can't seem to shake this headache," June says, her face drawn. She glances down at the unopened envelope. "It could be such an adventure, living abroad. Imagine the opportunities."

Appalled, Alec stares at her. "A bloody adventure?"

June's brow furrows. "But, Alec—"

"No," he says, frustrated and upset, and struggling to keep his voice low so Penny won't hear. "Imagine—those people carrying on in German all the time?"

There's a beat of silence, and then the flash of comprehension in her eyes. "Of course," she says quietly then. She puts a hand to her forehead for a moment. "You're right. I'm sorry. I wasn't thinking."

. . .

As winter fades and the days lengthen, Alec's worry gives way to hope. Whatever June has been gnawing at in her solitary way seems to have resolved, and he feels the determination of her return like the bright gleam of clouds opening after a storm. It has been a long time since she felt so present. And as he feels closer to June, the blur of Halifax recedes into memory, and Alec's horizon clears for the first time in ages, as if the stars are guiding him true again at last.

With spring, the city explodes into bloom. Sometimes, to his surprise, Alec misses the marsh flowers and willows of the Fenlands, but that small ache is soothed when he walks through the city with Penny, who has never known any home but Shakespeare Close. She and Alec are in the habit of meandering over to Blackford Pond and looking for the foxes they have sometimes glimpsed in the filigree of thickets or climbing all the way up the hill to the ancient fort that sits at the summit. Alec is glad to have had the winter to get used to being without Ursa.

At midsummer, they take a weeklong holiday at an old croft cottage at the base of the Cairngorms in Scotland's wild north. The cottage is gray and white stone, two rustic bedrooms and a kitchen warmed by an elderly stove that reminds Alec of the cottage in Fenbourne, and an old oaken table where he sits and writes postcards for Maeve and Cullen, Roger, and Sanjay. It's not quite a hundred yards up the hill from the shores of Loch Morlich, and in the mornings Alec and June take their coffee sitting on the narrow slate terrace and watch the high summer clouds scud across the clear surface of the loch. The cottage is surrounded by trees, juniper and oak and ash teeming with wildlife; on their second day, Penny spots a badger trundling through the blackthorn scrub and a pair of otters frolicking in the loch's shallows. At night, Alec lies next to June with the skein of stars visible through the window, listening to her breathe. The aurora comes once, gleaming waterfalls of blue and gold and green parading the night sky. That night, Alec turns on his side to find June awake too, and when he lays his fingers along the tender bones of her wrist, she smiles and puts her palm to his belly, smiling when he trembles.

It has been a warmer summer than usual, even this far north, the long twilight stretching out past ten, which means more time on the loch. Alec had nearly forgotten how well June swims, and he watches her slice through the water, mesmerized. Sometimes he sits with Penny in the golden sand and builds elaborate castles with walls that crumble away as fast as he can make them, the sand hissing against itself. Penny laughs and shores up the walls with stones. He watches them both, replete with all the ways one man can love.

At the end of the week, sun-pinkened and happily exhausted, they pack up the Zephyr and head south for the three-hour drive back to Edinburgh. Penny, in the back seat, is quieter than usual, and Alec thinks she's fallen asleep until she erupts into noise just outside Kincraig.

"Daddy! Look!" She points out the window at the broad sweep of field and hillock alongside the road, where an elderly shepherd and his pair of farm collies are working the sheep. For a moment he's puzzled—they've seen more sheep than he can count during their holiday—but then he realizes she's focused on the dogs just uphill from the road when she cries out, "I want to see!"

Alec glances at June, who shrugs, her face crinkling into a smile. "Very well," he says, and pulls over, careful not to park too close to the crumbling stone wall that borders the field. Penny piles out of the car and peers over the wall, and Alec lifts her up and sets her atop it, where she can sit and he can keep a grip on her.

"I love them," Penny says, regarding the dogs adoringly. The dogs are impressive indeed, responding either to their own instincts or cues from the shepherd that Alec can't identify, and before long the sheep are gathered in a pen at the far side of the field. His business done, the shepherd turns and lifts his cap to Alec, June, and Penny. Penny claps, and after a moment the shepherd whistles to the dogs and leads them across the green, pointing at a gate not far from where Alec's parked.

Alec lifts her down from the wall, and they walk over to the gate to meet the shepherd. Up close, Alec is startled by the intensity of the dogs' eyes, and wonders for an instant if they somehow hypnotize the sheep. Penny bends to pet them, gently tangling her hands into their soft, slightly shaggy black-and-white coats.

"They're good lads," the shepherd says in his thick Highland accent.

"Amazing to watch," Alec says. The tiny whorls of cowlick at the larger dog's withers remind him of Ursa, and he's afraid that if he reaches out to pet this dog it will just make him sad. Penny, though, seems almost starved for that contact.

June says, "It hardly seems as if you're giving them commands at all."

"Some," the shepherd says. "Most of it's sign and whistle, rather than words."

"Our dog went to heaven," Penny says morosely.

The old man's face softens. "Terrible thing."

"She was old," June says softly, laying her fingers across Penny's shoulder. "Such a good dog, though."

Penny nods and bends to hug one of the sheepdogs around the neck, and he wags his tail.

"That's Tip," the shepherd says. "Got another back to the barn with a litter by Tom, there." He gestures with his walking stick at the second sheepdog.

"I can't get over how clever they are," June says, her eyes roaming the dogs. "Thank you so much for letting us say hello to them."

The shepherd, his eyes twinkling, says, "Aye. Be a treat for the lassie to come see the pups, I reckon."

Penny lets out a delighted squeal, and Alec exchanges a glance with June. "No harm in looking, I suppose."

Not twenty minutes later Alec finds himself crouching by the flat stone stoop of the farmhouse, puppies clambering over his shoes. Their dam lounges watchfully nearby while Tom and Tip drink thirstily from a trough at the side of the house. Two of the puppies have glossy black-and-white coats like the larger dogs, but the third is a rich blue merle, swirls and gobbets of black mixed through the silver, one sharp eye nearly copper in the sunlight and the other a pale blue.

"Daddy," Penny says breathlessly, "look at his *eyes*. And his *ears*."

"They're all akimbo," June says.

Alec laughs, and the puppy tilts his head, watching the three of them intently, one ear tipped brightly skyward, the other flopping rakishly down toward the patch over his blue eye.

"He's so little," Penny says, dropping to sit on the ground. She takes the puppy's paw and shakes, her face serious. The puppy regards her hand, pawing at her knee when she lets his paw go, and she giggles.

A silver-and-white tomcat creeps out of the barn, pausing when he sees them all, and all three puppies lunge toward him, barking madly.

June smiles at Alec, her eyes bright. "They're awfully silly, aren't they?"

Alec nods. The two black-and-white puppies are barking at the cat as if they're trying to tree him, but the tom, nearly as tall as they are, ignores them as he sits and pointedly washes his forepaws. Alec gestures at the small silvery pup, who has crouched low and is staring at the cat the way the older dogs had stared at the sheep, stalking ever closer. The cat turns to regard him and puts his ears back before retreating back into the barn.

The shepherd points at the merle. "Canny, that'n."

"I wish I had sheep," Penny says. The shepherd laughs.

"I think sheep might be more bother than we probably need at home," Alec says. June chuckles.

Penny eyes them both reproachfully. "But I love him."

"I know," June says, "but he's got a job to do when he's older. He's not really a city dog."

"He's special," the shepherd says. "Runt of the litter, and sickly to boot. Weren't certain he'd come through."

"But he's the best one," Penny says. "He's the prettiest and the best."

"I really do love his color," June says. She kneels and claps her hands, and all three puppies gallop back to her, all paws and noses and tiny pinprick teeth. She glances at Alec. "Penny, perhaps we should say hello to the puppies' mother, don't you think? We've talked to all the dogs but her." When Penny scrambles to her feet and darts off to the adult dogs, June turns to Alec. "You had such fun training Ursa," she says, quietly enough that Penny won't hear. "Think what you could do with a dog like this, or what Penny could do."

"God, yes," Alec says, wondering if the shepherd might be willing to part with the puppy. "But you said it yourself. These are working dogs."

"Yes, they are. But, Alec? If you want to do this . . . I should think it's time."

He looks down at the swirl of puppies, warmed by this sudden swell of possibility. Nothing could be less practical than getting a puppy on impulse, from a farm in the middle of nowhere, three hours from home, but what a thundering great joy it would be, having a dog in the house again. He glances at Penny, now crouched on the ground with all three puppies and their dam, listening to his daughter's delighted giggles as the merle puppy licks her nose. He is so unlike Ursa, except for those whorls and feathers, but Penny's right—he is far and away the best of the litter, runt or not.

When he turns back to June, she is smiling broadly at him. Alec turns to the shepherd, trying to organize his thoughts around the pleasure moving through him like breath. "So. Any chance?"

B y the time they reach Shakespeare Close, Penny has named the pup Lucky, after her favorite of the 101 Dalmatians, and taught him to shake hands with her. He has proven to be remarkably steady in the car, and back at home Alec finds him extraordinarily responsive to training. Lucky is deaf in one ear, and so Alec works him with visual cues, the way he'd seen the shepherd do with the other dogs. Mrs. Nesbit regards Lucky suspiciously at first, until he learns to stop messing the floors, and when Penny teaches him to greet her by sitting and offering his paw, the housekeeper is as charmed as the rest of them.

Alec hasn't felt so close to June in years, as if she had hidden behind her crossword puzzles and mathematics and the chores of academia. He feels her presence differently now that she doesn't seem to be listening for something else. Whatever has distracted her from him— from them—has been let go. They talk more now, like they used to. And even when they're not talking, they spend more time close together, Alec's head in June's lap while they read on the sofa, her hand flat against his chest or curling through his hair. The world outside Shakespeare Close is full of confusion, but for the first time in a very long while, Alec's world feels whole.

. . .

A few days into August, Alec and June sit down at the kitchen table for a Sunday night game of cribbage. He takes his time readying the board and the deck of cards while June pours them each a cup of tea. He shuffles twice, and as he's laying the deck facedown to wait for June to cut for dealer, her hand jerks away from her, and the tea spills across the table.

"Bloody hell," she says, her face tight, as Alec lunges to his feet and takes the teapot from her, setting it on the counter. He grabs a cloth and turns to sop up the spilled tea, but June is still standing, watching her hand shake. "I can't make it stop. This happened last week, but only for a moment."

"Why didn't you say anything?" Alec throws the wet cloth into the sink and steps closer, taking her hand in his. The shaking slows, but her fingers are still trembling like a sparrow in his palm.

"It was only a moment," she repeats.

"Has it happened before that? Anything like this?"

"Not exactly this, no. The shaking . . . Every now and again, I suppose? But last week was the only other . . ." She frowns. "I suppose you'd call it a convulsion of sorts?"

"Perhaps," Alec says. "We should get you to the doctor, June."

June sighs. "Yes, you're right. I'll ring the surgery tomorrow."

Alec nods. The small animal of June's hand seems so separate from her, and he closes his own hand around it as well as he can and leans close to her, touching his forehead gently to hers, as he used to do when they were much younger. Sweet June. He tries to put on a brave smile for her. Whatever this is, they'll suss it out and make it right.

The next morning Alec, against his better judgment, lets June send him off to work. June's hand is open again, and the quiver has gone; she promises him she'll ring the doctor and make an appointment, that she's fine, that he'll miss nothing. He makes his fretful way to Leith, the roads and buses half-empty with so many people off on holiday, and at the shipyard he sits with Sanjay, talking about the racing sloop that's finally starting to come together after a year of planning since Halifax. The day creeps on until, using the summer holidays as an excuse, Alec leaves Livingstone & Gray as early as he can and heads back to the house. He knows he could have picked up the telephone and rung June for an update; he knows as well that if she had had something to tell him she would have called. But he feels sure that there is a fine line between asking her to make an appointment and doing anything that she might consider hounding her about it. Somehow, arriving home early feels less pushy.

But when he gets home, he finds that June has gone out. Lucky and Penny are in the garden, and Mrs. Nesbit takes him aside. "Mrs. Oswin tried to ring you, but you'd started home already." She pulls a folded note from her apron pocket. "She left this for you."

Alec thanks her and takes the note—June has gone to see a doctor whose name he doesn't recognize at the hospital pavilion up the road. Alec frowns down at June's careful printing, seeing shakes in the lines of letters where perhaps there are none. Why hasn't she gone to the family's GP? He folds the note into his pocket, hugs Penny, and tells Mrs. Nesbit he'll be back as soon as he can, then sets off.

At the hospital, he makes his way through the maze of corridors in the new wing, looking for the right suite of rooms. His steps slow as he realizes that the hallway he's in connects to the old military pavilion, where he used to come for his appointments with Captain Carnaby. Why is June here? His heart is beating too fast; nothing makes sense, and the sounds and bustle of the hospital are increasingly distracting with their glaze of memory. When he finally finds the right office number, he pushes the door open.

The receptionist, an older woman with steel-colored hair, looks up at him with a brisk smile. "May I help you?"

"I'm here for my wife," Alec says, trying to keep his voice even. "June Oswin."

"Oh, yes, of course," she says, her tone softening just a bit. "If you'll take a seat. I will let Captain Grayson know you're here." The receptionist nods and picks up the phone. After a short pause she tells the doctor that Alec's waiting, then hangs up. "He'll be with you as soon as he can."

"Thank you," Alec says, resigning himself to what he hopes is a short wait. He stares around the room—the clock is ticking too loudly, and the blinds have settled crookedly against the windowsill. All of it serves to make him more on edge, and as the clock's hands jerk from second to second, he can't help turning his focus back to the receptionist.

As if she feels his eyes on her, she looks up, meeting his gaze placidly. "It shouldn't be much longer," she says. He can't tell if it's meant to be soothing or an admonishment.

Her phone rings, and Alec looks up hopefully.

"Captain Grayson's office," she says into the phone, and pauses. "Very well, please hold." She pushes buttons on the phone, and after another short pause says, "Captain? I have Alistair Corbett on the line for Mrs. Oswin."

Alec's head comes up hawk-sharp, his whole attention on the receptionist. Floss? Why is June taking a call here, of all places? Confusion avalanches over Alec as he processes the rest of what the receptionist has said. Why is Corbett calling June, and how can he possibly know to ring her here?

BOOK FIVE

1960, *Edinburgh*

The examination room smells of iodoform and something cold and metallic that June can't quite place. It's an uncomfortable smell, but that seems correct, somehow, under the circumstances. Her telephone call with Floss has left June feeling entirely on edge—bad enough that she's been ordered to lie down in a hospital room just off the surgery of a doctor Floss has chosen and June doesn't know at all, with a complaint that frightens and worries her. Just that would set the anxious nerves in her belly to fluttering. But Floss has not helped. She had not felt that she had a choice in whether to bring him into this—any medical examination with possible neurological implications would reveal the scar the Zero attack had left on the back of her head and raise questions she's unable to answer. Floss had not been encouraging, and even with his reluctant permission there are only so many things she can say, and any number she can't. Floss was quite clear—if absolutely necessary, she can tell Alec about Ceylon in the vaguest possible terms, as if she'd gone in a clerical capacity of some sort with the Wrens. But not a word about Bletchley Park or the Y stations—those places are still closely guarded secrets, any mention of them or the work she'd done there still absolutely forbidden.

The door opens, and Alec leans in. "June?"

"Alec," she says. "I'm so glad you're here." She puts out her hands, and he comes close, leaning down to wrap his arms around her.

"I've been so worried," he says, pulling back and meeting her eyes. "Are you all right? Have they told you what's wrong yet?"

Relief that he's there at her side wars with her dread of what's about to happen. Of what she must tell him, and what she knows it will do to him. "It's a bit complicated, Alec. They've run a series of tests, and I expect there are more to come." All she wants is to find an answer he'll be able to accept. And she can't.

He tries to smile, but it doesn't quite reach his eyes. "Whatever it is, June, we'll take care of you."

She just wants to cling to him. Such a dear, sweet man. He's been looking at her with this same wide gaze for most of his life, and now she is going to tell him things that will change the way he sees her, the way he feels about her.

"It's likely something neurological," she says, "although they're not at all certain what, exactly."

"Okay," Alec says slowly. "Have they offered any possibilities?"

June hesitates, trying to prepare herself for the possible trajectory that everything she says now may take—the questions he may have, the answers she may or may not be able to provide, the consequences of all of it. "One scenario he mentioned was Parkinson's disease," June says, though everything in her screams away from the idea of her symptoms getting worse until eventually they cripple her.

"Good God," Alec says, his frown deepening. "So that . . . Is there a cure?"

"Not as yet."

Alec chews on this a moment. "All right. What else might it be?"

She pauses. "Some kind of tumor, perhaps."

Alec blanches. He shakes his head as if he's trying to shed the idea. She can't blame him, but as much as she fears a tumor lodged deep in her brain, she resents even more the notion that something could invade her mind like that.

"Or," she says, very carefully, wrapping her fingers more tightly around his, "it might be a leftover of sorts from a brain injury."

Alec's head tilts. "But . . . What kind of brain injury? You've never had anything like that."

"Alec . . ." She pauses, collecting herself. "It might be best if you sat down. There's such a lot I need to tell you." As he settles on the edge of the hard chair beside the bed, she searches her mind for the most minimal ways to convey her history.

"What is it, darling?"

"During the war," she says. She hovers there, trying to find the words. "There was a plane crash . . ."

His brow furrows. "You were in a plane crash during the war?"

"Well. Not exactly."

"No, of course. I would have known." He hesitates. "What, then?" He looks so confused, and she hates it. She doesn't want to unravel their life. She doesn't want to hurt him. But she has no choice now.

"Oh, Alec," she says helplessly. "Things weren't quite as you imagined, I'm afraid. You see, I wasn't in London the entire time." She pauses, wishing for a way out, but there is none. "The Foreign Office sent me overseas."

"Overseas?" Bewilderment rises in his face. "Overseas where?"

She takes a breath, then exhales. "Oh, Alec," she whispers.

He watches her, his expression purely mystified. "June? Where?"

She struggles to meet his eyes. "Ceylon."

Alec blinks. It's an agony to watch him try to understand these impossible words, to say nothing of how it feels to be responsible for this betrayal, and all the pain yet to come.

"But you were in London," he says slowly. He lets go of her hands and pulls away. "You can't possibly have been injured in Ceylon, June."

"I know how confusing this must be to hear," she says.

"I'm sorry," he says, "but I don't understand."

Her hand begins its tremor again, and that brittle gray feeling is coming back behind her eyes. "It was while you were in Germany."

"While I was in Germany?" Before she can answer, he continues. "You were Corbett's secretary, at his office in London. Safe."

"At the beginning, yes," she says. "But I was attached to the Admiralty through the Foreign Office, and they sent me to Ceylon. There was a Japanese attack."

His brow furrows again, and he says with more conviction, "But you would have told me if you'd been wounded."

"I couldn't," she says.

"But whyever not? Surely the Foreign Office doesn't just send people halfway around the world and not tell anyone."

"I'm sorry," she says imploringly. "Oh, how I wish I could have told you."

Alec's expression shifts to something she can't quite parse, and he leans closer. "Perhaps you're mistaken," he says with an effort. "Isn't that possible, with brain concerns? That you're somehow imagining all this?"

"Oh," she says, her heart aching for him. "No. I'm sorry."

He shakes his head, thinking it through, bafflement creasing his face. June braces herself for the next question.

"Christ," he says after a while. "Ceylon?"

June nods. She's mired in the ghastly space of wanting to get this over with as quickly as possible and wanting to stop before it all gets worse. "There was a Zero attack, and there was shrapnel . . ." She goes on quickly, although she had hoped to soften the blow. "The explosion knocked me out for a bit."

He blinks at her, as mystified as if she were speaking another language. "You were unconscious in bloody Ceylon and you didn't tell me?"

"I'm so sorry," she says. "I couldn't."

"Was Corbett there as well?" He shifts in his chair. "I mean, if you were actually working for him?"

She flinches at the doubt and suspicion in his voice. Her own presence in Ceylon is only just barely information she can share with Alec; Floss's few visits to HMS Anderson are presumably still off-limits.

"I was always attached to his office," she says, trying to navigate this delicate space, "even when I was with the Admiralty."

"But why were you in Ceylon in the first place? I don't understand."

She wants to find a way to make this easier for him, but there's nothing. "I can't tell you that."

"I don't understand what that means." He shakes his head wordlessly. "Ceylon? I don't . . . For how long?"

She tries to meet his eyes, but she can't. "Three years."

Alec looks away and back again, his eyes dark and narrowed. "You were in Ceylon for three years? And you never told me?"

"I couldn't," she says.

He doesn't say anything else for a moment, just stares at his hands as if they contain the answers. "But Corbett knew?"

June shrugs helplessly. "I worked for him."

"And of course he knows you're here." The distance in his voice creeps along June's shoulders like ice. He gestures toward the waiting room. "I heard them put his call through while I was waiting. Before I knew anything." He stares at her, holding her gaze. "You spoke with him before anyone had spoken with me. And now . . . Ceylon, June? You could have been killed! I could have lost you, and you never said a word? In all these years?"

She can't bear the look on his face, the abject puzzlement and hurt.

A knock comes at the door, and Captain Grayson comes in. Alec stands, and the men shake hands.

"Mr. Oswin," Grayson says, "good to meet you."

"Can you tell us what's wrong?" Alec steps closer to the doctor.

"We'll need Mrs. Oswin to stay tonight for another set of scans, and so we can keep an eye on her." The doctor glances down at June's chart, then at Alec. "Unfortunately I'm only at liberty to share anything more with Mrs. Oswin or her senior officer."

"Officer?" Alec crosses his arms over his chest. "She wasn't military." Something passes over his face, and he tilts his head at June.

"No," she says. She can hardly look at him through the searing guilt that's settling over her.

"And yet we're in the military pavilion of the hospital," he says. "Curious."

"Mr. Oswin," the doctor says, "you were a military man, I'm sure you understand we have protocols. Some of what I need to speak with Mrs. Oswin about is of a sensitive nature, and I'm afraid I must ask you to give us the room for a moment."

"Sensitive?" Alec says, his voice rising. "She's my wife!"

June says, "Alec, please."

He stares at her, then relents, his voice sagging. "I'll be outside."

When he's closed the door behind him, June turns back to the doctor, who regards her sorrowfully.

"Very difficult situation," he says.

"It is," June says.

He takes her hand and lays his fingers against the too-fast pulse in her wrist, then adds a note to her chart. "There are scans we will perform, see what we can find. But it does seem as though this may be connected to what happened to you in Ceylon. We're finding that some types of brain trauma linger for years longer than previously thought, and everything you're describing about both the event itself and your symptoms now suggests that may well be what's happening."

"Is there a cure?"

He grimaces. "We've had some patients who were able to manage their symptoms effectively through a combination of medication and occupational therapy. We'll talk about that after the scans, though, yes?"

"Very well," June says wearily.

"Now then," he says, "my nurse will be in shortly to show you to your room and make sure you're squared away for the evening, all right?"

"Yes," June says. "Thank you." Grayson shakes her hand and leaves, and a moment later Alec comes back in.

"You were home when I came back," he says without preamble. "You were in Fenbourne."

"I was," she says, trying to predict where his thoughts are leading him.

"But you were in Ceylon before that," he says. It's a statement, not a question. "Three years, you said?"

"Yes." She wants to reach for his hand, but the idea that he might refuse her is too awful, so she folds her fingers tightly together. Instead of her hand she offers more information. "I came back not long after VJ Day."

"I was in Odessa by then," he says tightly. "I thought you were safe, here. You wrote me letters. In the camps."

"I did," she says, glad to be able to confirm something he already knows even as she tries to quash the memory of how hard it had been to write, sometimes, given both the secrets and their very different experiences.

He shakes his head. "So you wrote me letters from a place I had no idea you'd gone to. Was any of it real?"

"All of it was real," she says. "There was so much I couldn't—can't—say, but how I felt, how I missed you, all of that was true."

Alec glances around the room, his face grim. "How did you get there? To Ceylon?"

"By ship," she says, wretched.

Another long pause. "Did you . . ." He stops, swallows hard. "By way of India?"

She can't bring herself to say it.

"Answer me, June," his voice soft but sharp.

"Bombay," she says, almost whispering now, "and then a train to Madras."

"Christ," he says, bringing his hand to his forehead. His resentment and confusion are palpable, running around the room like a frightened animal. "Nothing you've said tonight makes any sense to me at all."

"I know. I understand that. But you can't imagine how badly I've always wanted to share this with you," she says, her tone entreating.

He regards her wearily. "I wish you could tell me the truth. That you had told me the truth all along." He sits and slumps forward, his head in his hands. "You're in hospital because of a war injury you never told me about, in a place I had no idea you'd ever seen, and I don't understand any of this."

"I know," she says. "I've felt unspeakably dreadful about it all this time—more than you know."

"I suppose I don't know the half of it." He gets to his feet.

"Alec," June says, alarmed.

"I should get home and make sure Penny's all right," he says coldly, not meeting June's eyes.

She isn't ready for him to go—not like this—but of course he's right. Penny needs him. And a bit of time may help him process some of this. "Of course," she says.

He shakes his head ruefully. "Ah, Christ. What will I say to her?"

"You can't tell her about Ceylon. Not now, in any event," June says, although the idea of building a new layer of secrets, with Alec implicated in them, makes her feel ill. "Alec—you can't say anything to anyone, about any of this. We'll need to sort that out later. But for the moment you might tell Penny they just want to make certain I'm all right, and that there's nothing serious, okay? And they'll let me come home tomorrow."

"Nothing serious," Alec repeats. "June . . . Would you ever have told me any of this, if this hadn't happened?" He gestures at her hand. "You could have died and you never said a thing. And Ceylon . . ." His face is awash in hurt. "You've seen India?"

"I'm sorry. I wish . . ." But she doesn't know what she wishes. She can't wish she hadn't done the work, saved those lives, served her king and country. But she wishes it hadn't hurt Alec. She wishes she could do anything at all to quiet the storm of hurt that keeps clouding across his face. She wishes she could fix it, and she can't.

He takes another look around the room, and grimaces. "Try to rest, June." He hesitates as if to figure out whether to come closer, but instead he says, "Right. I'll see you in the morning, then."

He ducks his head in a nod and leaves the room. The door snicks shut behind him, and June is left alone in the dim antiseptic quiet to wait for Grayson's nurse.

S leep comes only in moments. The scans and the fluorescein dye Grayson employed to examine her brain have left June exhausted and dizzy, nausea coming in steeply cresting waves, and in the confused half-light of the ward she's trussed as well to the unkind noise of machines and the crinkle of ill-fitting sheets, which whisper like Banquo's ghost whenever she closes her eyes. But even without all that, rest would have evaded her. All she can see is Alec's face and the way it had closed against her. Inevitable, really, that her choices would have led her here. And yet . . . and yet she had kept hoping that perhaps this moment would never come.

By morning, neither the nausea nor the guilt has subsided, and she sits back in the rigid hospital bed listening to the ward wake up. It's a private room, although the blessing of privacy is measured dubiously against the lack of distraction it provides, but the sounds still trickle in—the rattle of carts and the soft shuffle of nurses' shoes on the linoleum, an orderly's tuneless whistling growing louder as he passes her door, a woman crying.

Unbidden, her mind loops out a memory of a hot Saturday afternoon when she was a child, itchy in a too-heavy dress, crossing the summer-burned fields with her mother to pay a visit to a Plymouth Brethren family in their home outside the village. There was a new baby in the cottage, and the mother's quiet refusal of Mrs. Attwell's offer. What she'd offered June no longer knows, if she ever had. But she remembers the woman's husband blustering red-faced into the small front room, shouting at June's mother that the village had sowed the wind and now would reap the whirlwind. June hadn't known what he meant, although her father had preached the next day from the Book of Hosea and the phrase had hung in the air. It comes back to her now—for that's what she's done, isn't it? She sowed the wind of deceit as well as service, and now the whirlwind has come to collect.

The dawn light is pale on the dewy thick grass of the hospital's grounds. Last night June had looked out the window at the deepening twilight, watching the silhouettes of unknown animals skitter across the low horizon; now she wonders where they go when the light comes out, when the sun reveals their sly shapes for what they are. At Anderson she had wondered where Box slept too, and thinking of Box leads her to the guilt again, and Alec. She closes her eyes—what had her father told the congregation that morning at St. Anne's? His dry, reassuring tone comes back to her: *The whirlwind will always come, but it will never last,* he'd said, *and the righteous shall find their path lit with forgiveness.*

Is she righteous? She can hope so; the omissions were for a reason, after all, not the capricious whim of a duplicitous soul. But even so, who knows when the whirlwind will end.

. . .

The morning fills with tests, more hemming and hawing from Captain Grayson, more nothing. When visiting hours start, every set of footsteps in the corridor sends her heart into her throat, but it's always someone else, never that amble of Alec's. It had driven her mad when they were children, the way he was always stopping to look at something or sketch something in his book. Now, though, when the footsteps stop just outside her room, the silence left behind filled by a nervous cough she's heard a thousand times before, she's just relieved he's come.

"Good morning," he says as he comes in. "How are you today?"

He looks so tired, his eyes shadowed and bleary, and she's not sure what to say. Platitudes seem misplaced at best, but telling him how exhausted she is would be little more than whingeing. "I'm all right," she says. "How's Penny?"

"Worried," he says shortly.

"Captain Grayson has cleared me to go home today," she says, venturing a smile. "So that's quite a relief."

"Brilliant," he says, nodding. "Did he have any new information for you?" He pauses, and his face closes. "If you're able to share, I mean?"

June's heart sinks, but she presses on. "He's run a lot of tests, but we haven't the results back on most of them yet. The film they took last night has almost certainly ruled out a brain tumor, though."

Relief washes over his face for an instant, and then it's gone, replaced by that terrible new wall he's put up between them. "I am very glad to hear that," he says quietly. "Penny will be awfully relieved to have you back at the house." He glances back at her. "She wanted to come along this morning, but . . . I persuaded her to work on a project for you with Lucky instead."

June smiles, grateful for the way Alec has focused Penny's attention away from this surreal situation. It will be good to get home and see her daughter again and try to move forward through all of this as a family.

"So," Alec says, turning back to her, his face worried again, "what does he want you to do about whatever this is?"

For an alarming moment, June thinks he's talking about Floss, and it floods her with relief when she realizes he means Captain Grayson. "Oh," she says, "well, mainly he wants me to rest, and he's given me some pills for the headaches. If it's a brain injury issue . . ." She pauses, watching the way Alec's face changes when she reminds him. "When I spoke with him this morning he suggested that resting the brain can work much as resting an injured bone or muscle can."

He nods pensively. "What are you meant to do, though?"

"I don't know," she says. "At any rate, I need to have one last check-in with the nurse, and then I can go." She hesitates. "It will be awfully good to be home again, Alec."

"Yes," he says, but he's looking just past her, not meeting her eyes, and June isn't sure at all that he means it the same way she does. But she can't think of all the permutations and possibilities, not now. She's overtired, and the air between her and Alec feels as brittle as the ice on a newly frozen pond; she doesn't want to push too hard, or go out too far, and fall through.

But it is apparent from her first moments back on Shakespeare Close that things are at least as fraught as she'd feared. There's the querying look Mrs. Nesbit gives her, concern mixed with something else June can't quite identify. Not pity, exactly, but something closer to that than she would like. And there's Penny, who oscillates between an unfamiliar clinginess and keeping June at arm's length. June knows Alec hasn't said anything to Penny that would alarm her, but here they are in the drawing room, Penny trying to make Lucky do tricks for June, Alec seated in the armchair on the other side of the fireplace with studied nonchalance.

Even when Penny is done putting Lucky through his dubious welcome-home paces, and June goes upstairs to bathe and change her clothes, everything still feels just a degree or two off. It's less the barometric drop of a coming storm and more the first ripple of silence in a forest when the birds sense an intruder. As she stands in her dressing gown, running the hot water into the tub, June finds herself thinking about the way Alec's eyes had looked at the hospital, the way he had pulled away.

June settles into the tub, but she can't wash away the dark stain his odd, confusing blend of civility and distance has left. And it doesn't help that she knows his behavior is a result of her choices. For a moment she wishes she could go back in time to solve all this, but where would she go? Or when? She can't imagine going to that meeting in the drawing room with Sir Reginald all those years ago and deliberately walking away from his offer, even knowing what it would entail. And going further, as distant in her past as university, that first meeting with Floss at the special maths lecture . . . Indeed, the best thing, for Alec at least, would be to go back all the way to India, before the cholera that destroyed Alec's family. Save his parents, save his home. Let him have the life he had been intended for, all polo and cricket and summers in the Himalayan hill stations. Let him follow his father into the army and never fly a plane, never crush his hands. Never know her. He could have had his glory, and she hers, without this great sundering.

But the image will not hold—it's not merely that it's impossible, a foolish daydream. It's the idea of choosing a life in which she would never have been loved by the sharp, fierce arrow of his heart. She cannot change what she's done to him, and she cannot fix it. But she can see far enough into the future to know that the damage her choices have done is the lasting sort, calamitous and bewildering. There is no right answer, has never been. That small quake of doubt she felt talking with Sir Reginald in his office in the City, realizing that she would never be able to share with Alec . . . that's borne fruit now, hasn't it? The inevitable has come to pass.

She scrubs with a flannel at the patches where Grayson and his people stuck their instruments and electrodes to her chest and temples, trying to clean herself of hospital as well as guilt. Through the window the scent of larkspur wafts up from the back garden, reminding her of the vicarage and her childhood and Alec, back when they were happy. Or at least when the ways they were unhappy were so much more manageable. She scrubs harder, but nothing changes. It's all too much, and not enough, and she hasn't the faintest idea how to set anything right again.

I t's late when Mrs. Nesbit, who has stayed through supper to make sure they're all right, finally bustles off to her home and June and Alec settle Penny into bed, Lucky curled up in his basket in the corner of her room. June sits on the edge of her daughter's bed, stroking the flat bony wing of shoulder blade through Penny's thin cotton pajamas.

"Daddy," Penny says, yawning and hugging her bear to her chest, "you should tell me and Mummy a bear story."

Alec glances at June and away again, but in the lightning-quick blaze of his eyes June sees the calamity continuing to unfold. He pauses, then shakes his head. "Not tonight, love."

"But, Daddy," Penny argues.

"Mummy needs her rest," Alec says, his voice quiet but firm.

June's stomach flutters with alarm. "Perhaps tomorrow."

Alec leans down and kisses Penny's forehead. "Good night, Princess Penny. It's late. You sleep."

"Good night," Penny says, too sleepy to put up a fight. "Good night, Mummy."

"Good night," June says. She too kisses Penny's forehead, then follows Alec out, leaving the door open a sliver.

As they step into their room, Alec says gruffly, "You must be exhausted. You should sleep soon, too." June nods, grateful that he understands. He reaches for his dressing gown where it hangs on the back of the door, pauses. "I think it would be best if I slept in my workroom for now. Better that you should be undisturbed."

June stares at him, shocked into silence. The third bedroom has always functioned as a sort of office for him. Alec gathers up the dressing gown and his pillow, and June watches as he takes them to the other room. He steps back out to the landing and retrieves a light coverlet from the linen closet.

"Alec, no." She steps closer to him, meaning to take his hand or somehow stop the momentum he seems to have built away from her. But that wall she can't see, like a moat he's projected around himself, keeps her from completing the motion.

Alec finally looks at her, his gaze steady but wounded. "I'm sorry. I feel as if I don't know quite who you are," he says, so gently she has trouble aligning his voice to his words.

June's heart goes leaden. There is no one on earth who knows her better than he does. But this wound is her fault, isn't it?

"Anyway," he continues with that same dreadful soft tone, "good night." He picks up his book from his bedside table, and goes back downstairs.

The next day Alec stays home from work again, offering to drive June back to the hospital for a follow-up appointment. She could drive herself, or walk, but she can't help but wonder if perhaps more time at her side will help him as they find their way through this awful new landscape. Or perhaps it will just help her. But she's happy to accept his offer and have the time with him, although his excessive politeness does not warm her in the least.

At the hospital, he takes his place in the waiting room without being asked. And when she emerges after her appointment, shaken by Grayson's certainty about the absolute necessity of resting her mind, Alec stands and regards her with a quiet, puzzled sorrow.

"I don't know how to do nothing," June says, wishing she didn't sound so plaintive.

"No," Alec agrees. "But if this is what he's ordered . . . Do you remember when we found Carnaby, and everything he asked me to do just hurt more?"

"I do," June says softly, wanting again to reach for him. But she doesn't.

"Grayson is your Carnaby," Alec says. "Bloody army surgeons." He cracks a wan smile. She returns it, his humor giving her a moment of hope.

As they walk out to the car, she says, "He wants me to take the fall term off."

Alec glances sharply over at her. "Is he quite serious? What will you do if you're not teaching?"

"I don't know," she says.

For the rest of the day, every interaction feels buffered and at a remove. Around Penny and Mrs. Nesbit, Alec seems almost normal, but if it's just the two of them . . . Well. It rarely is, and isn't that part of the problem? And Penny . . . How is June meant to explain any of this to her daughter? The larger question of Ceylon and the injury aside, the diagnosis itself is fresh, confusing, and hardly assured. She wants to communicate clearly with Penny, but it seems at the same time as though there's no point until she knows more.

O nly Wednesday, but already the week has that feeling of being torn between too many masters. There have been letters to write and telephone calls to make, the department chair to contact, and so much else.

That evening, Penny droops over her jacket potato, nudging a piece of carrot around her plate. When she emits a tremulous sigh, Alec lowers his fork and turns to regard her. "What is it, love?"

Penny shrugs. "I was just wondering if Mummy's going to be all right," she says quietly, her eyes on the potato.

June sets down her water glass. "Of course," she says. "You and your father are taking such good care of me, Penny."

"But . . ." Penny pauses. "Daddy, why do you have to sleep in your workroom? Is Mummy contagious?"

June's heart plummets as she and Alec exchange a glance. She had hoped, perhaps unrealistically, that Penny wouldn't notice, or that Alec might be back where he belongs before this question arose.

"I'm not contagious even a little," June says, with what she hopes is a reassuring smile.

Penny looks at her and back at Alec, who leans closer to Penny. "She needs a particular sort of rest," he says, "and if I'm there, lolling about and tossing and turning and whatnot, well, she can't possibly sleep through all of that, can she?"

Penny giggles. "And snoring, Daddy."

"I never," he says with an exaggerated umbrage. "Perhaps tonight I should sleep in your room with you and Lucky."

She rolls her eyes. "Oh, Daddy."

He grins at her. "Eat your dinner, princess."

Penny wolfs down the rest of her potato, excuses herself, and slides off her chair to vanish into the back garden with Lucky. Alec stands and clears the table, stacking the dishes into the sink.

"Thank you," June says. He nods, looking at her with that same ghastly, cordial blankness, and her heart sinks again. For a moment, it's all June can do not to lay her head on the table and weep. Instead she goes to the drawing room to have the lie-down her doctor has insisted on. The specter of a brain injury is worrisome, of course, but the practice of trying to heal it is rather dull, not to mention frustrating. Her main amusements are unavailable to her except in small parcels of time throughout the day, and it can't possibly be good for her to be locked into this loop of fretting about Alec, can it?

The sound of dishwashing trails off in the kitchen, and Alec appears in the drawing room doorway, his book clutched in one hand. "India," he says tersely. "Bombay? The Gateway and the docks?"

She hesitates. What she sees in his face is far too damning. "Yes."

"What was it like?"

"Hot," she says, hoping a stab at humor will help. It doesn't; he regards her with his lips tight. She takes a breath and tries again. "It was awfully crowded. And I'd never seen such colors."

His face closes off again. "Did you think of me? When you were standing there?"

"Oh, Alec . . ." Her voice breaks a bit on his name. "Of course."

"India," he says again. He pushes his hand through his hair, starts to say something, stops. "All these years." And then he's gone, his footsteps quick and measured up the stairs, and June is alone again in the drawing room, sick with regret. He has loved her his whole life, and she has chosen a path that has, in the end, broken his heart.

1960, *Edinburgh*

The smooth scratch of slide rules and thick wax pencils against the watermarked Livingstone & Gray drafting paper feels to Alec like an anchor, as does the impenetrable scent of oil and scum coming off the water by the docks. He breathes the heavy air, mostly relieved to be back at the office. June has insisted she's well enough for him to go, pointing out that it's not as though anything is different, exactly; the diagnosis, such as it is, has not created new symptoms or worries. Besides, the office is a respite, a moment of normal life in which he can set himself straight again. Or it was meant to be; Alec hadn't counted on what it would be like when Sanjay and the other fellows asked after June. Half-strangled with confusion and a bright spark of anger, Alec had muttered something gruff about doctors and tests, and let the other men think what they would. Easy enough to avoid the bewildering truth, especially when one of the design team starts in about the bloody Tories and the NIIS. Easy with almost everyone, that is—but with Sanjay, the secrets taste bitter and dark in the back of Alec's throat. How many times have he and June had dinner with Sanjay and Parvati? Every time they tore a roti or spooned up a bit of chutney, thinking June had never known such things, how did she just sit there, pretending?

When Friday afternoon comes, he's more or less back in the swing of things at the office, and he almost wishes he could stay longer—but the ups and downs of worry for June are relentless, and Penny is already confused. The last thing he wants to do is make things harder for his daughter. So he goes home when he's meant to, traversing the familiar bus lines and streets to the house he knows so well. It feels like a dreadful game of sorts, picking out the things that are still true. The things he knows are real.

How many times has he come up the walk on an afternoon like this, caught in an end-of-day rain shower, the fat black handle of his umbrella awkward in the curl of his hand? It never keeps him dry enough. Already damp, he pauses with the weather soaking into his hair, basking in the rich scent of the rain striking at Edinburgh's peculiar summer dust, that harsh bite of lime and granite. Still, though, he's not quite ready to go inside. Outside is so uncomplicated. Alec straightens his umbrella and goes around the back, taking his time. The trees provide a bit of shelter, and he skirts the puddles, but he can't help pausing to admire the raindrops beaded against the lush purple velvet of the larkspur. The garden plucks at his trouser legs like a greedy child, unencumbered, laden only with pollen and rain, and for now he is content to wallow in the quiet.

When he does finally make his way damply inside, Penny looks up from her book and grins at him. "Daddy!"

"Hallo, princess," he says. He tips the umbrella into the old blue-and-white porcelain stand and hovers on the mat.

"Mummy is resting," Penny says gravely.

"All right," Alec says. "Thank you for letting me know. I'm going to go up and change, but I'll be back in half a tick."

"Okay," Penny says.

"Shall I put on the kettle?" Mrs. Nesbit asks, eyeing the way he's dripping.

"That would be lovely," Alec says. "Thank you." She nods briskly and sets to the task, and Alec leaves the room and goes upstairs, where he hangs his wet clothes in the bathroom and puts on his dressing gown.

He pauses as he moves back into the hallway—if June is sleeping, he doesn't want to disturb her, but most of his clothes are still in their bedroom, and that door is closed. As he's wrestling with this, the door swings open, and June steps out.

"I thought I heard you." She sounds tired, and she's rubbing the heel of her hand against her forehead as if another headache has come to roost.

"Yes," he says. He looks down at himself, then plucks at the dressing gown and tries to smile for June. Perhaps if he acts as if things are normal, they someday will be. "Got a bit wet out there. Thought I should change."

"Oh, of course," June says. She moves back into the bedroom and sits on the edge of the bed. The blinds are pulled closed, and what little of the rain-wet sunlight there was has gone gray in the half-dark.

He gathers dry clothes and changes quickly. As he heads back to the bathroom to hang up the robe, he pauses and turns back. "Mrs. Nesbit is making tea, if that would help." He gestures at his temple, and June gives him a faint, sad smile.

"Thank you," she says. "I'll be right down."

He makes his way downstairs, and just as he's about to go into the kitchen, the phone rings. He reverses himself and goes to the front hall to answer.

"Ah, Oswin," Floss Corbett says, his voice silky and unwelcome. "Corbett here."

Something bounces wrong in Alec's chest, and he glares at his reflection in the small square mirror on the wall above the telephone table. "Good evening."

"I wondered if I might speak with June," Corbett says.

It's impossible for a moment to craft a civil response, and he's gripping the handset so hard his fingers have already begun to ache. He glances at the stairs.

"I'm not sure she's finished her rest," he says.

"She's been resting? Good, good." There's a small silence, then the click and hiss of a cigarette being lit on the other end of the line. For the first time in years, Alec thinks about the last cigarette he had, in Algeria. But that stops him in his tracks. When he was in Algeria, June was already in Ceylon. And Corbett had known it. Corbett had told him she was out of town for the Foreign Office, and Alec had never been the wiser. That had been, what, the autumn of 1942? All he can think of is that moment when the truth could have come out and didn't. What a bloody imbecile he feels, remembering the happy optimism with which he had returned from Ottawa and gone to find his June. God.

"Hold just a moment and I'll let her know you're on the line," Alec says coldly.

"Look, Oswin, I know this must be bloody difficult," Corbett says at last, his voice languid and not, Alec suspects, entirely sincere. "It can't be helped, of course."

Alec tries to speak, but words won't come. This man is part of his betrayal, and, even worse, the reason June was there at all. Corbett is to blame for all of this; he should never have put her in harm's way and risked her life.

"You have no idea what you've done to us," Alec says at last, too loudly, his throat clotted with resentment. "'Can't be helped'? Are you quite mad? You could have helped all of it if you hadn't sent her off to your bloody war!"

June appears on the stairs, and he shoves the handset at her. "It's Corbett."

"Thank you," June says. She looks at him warily—she must have heard everything. Alec drops his gaze, embarrassed and angry.

June takes the phone from him. "Floss?" She listens, then tells him to hold on for a moment, then cups her palm over the mouthpiece and turns to Alec. "I'm sorry," she says, not quite meeting his eyes, "but . . ."

"No, of course," he says stiffly. Feeling like an ass and a fool, Alec goes to see if tea with his daughter and her dog will help.

The next day is his birthday, and Alec awakens to more rain, the fat drops shattering against the gleaming leaves of the pear tree and the patch of daisies where he'd buried Ursa. It's been another nearly sleepless night in the wrong bed; the Saturday morning light falls awry on this side of the house even on a brighter morning, and he doesn't like it. The rain magnifies his disorientation as the windows run inky with water. It's been a cool, wet August, and Edinburgh has gone riverine and florid with poppies and phlox interrupting the relentless green and gray. There's something about the ruffle of it against the roof that reminds him of India. Has June heard that monsoon rain as well?

He closes his eyes. He's in no hurry to get up. It's another birthday, and he's old enough now that they seem less noteworthy than they used to. Forty-one is not half so interesting as nine, or six, or fourteen. When he was very young, his mother would greet him on his birthday morning with the same hug she always had for him and one of the small spiced biscuits layered with almonds and coconut their Kashmiri summer cook would make just once during the season. In the afternoons Alec and his parents would go riding through the hills around the camp. He remembers still the way his father had seated him snug against the sleek black gelding's shoulders at the front of the cavalry saddle and nudged the horse to a canter. He can't have been more than five or six years old, but the rush of Himalayan wind in his face, the thick heathering of rust-colored hair on his father's forearm, the smell of the horse's sweat . . . so many other memories have come and gone, but those have stuck. Not for the first time he wonders if he's held so close to those because they were so happy that summer, the three of them, or if the series of images fits the idea of the life he might have had if they had lived. But memory is a peculiar beast; he cannot remember the horse's name to save his life. He can't remember if his mother had laughed or told her husband to be careful. It doesn't matter, exactly; he remembers that he was safe, then, or thought he was.

He frowns. Perhaps he'd been seven that summer, not five. Perhaps it had been that last summer before the cholera came and burned his home and his family and every security to ashes. It had been a long time until he'd felt that safe again, and then the war had taken that away, and it had been quite a job finding it again. But he had, and even when he and June had struggled with one thing or another—distance, his recovery, whatever it had been—he had felt as if he knew where the ground beneath him lay, where it tipped and angled and where it ran true and level. As much as she's told him, the galling reality is that there are a thousand times as many things she has not. It's worse since Corbett's call last evening; Alec had barely been able to speak to June at dinner, pushing through gamely as well as he could for Penny's sake.

On Monday it will have been a week since that awful day at the hospital. Confusion inhabits him, always infected with some other feeling, whether the general weight of it made spiky with anger or more a sorrowful echo. He is her husband, yes, but he is not the man who knows her secrets. That honor belongs to Corbett. And who knows, maybe others.

If he can put aside the hurt this has done him, Alec can focus on what is really important, which is that this brain injury or whatever it is—he skitters away from that, trying not to fall into the maelstrom of bewilderment—is to blame for the spasms and headaches. He gets the sense June hoped the diagnosis, however rudimentary and tentative, might have led to some form of progress by now. Alec knows June well enough to know that she is afraid of worse. And well enough to know that she is pretending—for herself, for him, for Penny—to be better with this than is actually the case.

Alec sighs and swings his legs over the edge of the sofa. He can't stay there forever, for any number of reasons. His heart gladdens as he hears Penny laughing downstairs, accompanied by the ridiculous shrill bark of the puppy. Alec sits and rubs his hands together, the left bolstering the right, and as one thumb creases across the opposite palm he pauses, frowning down at the frayed edges of the rug. Buried somewhere in the betrayal is something else—a story he doesn't understand. Can't understand. When he tries to imagine what June means when she speaks of a Zero attacking wherever she was in Ceylon . . . How could he not have known she'd been hurt so badly? It's impossible to say which moments in all this are the worst, but he's struck now with a new epiphany. He looks at his hands again, appalled.

All this time, she's been helping him recover from his wounds, and he'd never known she had war wounds of her own. She had worked so hard to bring him back to England from Odessa, and then back to himself from what the camps had done to him. And all this time, through his endless complaints and confusions, through the years of nursing him back to something resembling the man he'd been before the war . . . Christ. She's never said a word, never complained except occasionally when her headaches have been too punishing to ignore. God knows what she's seen, what she's heard and smelled and felt.

For the first time he considers the scenario June has alluded to, rather than his resultant fears and worries, and his mouth goes dry. The whole Pacific war had been full of Japanese pilots and their immensely maneuverable Zeros. Kamikaze or otherwise, the sleek little fighters had done enormous damage. What can that have been like for June, to have lived a life in which something like that could happen? To have been left wounded in an attack like that . . . She'd said "uncon-scious," but for how long? Was she in hospital, out there in Ceylon? A brain injury . . . nothing bleeds quite like a head wound, and he can't for the life of him imagine June like that, felled by a piece of metal, covered in blood. How does she stand the memories? He can't quite comprehend any of this.

June has had her own war, her own horrors. It casts a new light on her efforts to be strong and brave for Penny—and for him, for that mat-ter. Just a year ago—God, a week ago—her pretending would have made sense to him, although it would have made him sad for her, that she felt like she needed to be so stoic. But now . . . The stoicism feels different through this new and alarming lens. Now he notes the fear and notes how brave June is being, how calmly she steers Penny away from the prognoses she is not yet ready to discuss. It's like Jekyll and Hyde in Alec's head all the time now: he looks at his wife, sees the cour-age and the trepidation and the dogged determination to heal; at the same moment he sees her carefully and quietly building a layer of un-truth. And through it all he wonders whether she shares the fear with Floss Corbett. Whether Corbett has been allowed to see her vulnerable.

The night before, Alec had come out of the bathroom after cleaning his teeth and found her standing in their bedroom doorway as if she were waiting for him. He'd paused, the Jekyll in him throbbing with concern for his wife, wanting her to be okay more than he's ever wanted anything. *Come to bed*, she'd said, almost a whisper. He'd seen what it had cost her to ask, and then the Hyde in him had laced his mind with the fears again, and he'd shaken his head, murmured a hasty apology, and gone into his workroom. He hates sleeping there, hates being away from the warm stillness of June, of this woman he's loved for as long as he can remember. But she has hurt him as deeply as she's loved him, and the undulating animal of sorrow in his chest makes it impossible yet for him to go back to something that will never be normal again.

He washes and gets dressed, then goes downstairs to see about a coffee.

"Happy birthday, Daddy," Penny says when Alec joins her at the dining table. She puts her hands across a sheaf of paper on the table in front of her to shield it.

"Thank you, love," Alec says, squeezing her shoulder. "What's that you're working on?" Mrs. Nesbit brings him a cup of coffee from the kitchen, and he accepts it, and her birthday wishes, with a grateful nod.

Penny goes rather pink and beams at him. "I'm making you a story for your birthday."

Alec's chest flutters with love and memory. "Are you indeed? That's splendid."

June comes in. "Happy birthday, Alec." She kisses him quickly on the cheek and takes her seat across from him.

"Thank you," Alec says. He looks up, girding himself for the punch of meeting her gaze. Her ocean-glass eyes look right through him, knowing everything, just as they always have.

Penny looks from one parent to the other and pointedly stacks her papers more neatly, lining up the edges. "It's about a bear," she says proudly. "And also Lucky."

"That sounds wonderful," June says. Alec nods, grinning at his daughter.

"But you have to wait," Penny says to Alec. "It's not finished just yet."

"I shall do my best," Alec says solemnly.

Mrs. Nesbit appears with a coffee for June and a bowl of oatmeal for Penny. "May I move it off the table for a bit, Penny?"

"Thank you," Penny says, watching intently as Mrs. Nesbit carefully shifts the papers to the top of the sideboard. She turns to Alec. "Don't look, though."

"Upon my honor," he says, and she grins at him before turning her attention to her oatmeal. Alec smiles to himself, a little overcome by the idea that she's written him a story. She's made up her own stories before, but this feels different. More organized. And, he realizes, glancing across at the stack of paper, longer.

Penny finishes her breakfast and bounces out of her chair. She collects her papers and Lucky, then turns to Alec. "Stay in here while I finish, Daddy."

"I'll keep him here," June says with a smile. Penny nods agreeably and goes off to the drawing room.

Mrs. Nesbit brings Alec his newspaper. "Would you like eggs this morning?"

"Yes, thank you," he says, "but I'd been hoping for one of yesterday's scones as well. Those currants went down a treat."

She smiles at him, pleased. "We have a few left, certainly." She turns to June. "Eggs for you as well, then?"

"That would be lovely," June says.

Alec's jaw clenches—every time June speaks, he feels raw, and she's not even saying anything that hurts. He just wants to read the paper but opening it now and blocking her out with it would be unkind. With an effort, he lays the paper aside. "You look as though you're feeling better," he says, trying to make his voice less stiff.

"Yes, thank you." She looks up and smiles at him tentatively. "I was thinking perhaps Penny and I would try our hand at making you a cake today. A Victoria sandwich, like Cook used to do for you."

Alec blinks. She couldn't have startled him more if she'd tried. "I'm sorry, what?"

June's smile wavers. "Well, it seemed to me that if the doctor means me to be around the house more often, perhaps I ought to find ways to occupy myself. And then I thought about your birthday and the sponges."

"I see," Alec says, his mind roiling with too many feelings to count. It's not even rational, yet he has a flash of wondering if she had also learned to bake in Ceylon. Or wherever else she was. He has no idea if there are more places, more injuries, more secrets waiting in the wings. He bites back a question and tries to focus, but what comes to mind instead is Maeve and Cullen, all those mornings with fresh bread or perfect little cakes in that grand old kitchen, that gorgeous Victoria sandwich at the end of his time in Halifax. "That seems a bit outside your purview. Don't trouble yourself. But thank you."

Her smile drops away entirely, and Alec looks away, ashamed that he's chosen to say something he knew would wound her. But it's as if the past week has built up behind a dam in his chest, or in his throat, and before he can stop himself, he adds, "When I was in Halifax, Maeve used to make cakes rather often. She made a marvelous Victoria sandwich for my going-away party."

Hurt flashes over June's face, and she lowers her eyes. It's a long moment before she responds. "You never said."

"When I got back you were in the midst of planning for Oxford, weren't you," Alec says. The ice is seeping back into his voice, and for a moment he doesn't want to make the effort to sound better. "Didn't really seem like the time to mention a cake."

The rain has picked up, and Alec can hear it on the window behind him, the raindrops clicking and clacking like the hooves of a thousand tiny horses against the glass. Hardly a monsoon, but the rain this month has started to feel like it may never end.

Mrs. Nesbit comes back then with their breakfast plates. She's included a little ceramic pot of the homemade strawberry jam she brings only on special occasions, and Alec smiles at her gratefully. He and June eat in silence. Alec glances at the newspaper, although his mind is racing so fast that the printed words are meaningless. Perhaps the rain is getting to him. June has seen the rainy seasons too, hasn't she? He can't shake the idea of it, and wants to ask, but doesn't dare—there isn't an answer that won't hurt and confuse him. The worst of it, this time, is that he wants to share stories, compare experiences. But his India is a lifetime ago, and hers . . . Well. It's been nearly twenty years, hasn't it? They can't really compare the Bombay of the eight-year-old boy he'd been when his India ended in conflagration with the Bombay through which June had entered the East as . . . Well, what had she been? A spy? He's asked so many questions, and the answers have left him cold and confused: *I'm sorry, I can't tell you. I can't explain. I'm sorry.* He can't ask if she was a spy, because he knows she won't provide a remotely satisfactory answer, if there even is such a thing at this point.

Lost in the burden of wanting to ask June questions he can't yet even devise and already knows she won't answer, Alec is unspeakably relieved when Penny and Lucky march into the room.

"Daddy," Penny says, the serious expression on her face belied by her shining eyes, "are you ready?"

"I am indeed," he says, folding his newspaper away.

"Shall we come into the drawing room?" June asks.

Penny nods and guides them to the sofa with a munificent bow. "All right," she says. She claps her hands and tells Lucky to sit, and he drops to his haunches beside her. She pats his head with a smile, then turns to her audience, ruffling her pages grandly. "Once upon a time," she intones as seriously as can be expected through a cascade of giggles, "there was a bear."

Alec grins at her, delighted. Penny beams and keeps reading. "One day a group of soldiers found him and took him on their ship. The bear loved being on the ship and looking at the porpoises and birds, and he liked eating the snacks and biscuits the soldiers gave him. They named him Wojtek, and he was a very good bear. But what he really wanted . . ." She pauses, her eyes shining. "What he really wanted was a hat!"

June laughs, and Alec can't help but exchange a smile with her. Penny refers to her sheaf of papers. "The ship sailed and sailed, until one day it got to Scotland. By then the soldiers had run out of biscuits, but they wanted the bear to get more, so they dressed him up like a soldier. But he still didn't have a hat, and so the people on the dock knew he was a bear. 'No,' the chief soldier said, 'he is a soldier, like us. See? He knows how to act like a soldier.'" She pauses and clears her throat, nudging Lucky. He leaps to his feet, ears pricking attentively in different directions. "But the man on the dock wasn't sure, so he grabbed a rifle and pointed it at the bear. The soldiers yelled! But the man didn't shoot. He pointed the rifle and said 'BANG!'" She glances down at Lucky, whose eyes are fixed on her, and sighs. "BANG!"

To Alec's astonishment, Lucky collapses to his side, largely still except for the lolling tongue and the delighted tail.

"Good boy," Penny whispers, bending for a moment to pet him. "The bear did not care one bit about the rifle or the man on the docks, but he liked the man's hat, so he took it!"

"I daresay he did," June murmurs. "Good job, Wojtek."

Penny regards them sorrowfully. "'You can't just take someone's hat,' the chief soldier said to the bear. So Wojtek was sad. Then the soldiers took him to the zoo so he could have all the snacks he liked and not be able to take any more hats." She turns to the puppy, who is still watching her, and whispers, "Go to the *zoo*, Lucky." His ears twitch as he ponders this, and then after a small pause Lucky crawls under Alec's armchair. Penny, grinning ear to ear, pulls the corner of a scone out of her pocket and tosses it to him.

"Oh, well done," Alec says, clapping, his heart pushing too hard. This is unlike every other bear story, and yet. What a brilliant girl Penny is, and how hard she must have worked with Lucky. "That's grand, Penny."

"So, Daddy," she says, "today we must go to the zoo to see if we can rescue the bear!"

Alec smiles. "You think they'll let us rescue Wojtek?"

Penny shrugs. "Perhaps not," she says, "but we ought to give it our best, oughtn't we?"

"Rather," June says. "Shall we see if it stops raining, or slows at any rate, and go after lunch?"

"Perfect," Alec says.

"Yes, perfect," Penny echoes.

Alec opens his arms, and Penny scoots into a hug. "That was brilliant," he says. "Absolutely marvelous. And Lucky was terrific."

Penny glances back at the dog with a proud smile. "He's awfully clever."

Alec grins over her shoulder at June, who looks as bemused and astonished as he feels, and for just a moment the world feels less on the edge of disaster.

The rain clears in the early afternoon, and the three of them take the tram to the zoo. As they alight at the gatehouse on Corstorphine Road, Alec catches a glimpse of their reflection in one of the puddles gleaming along the cobblestones: the two of them as tall as church towers, Penny the portals and facade between them. He smiles to himself—if Lucky were here, would he be the clerestory or the nave?

June catches him smiling, returns it tentatively. "What's funny?"

"It's nothing," he says, and her smile loses its balance. He hadn't meant it to sting, but perhaps everything they say to each other will be laden like this from now on, weighted for one in ways the other can't hear.

It has turned out to be a beautiful afternoon, and they are joined at the zoo by what feels like half the city. But while most of the families mill about and try to organize themselves, Penny takes her parents by the hands and tugs them up the hill toward Wojtek's enclosure. They are nearly there when an elephant's trumpeting burnishes the after-noon, and Penny stops in her tracks.

"Sally!" She hovers for a moment, undecided, then changes course. "We must see Sally, Daddy. Maybe you can have an elephant ride for your birthday!"

"I think I'm a bit larger than her usual sort," Alec says mildly.

Penny rolls her eyes. "Well, yes, but you're not bigger than four chil-dren, are you?"

"You make an excellent point," he says, "but I think I'll take a pass if it's all the same."

"Okay," Penny says. She comes to a halt outside the elephant's home, the sun steaming out of the acrid hay. June wrinkles her nose, but Penny digs in her pocket and pulls out another bit of scone. She tosses it to the elephant, who flaps her massive ears before delicately taking the morsel from the ground with her trunk.

"I see Sally likes the scones as well as Lucky does," Alec says.

"May I have an elephant ride?" Penny regards them plaintively. "I haven't in ages."

"Of course," Alec says.

Penny pauses again. "Have you ever ridden an elephant, Daddy? When you were small?"

"Yes," he says after a moment. "When I was just about your age, I suppose. My parents knew an old mahout, and one morning they let him take me out on his elephant, up in the hills. Indian elephant, of course, much smaller than Sally." Almost unconsciously his hand steals out in front of him as if the rough gray-and-pink forehead might still be within reach. "He said that when his elephant was young he'd smelled like honey."

Penny looks up at him, her face dubious. "Sally doesn't smell a bit like honey."

June chuckles. "No, it's just the young males that smell sweet. Once they get a little older . . ." She gestures at Sally. "Well, you know. Rather much, aren't they?"

"I didn't know you knew about elephants, too," Penny says, regarding June curiously. "Did you ever ride one, like me and Daddy?"

June looks out over the zoo, sloping away toward the city below them. Beyond Sally, giraffes sway across a paddock thick with grasses, and for a moment Alec thinks she's staring at them, until he realizes that she's gazing off toward something he and Penny can't see. The elephants of her past, presumably. At last, June turns back to Penny with a too-bright smile. "I've never ridden an elephant, no."

Alec doesn't know what to think. Is she telling the truth? She wouldn't just lie, would she? Not now, not after everything that's come out in the last week. But even if she hasn't ridden an elephant, surely she's seen one. Surely.

What is he meant to do when the truth is couched as unbearably as the omissions and untruths that led them to this point, and everything his wife says is laced with doubt? How is he meant to be part of this?

Alec looks down at Penny again, trying to fix his smile. He knows the answer lies with her, and someday perhaps he will be able to see it more clearly. For today, he turns and looks back at Sally, the leisurely switch of her tail.

"Let's get you a ticket," he says to Penny, "and I'll tell you more about the mahout and his elephant while we wait."

1963, *Vienna*

The path to the restaurant runs as straight as a Fenlands lane, the pale gravel walkway lined with horse chestnut trees with leaves as bright as tigers. June walks slowly through the Stadt-park, listening to the rattle of crows lighting on the iron fence, their wings mahogany in the setting sun. An elderly couple crosses not far in front of her, a fat white dog pulling them along through the gloaming. The woman's left elbow loops through the man's right; his own left arm is just a sleeve pinned tidily up to the shoulder. June pauses to let them pass, wondering about the old man's war.

She gazes around her, shaking off the momentary disquiet before she continues on her way. There are people everywhere, but it's not noisy; Vienna is a staid old city, a dowager on the banks of an ancient river. Although quiet is relative, isn't it? There is the crunch of her foot-steps on the gravel, the wind in the branches of a linden tree where a squirrel runs headlong down the trunk to chatter her away, the trill of a sparrow somewhere off in the distance.

And, at the end of the walk, a meowing gray cat who arches against June's calf and presses its forehead to her palm when she stoops to pet it. She makes a note to tell Penny about the small cat later, and the relief catches at her again that Penny is well, that the fever that raged through her over the summer has gone away, that her daughter is heal-ing and gaining back her strength. It had been terrifying, to say the least. Alec had aged visibly through the course of the illness, and June has no illusions that she is any more unscathed than he. Even once Penny had turned the corner and started to recover, it had been a hard road, and for a while it had seemed that June would be unable to accept the invitation to the mathematics symposium that's brought her to Vienna.

She forces herself back to the present and straightens up to regard the restaurant. Tucked between two old stone edifices, it might have been a stable once. Or perhaps this place with the low yellow walls and the guttering gaslit lantern over the doorway has been serving Vienna since the Turks were here, or the Romans. Café Leo looks like something out of an old story, the kind of place where travelers might have stopped and exchanged tales on a stormy night. But truly, everything on this visit has felt like a fairy tale, all castles and swans and light dappling through trees.

But fairy tales never come to good ends, do they? The cost is always too high, the dragons too strong, the obstacles too mighty. Her time with the Foreign Office had been like a fairy tale as well, and she the heroine counting seeds or spinning straw to defeat the enemy. And she had been damn good at it, too. But the cost . . . The cost had been calamitous; she had almost lost Alec, and although, in the end, he had stayed, and their life had evened out, he had never looked at her quite the same again.

June steps inside and pauses, letting her eyes adjust to the way the fading light appears in pockets through the deep-cut windows. Most of the oaken tables are full, old men, mostly, sitting in clusters with heavy jugs of wine. Smoke from cigarettes and heavy pipes curls through the air, the fug of it thick and autumnal. The men glance up curiously at her and then away again. For just an instant, June shivers—some of these men may have served in the first war, but what of the others? Are there former soldiers or sailors here whose fates she held in her hand?

Are there pilots here who confronted Alec in the midnight skies over the Channel? She can't help but think of that awful moment, years ago now, when Alec bridled against the idea of living in a German-speaking world. She had understood enough, then, to change her own trajectory forever. But now, standing here on the thick wooden planks of the café's old floor, listening to a young waitress chat in German with one of the patrons, she understands the long reach of Alec's war differently.

Across the room, Wendy Fairchild rises from her seat by the fireplace and raises a hand to catch June's eye. "Over here," she says, her voice carrying through the hubbub. June smiles and makes her way to the table, and Wendy comes around and embraces her. "God, it's good to see you. You had me worried, Attwell." She steps back and eyes June critically. "You look good. Better than last time."

June smiles. "Thank you." The last time she'd seen Wendy had been, what, two years ago? Wendy had been on her way to Vienna in some capacity, nominally connected to the embassy, and had come through Edinburgh as part of her leave. "You as well, though. Vienna agrees with you."

Wendy gives her a toothy grin. "Grand old city, really." She gestures at the table. "Here, I'll get us some wine."

They sit, the fireplace beside them raked clean and cold of the prior night's ashes. A sleek black-and-tan Doberman lying in the shadows beneath the table looks up and regards June with mild interest before lowering his head back to his paws. Wendy drops a hand to his head. "That's a good boy, Jaeger." The dog pushes his face against Wendy's palm. There had been Dobermans at Anderson near the end, when the Americans joined them with their solid, clever war dogs. Wendy had wanted one then; it was no surprise when she'd got a puppy soon after her transfer to Washington.

"He's your third, is that right?"

Wendy nods. "I'd just lost Blaze before I transferred here, and then there was a chap we worked with at the, ah, embassy, whose bitch had a litter, and it seemed like the time."

"He looks so intelligent," June says.

"Rather," Wendy says, regarding her dog proudly. She pats him again and turns to the waitress hovering nearby. "Ein Flasche rot, Greta, bitte sehr." The waitress nods, her coiled blond braids bobbing, and vanishes through the doorway into the next room.

"Really, though," Wendy says to June, "you're well now?"

"More or less," June says. "It wasn't as bad as all that, honestly, after the beginning. And I got used to it." She shrugs, and lays her hand flat on the table, the fingers quivering lightly. Alec said once that it reminded him of a hibernating dormouse, and now she can't think of it otherwise, although it has also seemed a softer, less brutal echo of Alec's injuries. The tremor never really stops these days, the dormouse's lungs forcing motion like a bellows, but she's found ways to work around it, especially since there has been no further deterioration, nor a clear diagnosis beyond the suspected consequences of that long-ago head injury. The endless therapy has helped as well. And Alec. Always Alec.

"I'm glad, June. Gosh," Wendy says with a shudder. "I thought you were done for that day. Always admired the way you came back to the work at Anderson. You and Lucy Kent both. A lot of people would have copped a Blighty and gone home, but not our Attwell."

June glances down at the table, pleased and a bit embarrassed. "It was a long time ago," she says. "Things were different then. But you're right, I couldn't wait to get out of hospital and get back to the wireless."

"I'm sorry you had to give it up in the end." Wendy shakes her head with an affectionate smile. "Never thought you'd turn out one of those family girls, like old Pamela."

June forces a smile. She would never in a million years have compared herself to someone like Pamela Glynn, so determined to leave the Foreign Office and marry her officer fiancé at the first possible opportunity, but here she is, isn't she? Not Pamela, but something else, without so clear a category.

Wendy's smile fades as she seems to realize what she's said. "Oh, gosh, June, don't look like that. It's just . . . you were always the best of us. That's all."

Whatever she is, June's not here working with Floss and Wendy in Vienna. She knows Wendy meant no harm, but the other woman's words leave a hollow spot nonetheless.

Wendy goes on in a rush. "And Alec's a good man, isn't he? A good father?"

June sighs. "A splendid father, yes. He makes everything work as well as can be expected."

A silence falls between them. June doesn't want to talk about the schism between her and Alec, which has never quite healed, and doesn't know what she would say even if she did. It was a long while before Alec came back to their shared bedroom, and even then they were awkward together until they each learned to negotiate the new landscape. And, while June hates to admit it, Penny's illness had brought them closer as well. But even so, they are still not the same as they were before she had told Alec about Ceylon. Three years now, and it still creates ripples in their lives like a stone skipping across a pond.

The waitress returns with a carafe of dark red wine, and there's a moment of spirited conversation between her and Wendy. June's German is more technical, less . . . Well, less like this. Less like the German of someone who lives and works and orders food in Austria. And like everything else, it's a bit discomfiting, another echo of the life June might have had. Finally Wendy thanks the girl, who vanishes again. Wendy pours wine for June and then for herself.

June lifts her glass and watches the wine move in the light. It glints purple, the liquid clinging to the sides of the glass, and she pauses to breathe in the dark fruity scent before taking a sip. "This is marvelous."

Wendy grins at her. "The drink is not the worst part of being posted here." June nods, regarding her friend more closely. For decades Wendy has seemed practically ageless, but suddenly now when she smiles there are new lines around her eyes, and her coppery hair is heavily threaded with silver, as if this new war is somehow harder than the last one, despite its lack of obvious battlefields. June falters, viscerally aware in a way she can usually quash that this war is not hers to fight. Whatever those challenges are . . . She is free to speculate all she likes about what it is to work against the Russians from this strange old city just at the border between East and West, how the scares in Cuba and other places might have affected what Wendy does here. June would love to know more, but she cannot ask. She doesn't even know where Wendy works, or if she rattles its corridors with her deck of playing cards like she always had in Scarborough and Ceylon.

"Is there a worst thing?" She smiles with an effort. "Everything I've seen of Vienna so far has been lovely, and I imagine there are all sorts of benefits to working at the embassy."

Wendy's gaze roves around the restaurant, looking anywhere but at June. "Yes," she says, "but everything is a mixed bag, isn't it? In any event," she says too brightly, finally meeting June's eyes, "academic life seems to be treating you all right these days. I read your piece on linear inequalities. Hardly understood a bit of it."

With a shock, June recognizes the tactics she's used herself for years to steer conversations away from secrets. Disoriented and trying to recover, June smiles an acknowledgment of Wendy's comments and raises her glass in a toast. "To old friends," she says, "in new places."

"Old friends," Wendy echoes, and they clink their glasses. The waitress comes back, laden with plates she sets down on the table between June and Wendy. Jaeger raises his head again, scenting the air with interest. June leans forward, breathing in the rich scents of onion and paprika steaming up from the dishes.

Wendy regards the plates happily. "Thing I like about Café Leo, though, is one of the cooks—Greta's aunt, I think," and she pauses, gesturing at the waitress, "she came across from Budapest right after the first war. So you've got your schnitzel and whatnot, can't very well come to Vienna without getting that, but also a grand goulash." She points at the deep bowl full of thick, bricky soup with its chunks of beef and potato.

"It looks delicious," June says, taking another deep breath of its earthy aroma.

Wendy beams, as proud as if she'd cooked it all herself. "I figured you'd like some real food after two days of conference, and I know there are a thousand places we could have gone that would have been more posh, but . . . This seemed more our speed." Her face lights up. "Remember that pub we used to haunt in Scarborough, by the harbor?"

"The Scarlet Hen." June laughs, relieved to be able to talk about their mutual past, and as they tuck into the food, she and Wendy drift into memory. It's so much easier to talk about days long past than about the present, and June, caught as she is in a life where so much of the past is encoded and locked away, is glad to find her footing here. The absence of the present is a different issue, a pinprick that won't let up, but she's known Wendy a very long time now. There are enough old stories to fill some of the glaring empty spaces left behind by topics that are suddenly, jarringly taboo.

After a while, as the plates and the carafe of wine empty, the stories taper out as well. Wendy slips a last bite of schnitzel to Jaeger, who takes it more gently than June would have expected from such a large dog.

"Penny's dog is gentle like that, too," she says. "Of course, she makes him do tricks for his treats."

"Fair enough. They certainly seemed well-matched when I last saw them, though. Pair of cleverboots." She finishes the last sip of her wine.

"I expect she's not looking forward to not having Lucky about when she goes off to school, eh?"

"Ah," June says. The happy mood feels dampened suddenly, her real life too real. "After last summer . . . Well, it's a lot of things, really. But we're going to keep her at home a bit longer. She's got a lovely grammar school in Edinburgh, and Alec never thought she should go away even before she took ill."

Wendy frowns. "But don't you think she needs those opportunities? Those connections?"

June looks down at her own empty glass. "I had thought so, yes. But she was so ill, Wendy." She shakes her head, unsure how to explain the fear in which she and Alec had dwelled for those weeks this past summer with Penny in the relentless grip of a hepatic fever. "I didn't go until I was fourteen, Alec either, and while I had hoped to start Penny earlier . . . It's hard to consider letting her that far out of my sight, if I'm honest. I wasn't sure I'd even be able to be here, and it was only after Alec swore they would be all right, and Floss promised he would get a plane to fly me back at a moment's notice if I had to go . . ."

Wendy's mouth twists sadly. "I'm so sorry," she says, reaching over and laying her hand over June's, just for a moment. "I can't imagine what that must have been like."

"She's only ten years old," June says, her voice breaking. "And I was so afraid." She turns away, watching the other diners. Café Leo has filled with people since she arrived; every table is full now, and a cluster of men stands at the bar, heavy steins of beer and plates of sausages and mustard in front of them. It's been a long time since she found herself somewhere that feels so full of camaraderie. All these men and women talking and laughing with one another . . . It's comfortable here in ways June had not anticipated, and it steadies her even as it makes her miss her family more. She glances at Wendy and away again, wondering if Wendy, with no family at all, is lonely here.

Wendy catches her eye, nodding as if she can read June's mind. "It's good here, isn't it? The Hubers, Greta's family . . . I know it's complicated, what with the war and all that, but everyone here has been very welcoming."

"I'm awfully glad," June says. She takes a deep breath, lets it out. She feels steady enough, as long as she doesn't try to look over the confusing wall that keeps her from asking, or Wendy offering, more information about the work here in Vienna.

Later that evening she stands at the window of her hotel, watching the streetlights come on. A horse-drawn carriage clops along the street below her window, and the evening light falls across the pale dun flanks of the horse like muslin. What must it be like closer to Christmas, when the city lights up for the holiday and the back streets fill with markets and vendors? Already the corners near the Ringstrasse are occupied by old men turning chestnuts or potato wedges in heavy black kettles, and as they'd walked from Café Leo back to June's hotel, Wendy had stopped to buy a tiny sack of chestnuts to carry in her pockets and warm her hands. It had been a good stroll in the growing dark, much like the walks they'd taken together in Scarborough and Colombo, except for the lean, dignified dog at their side.

It has been a grand trip. She has enjoyed the conference immensely, particularly a panel on algebraic vs. analytical semigroups, led by an elderly Polish professor and one of his protégés. She's learned so much and spoken with other researchers and professors who share her interests, and it's only reasonable that there will be other conferences, other boons of this academic life that somehow seem to make up for the rut she's in at the university.

And, when the bustle of the conference has proven too much, she's had ample opportunity to explore. The day before she had had lunch with Floss at a Heurige attached to one of Vienna's small vineyards on the northwest fringe of the city. Below them, coated in the gossamer haze of the October afternoon, Vienna had spread down across the valley like a bicycle's broken wheel. Squinting, June had been able to see the Danube, and there had been a hard moment when she'd wondered if she were imagining it, overlaying reality with the maps she carries in her mind.

But then he had paused in front of the tavern, and she had been able to smell the hazy bite of the fir twigs hung over the doorway to tell passersby that the Heurige would be serving wine from its vineyard. It had been a bit rustic, a reminder of an older Europe that she didn't quite understand, and knew she never would. The twigs' scent had dug into her chest with the sharpness of a memory, but for a life she'd never had.

It transpires that she loves Vienna, not least because she has enjoyed her conference so thoroughly, and because Floss, the day before, had taken such pains to show her the old city at its best. In the time she's been here, Floss has worked his magic as if he were Prospero and she Miranda; the Vienna he's giving her for this short visit is glossier, more enveloping, than the Vienna she would have had if she had chosen it. But that door is closed, and has been for some time. This Vienna is mostly a gift, but increasingly it feels like an admonishment as well, a pointed reminder of a life she would have loved.

That blurry, upsetting sense of dreams unfulfilled sticks with June the next morning. With the conference at an end, her last day in Vienna holds lunch with Floss and then, in the early evening, her flight back to Edinburgh. With the rest of the day empty, she elects for a walk; her whole visit the spire of Stephansdom has called to her, and now she is finally able to take the time to explore. Standing in Stephansplatz and gazing up at the old cathedral makes her stomach hurt, and she's not sure why—the great Gothic towers are more ornate, and more tragic, it seems to her, than those of other churches she's known. But it's also true that she can hardly see a cathedral without thinking of the vicarage and her parents. This church was nearly unscathed by the war, even when the Allies bombed Vienna so doggedly that nearly a quarter of the city was destroyed. But its bells share a tone with the bells of her childhood, and perhaps that is enough.

June is on her way back to her hotel when she's brought up short by a stunning gold-and-white memorial in the middle of the Graben, where pedestrians mill about through shops in the great cathedral's shadow. She steps closer, mesmerized by the baroque immensity. On further examination it turns out to be a memorial column set in place hundreds of years earlier, both to commemorate the victims of the last great wave of plague to scour Vienna and, if she's reading it right, to celebrate the final expulsion of the Turks at around the same time. It's a remarkable work, dozens of feet of marble coursing upward and telling a story through its statues. She peers closer, noting the emblems of emperors and nation-states. It's glorious but grisly as well, especially the tragic fallen figure of a plague victim, suffering writ across his stone face and empty rib cage.

June shudders. The stone man reminds her of the men she met at Anderson when the war ended and the Japanese camps were liberated— gaunt, damaged, hollow. God. Alec would have hated it here; it would have hurt him every day. She looks around, trying to get her bearings though she feels vaguely ill. A cluster of schoolchildren in thin gray blazers brushes past her, a woman June assumes is their teacher pointing out the different historical figures on the column. The children are Penny's age—if June had brought the family to Vienna, perhaps the teachers at the English School would have brought their students down to the Graben to parse the city's memory as well. Perhaps Penny would be one of these children. June looks away, hard-pressed to contain the quickening of loss.

Vienna's memory is so long, and yet she herself will be only the tiniest blip on it, less than the fallen feather of a swan in the Danube. The realization hurts. It's all too much, suddenly—the plague column, the children, even the sharp midday shadow of the cathedral . . . There are too many reminders, too many emotions, and she makes her escape into a toy store not far from the column. JOSEF KOBER, SPIELWAREN, the sign reads. June steps inside, takes the clattering lift upstairs. It's quieter there, and looking at the toys and stuffed animals gives June something to focus on beyond the ravages of her own confusion.

She drifts back through the store, trailing her fingers across the shapes and textures of the toys she encounters. The shop seems to have everything, but even through her delight at the idea of finding something for Penny, June is also wary of bringing back anything that will trigger another round of questions and worries from Alec. Better to keep it simple. She eyes books and a series of models, looking for exactly the right thing. Penny is almost eleven, in that odd in-between place where she is no longer a little girl, but not remotely an adolescent, either. Too, her illness last summer had resulted in more than enough stuffed animals from classmates and friends. June pauses to thumb through a set of adventure books of the kind Penny loves best, but they're in German, and June suspects they might provide a somewhat different angle on the recent war as well. That would never do.

At last her eye is caught by a stand of soft animal puppets with the tiny brass Steiff tag in their ears. She hovers there for a moment—they're stuffed animals, certainly, but Penny loves to tell stories, and perhaps these hand puppets would help her in that endeavor. June looks through all of them, eventually settling on a silvery wolf and a tiger with pale yellow and black stripes. She can almost hear Penny coming up with a narrative that will suit these characters, or some elaborate task for Lucky to perform with them and, satisfied, she purchases the puppets and turns her steps back to the hotel.

The man at the front desk flags her when she walks in. "Frau Doktor," he says, "I have here a message for you." June thanks him and takes the thin envelope he's offering, pale cream stock with the golden sigil of the embassy, and her name on the front in Floss's unmistakable scrawl. Her heart sinks as she slips it into her pocket to read once she gets upstairs to her room.

June, the note reads, *I'm afraid I must cancel our lunch. Postpone, rather, as we can make it up when next I'm in Edinburgh. But there are great doings just now, and I'm needed here. I know you understand. More to follow. F.*

She looks up and out the window at the stately opera house across the street, a bitter taste in the back of her mouth. Certainly she can lunch by herself, but . . . There's a difference between knowing Floss has carried on without her and actually hearing it firsthand—she could not feel more aware of her own obsolescence now than if Floss had done this deliberately.

June washes her face and hands, eyeing herself sadly in the mirror before going back downstairs. If she regards the rest of the day as a list, maybe it will mitigate this gnawing feeling in her chest. *Very well,* she thinks. Soup, a glass of wine, perhaps a slice of Sacher torte. Then she will collect her belongings and take a taxi to the airport and the plane that will take her back to Scotland, her family, and her research, as if those glorious days at that ghastly old mansion and its outposts had never even happened.

All those years of urgency, and the endless ripples of consequence. Lives saved, to be sure, but her marriage imperiled, her health chipped away at like a flock of sheep beset by wolves. And yet. Wouldn't she do it again, if she could, even knowing the cost? The codebreaking, that work . . . It had been home. Of course the house on Shakespeare Close is home as well, as is Alec, their family. But it's not the same. Perhaps she is ungrateful. But sometimes she thinks back on the life her mother had planned for her, the life June had tried so hard to avoid, only to realize that she's ended up more or less where Imogene Attwell had wanted her. And that is a bitter pill indeed.

1964, *Kenya*

Swifts wheel across the limpid green surface of the river. Alec lies back on the thick tartan camp blanket, watching the little black birds in the dusking African sky. They remind him a bit of the war, darting through space like tiny miracles the same way that he and the other pilots had had to conquer the air to fight the Germans. He can almost imagine the sound of engines overhead, until the illusion is scattered into prisms by the splash of a kingfisher's dive.

"We should be heading back," Roger says, coming up behind him with a cough that reminds Alec that his uncle, no matter how hale he makes himself out to be, is dying. "Ezekiel and his boys say there's been a leopard on the prowl lately, and we don't want to get caught in the dark."

Penny, not far from the water's edge, looks up, her eyes bright, and comes to join them. "Daddy, I should love to see a leopard!"

"Just like your grandmother," Roger says. "Can't tell you how many times Connie had to talk Pen out of larking off after a tiger or some such."

Alec laughs, then turns and grins at his daughter. He's glad they've come to Kenya, although he wishes they had come sooner, when Roger was healthier. "If I let a leopard get you, your mother will skin me alive, darling." June is back at Brightmere, having decided some days ago that riding horses out into the bush was not for her. She was reading on the verandah when they left, one of the farm's mostly tame zebras grazing the lawn nearby.

"You're just the right size for stashing in a tree," Roger says in a lurid tone, and Penny giggles. He has spent Penny's whole life indulging her taste for ghost stories and adventure, and since they've been in Kenya the old man has added animal tales and accounts of his childhood in India to his repertoire.

"Not if it gets you first," Penny says to Roger.

"Eh," Roger says with a shrug, "don't think any self-respecting leopard would go for a tired-out piece of leather like me."

Alec gets to his feet, gathering up the blanket, and goes to the acacia where they've tied up the horses. He loves the way Roger and Penny have bonded; they've always been as close as distance would allow, but this trip has created a new layer of connection. It will be hard for her to lose her beloved great-uncle, and when Alec thinks too closely about that future, how sad Penny will be, his insides knot with grief. They have told her Roger is ill—she's a bright girl, and eleven is old enough for the truth—but she has never seemed to dwell on it. Indeed, with Roger's influence, Penny has expanded, somehow, becoming more than ever the kind of child who would have thrived in the India of Alec's childhood. Watching her stride the foothills of Mount Kenya in boots and an Australian bush hat has been a wonder.

When Penny joins him, he gives her a boost and she settles into the saddle and pats Mfupi's neck. The stocky bay Abyssinian pony whickers softly at her, his ears alert, and Alec's heart warms. It had been an effort to convince Penny to leave Lucky with Mrs. Nesbit in Edinburgh; even June's point that Lucky would be miserable in the confines of an ocean liner for a fortnight had barely had any traction with Penny. Alec had understood her reluctance—being without Ursa while he had been in Halifax had been dreadful sometimes. Too, in the autumn after

Penny's illness, she and Lucky had been more inseparable than ever, the young dog waiting with his crooked ears at the gate for her to come home from school every day. But two weeks at sea had helped Penny adjust to this temporary life without her dog, and as they'd steamed ever closer to the equator his daughter had come more and more out of the quiet shell of healing that she'd been in for so long.

Alec pulls himself awkwardly into his own saddle and ties up the blanket behind him. Until this trip, it had been decades since he'd been on horseback, and his hands have been slow to adjust. The rest of him, however, has not. While their first canter out around Roger's farm had left Alec sore and somewhat chafed, it had been immensely gratifying to find the old muscle memory still alive and well. The pressure on his inner thighs from the animal's breathing, the comfortable bend of his knees when he'd slipped his boots into the stirrups, the sway of movement . . . That first day Penny had shared his horse; by the next morning she'd been clamoring at Roger to let her ride one of his sleek, fast polo ponies. He'd laughed and steered her away from the spirited South African geldings. Next year, he'd said, with a sideways glance at Alec. They both knew next year was a pipe dream at best, given the circumstances that had brought them to Kenya, what Roger had called his last hurrah. But, as difficult as it has been coming to terms with seeing Roger for the last time, it has been grand to watch Penny turn out to be as comfortable on horseback as Alec had once been on the cricket pitch.

Roger secures his shotgun in its holster beside his saddle, and the three of them set off down the hill toward the gleam of the house's thatched roof.

"We should race," Penny says, urging Mfupi to a trot so she can catch up with Roger.

Roger glances down at her with a warm smile. "Your uncle's a bit tired for that," he says cheerfully. He pats his horse's dappled gray roan neck. "And this terrain isn't ideal for Ajax the way it is for Mfupi, in any event."

"All right," Penny says, and she drops back into second place again, just ahead of Alec.

B rightmere sits nearly seven thousand feet above sea level, a sprawling home built of cedar and stone. The verandah looks out toward the distant western horizon, and to the east Mount Kenya looms against the amethyst morning skies. It had taken hours to get to Roger's farm from Nairobi, where they had spent their first night after coming ashore in Mombasa, and Alec had been startled and pleased by the thrum of recognition he'd felt in the highlands. It wasn't India, but the house, surrounded by white Mardan roses, brilliant sweeps of bougainvillea, and a bristle of blue and pink delphiniums, had reminded him of the kind of place his parents had loved in the hill stations of his childhood. It is unmistakably not England, though even with the country grasping its independence this year, Kenya still feels like part of the Empire.

But wasn't that why Roger had retired here after independence and Partition had erased their idea of India forever? As he'd put it, it had been time for him to retire in any case, and if the Indians didn't want him taking up space in Ooty or Kerala, he'd be just as happy to take up space in Kenya. After all, he'd said, you didn't see the Africans throwing a fellow out, independence be damned.

As they round the corner of the house, Roger's majordomo, Ezekiel, appears, two of the groom's boys just behind him. He gestures the two boys forward, and they hold the horses' reins close as Alec, Roger, and Penny slip down from their saddles. Roger's boots have no sooner

reached the earth than a tall, flame-colored dog lunges off the verandah to greet him.

"Ah, good lad, Mwezi," Roger says, running his palm along the backward ridge of hair on the hound's spine. Penny calls the dog to her, and
he obligingly steps close and leans against her for a moment, his tail
thundering against the ground, before returning his attention to Roger.
Penny watches the dog, how much she misses Lucky crystal clear in her
face, and Alec is relieved when she's distracted by Mfupi's whickering.

"I'll see you tomorrow," Penny tells her pony. She hugs Mfupi again,
kissing his soft, whiskery muzzle, then stands back as the boys lead the
horses back to the stable to rub them down and ready them for the
night. Roger and Ezekiel exchange a few animated sentences of Swahili, and the two men go inside, Ezekiel frowning, Mwezi trotting just
behind. Alec has only a handful of words of Swahili, if that, but he's
seen how carefully Ezekiel watches Roger, as if he's gauging how Roger's health is doing from moment to moment. Roger is unquestionably
diminished by the leukemia crawling through his veins, but equally
clear is his refusal to slip quietly away and let it take him.

"Let's go see what Mummy is doing," Alec says, and Penny follows
him out to the lawn. The zebra is still there—or perhaps it's another
zebra, Alec has no idea—but June is just coming back through the gap
in the plumbago hedge from the path that winds down to the shallow
pond that Roger and his staff have created in one of the river's curves.

"You're back," she says, smiling broadly at them, and Penny runs and
hugs her.

"We saw ever so many giraffes," Penny says, "and Uncle Roger says
it's all right if I try to pet a dik-dik next time I see one."

"They're wild animals," June says patiently.

"Oh, I know," Penny says, nodding sagely. "But they're awfully little,
and there was a girl who had one as a pet down at Lake Nakuru, Uncle
Roger said."

Alec laughs. "Nevertheless."

Penny shrugs elaborately. "That doesn't sound very wild to me."

At dinner, Penny chatters about the other animals they'd seen on their ride, June nodding and commenting. Roger is flushed with gin or the illness; they seem to manifest similarly, and both make him more inclined to bluff and bluster. Ezekiel hovers worriedly, choreographing the staff throughout the meal while Mwezi sprawls behind Roger's chair, watching everything. The food has been unexpected, an idiosyncratic medley of English and Indian cuisines with a decidedly East African twist; Suresh, Roger's cook, comes from an old Tamil family that's been in Nairobi for generations. Tonight is grilled chicken in a coconut curry, a richly flavored rice pilau, potato samosas, and a kachumbari salad. Penny eats hungrily, seeming to relish the smoky yellow kuku paka that reminds Alec a bit of mulligatawny, and Alec looks up to find June watching their daughter, a faint, warm smile playing at the corners of her mouth.

As she finishes her curry, Penny asks Roger if they can go out and look for the leopard the next day. He laughs. "Perhaps," he says, "but it's damn hard to find a leopard if he doesn't want to be found, particularly during the day."

She regards him patiently. "I mean quite early," she clarifies.

"I imagine Roger might want to sleep in," June says. Roger gives her a look but doesn't argue, to Alec's relief. Perhaps he really is too worn-out. Roger takes umbrage, sometimes, if there's any reference to his needing to take care of himself, as if he thinks they can't see the sharpness of his cheekbones or the gaunt line of his shoulders in clothes grown a size too large.

"We shall see," he says at last, and Ezekiel gestures to his crew to bring out coffee service and dessert—sweet, doughy mandazi, and a special treat sent up from the coast, mabuyu, baobab seeds coated in a thick strawberry-flavored sugar.

Later, Roger builds a small fire in a pit out at the bottom of the lawn, and the adults sit companionably around it while Penny and Mwezi chase fireflies. Frogs and nightjars chorus up from the lake. The sky overhead is almost too clear, and there are so many stars that Alec can barely find half-remembered constellations, a task made more complicated by the nearness of the equator. Polaris is nearly out of sight along the northern horizon, and if they moved not even a hundred miles south it would be gone entirely, replaced by the equally distant Southern Cross. Shadows lunge and swoop through the smoke, bats flitting across Alec's field of vision as they hunt through the air. In the distance, a hyena calls, its cry repeated by another until a whole pack of them is carrying on.

June shudders. "I can't seem to get used to that."

Roger grunts his assent. "Dreadful racket, isn't it?" He drops a hand to soothe Mwezi, whose ears have lifted as he regards the night with a growl.

"I like it," Penny says. She pauses, frowning into the darkness. "Well, I don't mean I like it, exactly, but I like how ferocious it is."

"I feel just the same," Alec says. "Reminds me how wild the world really is."

"I'm not sure I want to be reminded," June says, her voice wry. "But if I must be, I'd rather it wasn't hyenas."

Alec smiles at her. They have never seen the world quite the same—for him, wonder exists in the reality he inhabits. A rock is a rock; the sky is the sky. Wild and unruly are not the goal, exactly, but they are part of that reality. For June, it's quite different. Everything is patterns; she has always seen the world as a series of sets. It's part of what makes her such a gifted mathematician and part of why, over the years, as she's moved from teaching to research, she has built a name for herself in Fourier transforms. When she speaks of concepts like the harmonic analysis of topological groups, she lights up, and the language has a simple beauty to it, nearly musical in its orderly sequences of integers and signs, even though Alec rarely understands what she's saying. She has always seen patterns, and he imagines that whatever she was doing during the war, whatever secret work she carried out in Ceylon and beyond, that gift was part of it.

And Penny shares that sense—here on Roger's land she has pointed to the ways the landscape repeats itself, the intervals between patches of bare soil, the measured stroll of a giraffe. Alec finds a sort of peace in watching her find a path that seems to him to bridge the ways she is most like him and most like June all at once.

The next morning Alec wakes to find the clouds have lifted from Mount Kenya in the pink-and-golden dawn, the mountain dominating the entirety of the horizon and looming over a cluster of kudu standing hock-deep in the swirling waters. In the afternoon, raindrops the size of quarters churn the green-brown surface of the river into froth.

When the rains clear, Alec and June take their tea on the verandah. Tea at Brightmere is a more English affair than dinner, and on days when they're not out exploring it has felt like a decadent entrée to the end of the day. Today Suresh has baked scones riddled with sultanas, and one of the kitchen girls has brought the wide silver tray out to their table laden with the scones, a jar of hibiscus and papaya jam, and a dish of thick cream as well as a small pewter tray of the sticky sweet mabuyu. June pours the green tea into delicate Wedgwood cups and sits back. Alec takes a sip. The tea has a lush taste to it, but perhaps it's his imagination, fueled by knowing that it's come to Brightmere from the not-too-distant shores of Lake Victoria.

"I still can't quite believe this place," June says, gesturing before them, where a giraffe sways beside an acacia not twenty yards away, grazing as the sheets of rain move off across the savannah, the clouds towering beyond the mountain.

Alec smiles. "I can understand why Roger came here when he had to leave India," he says. The wound of India plucks at him again, and he sighs. It's been four years now since June's revelation, almost exactly, all of which they have spent trying to find their way back to the heart of the marriage, but that bafflement has never stopped rearing its head. And it doesn't help that there are so many other bewilderments here at Brightmere, not least of them the eventual loss of his uncle, which he can almost see on the horizon.

Does June have those moments too, where the world feels off its axis? Although she still sometimes falls prey to those staggering head-aches, she has seemed to find a stasis of sorts—at least where her health is concerned. There have been no new tremors, and no new symptoms. But despite that relative stability, Alec now and again has noticed flick-ers of what seems like discontent. But instead of asking why he has always tried to accept not knowing, again, as gracefully as he can.

A shift in the brush catches his eye, and a small herd of elephants moves out from the tree line, gray and shapeless at a distance and then suddenly disarmingly real. There are nine of them, led by their matri-arch, whose tusks are nearly as long as June is tall. A mother elephant lays her trunk across the haunches of her baby to move him along, and Alec says, "My mother used to nudge me along rather like that."

"Not surprising," June says. She regards him fondly. "I imagine you had stopped to look at a fern or something." Alec chuckles, and the wound recedes again. There is no way to foresee how he will feel from moment to moment, or what will slap at him, even after all this time. He still has too many questions, too many doubts, even if he doesn't often know what they are. It feels like days ago, not years, that elephants were an unbearable reminder, but now . . . Right now, sitting with June beneath the vast dome of sky, he's all right.

"Remind me to ask Penny how to keep track of which giraffe is which when she gets back," he says; Penny has gone off in the Land Rover to Nakuru with Roger, Ezekiel, and Mwezi to collect the post.

June nods, her mouth quirking up in a smile. "You asked her last night, didn't you?"

"Yes," Alec concedes, "but I have the very devil of a time remembering. And she likes having all the answers."

"True," June says. She turns and meets his eyes with that level stare that he's loved his whole life. "You know she's too clever for that school." She pauses, and for just a moment her gaze goes faraway. "I want her to have every opportunity."

"Of course," Alec says.

June gives him a long, considering look, as if she's weighing what to say. "She's the best of both of us, Alec. And she should never have to make impossible choices about how best to use her gifts."

She's right about Penny, though it's hard for him to think about what she means when she talks about those choices. He loathes the idea of sending his daughter away somewhere. June and Penny are his world; other than Roger, they are his entire family. The fear of losing Penny last summer had sliced through him like a winter storm and scared him worse than anything ever had. Worse than cholera or the camps or all the rest of it put together. But if he's honest, Penny is also too clever by half. And she has a bright future ahead of her, if he can let her go to it.

He glances back at June, now sipping her tea and looking out over the glinting surface of the river. Africa has been a glory, but there have been difficult moments as well, and he doesn't know if June has found peace here the same way that he has. The ways it reminds him of India are both soothing and challenging, and he can't ask if it is the same for her, if the terrain, the people, the food, any of it, brings to mind her years in the East. Even thinking the question is too painful, though, riddled as it is with the fear that she won't answer, or that asking will disturb their fragile equilibrium as it has so many times over the years. Instead he pushes it away. He has become adept at pushing away the doubts, and, especially since last summer, trying to be in the moment.

So, this moment now: tea, elephants, a white-necked raven swooping across the horizon.

I t's just past dawn a few days later when the klaxon cawing of a hadeda ibis wakes him. Alec lies still a moment, disoriented, June curled lightly on her side next to him, lost in sleep. He regards her tenderly—even in sleep, her hand has just the hint of a tremor—and arranges the light blanket over her before he steps out of bed. He's restless, and despite the early hour he dresses quickly and steps out onto the verandah. The ibis lofts into the morning, the iridescent green covert feathers lending its wings an almost supernatural gleam.

The air is chilly and breathlessly clear beneath the immensity of sky. The moon has begun its descent, and ghostly Orion hovers overhead, Sirius still brilliant at his heel. There are so many stars that the crepuscular sky is softened into something tactile, almost mobile, like an animal's pelt. He steps off the verandah, startled to find Penny outside already, crouching beside Ezekiel as they regard something on the ground.

Penny turns and waves at him, and he almost pauses to talk, but she's busy. Probably looking for leopard spoor, he realizes, although the idea that there may have been a leopard right outside the house leaves him anxious. For a moment he wonders where Roger is, then remembers that it's still early.

As Alec sets off down the path to the pond, birdsong ebbs and flows in the air: go-away birds, weavers, doves—so many Alec can't tell them all apart. Around him, the stands of flowers and bamboo quiver with life. A monkey races along a branch overhead, shouting a warning. The sun continues its ascent behind him, light licking at the path and at Brightmere as Alec descends to the papyrus swamp that lines the shore. Suddenly a thundering roar splits the morning wide open. The birds and monkeys fall silent, and in the moment after the roar, Alec is astonished by the matching thunder of his heart. He stands taller and moves back from the shore, a bit uphill, trying to see where the vast sound came from. There—a single, massive lion standing on the opposite shore, not a hundred yards away.

My God, Alec thinks. He turns to go back up the path to find his daughter—Penny will have heard the lion too, but he wants to be sure she can see the beast, that her Kenya is as rich with possibility as his boyhood in India had been. As he comes up the slope, there she is, staring out across the water through a pair of battered and oversize field glasses, the dawn lavendering her fair hair.

"Daddy," she says as he approaches, "did you see?"

"I did," he says.

She lowers the field glasses, her eyes enormous. "I hoped and hoped, but Uncle Roger said lions don't come very often." She bites her lip. "I wish we could stay here forever, like Elspeth Huxley." A pause. "Except we have to get Lucky and Mrs. Nesbit."

Alec laughs. She had read *The Flame Trees of Thika* on the ship out from London to Mombasa, and Huxley's memoir of growing up in colonial Kenya had apparently taken root in Penny's imagination. "I think

Mrs. Nesbit would rather stay in Scotland," he says, "and besides, what would your mother and I do for work?"

Penny shrugs, unbothered by the logistics of adulthood, and lifts the field glasses to her face again to scan the horizon. "Lucky would like it here, like I do."

"I expect he would," Alec says. He can almost see it too, the pair of them exploring the whole of the Rift Valley. He regards her again, teeming with emotion. Penny is a bit small for her age, all fawn legs and bird bones, but sound and strong. Sometimes he can see what she'll look like as an adult—June's eyes, his hair, and layered under everything else the profile of her namesake, Alec's mother. She had stood just like this with field glasses, all those decades ago, watching foothills and a horizon of her own.

When he turns to go back inside, he sees that June has come out to the verandah, her eyes shining as she too watches Penny. The morning sounds, and the lion, must have woken her. There is a clarity to her wakefulness that Alec has always admired; she doesn't bog in sleep the way he sometimes does. The way Penny does too, for that matter, as if the movement from asleep to awake involves a complicated border crossing of some sort. He takes a moment to regard June before he crosses to tell her good morning—how long has it been since he's really looked at her? Really seen her? The early sun sparks mahogany in her hair. There is silver there now, but not much, and the handful of shimmering threads just add to the welter he feels when he looks at her.

She turns and looks at him, smiling. It aches at him, and he stops to catch his breath, undone.

I t's likely he will never see Roger again; his uncle has seemed vital enough most of the time during their visit, but now and again . . .

now and again there has been something else, a peculiar droop to the shoulders that had seemed so broad to Alec when he and Roger sailed from India, a stumble where there should have been the long stride of a cavalry officer. Roger is Alec's last tie to India and the life he'd had there with his parents, and Alec is finding it hard to quell the mourning—already as tangible and brittle as a seashell, though Roger is still alive—through which he has no clear path.

Tonight he considers the evening from the verandah, watching the grasses move like ocean in the breeze. The setting sun turns the landscape a bright gold and green that reminds him of summer skies filtered through palm leaves. Quite different from the way the sun smooths along the mossy old stones of Edinburgh, or the often washedout Fenlands light of his adolescence.

He sits, watching the sun dip below the edge of the world, and the moon rise to greet the soft speckled velvet of the sky. Unbidden, a memory of India comes—mangoes and scraping the fruit from its skin with his teeth under a tree, the rock bees swarming overhead. They had gone to the hill station at Ooty to escape the desultory, oppressive heat of Bombay, and he had thought the rock bees were following them. His mother had explained migration to him then; the bees wanted cooler air, too.

He can taste the fruit and hear the bees, and his father talking with Roger on the verandah. Perhaps his father had thought him too far away, or perhaps there had been enough gin poured that the men had stopped quieting themselves. He remembers talk of trenches, of the maimed soldiers sent back to England, men he would see for himself later, in London, selling matches or fruit to eke out a living, masks carefully over missing jaws, long sticks standing in for legs, empty sleeves tucked out of the way. And he has his own war too, with its own sights and sounds. Christ Jesus, when the Americans had come, and they'd all been able to see what Germany had been doing all that time . . . Christ. It can't have been easy for June, either, in the Pacific, although she will never say so. Who knows what other scars and memories she has to which he will never be privy.

Alec looks up at the sky, wondering if June can navigate by the stars, as he used to himself during the war. Or even earlier. He has navigated by June for most of his life. She is his light and his lodestar, and she has been all this time, despite everything that has come between them. He stands and stretches, then turns to go inside and join her.

As he comes around the corner of the verandah, just before their bedroom's doorway, his eye is caught by something glinting in the light of the rising moon. The quick flash of reflection comes again, and he kneels. And there, tucked against the base of a giant pot of pink and yellow roses, he finds a careful arrangement of stones—volcanic black glass, a sheared oval of purple crystal, knobs of gypsum and limestone and basalt. Alec sits back on his heels, his heart larruping in a way it hasn't for a long time. He was there when she collected most of them, picking them like berries off the floor of the Rift Valley, the silver-shadowed foothills of Mount Kenya, the shores of geyser-warmed lakes. But when had she built the cairn?

Alec places the stones gently into the curl of his hand, letting the stars lend them new shapes and shadows, then closes his fingers as well as he can around them. The corners of the stones grip at him sharply even while their small flat expanses are smooth against the scars on his palm. So many scars, he thinks. Too many. The scars, the stones, the awareness that soon the three of them will sail from Mombasa to Leith, building new memories of a new ship . . . Everything has a weight to it that he cannot quite fathom, but perhaps he's never been meant to. Perhaps his task is to steward his family as well as he can, trusting that impossible serpents will not sink the ship, that the stars will continue to light his way, and that all the hurts they've done each other will eventually heal. Perhaps that is the best anyone can do.

A lone breath of cloud gossamers the moon above the foothills. Alec steps inside, closing the door softly behind him, and pauses, watching the moonlight settle on June's hair as she sleeps. Brightmere is quiet then, the night as safe as houses.

Acknowledgments

Every book has a whole world of people behind it, and *The Stars We Share* is no different. And I am extremely fortunate to have had such a stellar bunch along for this ride.

First, I cannot say enough great things about my agent, Danielle Bukowski—your patience, generosity, and big-picture thinking contributed hugely to *The Stars We Share* before it was even fully formed, and I am enormously grateful for your commitment to and advocacy for the novel.

Thank you to my wonderful and dedicated team at Pamela Dorman Books and Viking, especially Pamela Dorman and my editor, Jeramie Orton, whose faith in this book has been greatly appreciated. I would be remiss if I didn't express my deep gratitude to Brian Tart, Andrea Schulz, Kate Stark, Lindsay Prevette, Kate Hudkins, Sara Delozier, Roseanne Serra, Claire Vaccaro, Cassie Garruzzo, Carlynn Chironna, Fabi Van Arsdell, and everyone else who contributed to this project. Your enthusiasm, encouragement, and assistance have been invaluable. I'd also like to shout out my copy editor, Andrea Monagle, and her curiosity, wit, and extraordinary eye for detail.

My thanks also to my MFA faculty and classmates at the University of Baltimore, as well as my colleagues, past and present, in the UWP and the Second Chance Program at UB. I would additionally like to express my gratitude to the writers and book people who have helped me over the years; you are legion. Thank you to my family, particularly my much-missed dad, who loved airplanes and adventures, and told me an alarmingly long time ago that I too could write a book with secrets and spies in it.

Finally, I could not have written this book without the unflagging support and collie-ing of Paula Garner. Without you, this book and I would be a mess. Thank you for believing I could write a book like this, and for reading every draft of every chapter uncountable times and always finding ways to make the book better. Thank you for the billions of hours you spent listening to me go on about Alec and June and all their things, and for what you said that sparked it all in the first place. Thank you for understanding when I wanted to go write more dogs and bears instead of people, and for knowing what I was trying to do even when I sometimes didn't. Thank you for not ever letting me get away with coasting, and for not ever blowing smoke. Thank you for cookies. Thank you very much indeed for all the everything—so many things and places and fish would not have happened without you, and I am more grateful than I know how to say.